MS. MARVEL
METAMORPHOSIS

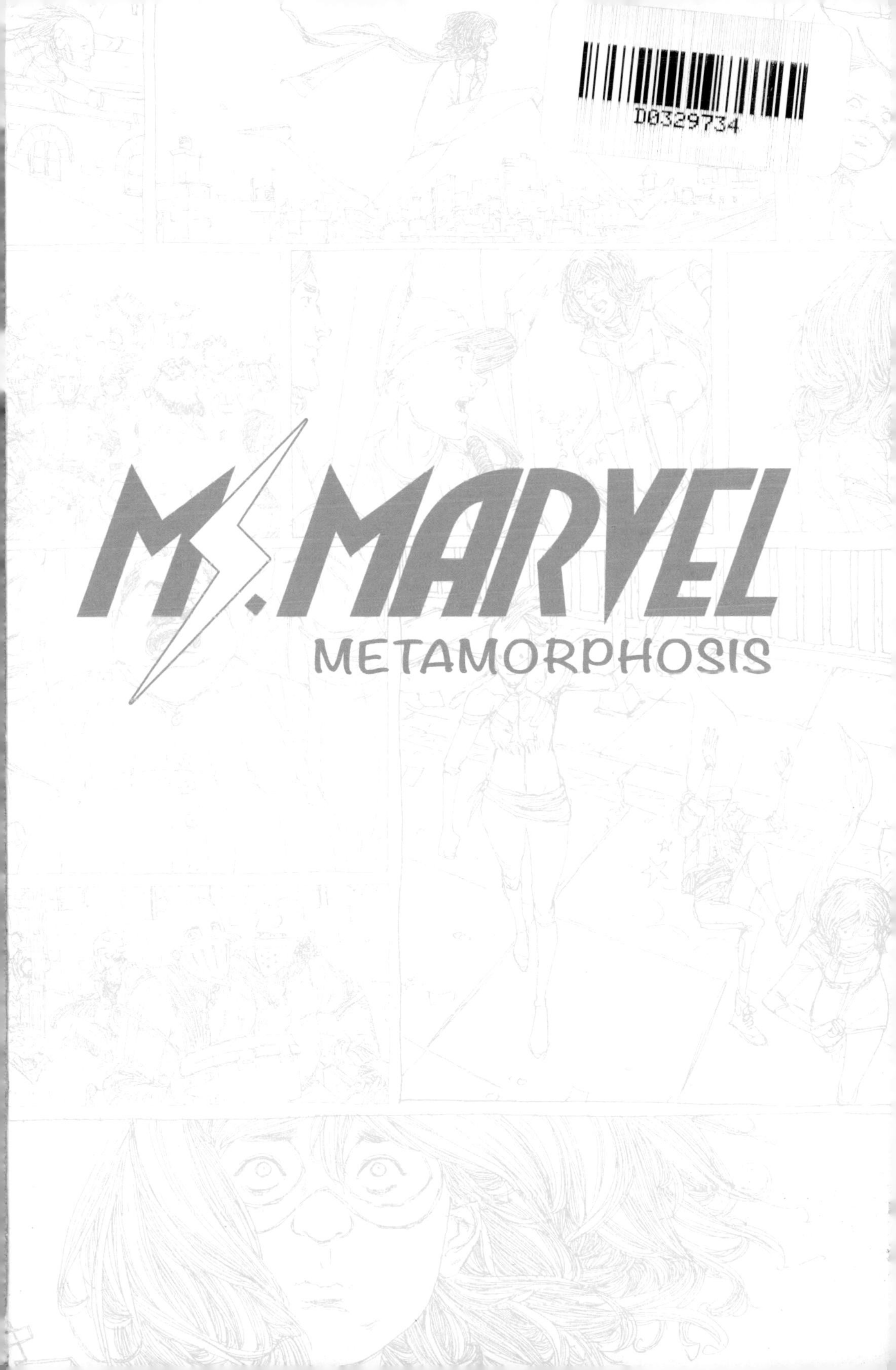

PREVIOUSLY

After a strange Terrigen Mist descended upon Jersey City, Kamala Khan got polymorph powers and became the all-new MS. MARVEL!

With strict parents on her case, her best friend Bruno by her side and a whole lot of weird ensnaring Jersey City every day, Kamala soon realized that being a super hero is...complicated.

collection editor JENNIFER GRÜNWALD
assistant editor CAITLIN O'CONNELL
associate managing editor KATERI WOODY
editor, special projects MARK D. BEAZLEY
vp production & special projects JEFF YOUNGQUIST

svp print, sales & marketing DAVID GABRIEL
director, licensed publishing SVEN LARSEN
editor in chief C.B. CEBULSKI
chief creative officer JOE QUESADA
president DAN BUCKLEY
executive producer ALAN FINE

MS. MARVEL: METAMORPHOSIS. Contains material originally published in magazine form as MS. MARVEL #12-19, S.H.I.E.L.D. #2 and AMAZING SPIDER-MAN #7-8. First printing 2019. ISBN 978-1-302-91808-8. Published by MARVEL WORLDWIDE, INC., a subsidiary of MARVEL ENTERTAINMENT, LLC. OFFICE OF PUBLICATION: 135 West 50th Street, New York, NY 10020. © 2019 MARVEL No similarity between any of the names, characters, persons, and/or institutions in this magazine with those of any living or dead person or institution is intended, and any such similarity which may exist is purely coincidental. **Printed in Canada.** DAN BUCKLEY, President, Marvel Entertainment; JOHN NEE, Publisher; JOE QUESADA, Chief Creative Officer; TOM BREVOORT, SVP of Publishing; DAVID BOGART, Associate Publisher & SVP of Talent Affairs; DAVID GABRIEL, SVP of Sales & Marketing, Publishing; JEFF YOUNGQUIST, VP of Production & Special Projects; DAN CARR, Executive Director of Publishing Technology; ALEX MORALES, Director of Publishing Operations; DAN EDINGTON, Managing Editor; SUSAN CRESPI, Production Manager; STAN LEE, Chairman Emeritus. For information regarding advertising in Marvel Comics or on Marvel.com, please contact Vit DeBellis, Custom Solutions & Integrated Advertising Manager, at vdebellis@marvel.com. For Marvel subscription inquiries, please call 888-511-5480. **Manufactured between 4/12/2019 and 5/14/2019 by SOLISCO PRINTERS, SCOTT, QC, CANADA.**

10 9 8 7 6 5 4 3 2 1

MS. MARVEL

METAMORPHOSIS

writer
G. WILLOW WILSON
artists
ELMO BONDOC (#12),
TAKESHI MIYAZAWA (#13-15)
& ADRIAN ALPHONA (#16-19)
color artists
IAN HERRING
WITH IRMA KNIIVILA (#13)
letterer
VC'S JOE CARAMAGNA
cover art
KRIS ANKA (#12 & #15-19),
MARGUERITE SAUVAGE (#13) & JAKE WYATT (#14)

assistant editors
**CHARLES BEACHAM
& DEVIN LEWIS**

editor
SANA AMANAT

S.H.I.E.L.D. #2
writer MARK WAID
penciler HUMBERTO RAMOS
inker VICTOR OLAZABA
colorist EDGAR DELGADO
letterer VC'S JOE CARAMAGNA
cover art JULIAN TOTINO TEDESCO
assistant editor JON MOISAN
editors TOM BREVOORT WITH ELLIE PYLE

AMAZING SPIDER-MAN #7-8
"Ms. Marvel Team-Up" & "Adventures in Babysitting"
plot DAN SLOTT
script CHRISTOS GAGE
penciler GIUSEPPE CAMUNCOLI
inker CAM SMITH
colorist ANTONIO FABELA
letterer CHRIS ELIOPOULOS
cover art GIUSEPPE CAMUNCOLI,
CAM SMITH & ANTONIO FABELA
assistant editor ELLIE PYLE
editor NICK LOWE

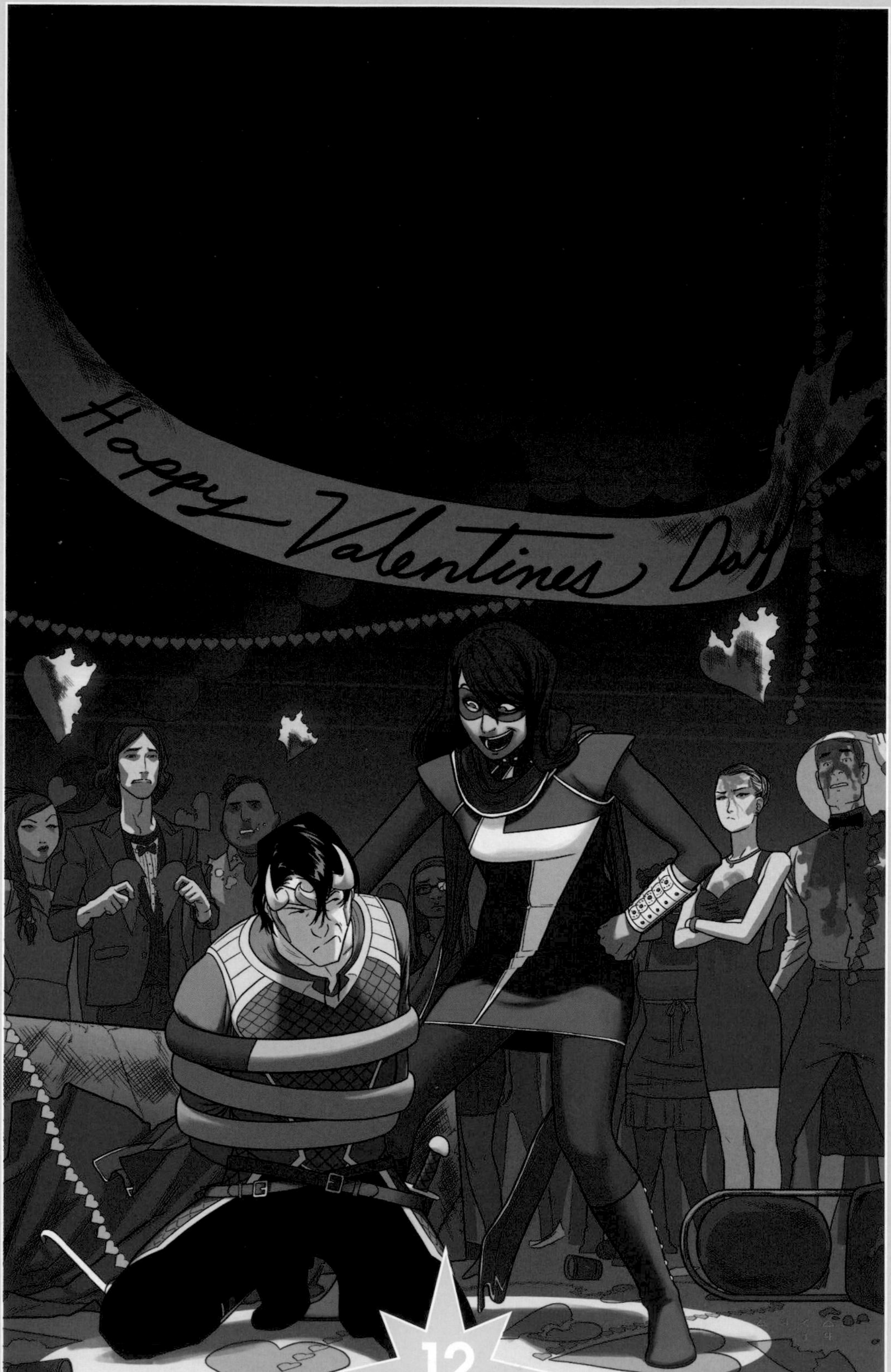
Happy Valentines Day
12

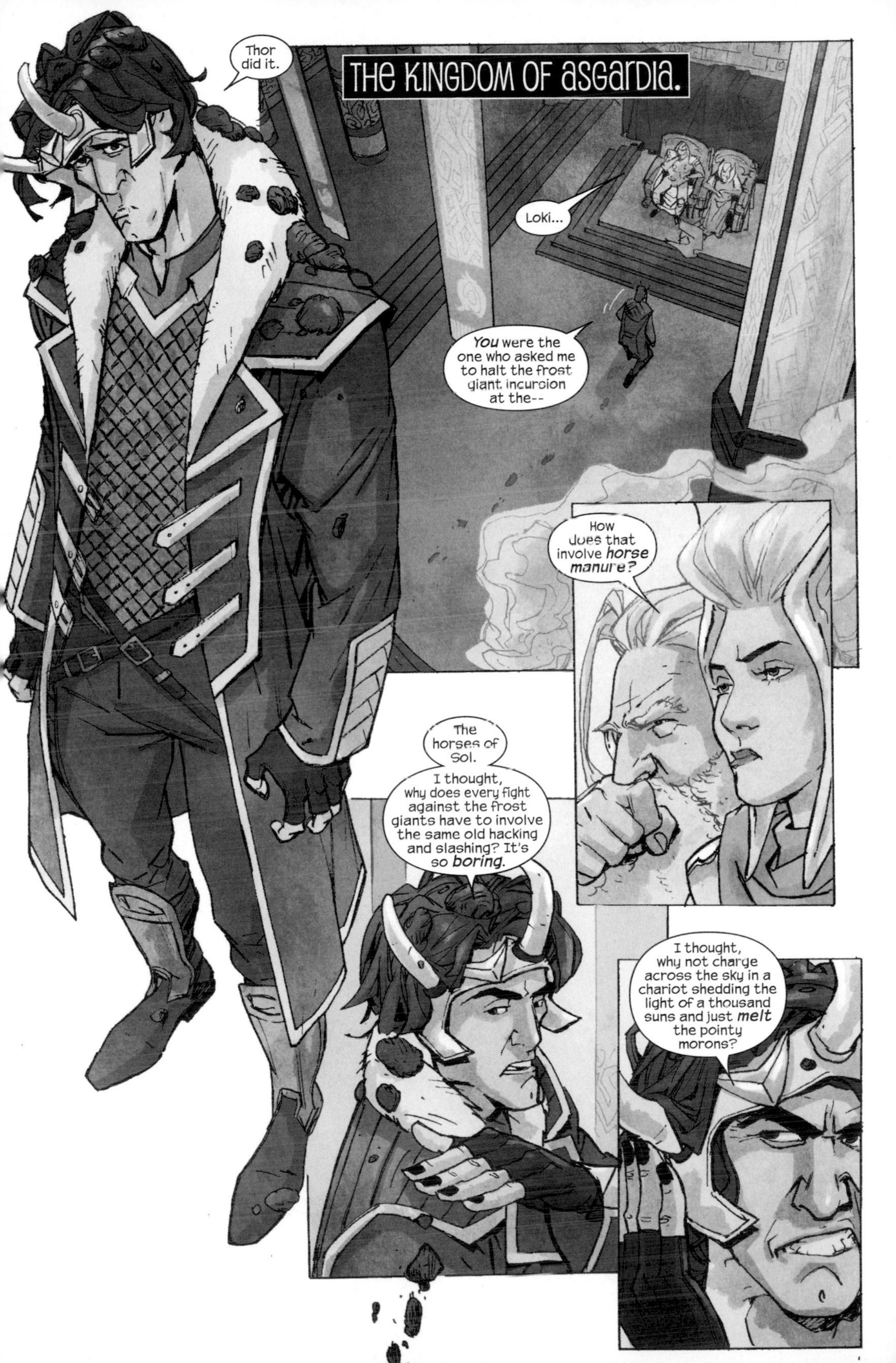
Thor did it.
THE KINGDOM OF ASGARDIA.
Loki...
You were the one who asked me to halt the frost giant incursion at the--
How does that involve ***horse manure?***
The horses of Sol.
I thought, why does every fight against the frost giants have to involve the same old hacking and slashing? It's so ***boring***.
I thought, why not charge across the sky in a chariot shedding the light of a thousand suns and just ***melt*** the pointy morons?

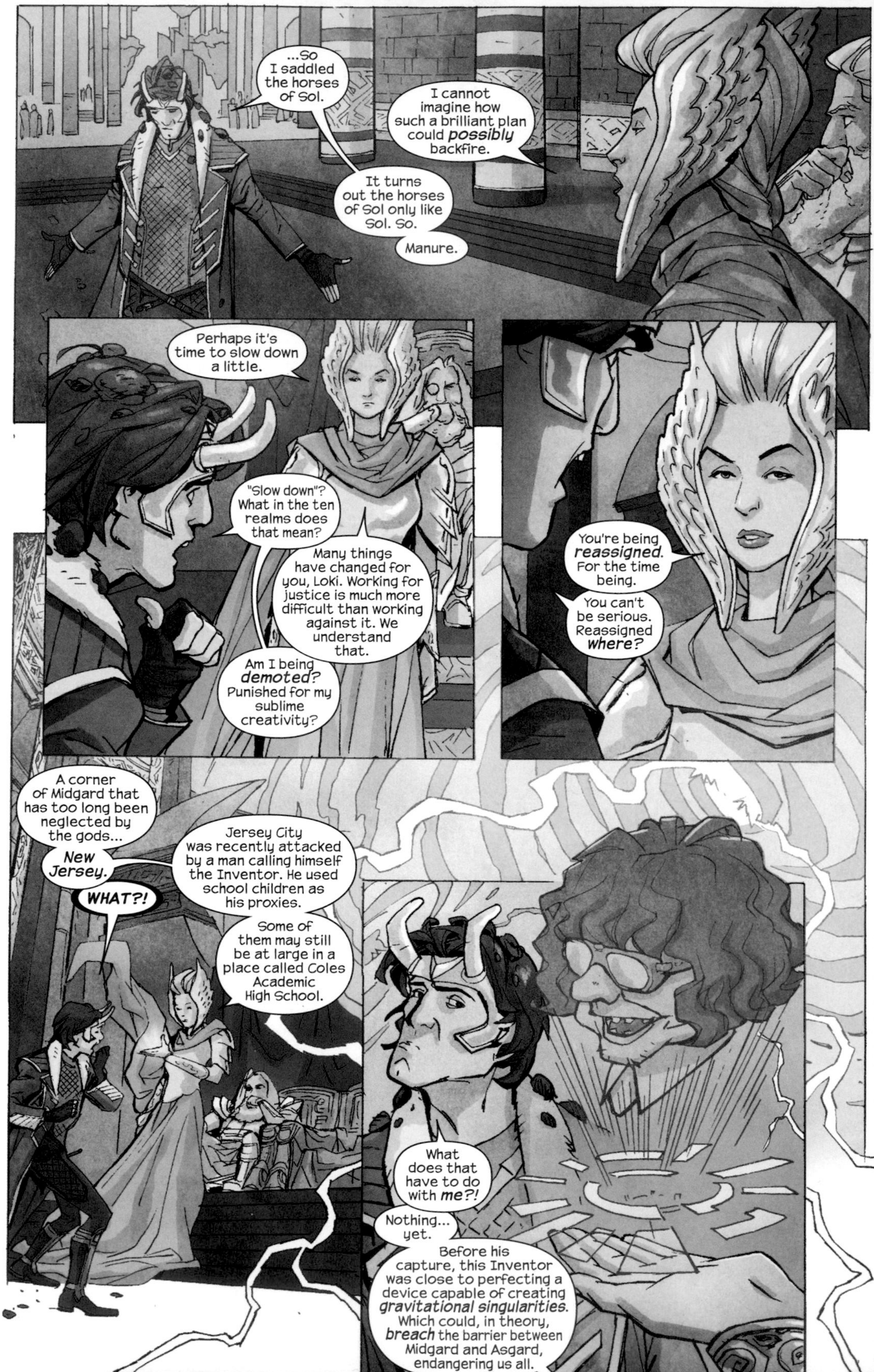
...So I saddled the horses of Sol.
I cannot imagine how such a brilliant plan could *possibly* backfire.
It turns out the horses of Sol only like Sol. So.
Manure.
Perhaps it's time to slow down a little.
"Slow down"? What in the ten realms does that mean?
Many things have changed for you, Loki. Working for justice is much more difficult than working against it. We understand that.
Am I being *demoted?* Punished for my sublime creativity?
You're being *reassigned*. For the time being.
You can't be serious. Reassigned *where?*
A corner of Midgard that has too long been neglected by the gods...
New Jersey.
WHAT?!
Jersey City was recently attacked by a man calling himself the Inventor. He used school children as his proxies.
Some of them may still be at large in a place called Coles Academic High School.
What does that have to do with *me?!*
Nothing... yet.
Before his capture, this Inventor was close to perfecting a device capable of creating *gravitational singularities*. Which could, in theory, *breach* the barrier between Midgard and Asgard, endangering us all.

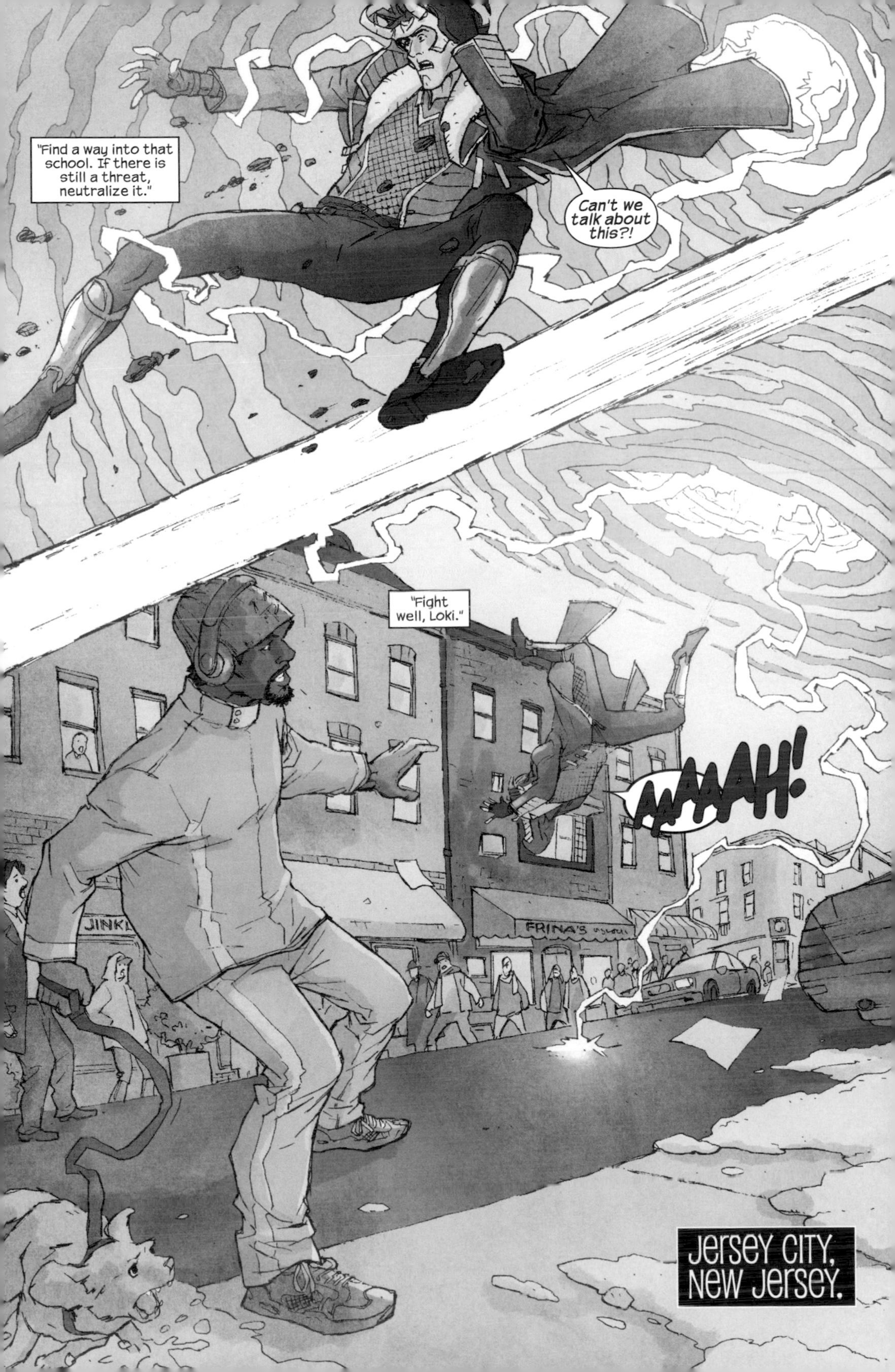
"Find a way into that school. If there is still a threat, neutralize it."
Can't we talk about this?!
"Fight well, Loki."
AAAAAH!
JINK
FRINA'S
JERSEY CITY, NEW JERSEY.

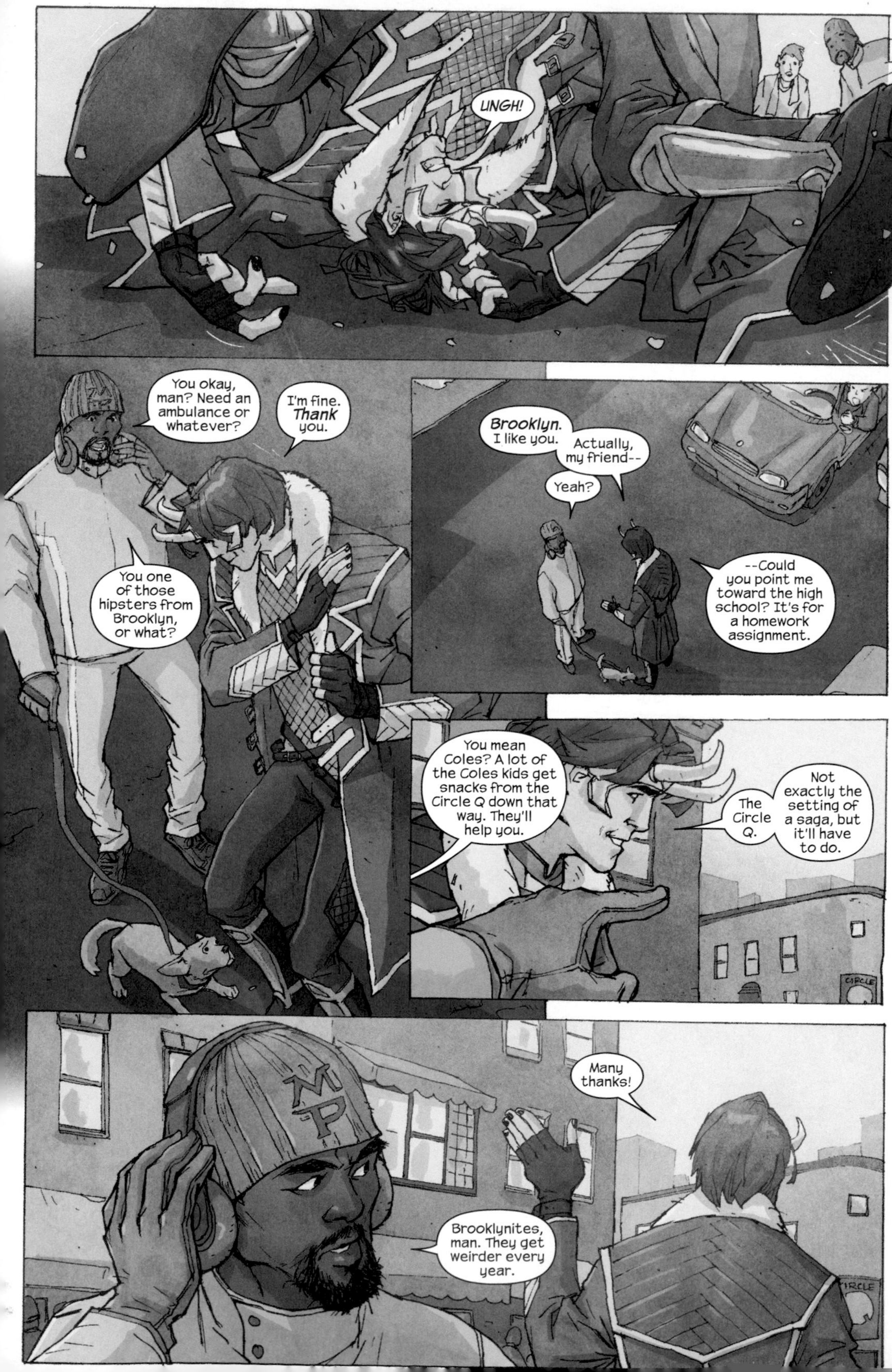
UNGH!
You okay, man? Need an ambulance or whatever?
I'm fine. *Thank* you.
You one of those hipsters from Brooklyn, or what?
Brooklyn. I like you.
Yeah?
Actually, my friend--
--Could you point me toward the high school? It's for a homework assignment.
You mean Coles? A lot of the Coles kids get snacks from the Circle Q down that way. They'll help you.
The Circle Q.
Not exactly the setting of a saga, but it'll have to do.
Many thanks!
Brooklynites, man. They get weirder every year.

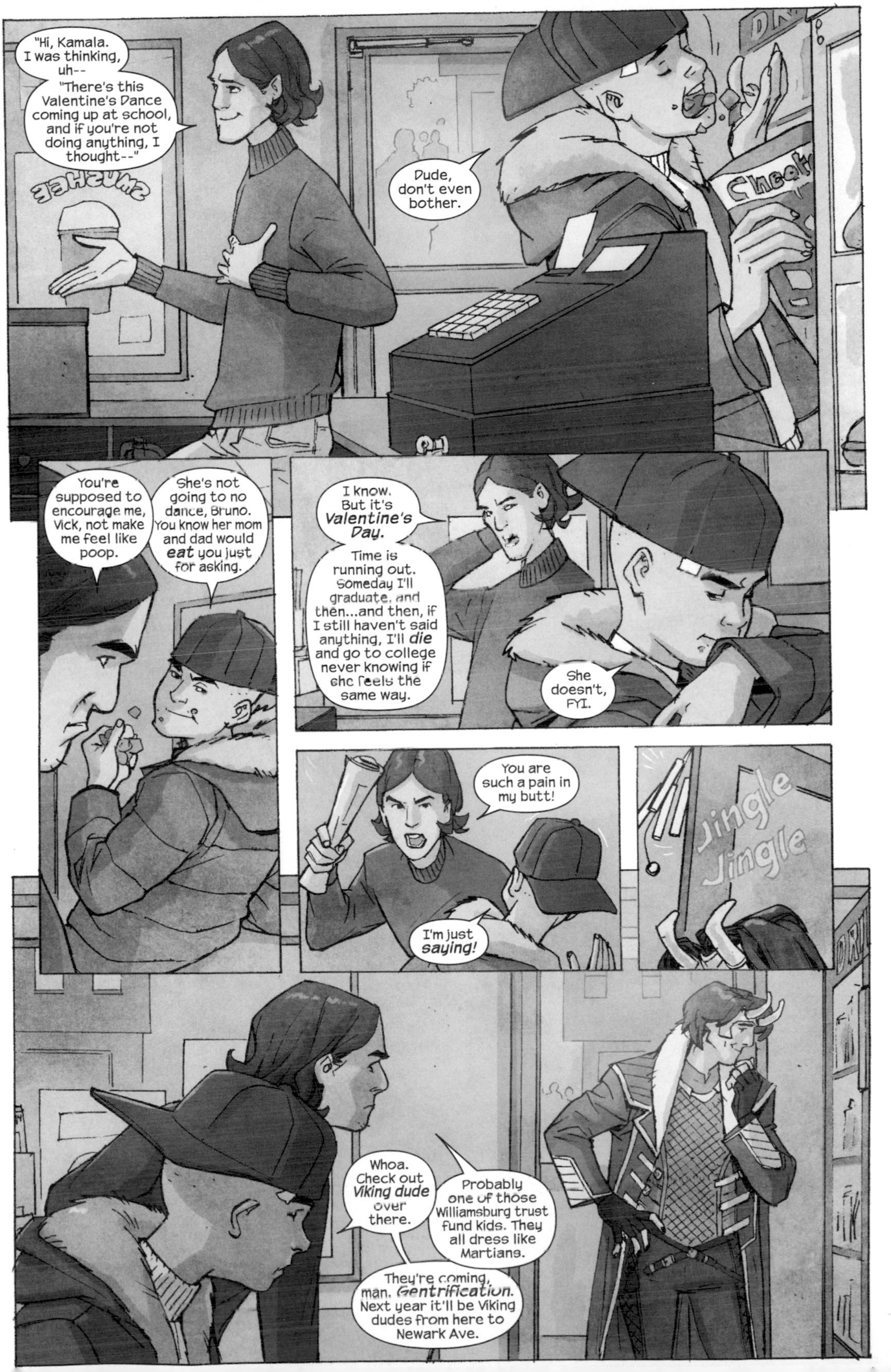
"Hi, Kamala. I was thinking, uh--
"There's this Valentine's Dance coming up at school, and if you're not doing anything, I thought--"
Dude, don't even bother.
You're supposed to encourage me, Vick, not make me feel like poop.
She's not going to no dance, Bruno. You know her mom and dad would *eat* you just for asking.
I know. But it's *Valentine's Day.*
Time is running out. Someday I'll graduate, and then...and then, if I still haven't said anything, I'll *die* and go to college never knowing if she feels the same way.
She doesn't, FYI.
You are such a pain in my butt!
I'm just *saying!*
Jingle Jingle
Whoa. Check out *Viking dude* over there.
Probably one of those Williamsburg trust fund kids. They all dress like Martians.
They're coming, man. *Gentrification.* Next year it'll be Viking dudes from here to Newark Ave.

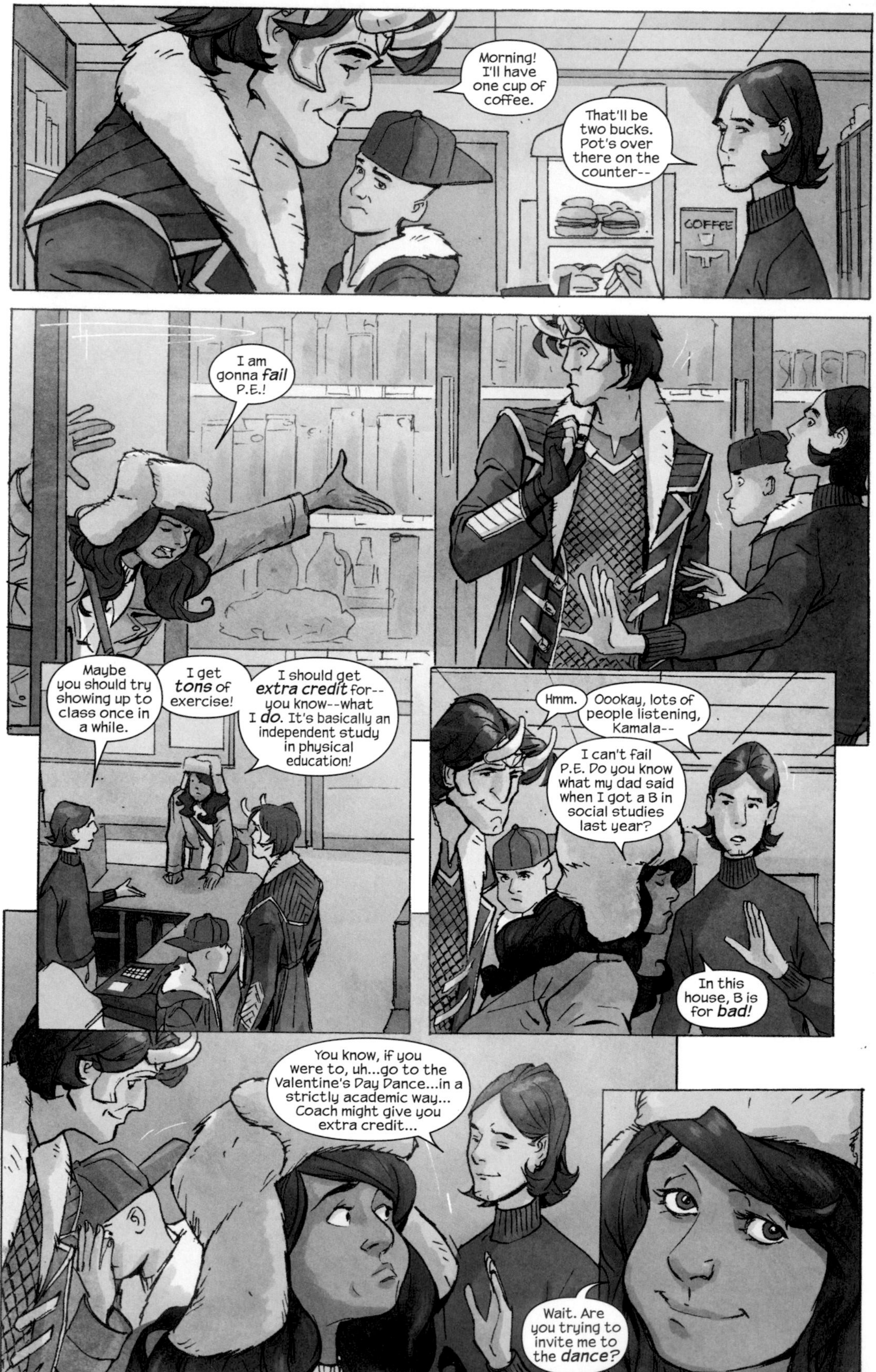

Morning! I'll have one cup of coffee.
That'll be two bucks. Pot's over there on the counter--
I am gonna *fail* P.E.!
Maybe you should try showing up to class once in a while.
I get *tons* of exercise!
I should get *extra credit* for-- you know--what I *do.* It's basically an independent study in physical education!
Hmm.
Oookay, lots of people listening, Kamala--
I can't fail P.E. Do you know what my dad said when I got a B in social studies last year?
In this house, B is for *bad!*
You know, if you were to, uh...go to the Valentine's Day Dance...in a strictly academic way... Coach might give you extra credit...
Wait. Are you trying to invite me to the *dance?*

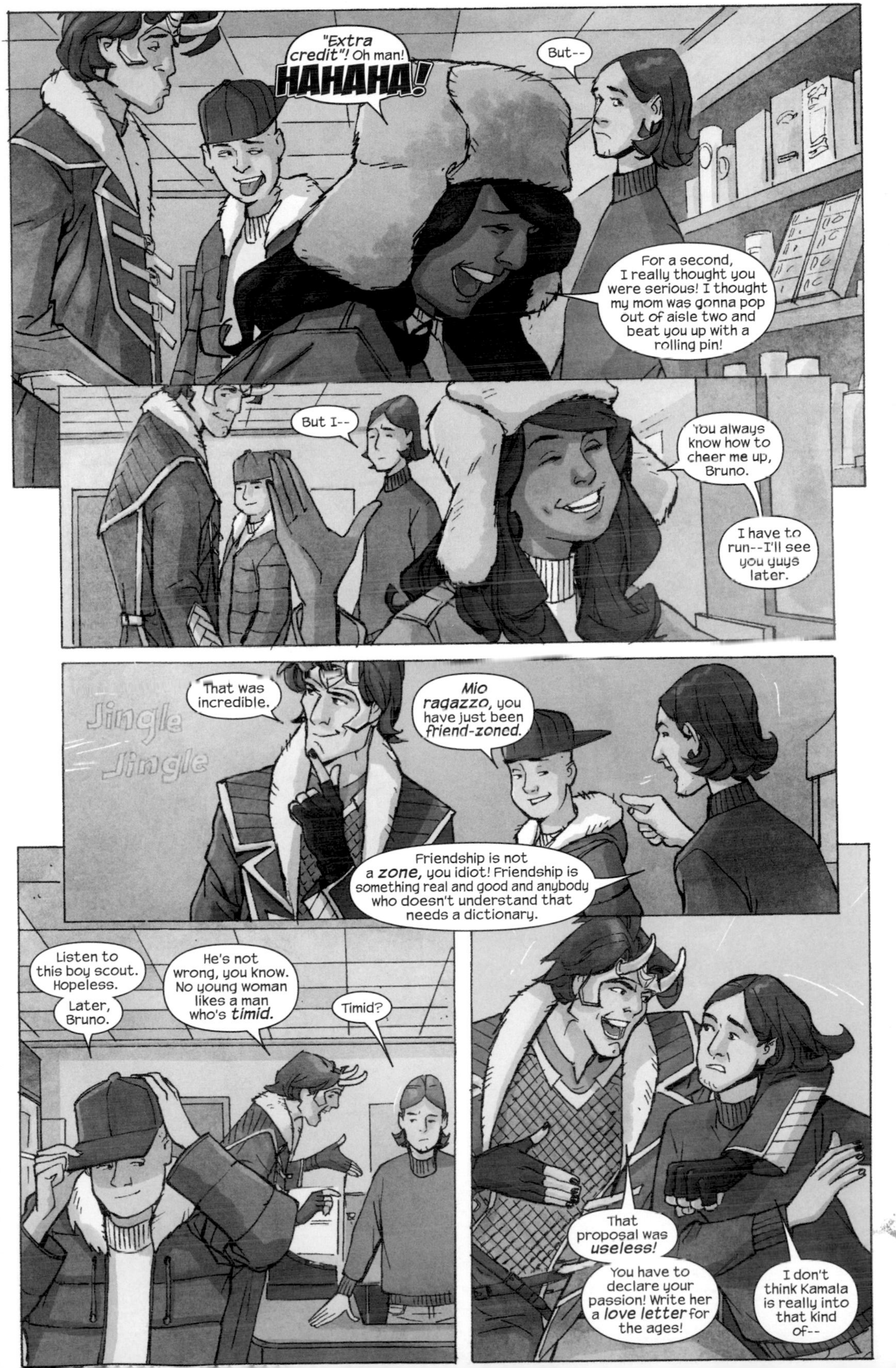
"Extra credit"! Oh man!
HAHAHA!
But--
For a second, I really thought you were serious! I thought my mom was gonna pop out of aisle two and beat you up with a rolling pin!
But I--
You always know how to cheer me up, Bruno.
I have to run--I'll see you guys later.
Jingle Jingle
That was incredible.
Mio ragazzo, you have just been friend-zoned.
Friendship is not a zone, you idiot! Friendship is something real and good and anybody who doesn't understand that needs a dictionary.
Listen to this boy scout. Hopeless.
Later, Bruno.
He's not wrong, you know. No young woman likes a man who's timid.
Timid?
That proposal was useless!
You have to declare your passion! Write her a love letter for the ages!
I don't think Kamala is really into that kind of--

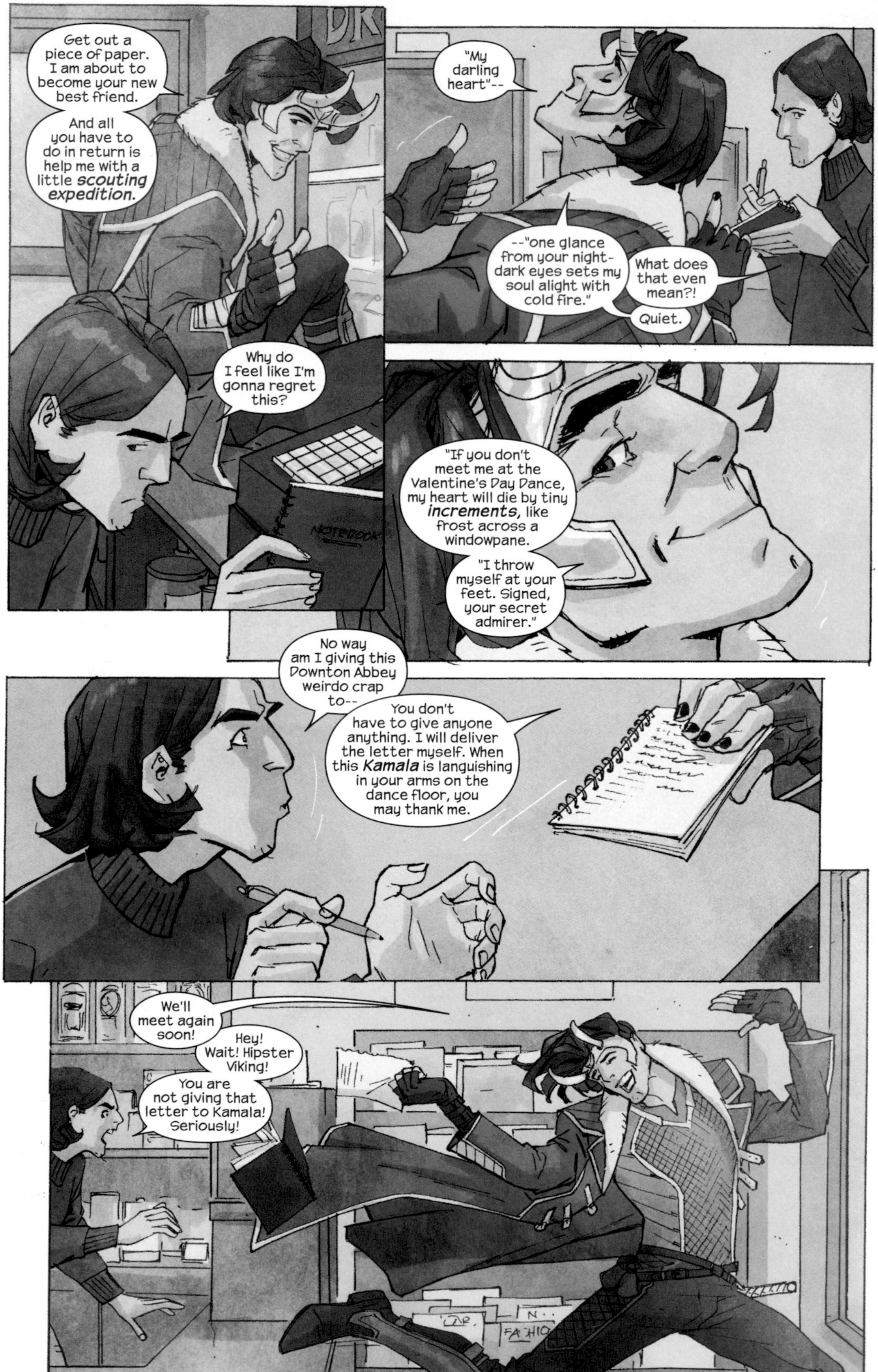

Get out a piece of paper. I am about to become your new best friend.
And all you have to do in return is help me with a little *scouting expedition*.
Why do I feel like I'm gonna regret this?
"My darling heart"--
--"one glance from your night-dark eyes sets my soul alight with cold fire."
What does that even mean?!
Quiet.
"If you don't meet me at the Valentine's Day Dance, my heart will die by tiny *increments*, like frost across a windowpane.
"I throw myself at your feet. Signed, your secret admirer."
No way am I giving this Downton Abbey weirdo crap to--
You don't have to give anyone anything. I will deliver the letter myself. When this *Kamala* is languishing in your arms on the dance floor, you may thank me.
We'll meet again soon!
Hey! Wait! Hipster Viking!
You are not giving that letter to Kamala! Seriously!

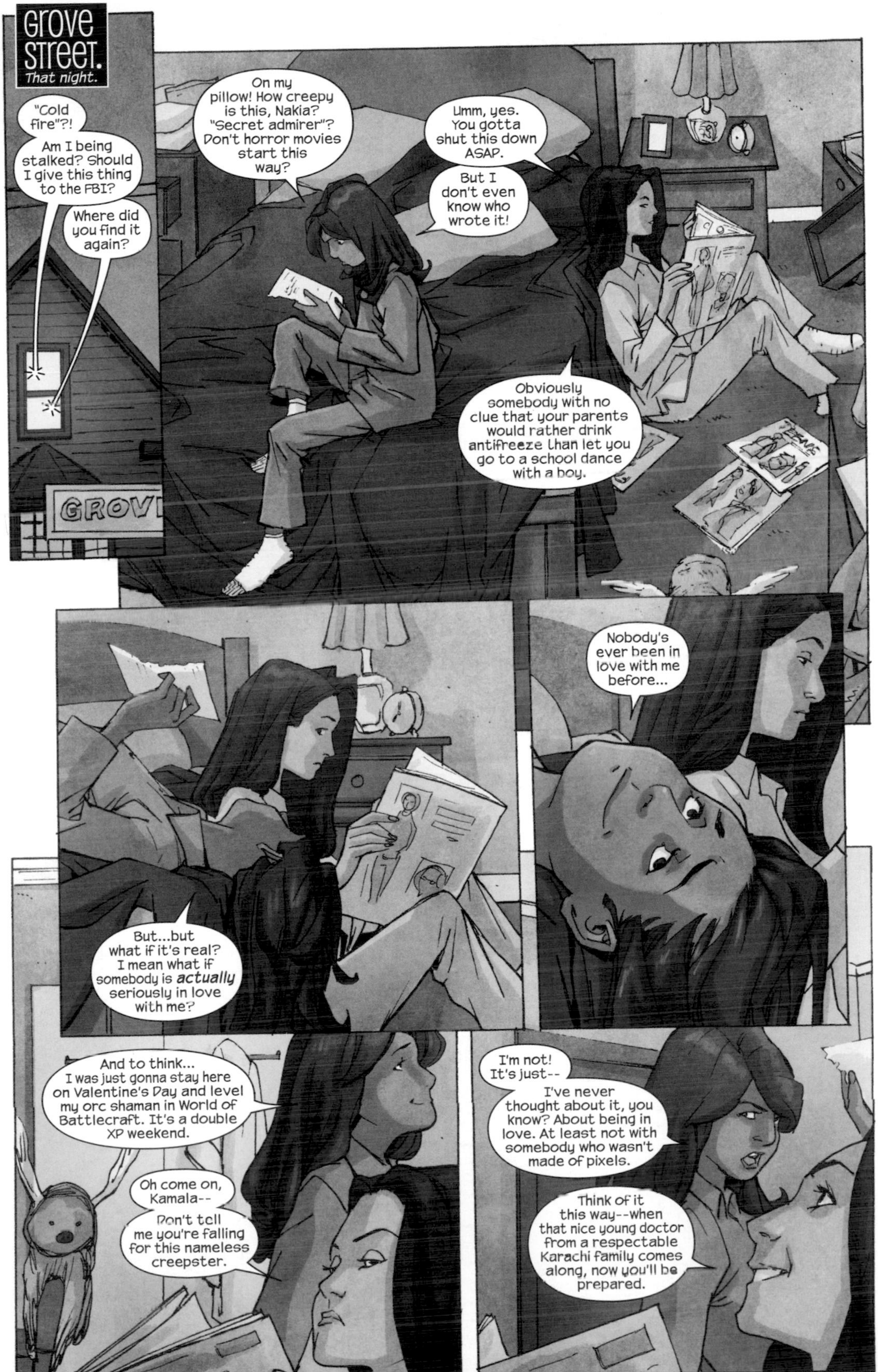
GROVE STREET. That night.
"Cold fire"?!
Am I being stalked? Should I give this thing to the FBI?
Where did you find it again?
On my pillow! How creepy is this, Nakia? "Secret admirer"? Don't horror movies start this way?
Umm, yes. You gotta shut this down ASAP.
But I don't even know who wrote it!
Obviously somebody with no clue that your parents would rather drink antifreeze than let you go to a school dance with a boy.
GROV
But...but what if it's real? I mean what if somebody is *actually* seriously in love with me?
Nobody's ever been in love with me before...
And to think... I was just gonna stay here on Valentine's Day and level my orc shaman in World of Battlecraft. It's a double XP weekend.
Oh come on, Kamala--
Don't tell me you're falling for this nameless creepster.
I'm not! It's just--
I've never thought about it, you know? About being in love. At least not with somebody who wasn't made of pixels.
Think of it this way--when that nice young doctor from a respectable Karachi family comes along, now you'll be prepared.

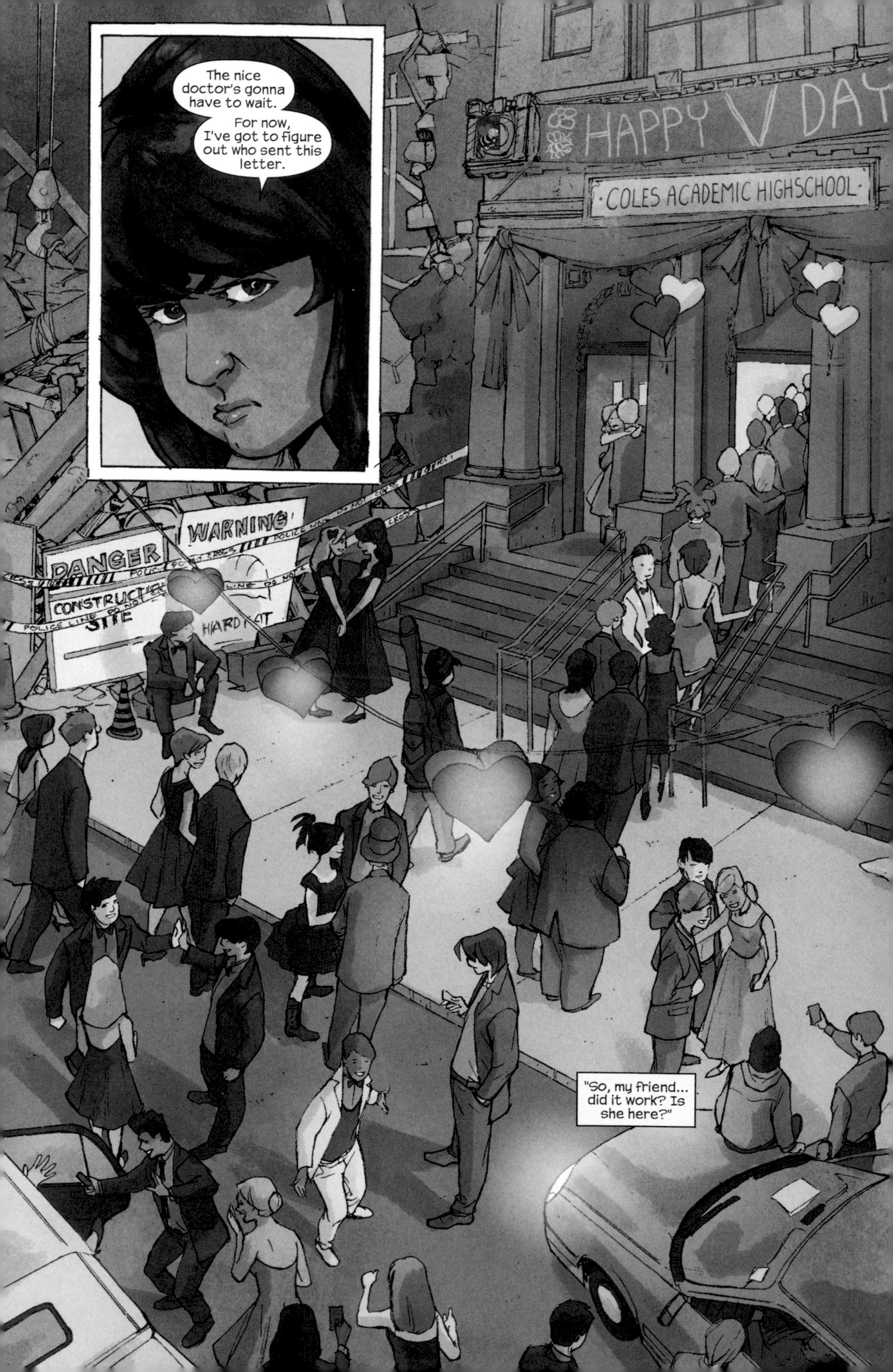

The nice doctor's gonna have to wait.
For now, I've got to figure out who sent this letter.
HAPPY V DAY
·COLES ACADEMIC HIGHSCHOOL·
WARNING
DANGER
CONSTRUCTION SITE
HARD HAT
"So, my friend... did it work? Is she here?"

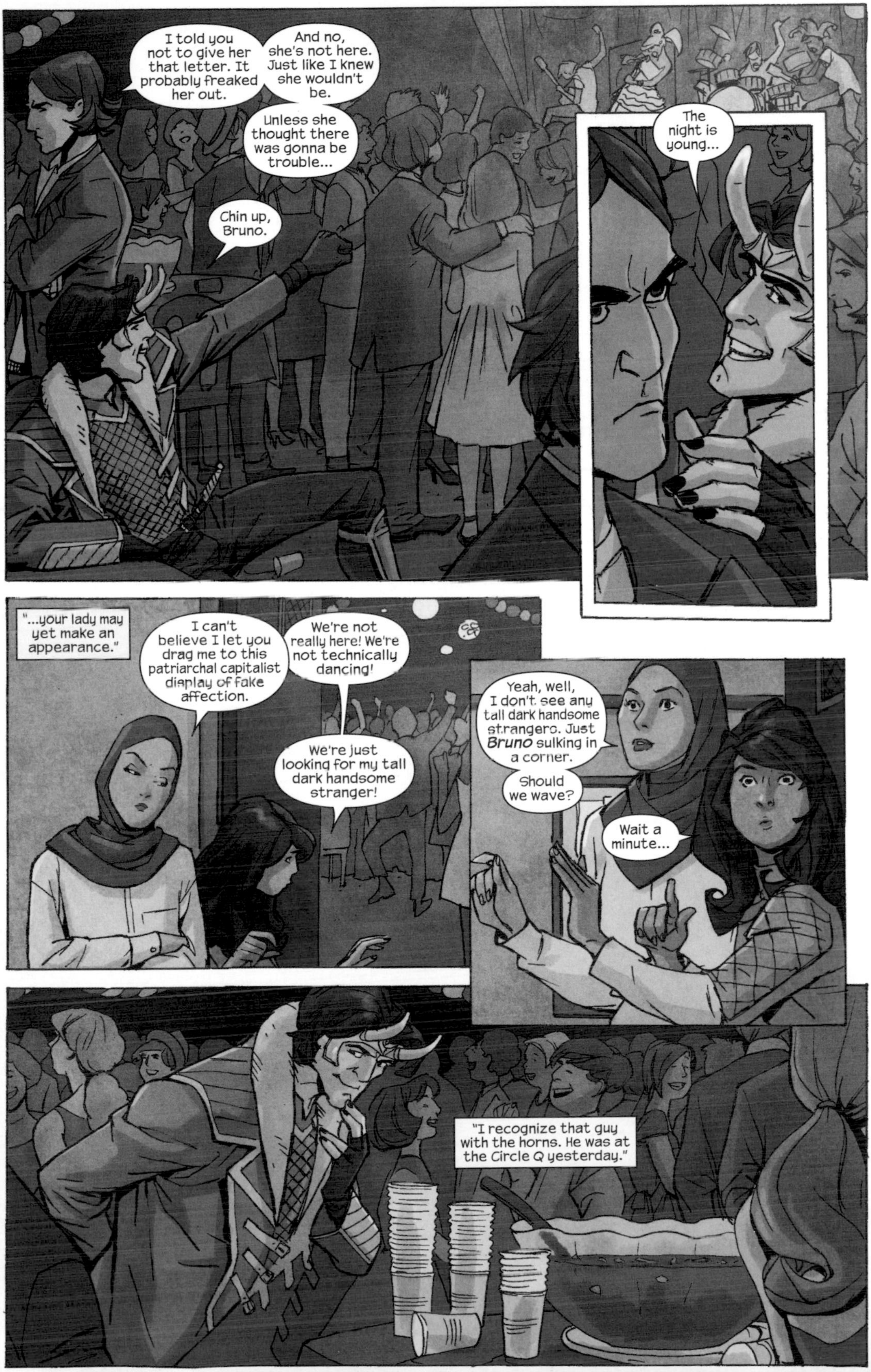
I told you not to give her that letter. It probably freaked her out.
And no, she's not here. Just like I knew she wouldn't be.
Unless she thought there was gonna be trouble...
Chin up, Bruno.
The night is young...
"...your lady may yet make an appearance."
I can't believe I let you drag me to this patriarchal capitalist display of fake affection.
We're not really here! We're not technically dancing!
We're just looking for my tall dark handsome stranger!
Yeah, well, I don't see any tall dark handsome strangers. Just Bruno sulking in a corner.
Should we wave?
Wait a minute...
"I recognize that guy with the horns. He was at the Circle Q yesterday."

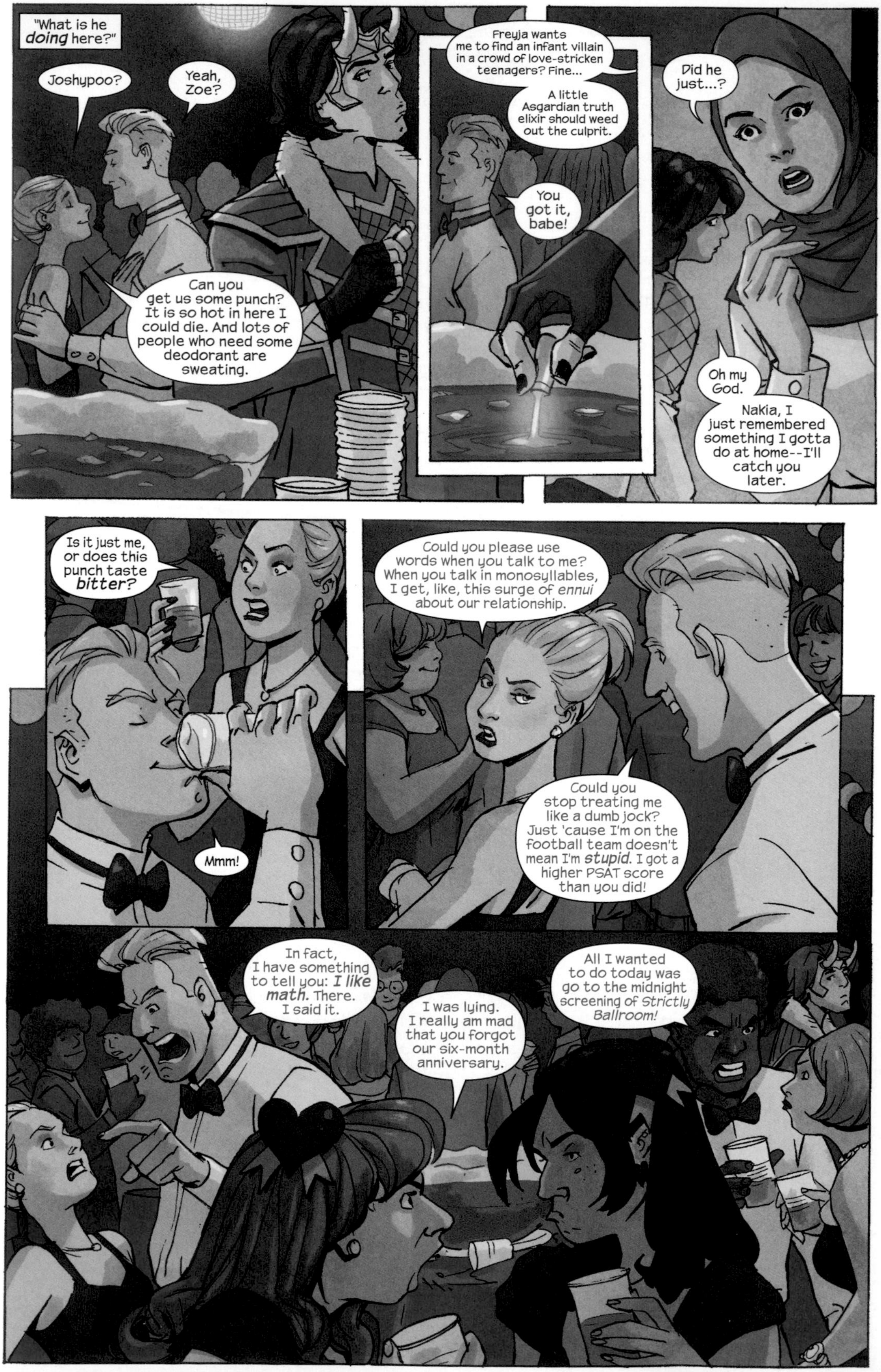
"What is he *doing* here?"
Joshypoo?
Yeah, Zoe?
Can you get us some punch? It is so hot in here I could die. And lots of people who need some deodorant are sweating.
Freyja wants me to find an infant villain in a crowd of love-stricken teenagers? Fine...
A little Asgardian truth elixir should weed out the culprit.
You got it, babe!
Did he just...?
Oh my God.
Nakia, I just remembered something I gotta do at home--I'll catch you later.
Is it just me, or does this punch taste *bitter?*
Mmm!
Could you please use words when you talk to me? When you talk in monosyllables, I get, like, this surge of *ennui* about our relationship.
Could you stop treating me like a dumb jock? Just 'cause I'm on the football team doesn't mean I'm *stupid.* I got a higher PSAT score than you did!
In fact, I have something to tell you: *I like math.* There. I said it.
I was lying. I really am mad that you forgot our six-month anniversary.
All I wanted to do today was go to the midnight screening of *Strictly Ballroom!*

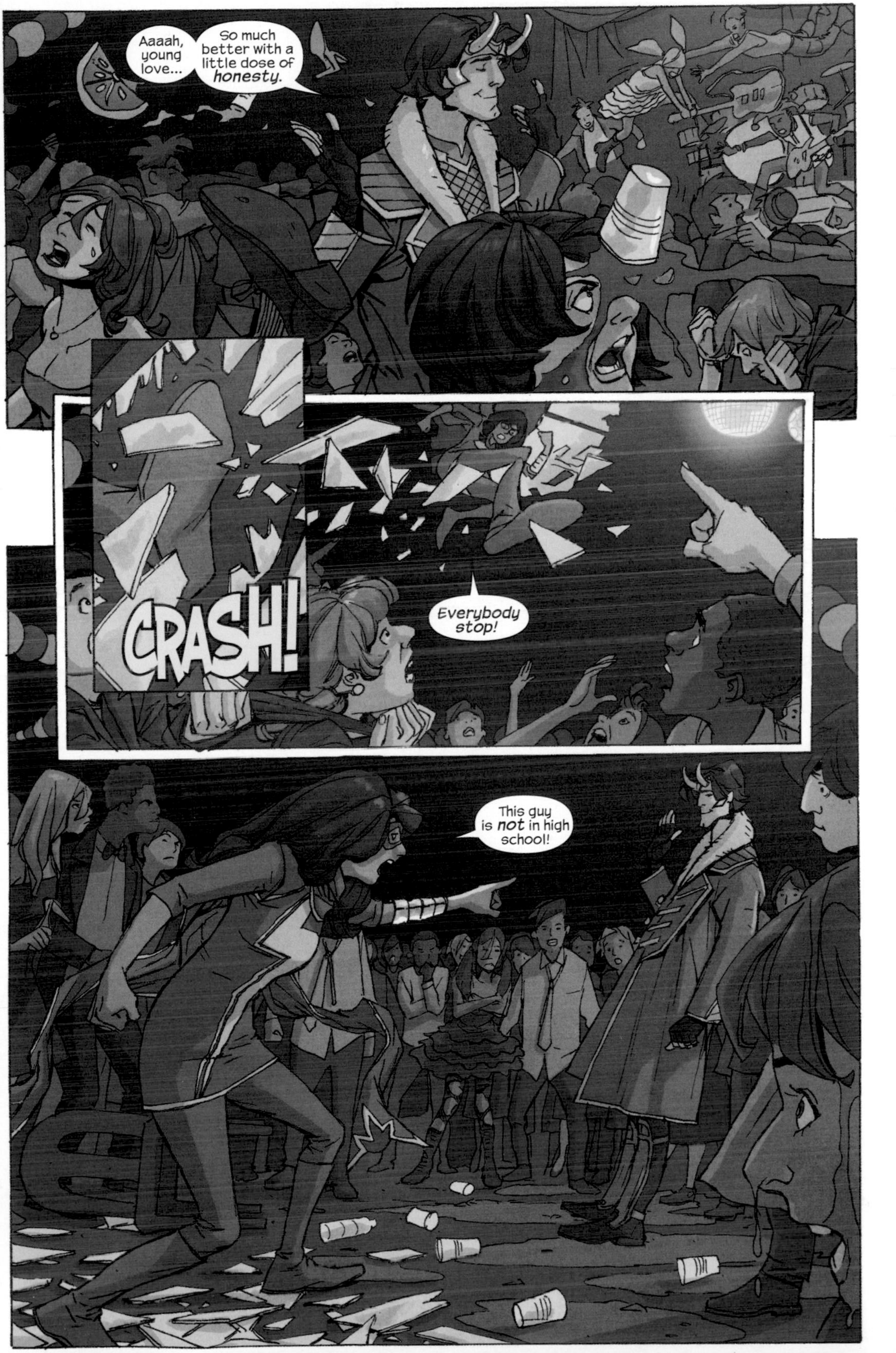

Aaaah, young love...
So much better with a little dose of *honesty*.
CRASH!
Everybody stop!
This guy is **not** in high school!

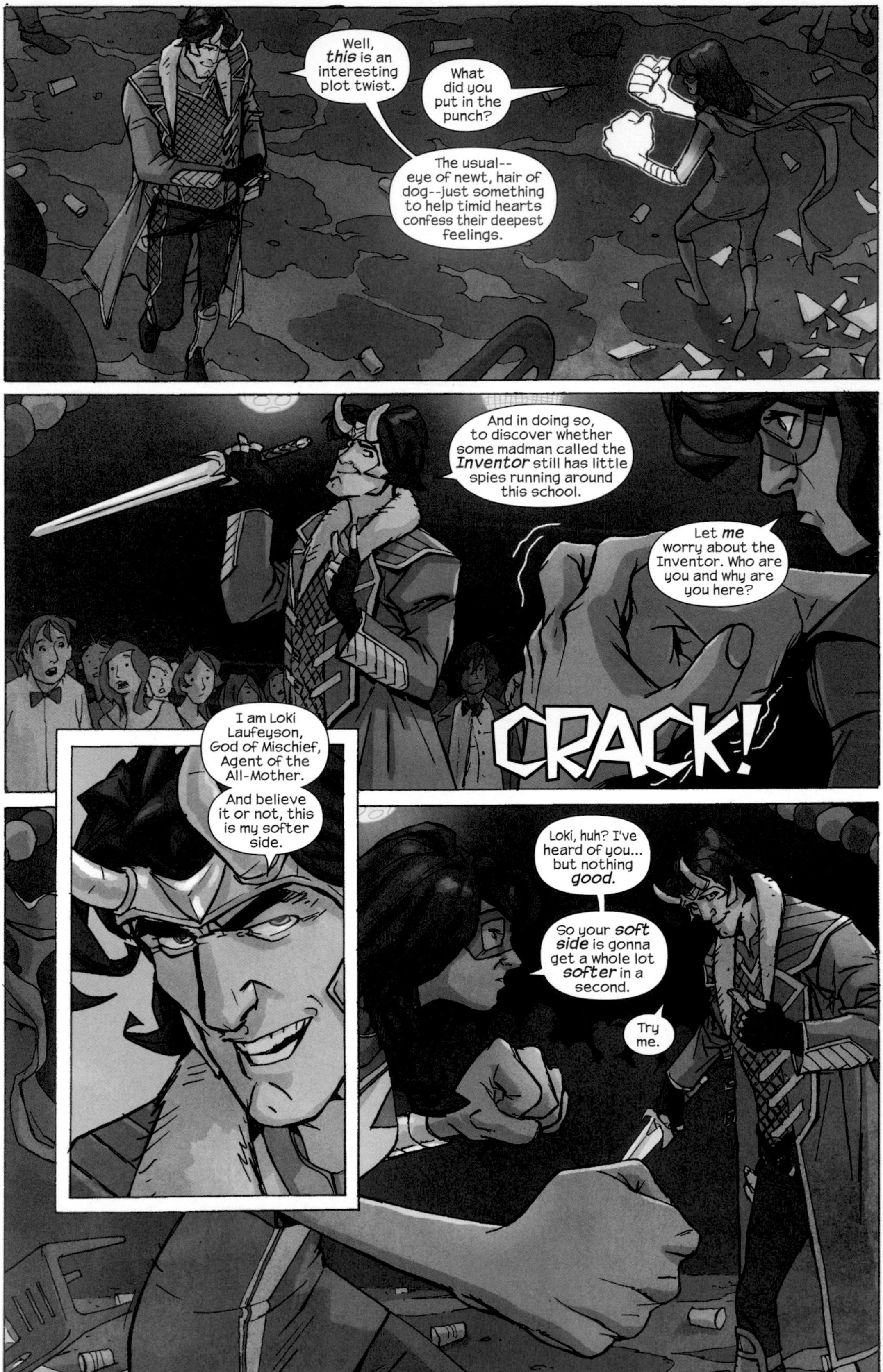
Well, *this* is an interesting plot twist.
What did you put in the punch?
The usual-- eye of newt, hair of dog--just something to help timid hearts confess their deepest feelings.
And in doing so, to discover whether some madman called the *Inventor* still has little spies running around this school.
Let *me* worry about the Inventor. Who are you and why are you here?
CRACK!
I am Loki Laufeyson, God of Mischief, Agent of the All-Mother.
And believe it or not, this is my softer side.
Loki, huh? I've heard of you... but nothing *good.*
So your *soft side* is gonna get a whole lot *softer* in a second.
Try me.

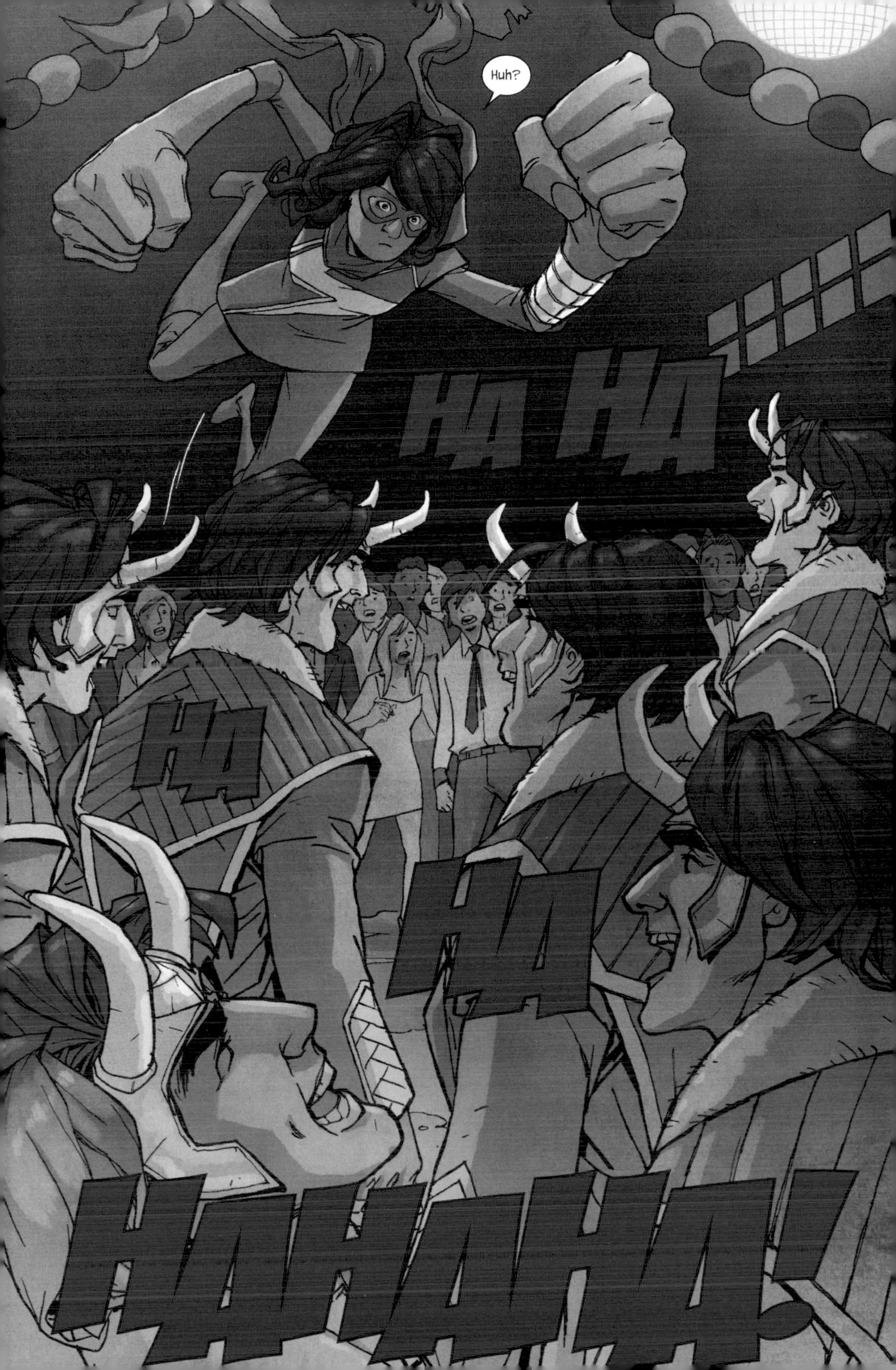
Huh?
HA HA
HA
HA
HAHAHA!

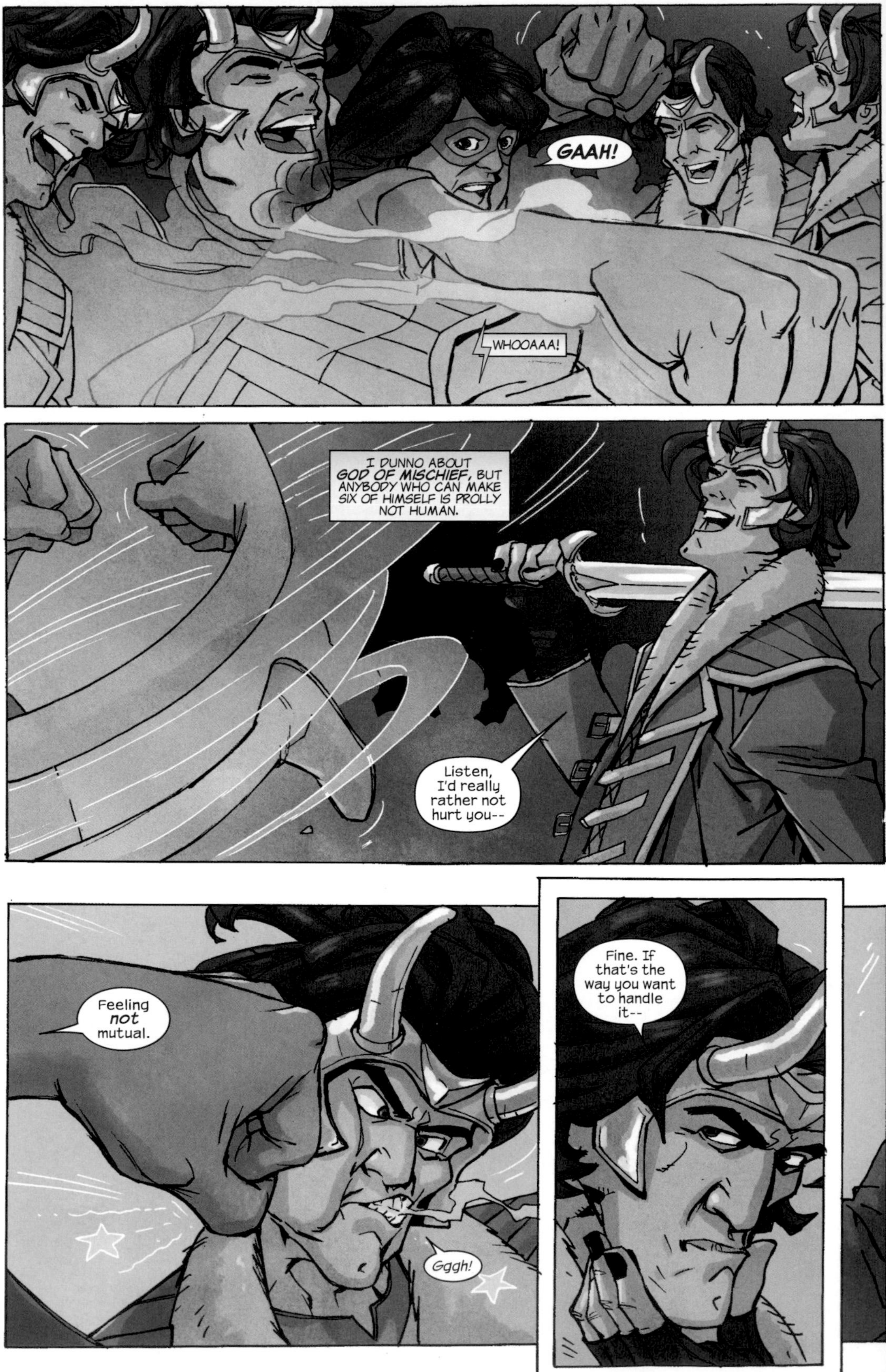
GAAH!
WHOOAAA!
I DUNNO ABOUT GOD OF MISCHIEF, BUT ANYBODY WHO CAN MAKE SIX OF HIMSELF IS PROLLY NOT HUMAN.
Listen, I'd really rather not hurt you--
Feeling not mutual.
Ggh!
Fine. If that's the way you want to handle it--

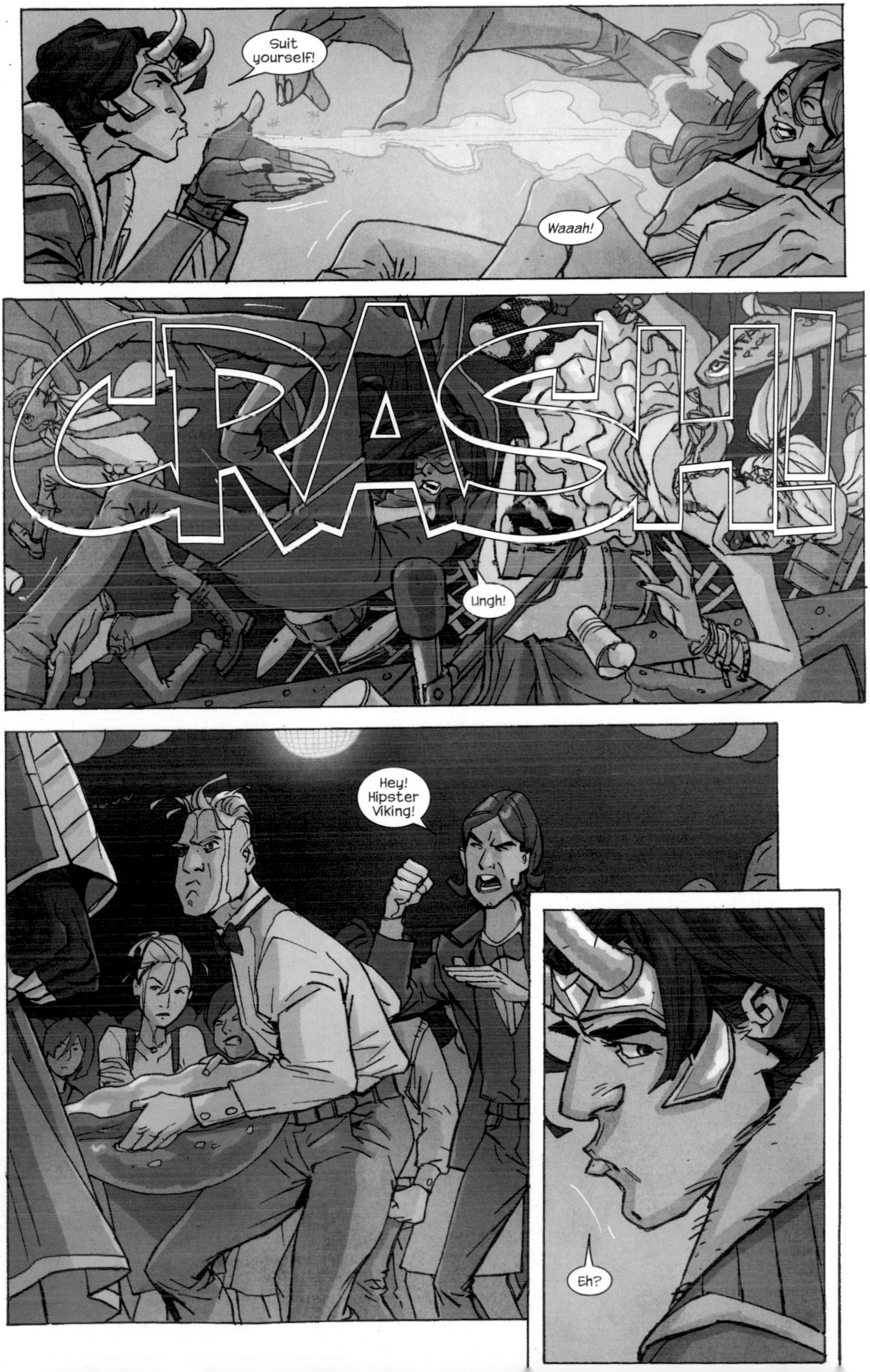
Suit yourself!
Waaah!
CRASH!
Ungh!
Hey! Hipster Viking!
Eh?

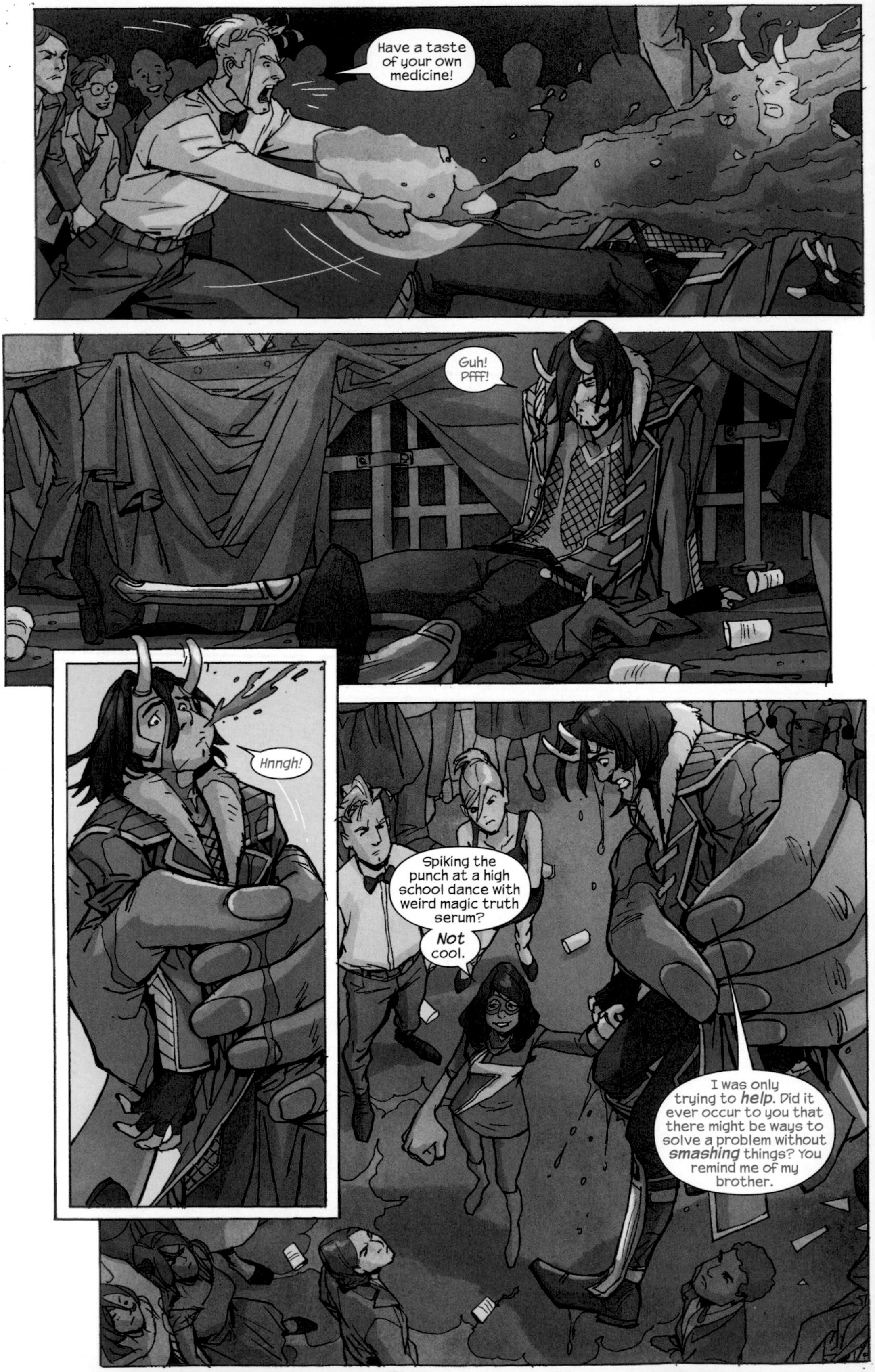
Have a taste of your own medicine!
Guh! Pfff!
Hnngh!
Spiking the punch at a high school dance with weird magic truth serum?
Not cool.
I was only trying to help. Did it ever occur to you that there might be ways to solve a problem without smashing things? You remind me of my brother.

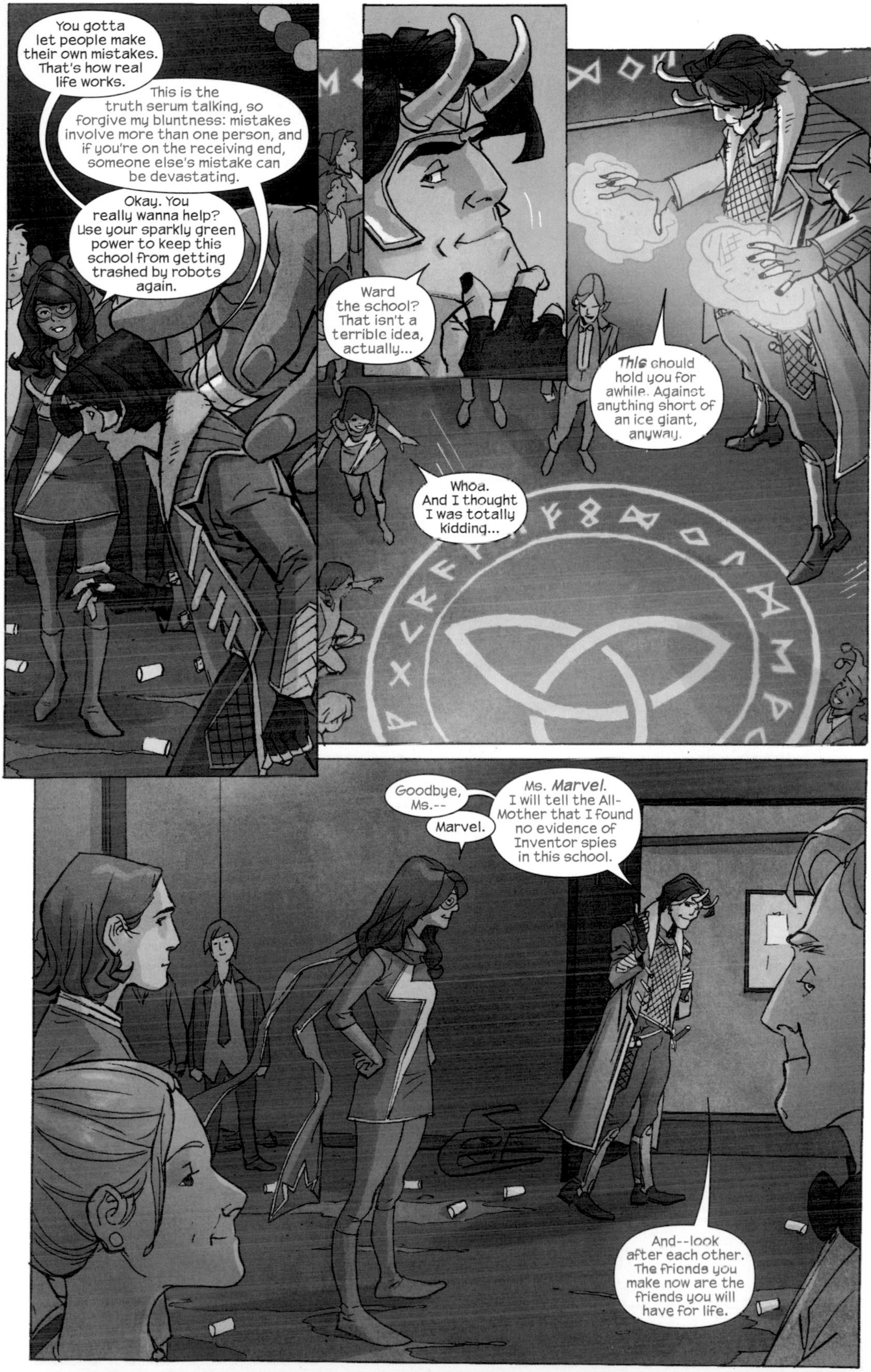
You gotta let people make their own mistakes. That's how real life works.
This is the truth serum talking, so forgive my bluntness: mistakes involve more than one person, and if you're on the receiving end, someone else's mistake can be devastating.
Okay. You really wanna help? Use your sparkly green power to keep this school from getting trashed by robots again.
Ward the school? That isn't a terrible idea, actually...
This should hold you for awhile. Against anything short of an ice giant, anyway.
Whoa. And I thought I was totally kidding...
Goodbye, Ms.--
Marvel.
Ms. Marvel. I will tell the All-Mother that I found no evidence of Inventor spies in this school.
And--look after each other. The friends you make now are the friends you will have for life.

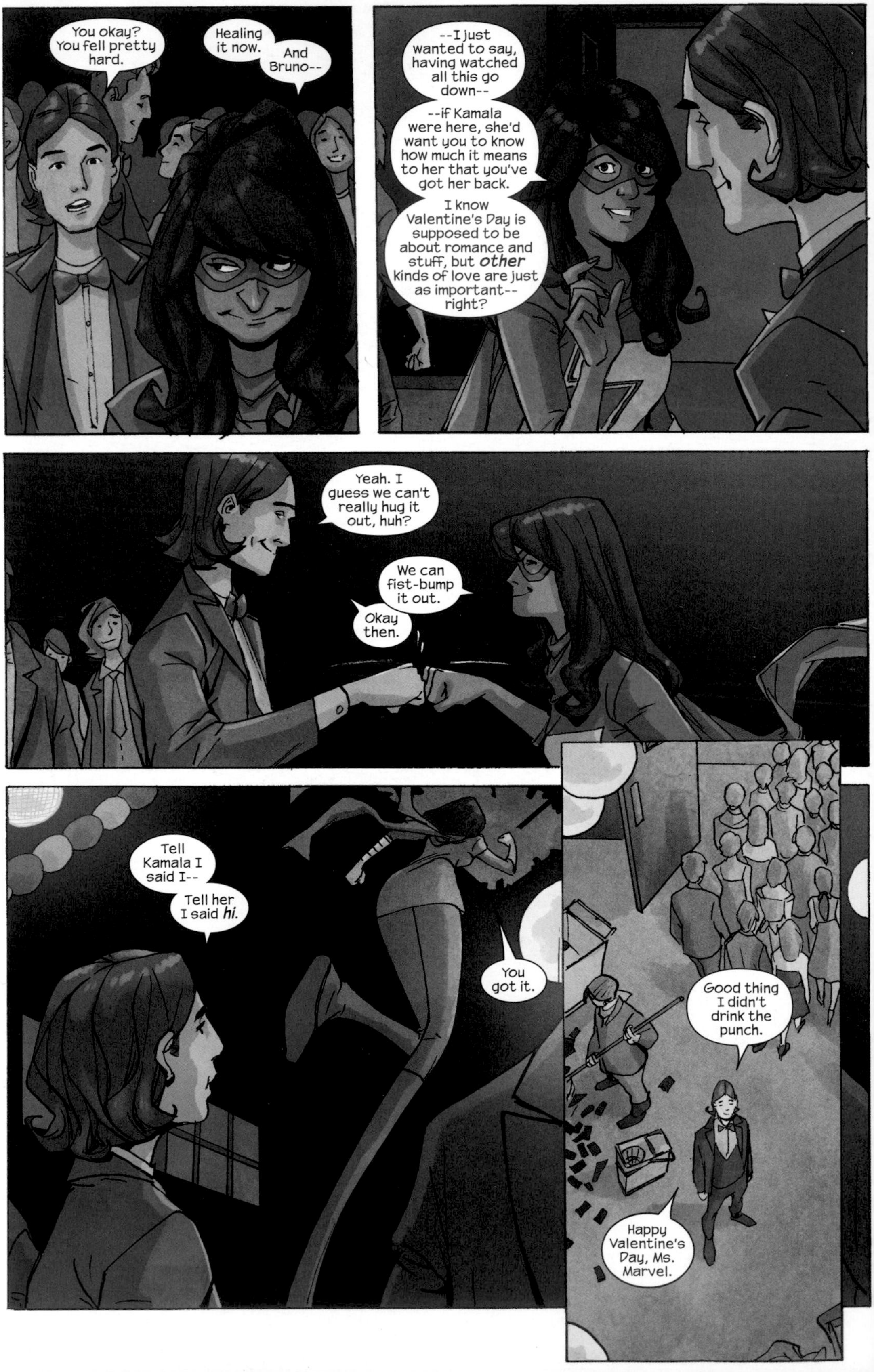
You okay? You fell pretty hard.
Healing it now.
And Bruno--
--I just wanted to say, having watched all this go down--
--if Kamala were here, she'd want you to know how much it means to her that you've got her back.
I know Valentine's Day is supposed to be about romance and stuff, but *other* kinds of love are just as important-- right?
Yeah. I guess we can't really hug it out, huh?
We can fist-bump it out.
Okay then.
Tell Kamala I said I--
Tell her I said *hi*.
You got it.
Good thing I didn't drink the punch.
Happy Valentine's Day, Ms. Marvel.

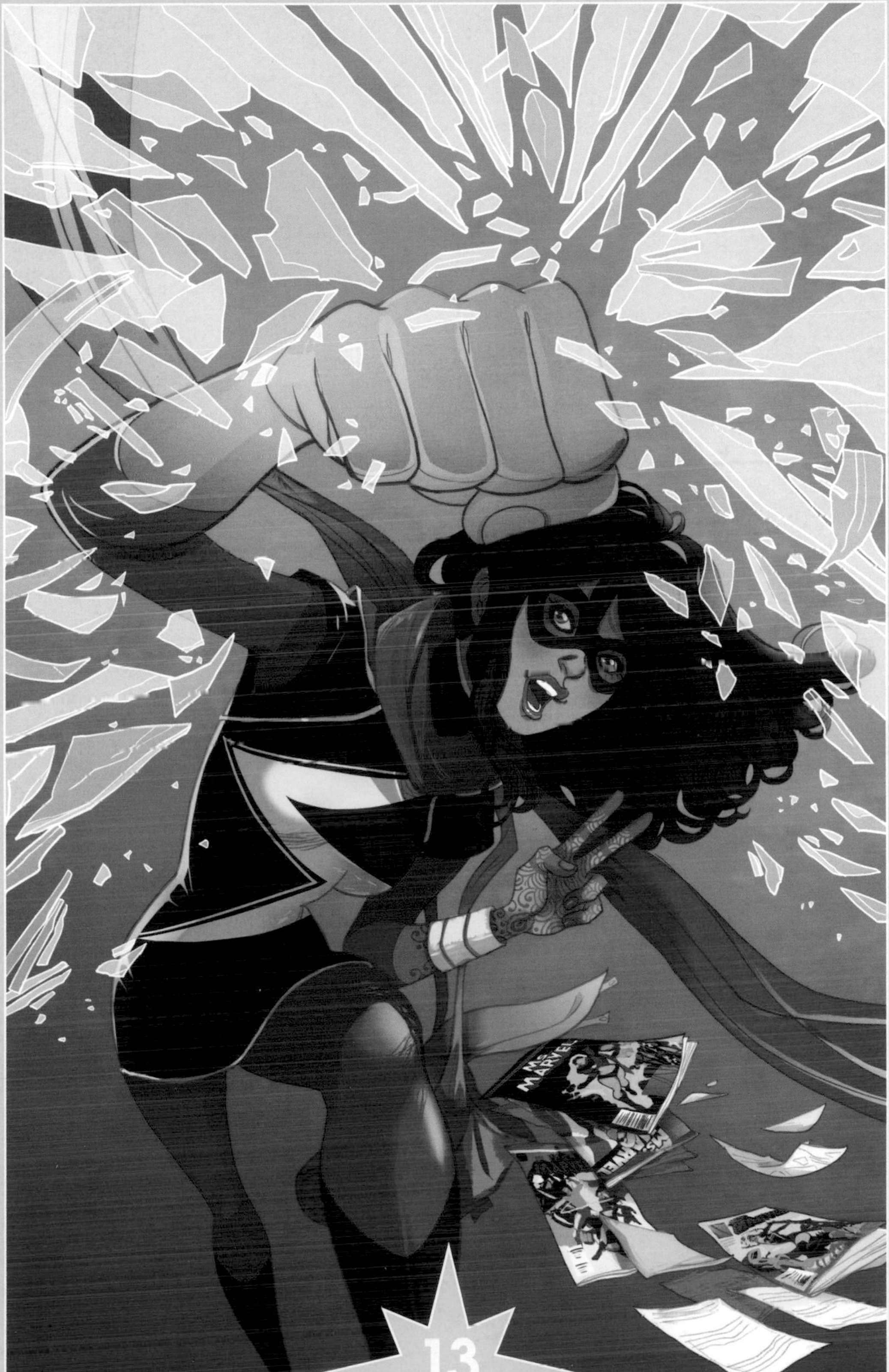
MS. MARVEL
13

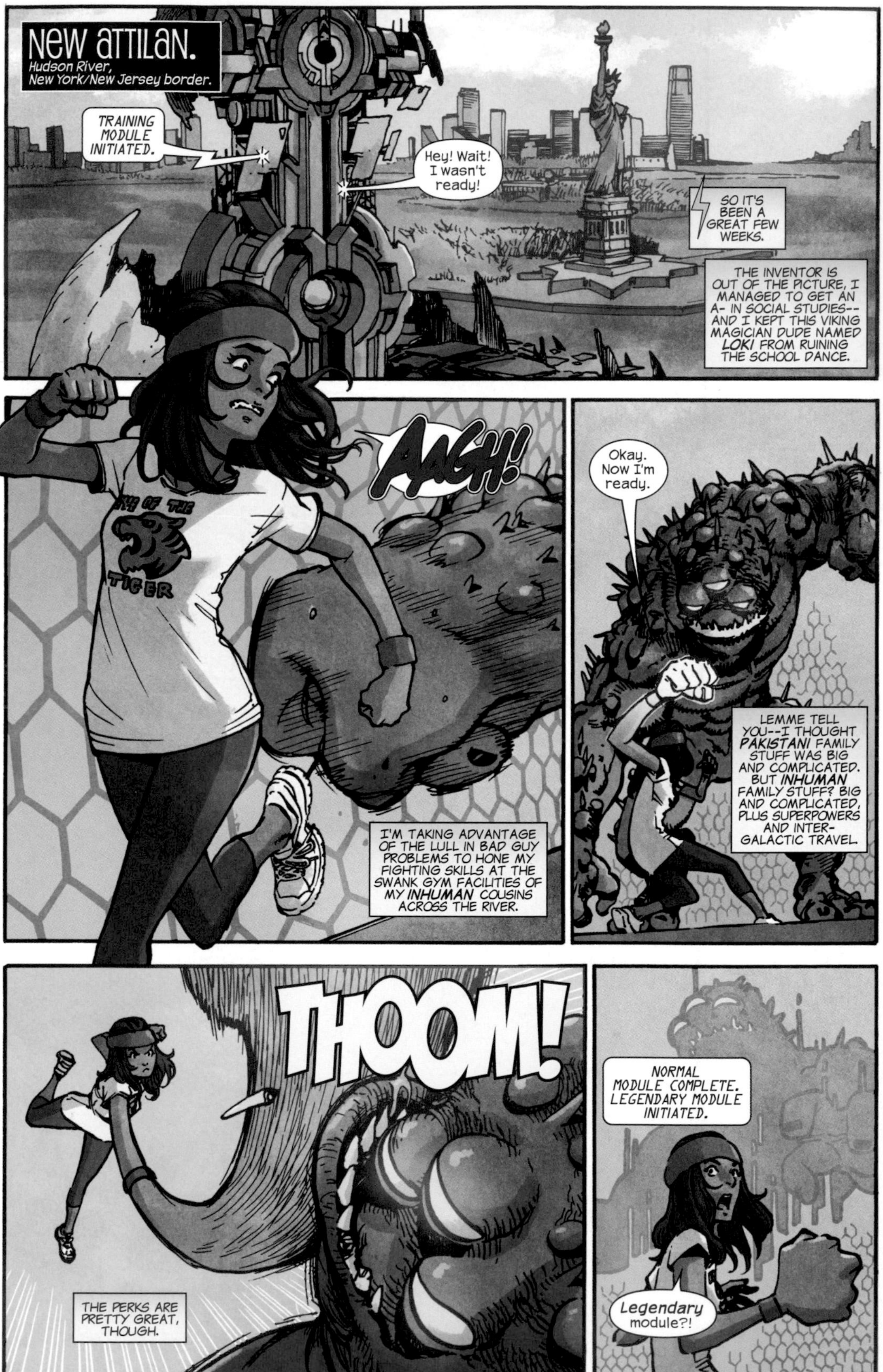
New Attilan.
Hudson River, New York/New Jersey border.
TRAINING MODULE INITIATED.
Hey! Wait! I wasn't ready!
SO IT'S BEEN A GREAT FEW WEEKS.
THE INVENTOR IS OUT OF THE PICTURE, I MANAGED TO GET AN A- IN SOCIAL STUDIES-- AND I KEPT THIS VIKING MAGICIAN DUDE NAMED LOKI FROM RUINING THE SCHOOL DANCE.
AAGH!
TIGER
I'M TAKING ADVANTAGE OF THE LULL IN BAD GUY PROBLEMS TO HONE MY FIGHTING SKILLS AT THE SWANK GYM FACILITIES OF MY INHUMAN COUSINS ACROSS THE RIVER.
Okay. Now I'm ready.
LEMME TELL YOU--I THOUGHT PAKISTANI FAMILY STUFF WAS BIG AND COMPLICATED. BUT INHUMAN FAMILY STUFF? BIG AND COMPLICATED, PLUS SUPERPOWERS AND INTER-GALACTIC TRAVEL.
THOOM!
THE PERKS ARE PRETTY GREAT, THOUGH.
NORMAL MODULE COMPLETE. LEGENDARY MODULE INITIATED.
Legendary module?!

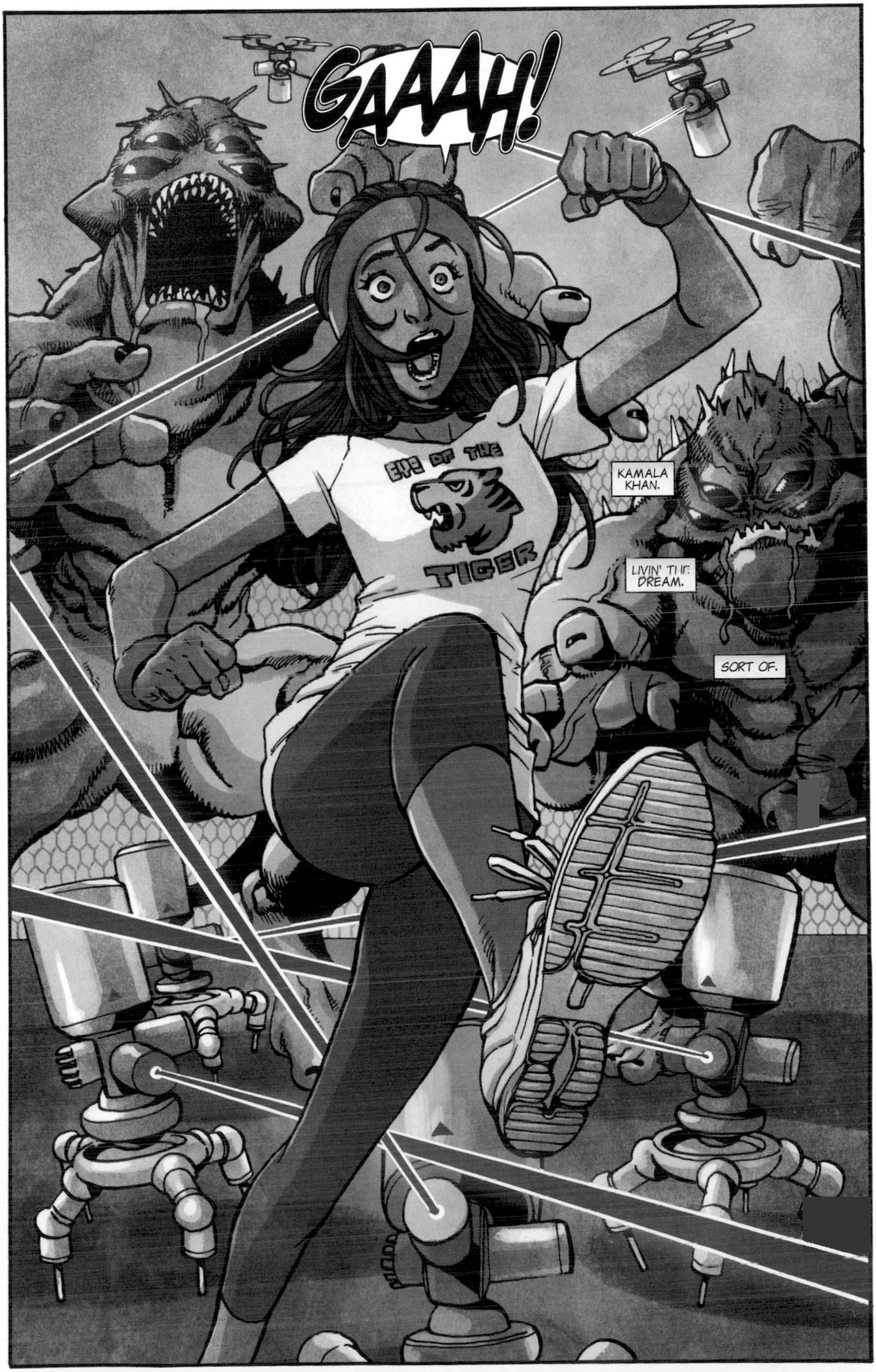
GAAAH!
EYE OF THE
TIGER
KAMALA KHAN.
LIVIN' THE DREAM.
SORT OF.

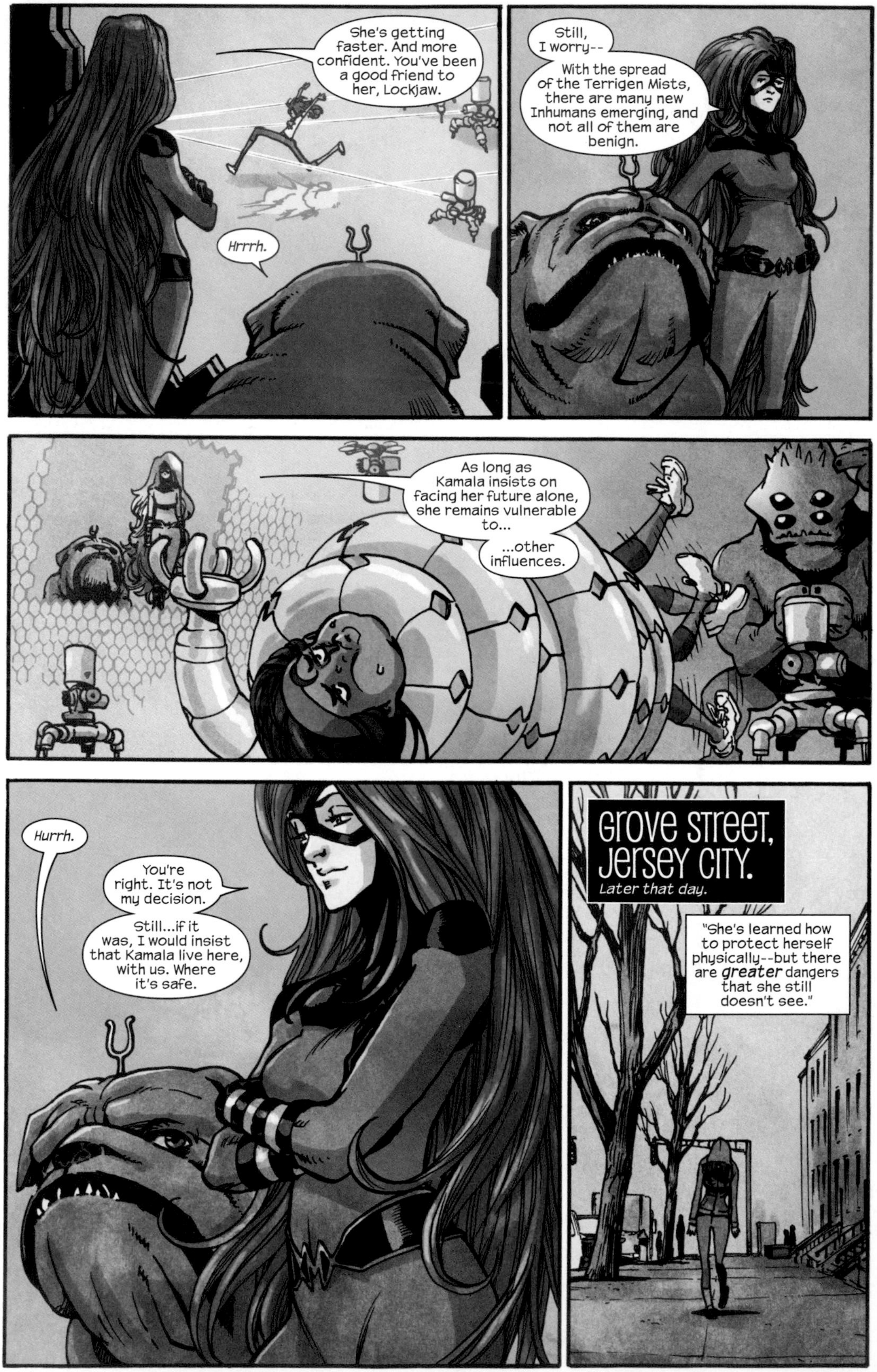
She's getting faster. And more confident. You've been a good friend to her, Lockjaw.
Hrrrh.
Still, I worry--
With the spread of the Terrigen Mists, there are many new Inhumans emerging, and not all of them are benign.
As long as Kamala insists on facing her future alone, she remains vulnerable to...
...other influences.
Hurrh.
You're right. It's not my decision.
Still...if it was, I would insist that Kamala live here, with us. Where it's safe.
GROVE STREET, JERSEY CITY.
Later that day.
"She's learned how to protect herself physically--but there are *greater* dangers that she still doesn't see."

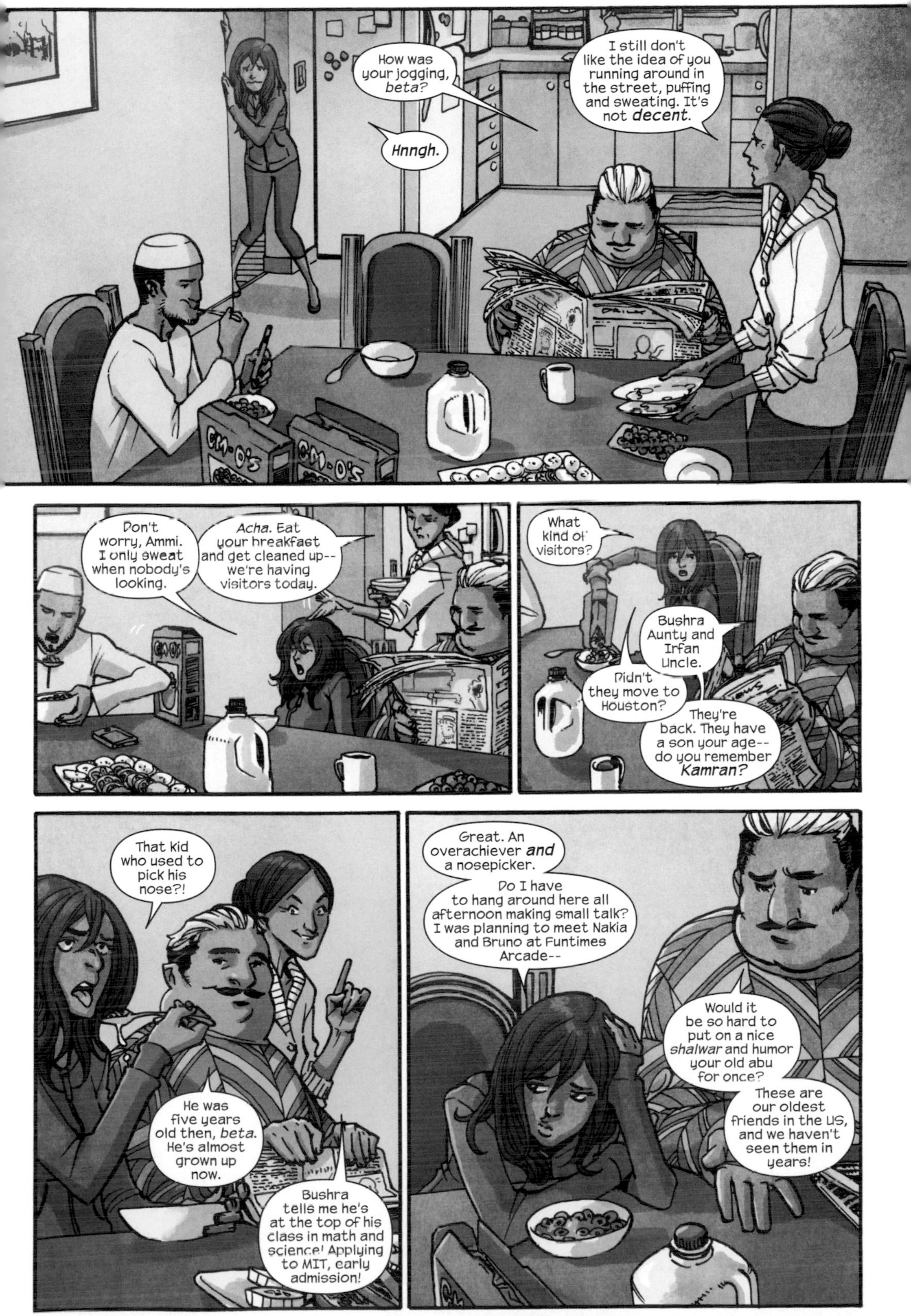
How was your jogging, *beta?*
Hnngh.
I still don't like the idea of you running around in the street, puffing and sweating. It's not **decent**.
Don't worry, Ammi. I only sweat when nobody's looking.
Acha. Eat your breakfast and get cleaned up--we're having visitors today.
What kind of visitors?
Bushra Aunty and Irfan Uncle.
Didn't they move to Houston?
They're back. They have a son your age--do you remember **Kamran?**
That kid who used to pick his nose?!
He was five years old then, *beta.* He's almost grown up now.
Bushra tells me he's at the top of his class in math and science! Applying to MIT, early admission!
Great. An overachiever **and** a nosepicker.
Do I have to hang around here all afternoon making small talk? I was planning to meet Nakia and Bruno at Funtimes Arcade--
Would it be so hard to put on a nice *shalwar* and humor your old abu for once?
These are our oldest friends in the US, and we haven't seen them in years!

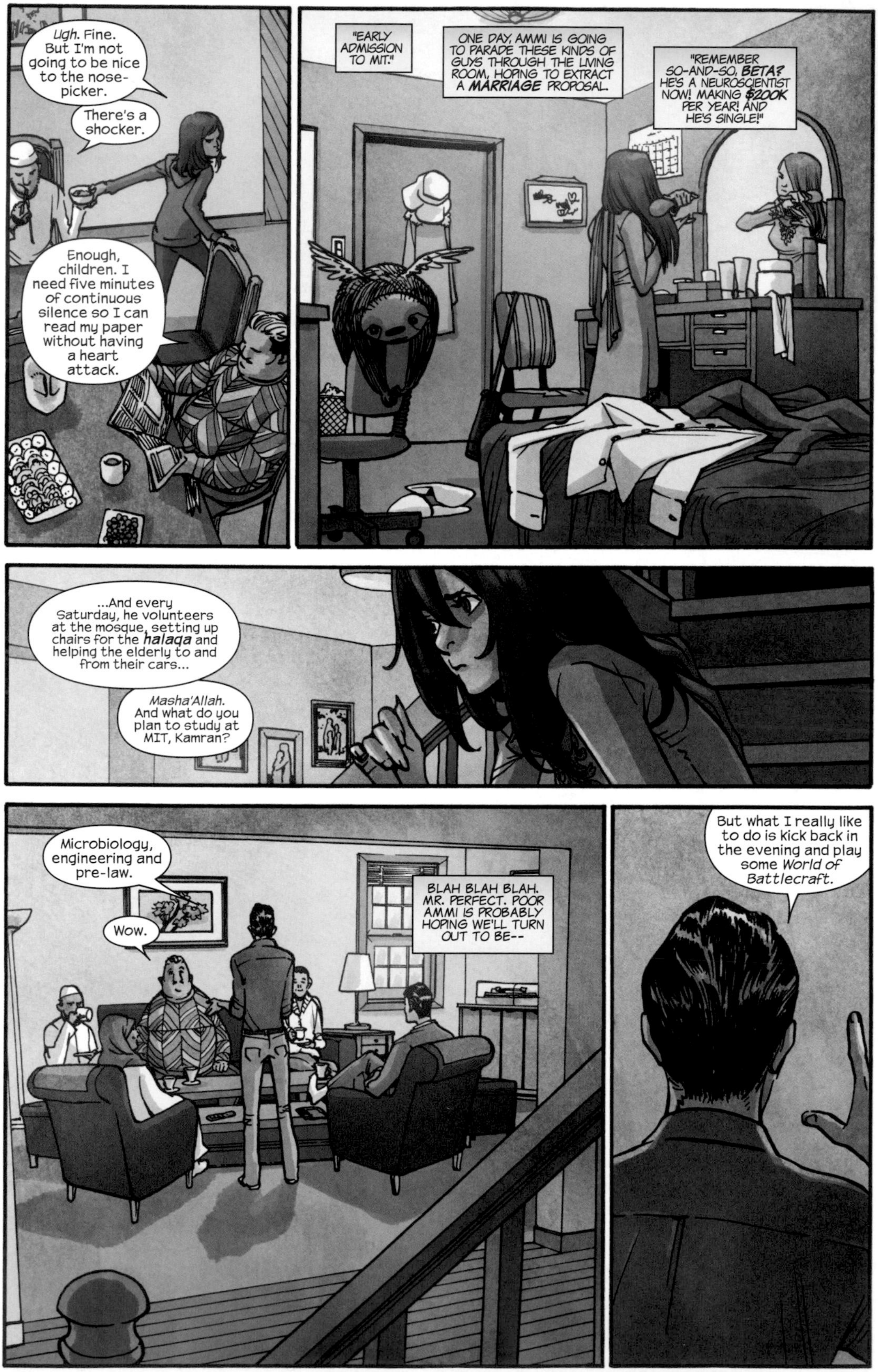
Ugh. Fine. But I'm not going to be nice to the nose-picker.
There's a shocker.
Enough, children. I need five minutes of continuous silence so I can read my paper without having a heart attack.
"EARLY ADMISSION TO MIT."
ONE DAY, AMMI IS GOING TO PARADE THESE KINDS OF GUYS THROUGH THE LIVING ROOM, HOPING TO EXTRACT A ***MARRIAGE*** PROPOSAL.
"REMEMBER SO-AND-SO, ***BETA?*** HE'S A NEUROSCIENTIST NOW! MAKING ***$200K*** PER YEAR! AND HE'S SINGLE!"
...And every Saturday, he volunteers at the mosque, setting up chairs for the ***halaqa*** and helping the elderly to and from their cars...
Masha'Allah. And what do you plan to study at MIT, Kamran?
Microbiology, engineering and pre-law.
Wow.
BLAH BLAH BLAH. MR. PERFECT. POOR AMMI IS PROBABLY HOPING WE'LL TURN OUT TO BE--
But what I really like to do is kick back in the evening and play some *World of Battlecraft*.

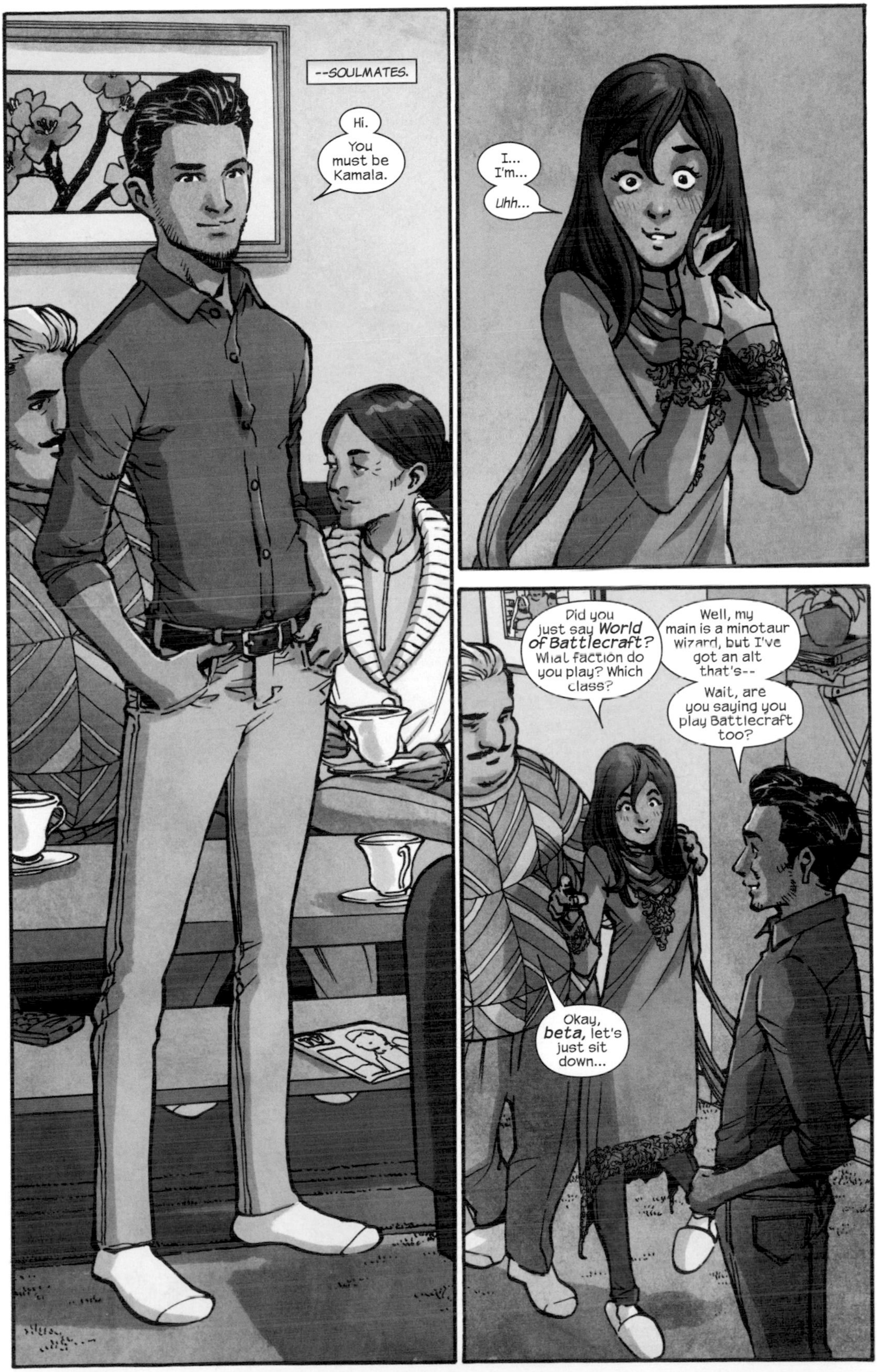
--SOULMATES.
Hi. You must be Kamala.
I... I'm...
Uhh...
Did you just say World of Battlecraft? What faction do you play? Which class?
Well, my main is a minotaur wizard, but I've got an alt that's--
Wait, are you saying you play Battlecraft too?
Okay, beta, let's just sit down...

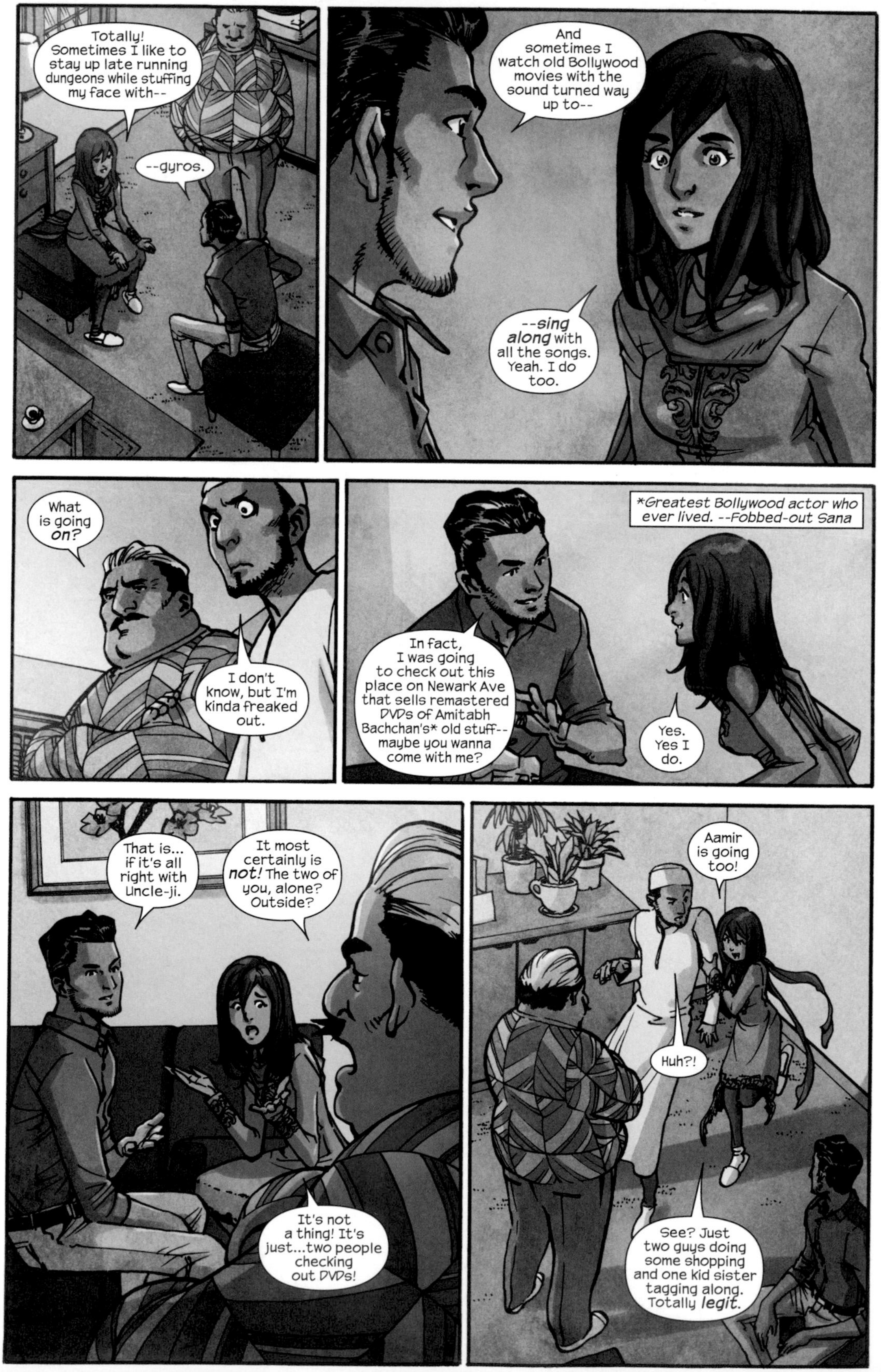
Totally! Sometimes I like to stay up late running dungeons while stuffing my face with--
--gyros.
And sometimes I watch old Bollywood movies with the sound turned way up to--
--*sing along* with all the songs. Yeah. I do too.
What is going *on?*
I don't know, but I'm kinda freaked out.
*Greatest Bollywood actor who ever lived. --Fobbed-out Sana
In fact, I was going to check out this place on Newark Ave that sells remastered DVDs of Amitabh Bachchan's* old stuff--maybe you wanna come with me?
Yes. Yes I do.
That is... if it's all right with Uncle-ji.
It most certainly is *not!* The two of you, alone? Outside?
It's not a thing! It's just...two people checking out DVDs!
Aamir is going too!
Huh?!
See? Just two guys doing some shopping and one kid sister tagging along. Totally *legit*.

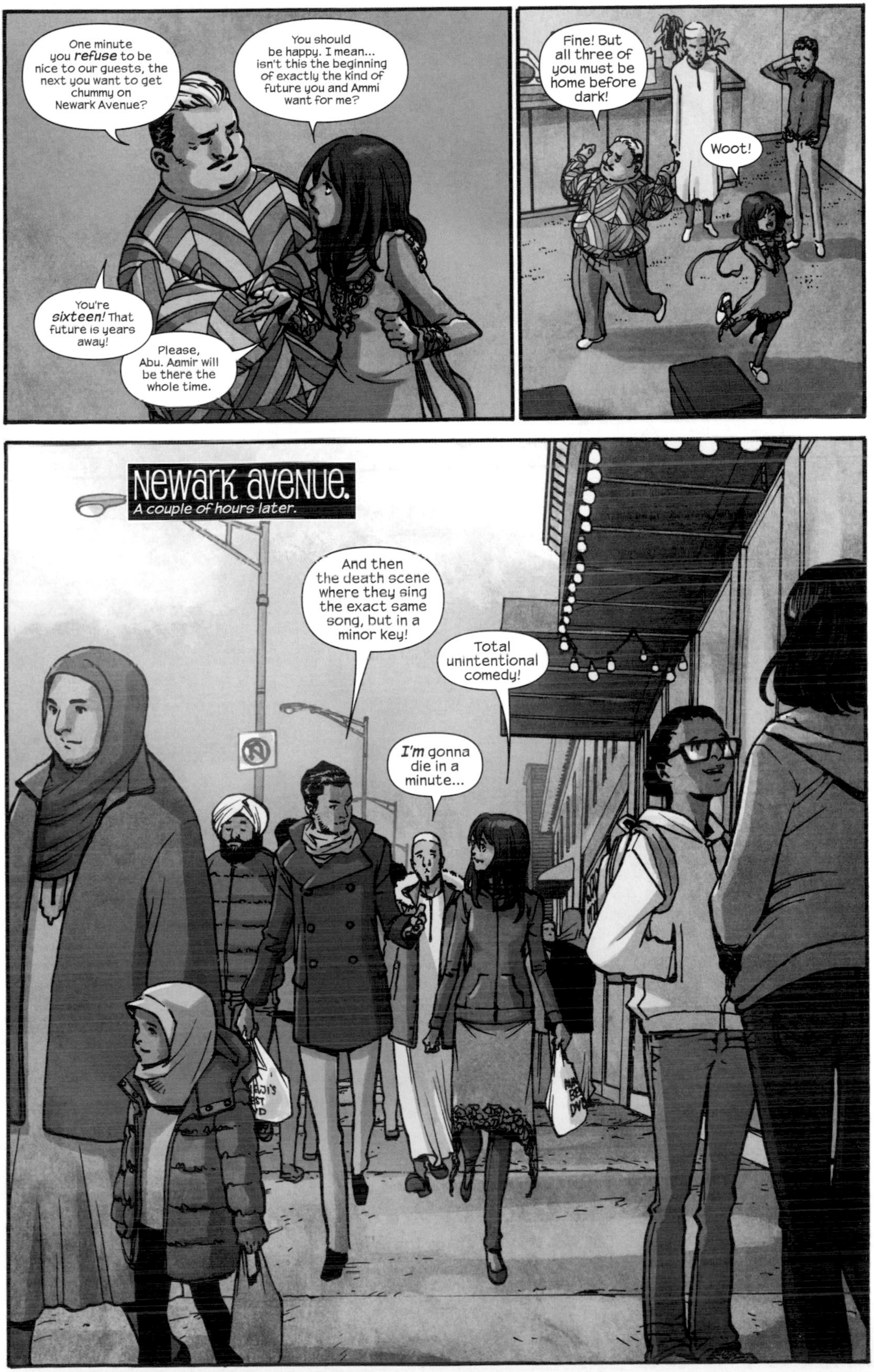
One minute you *refuse* to be nice to our guests, the next you want to get chummy on Newark Avenue?
You should be happy. I mean... isn't this the beginning of exactly the kind of future you and Ammi want for me?
You're *sixteen!* That future is years away!
Please, Abu. Aamir will be there the whole time.
Fine! But all three of you must be home before dark!
Woot!
Newark Avenue.
A couple of hours later.
And then the death scene where they sing the exact same song, but in a minor key!
Total unintentional comedy!
I'm gonna die in a minute...

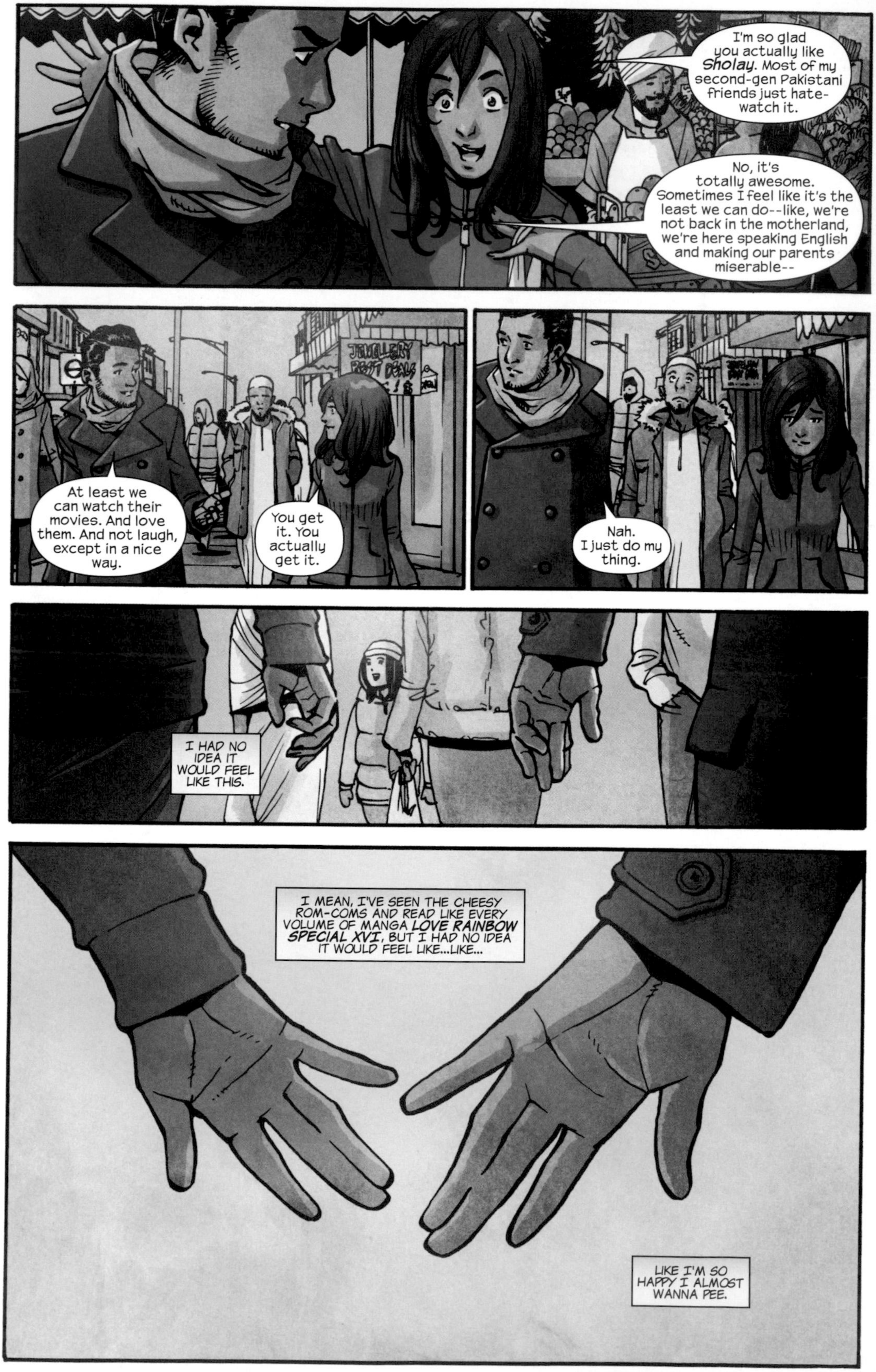
I'm so glad you actually like *Sholay*. Most of my second-gen Pakistani friends just hate-watch it.
No, it's totally awesome. Sometimes I feel like it's the least we can do--like, we're not back in the motherland, we're here speaking English and making our parents miserable--
JEWELLERY BEST DEALS
At least we can watch their movies. And love them. And not laugh, except in a nice way.
You get it. You actually get it.
Nah. I just do my thing.
I HAD NO IDEA IT WOULD FEEL LIKE THIS.
I MEAN, I'VE SEEN THE CHEESY ROM-COMS AND READ LIKE EVERY VOLUME OF MANGA *LOVE RAINBOW SPECIAL XVI*, BUT I HAD NO IDEA IT WOULD FEEL LIKE...LIKE...
LIKE I'M SO HAPPY I ALMOST WANNA PEE.

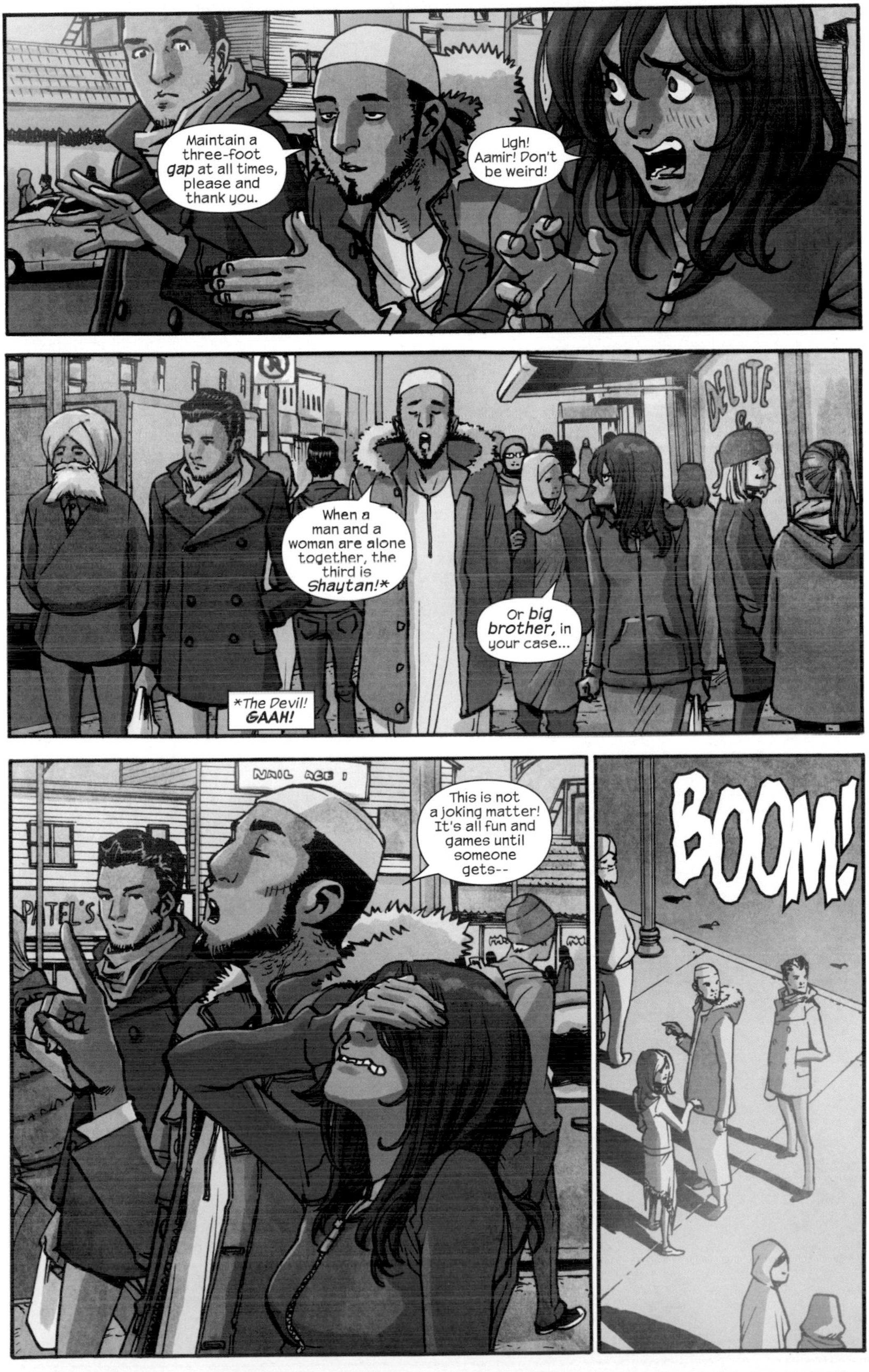
Maintain a three-foot *gap* at all times, please and thank you.
Ugh! Aamir! Don't be weird!
DELITE
When a man and a woman are alone together, the third is *Shaytan!**
Or *big brother,* in your case...
*The Devil! **GAAH!**
PATEL'S
This is not a joking matter! It's all fun and games until someone gets--
BOOM!

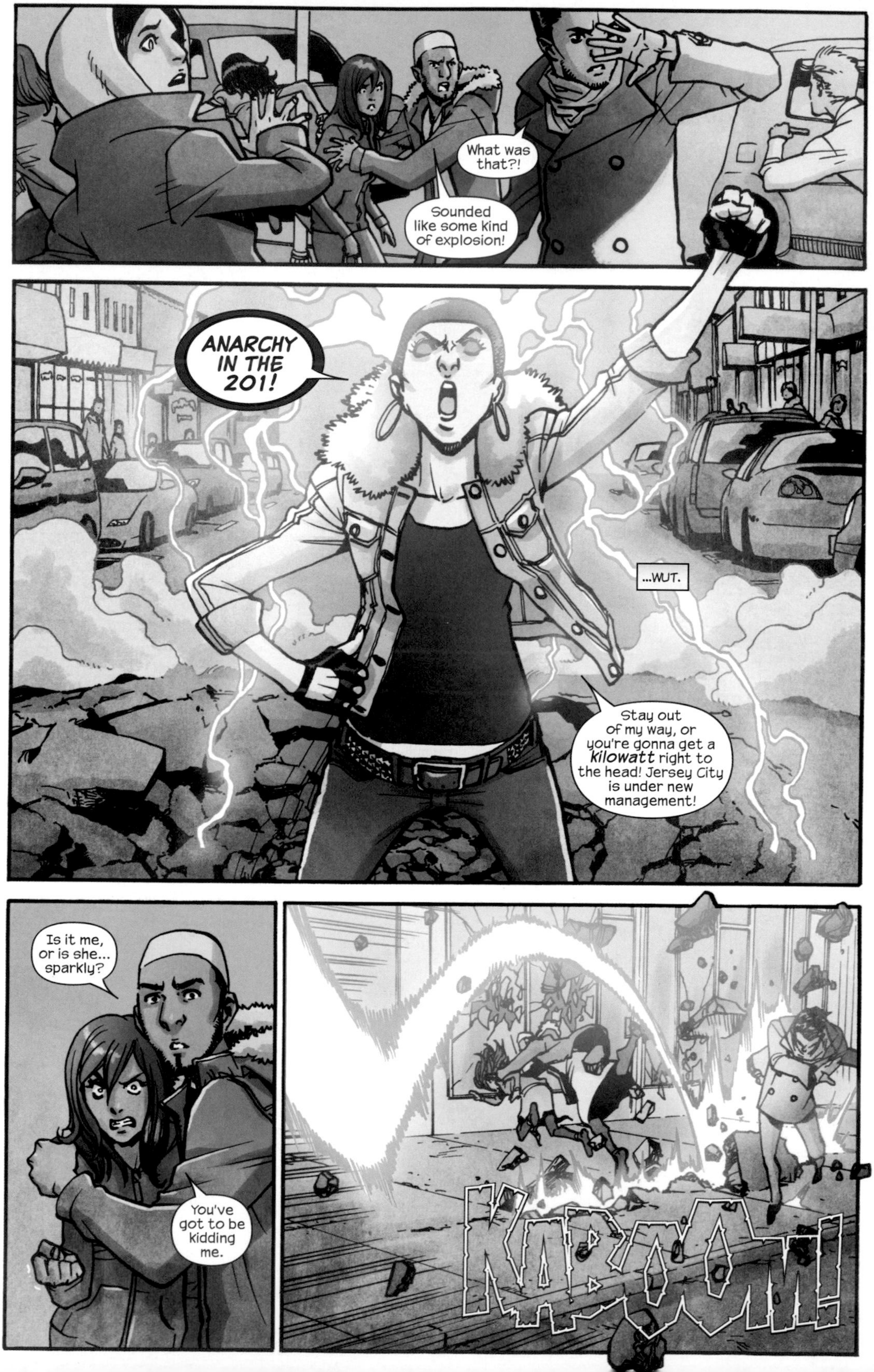
What was that?!
Sounded like some kind of explosion!
ANARCHY IN THE 201!
...WUT.
Stay out of my way, or you're gonna get a kilowatt right to the head! Jersey City is under new management!
Is it me, or is she... sparkly?
You've got to be kidding me.
KA-BOOM!

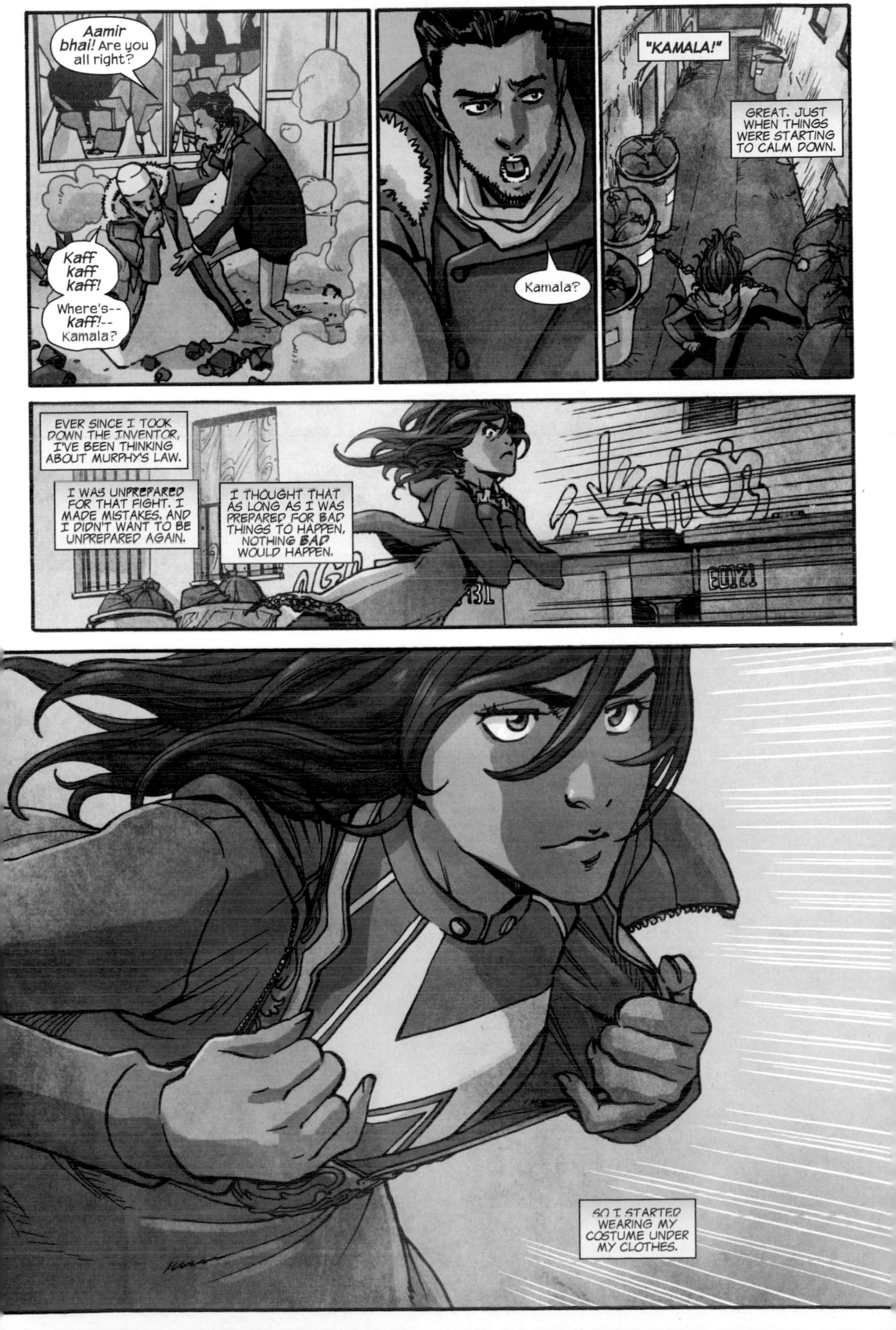
Aamir bhai! Are you all right?
Kaff kaff kaff!
Where's-- kaff!-- Kamala?
Kamala?
"KAMALA!"
GREAT. JUST WHEN THINGS WERE STARTING TO CALM DOWN.
EVER SINCE I TOOK DOWN THE INVENTOR, I'VE BEEN THINKING ABOUT MURPHY'S LAW.
I WAS UNPREPARED FOR THAT FIGHT. I MADE MISTAKES, AND I DIDN'T WANT TO BE UNPREPARED AGAIN.
I THOUGHT THAT AS LONG AS I WAS PREPARED FOR BAD THINGS TO HAPPEN, NOTHING BAD WOULD HAPPEN.
SO I STARTED WEARING MY COSTUME UNDER MY CLOTHES.

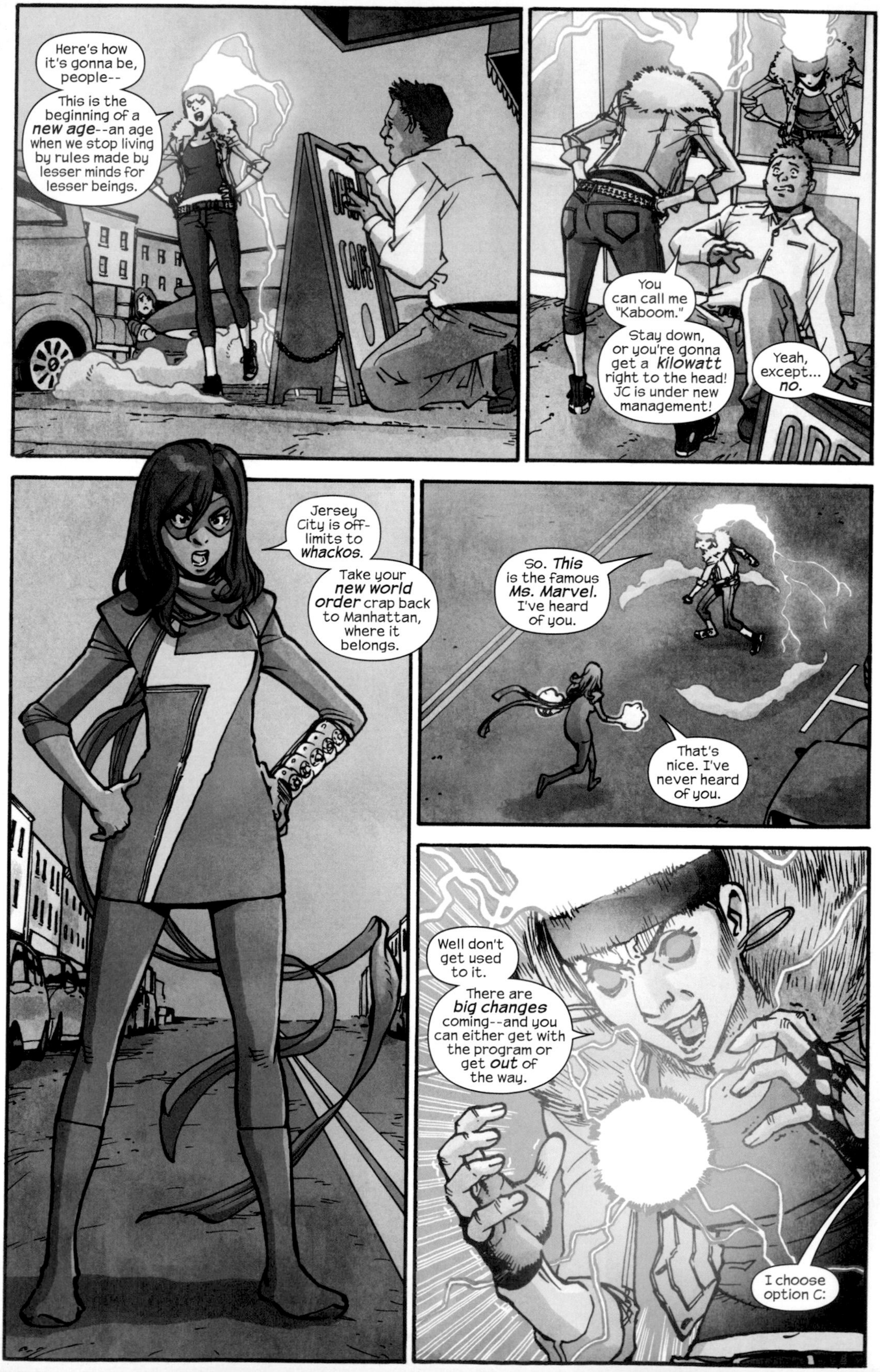
Here's how it's gonna be, people--
This is the beginning of a new age--an age when we stop living by rules made by lesser minds for lesser beings.
You can call me "Kaboom."
Stay down, or you're gonna get a kilowatt right to the head! JC is under new management!
Yeah, except... no.
Jersey City is off-limits to whackos.
Take your new world order crap back to Manhattan, where it belongs.
So. This is the famous Ms. Marvel. I've heard of you.
That's nice. I've never heard of you.
Well don't get used to it.
There are big changes coming--and you can either get with the program or get out of the way.
I choose option C:

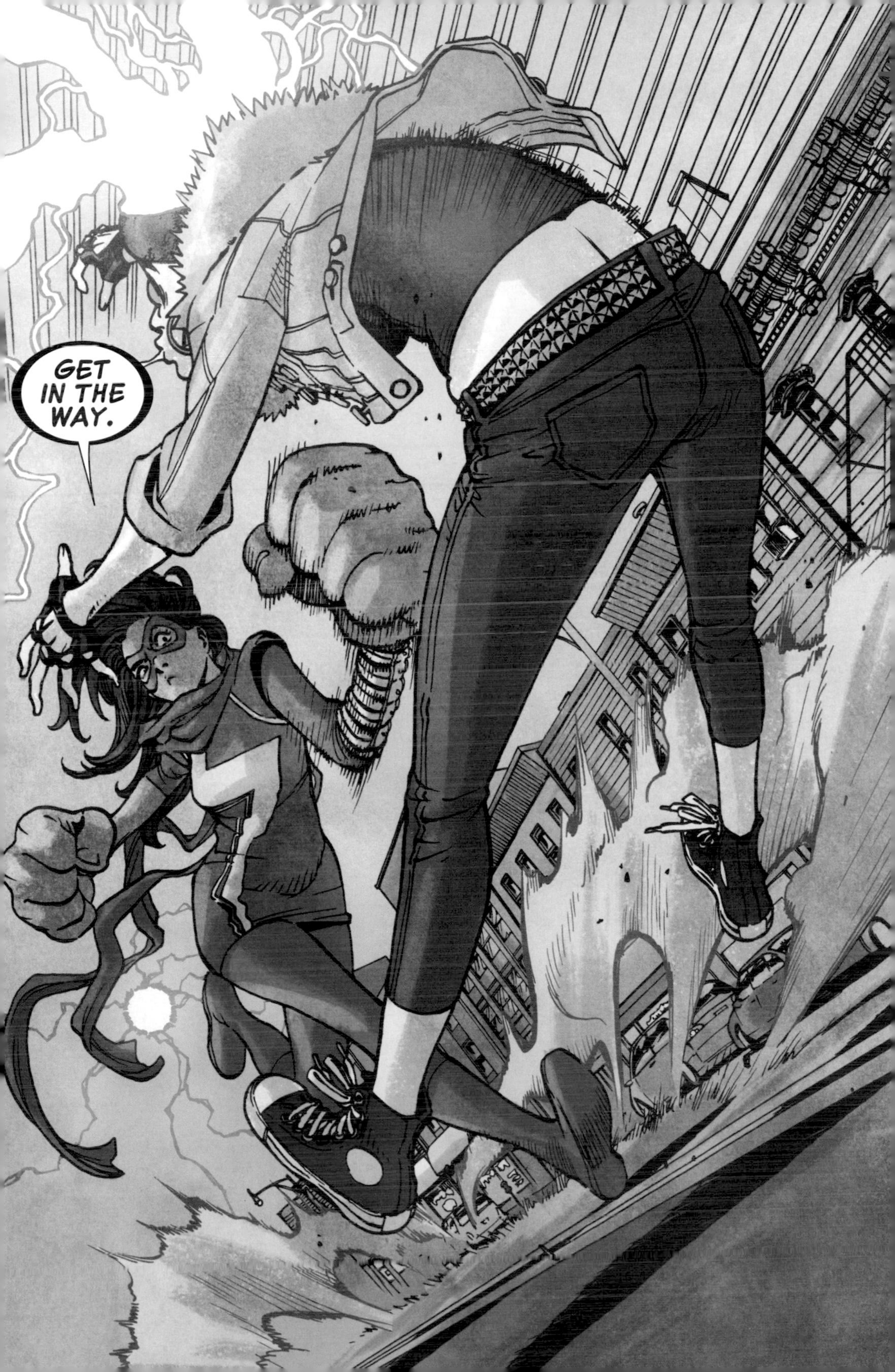
GET IN THE WAY.

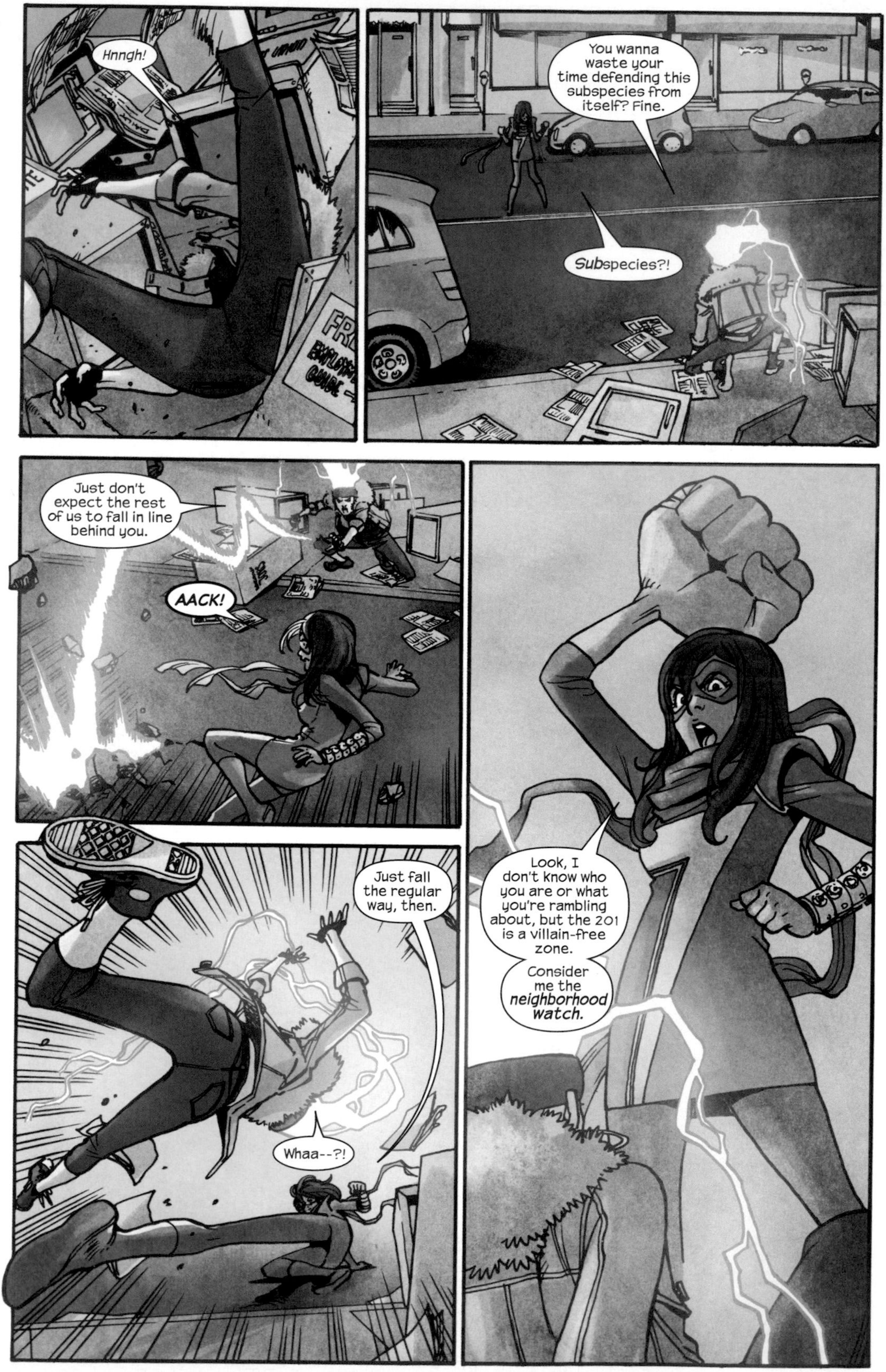
Hnngh!
You wanna waste your time defending this subspecies from itself? Fine.
Subspecies?!
Just don't expect the rest of us to fall in line behind you.
AACK!
Just fall the regular way, then.
Whaa--?!
Look, I don't know who you are or what you're rambling about, but the 201 is a villain-free zone.
Consider me the neighborhood watch.

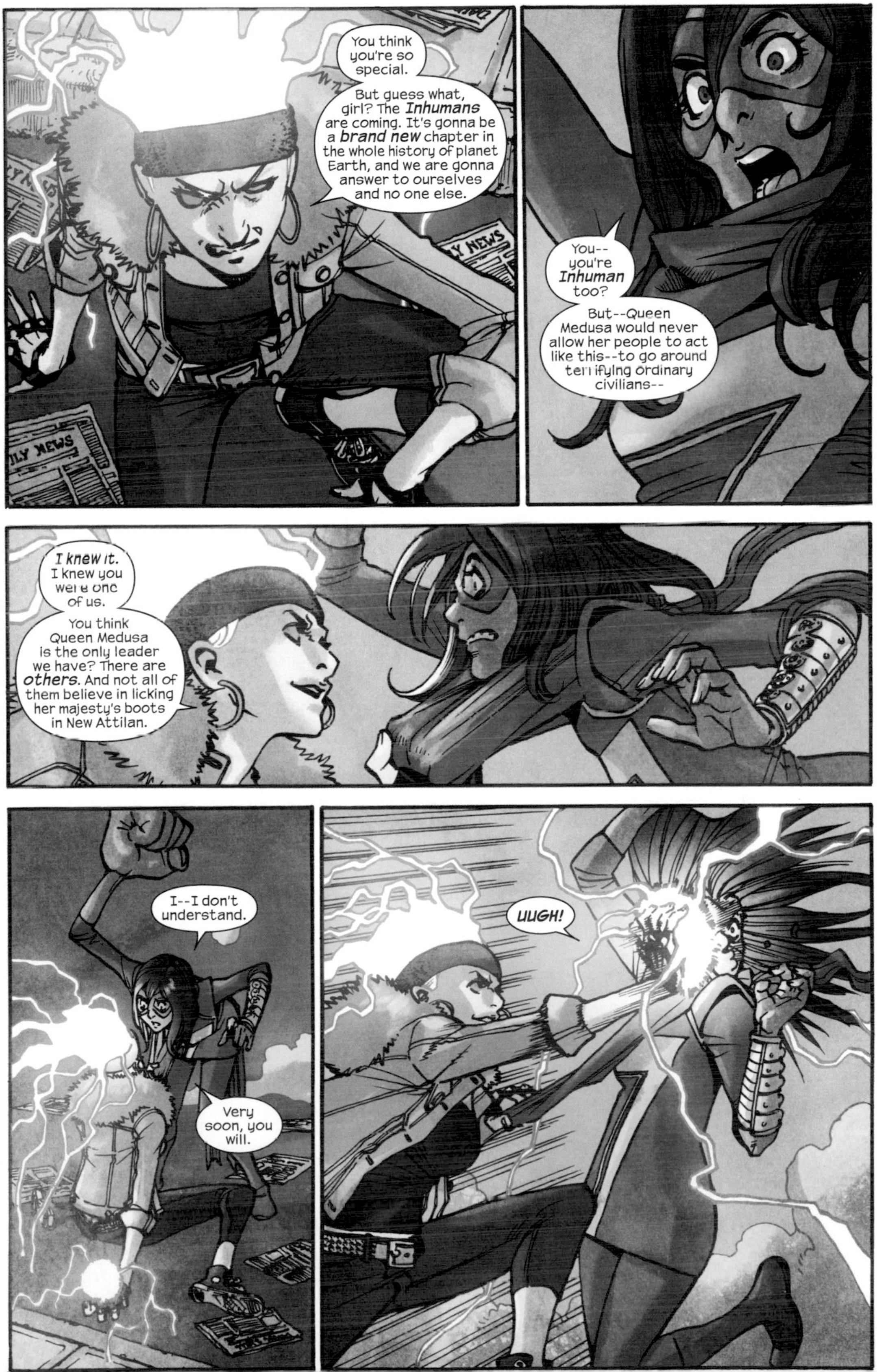
You think you're so special.
But guess what, girl? The *Inhumans* are coming. It's gonna be a *brand new* chapter in the whole history of planet Earth, and we are gonna answer to ourselves and no one else.
You-- you're *Inhuman* too?
But--Queen Medusa would never allow her people to act like this--to go around terrifying ordinary civilians--
I knew it. I knew you were one of us.
You think Queen Medusa is the only leader we have? There are *others*. And not all of them believe in licking her majesty's boots in New Attilan.
I--I don't understand.
Very soon, you will.
UUGH!

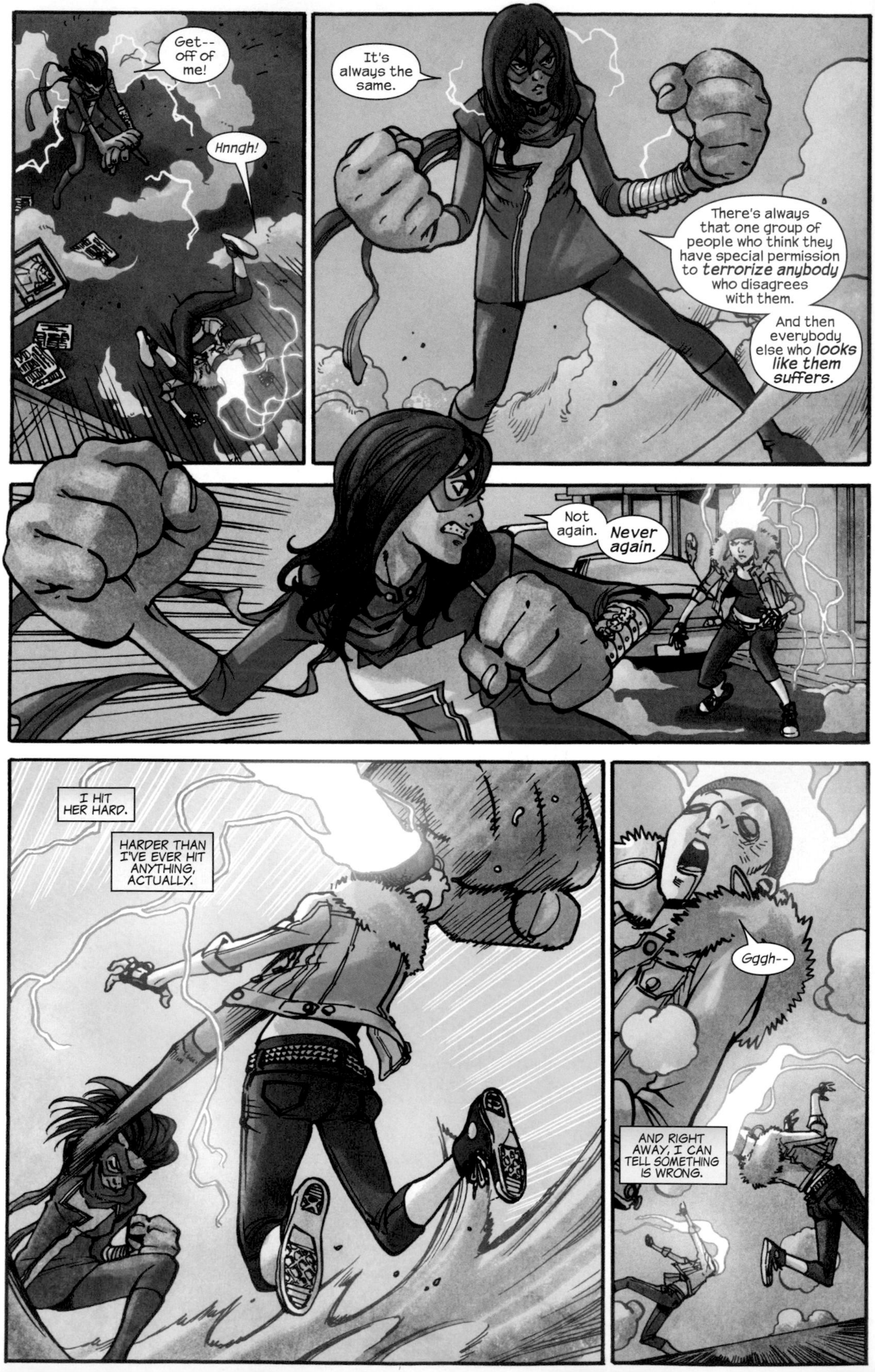
Get-- off of me!
Hnngh!
It's always the same.
There's always that one group of people who think they have special permission to *terrorize anybody* who disagrees with them.
And then everybody else who **looks like them suffers.**
Not again.
Never again.
I HIT HER HARD.
HARDER THAN I'VE EVER HIT ANYTHING, ACTUALLY.
Gggh--
AND RIGHT AWAY, I CAN TELL SOMETHING IS WRONG.

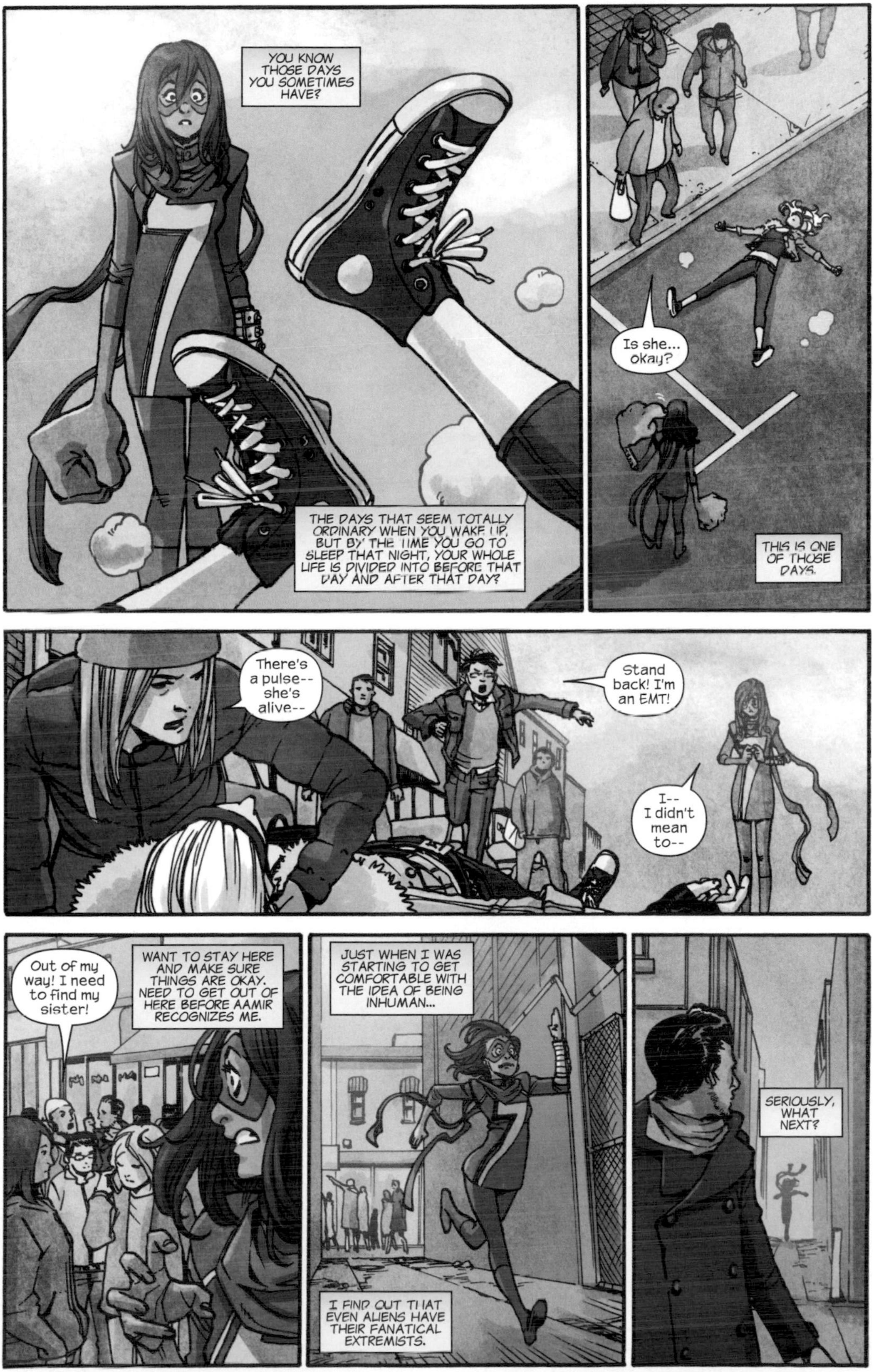
YOU KNOW THOSE DAYS YOU SOMETIMES HAVE?
THE DAYS THAT SEEM TOTALLY ORDINARY WHEN YOU WAKE UP, BUT BY THE TIME YOU GO TO SLEEP THAT NIGHT, YOUR WHOLE LIFE IS DIVIDED INTO BEFORE THAT DAY AND AFTER THAT DAY?
Is she... okay?
THIS IS ONE OF THOSE DAYS.
There's a pulse-- she's alive--
Stand back! I'm an EMT!
I-- I didn't mean to--
Out of my way! I need to find my sister!
WANT TO STAY HERE AND MAKE SURE THINGS ARE OKAY. NEED TO GET OUT OF HERE BEFORE AAMIR RECOGNIZES ME.
JUST WHEN I WAS STARTING TO GET COMFORTABLE WITH THE IDEA OF BEING INHUMAN...
I FIND OUT THAT EVEN ALIENS HAVE THEIR FANATICAL EXTREMISTS.
SERIOUSLY, WHAT NEXT?

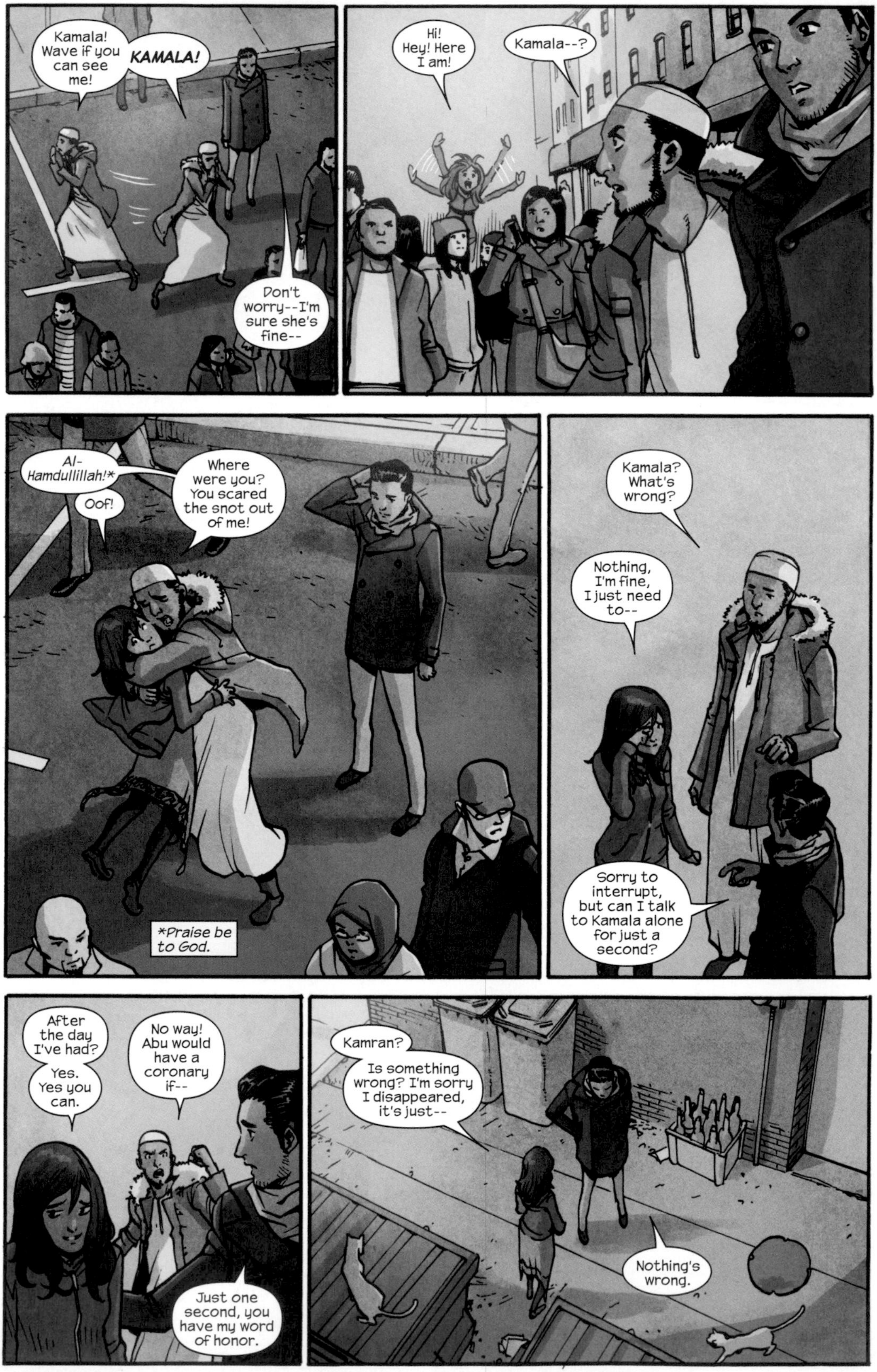

Kamala! Wave if you can see me!
KAMALA!
Don't worry--I'm sure she's fine--
Hi! Hey! Here I am!
Kamala--?
Al-Hamdullillah!*
Where were you? You scared the snot out of me!
Oof!
*Praise be to God.
Kamala? What's wrong?
Nothing, I'm fine, I just need to--
Sorry to interrupt, but can I talk to Kamala alone for just a second?
After the day I've had?
Yes. Yes you can.
No way! Abu would have a coronary if--
Just one second, you have my word of honor.
Kamran?
Is something wrong? I'm sorry I disappeared, it's just--
Nothing's wrong.

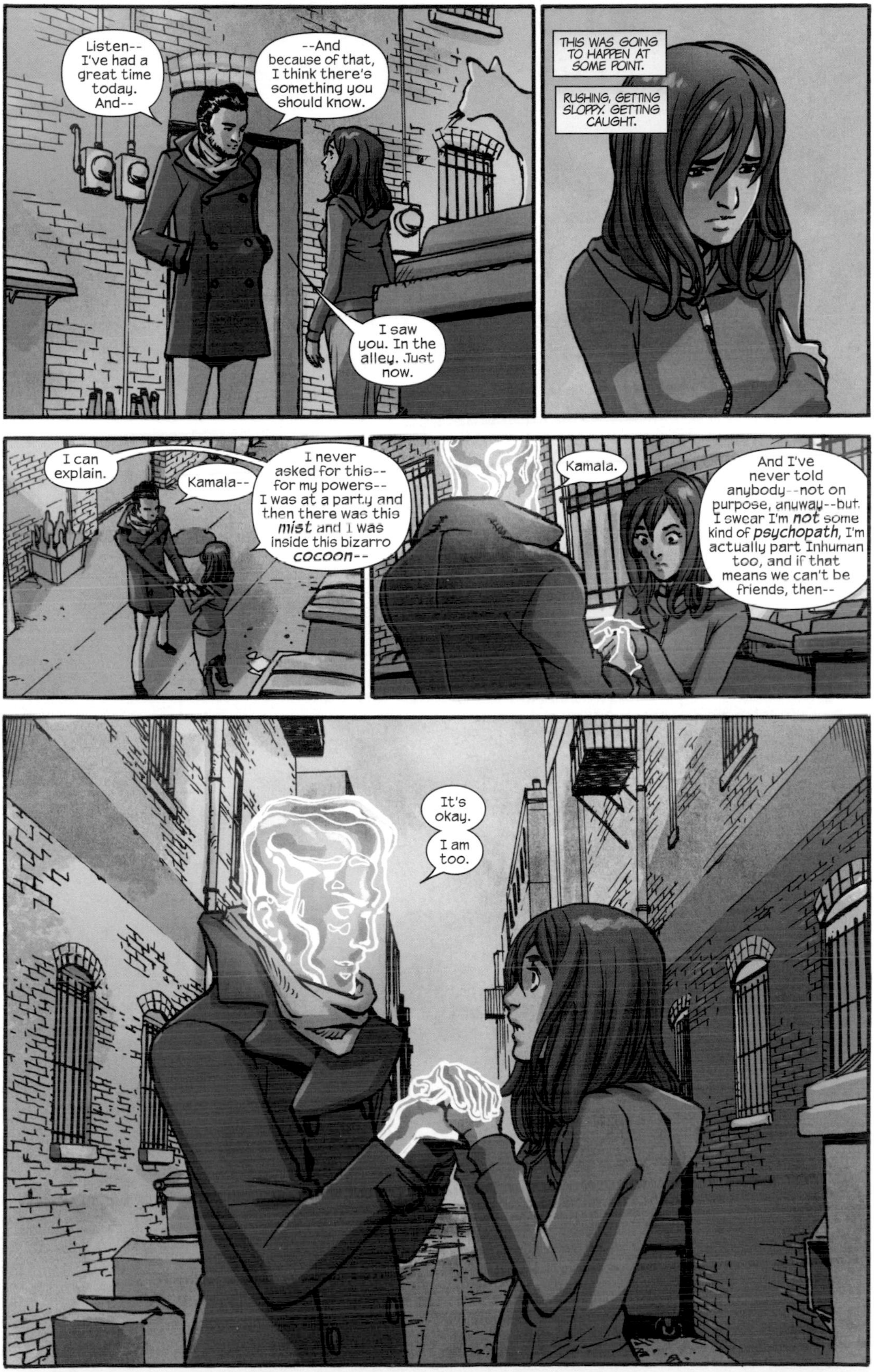
Listen-- I've had a great time today. And--
--And because of that, I think there's something you should know.
I saw you. In the alley. Just now.
THIS WAS GOING TO HAPPEN AT SOME POINT.
RUSHING, GETTING SLOPPY. GETTING CAUGHT.
I can explain.
Kamala--
I never asked for this-- for my powers-- I was at a party and then there was this mist and I was inside this bizarro cocoon--
Kamala.
And I've never told anybody--not on purpose, anyway--but. I swear I'm not some kind of psychopath, I'm actually part Inhuman too, and if that means we can't be friends, then--
It's okay.
I am too.

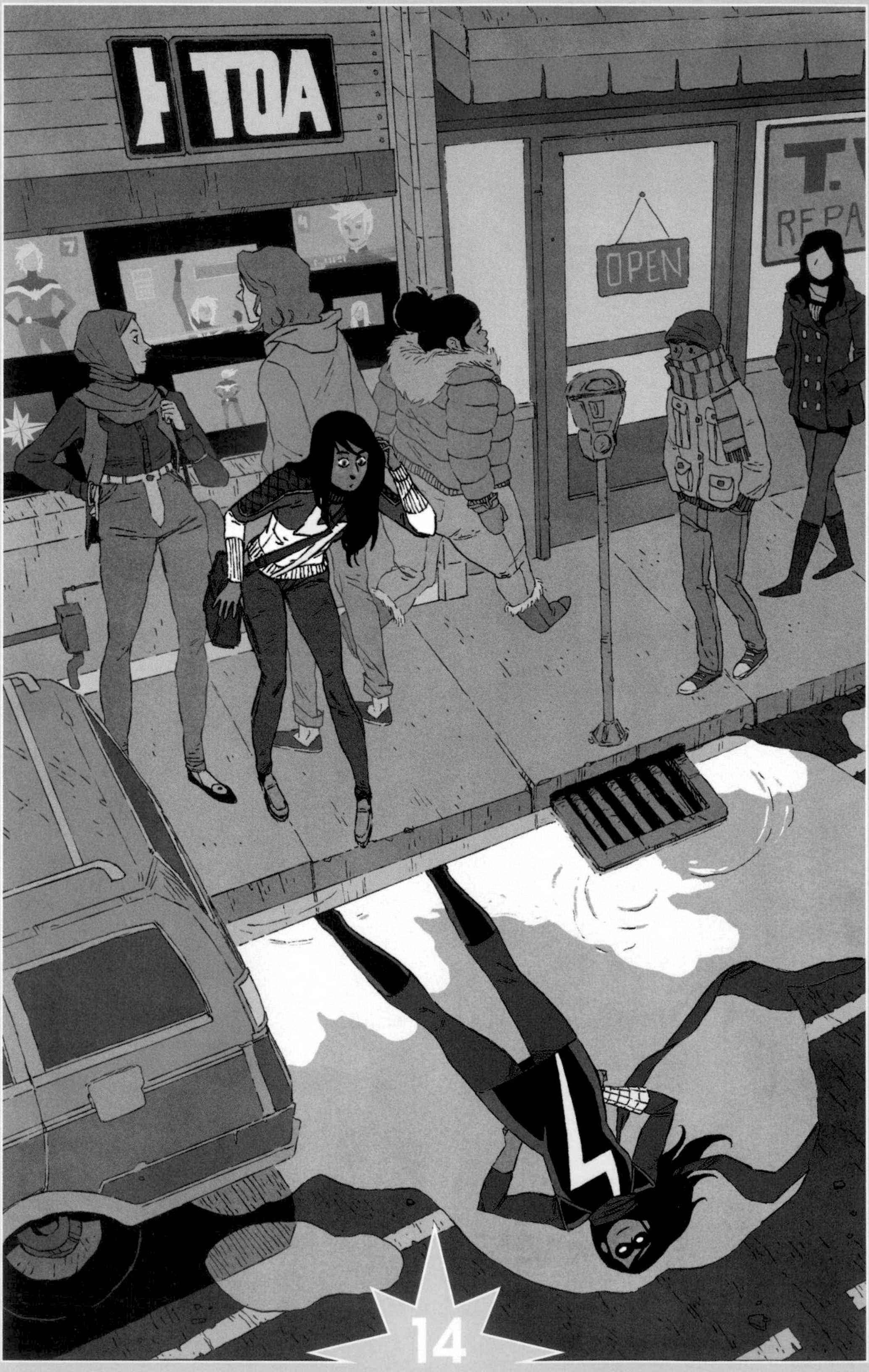
OPEN
14

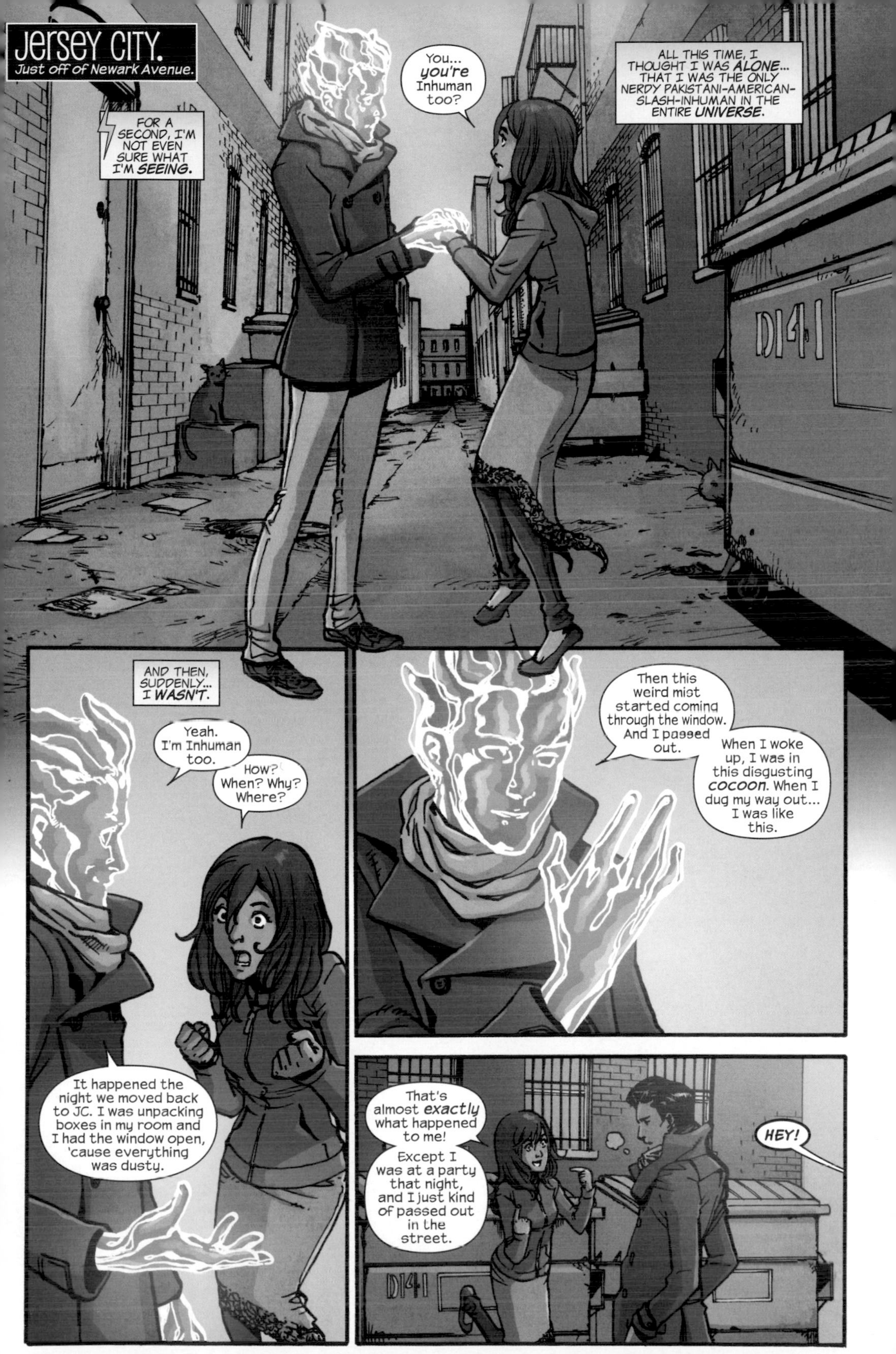
JERSEY CITY.
Just off of Newark Avenue.
FOR A SECOND, I'M NOT EVEN SURE WHAT I'M SEEING.
You... you're Inhuman too?
ALL THIS TIME, I THOUGHT I WAS ALONE... THAT I WAS THE ONLY NERDY PAKISTANI-AMERICAN-SLASH-INHUMAN IN THE ENTIRE UNIVERSE.
AND THEN, SUDDENLY... I WASN'T.
Yeah. I'm Inhuman too.
How? When? Why? Where?
It happened the night we moved back to JC. I was unpacking boxes in my room and I had the window open, 'cause everything was dusty.
Then this weird mist started coming through the window. And I passed out.
When I woke up, I was in this disgusting cocoon. When I dug my way out... I was like this.
That's almost exactly what happened to me!
Except I was at a party that night, and I just kind of passed out in the street.
HEY!
D141

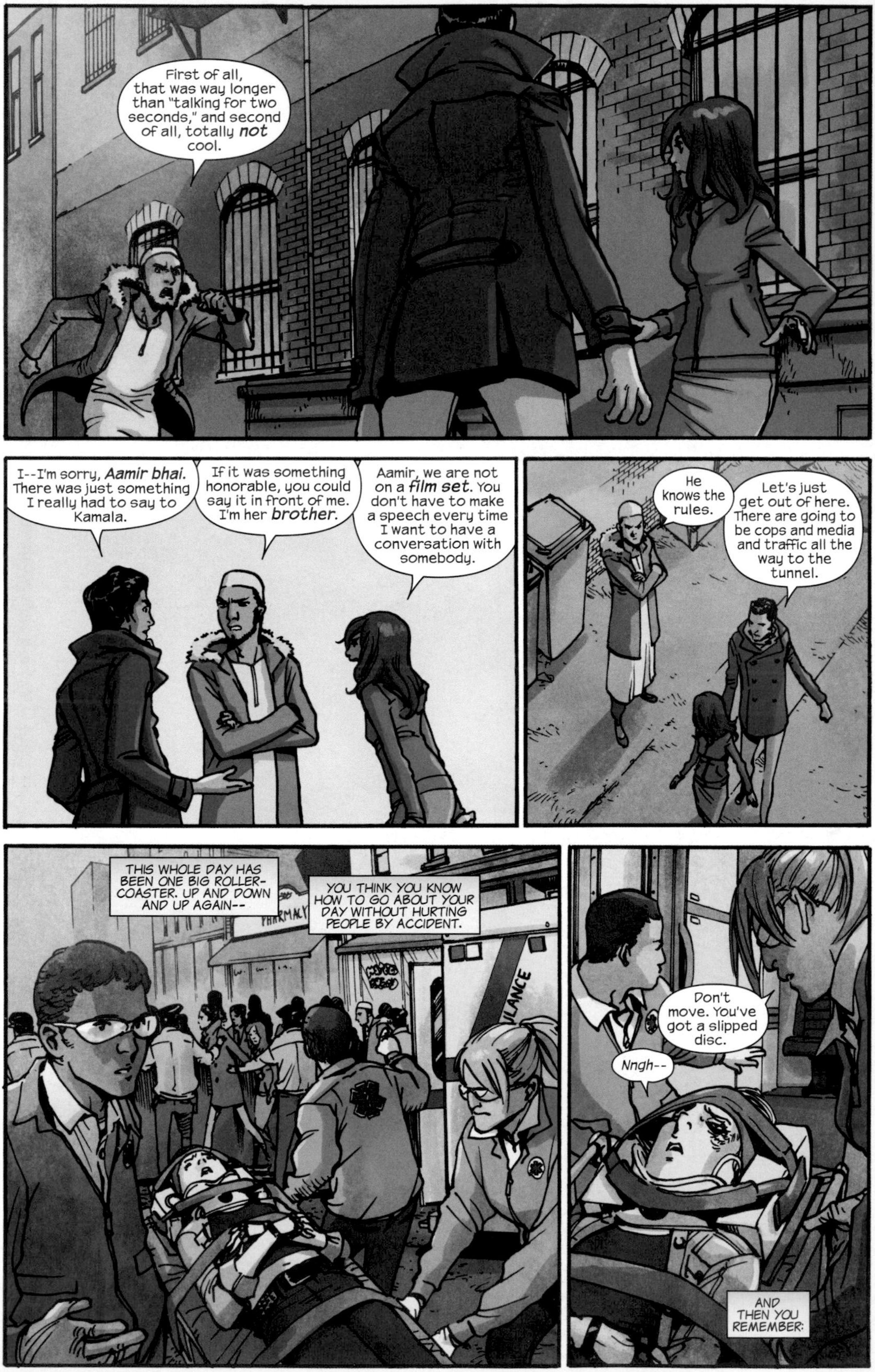
First of all, that was way longer than "talking for two seconds," and second of all, totally *not* cool.
I--I'm sorry, *Aamir bhai*. There was just something I really had to say to Kamala.
If it was something honorable, you could say it in front of me. I'm her *brother*.
Aamir, we are not on a *film set*. You don't have to make a speech every time I want to have a conversation with somebody.
He knows the rules.
Let's just get out of here. There are going to be cops and media and traffic all the way to the tunnel.
THIS WHOLE DAY HAS BEEN ONE BIG ROLLER-COASTER. UP AND DOWN AND UP AGAIN--
YOU THINK YOU KNOW HOW TO GO ABOUT YOUR DAY WITHOUT HURTING PEOPLE BY ACCIDENT.
PHARMACY
Don't move. You've got a slipped disc.
Nngh--
AND THEN YOU REMEMBER:

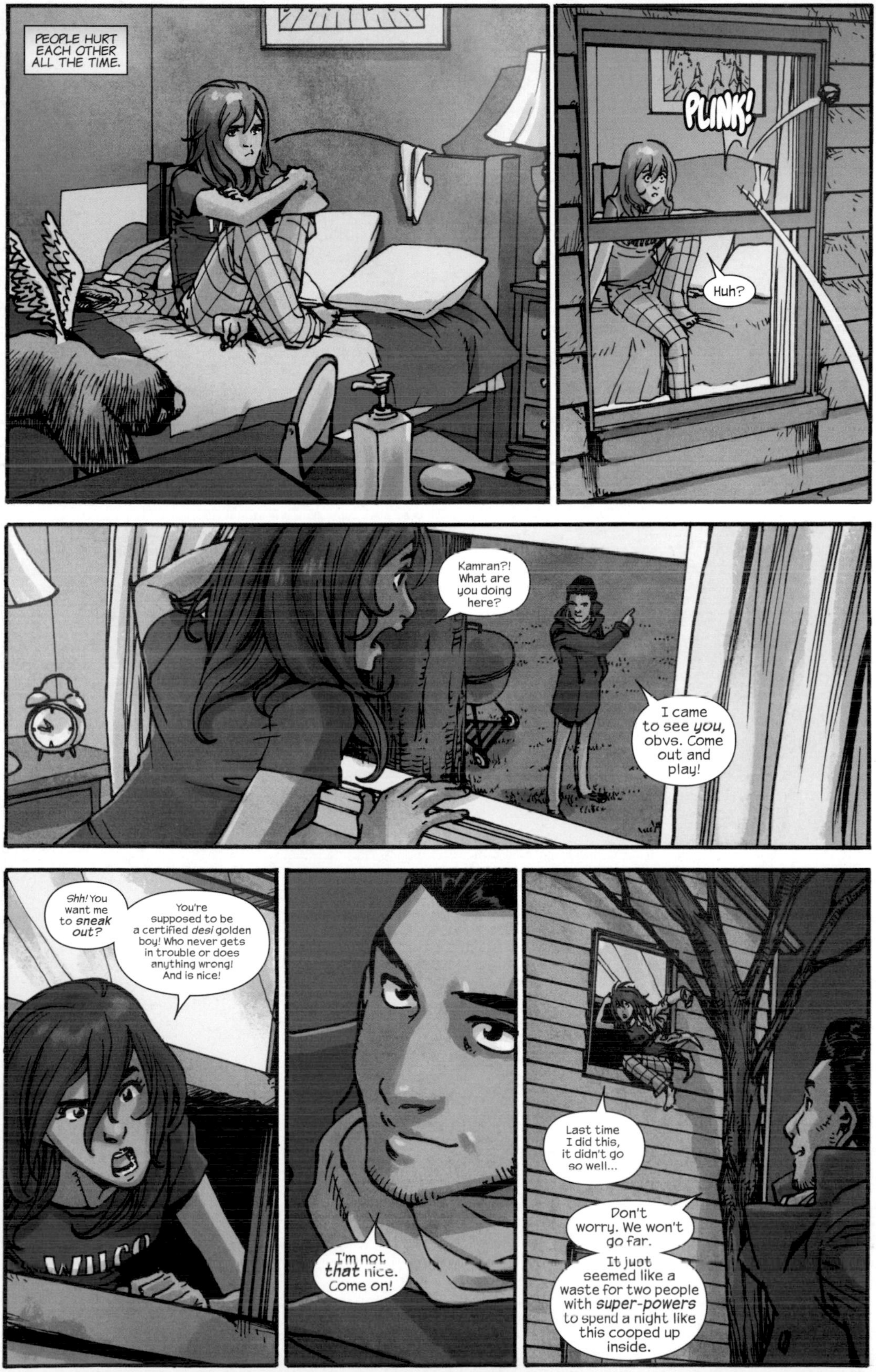

PEOPLE HURT EACH OTHER ALL THE TIME.
PLINK!
Huh?
Kamran?! What are you doing here?
I came to see *you*, obvs. Come out and play!
Shh! You want me to *sneak out?*
You're supposed to be a certified *desi* golden boy! Who never gets in trouble or does anything wrong! And is nice!
I'm not *that* nice. Come on!
Last time I did this, it didn't go so well...
Don't worry. We won't go far.
It just seemed like a waste for two people with *super-powers* to spend a night like this cooped up inside.

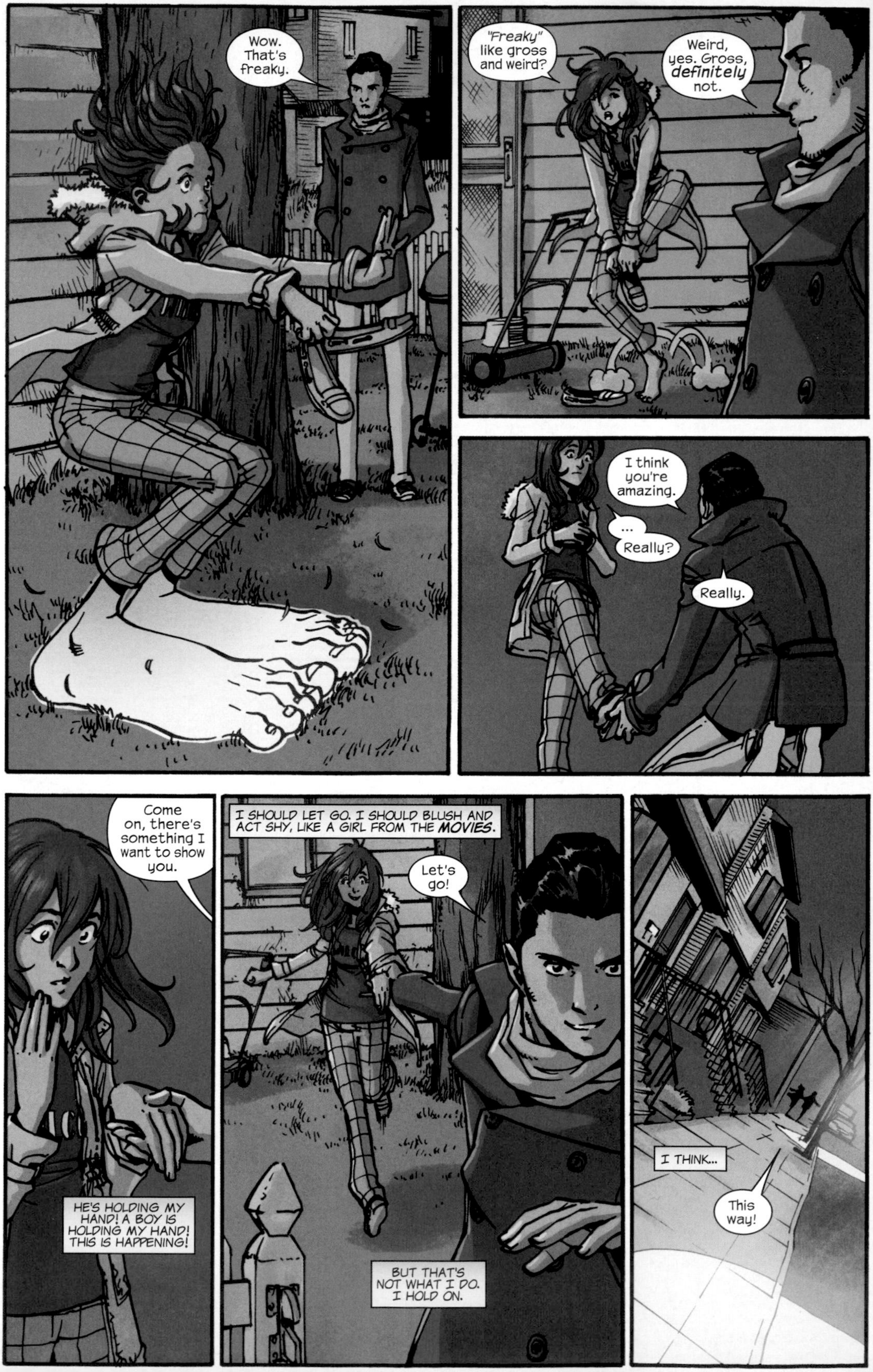
Wow. That's freaky.
"Freaky" like gross and weird?
Weird, yes. Gross, *definitely* not.
I think you're amazing.
... Really?
Really.
Come on, there's something I want to show you.
HE'S HOLDING MY HAND! A BOY IS HOLDING MY HAND! THIS IS HAPPENING!
I SHOULD LET GO. I SHOULD BLUSH AND ACT SHY, LIKE A GIRL FROM THE *MOVIES*.
Let's go!
BUT THAT'S NOT WHAT I DO. I HOLD ON.
I THINK...
This way!

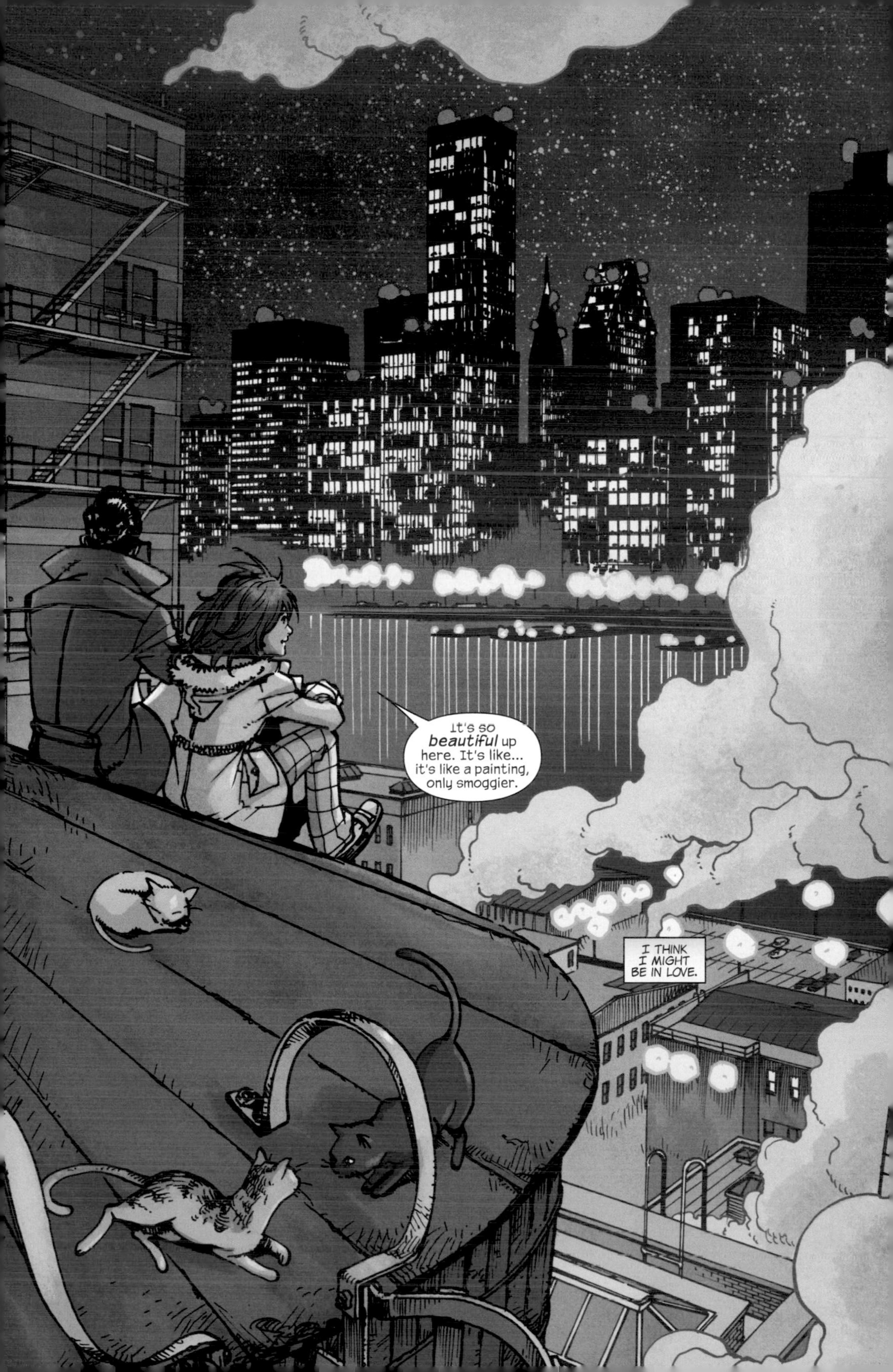
It's so beautiful up here. It's like... it's like a painting, only smoggier.
I THINK I MIGHT BE IN LOVE.

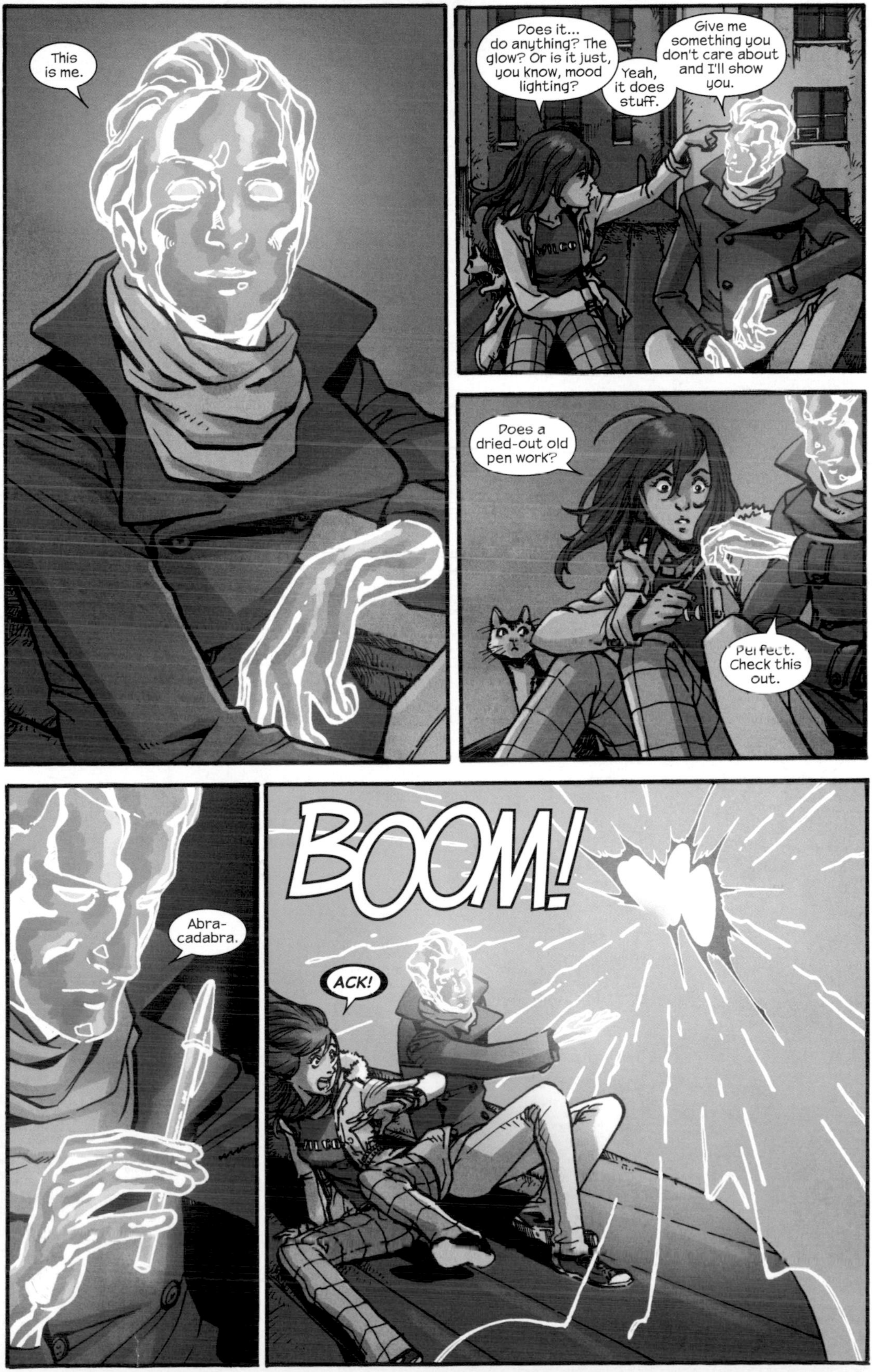

This is me.
Does it... do anything? The glow? Or is it just, you know, mood lighting?
Yeah, it does stuff.
Give me something you don't care about and I'll show you.
Does a dried-out old pen work?
Perfect. Check this out.
Abra-cadabra.
BOOM!
ACK!

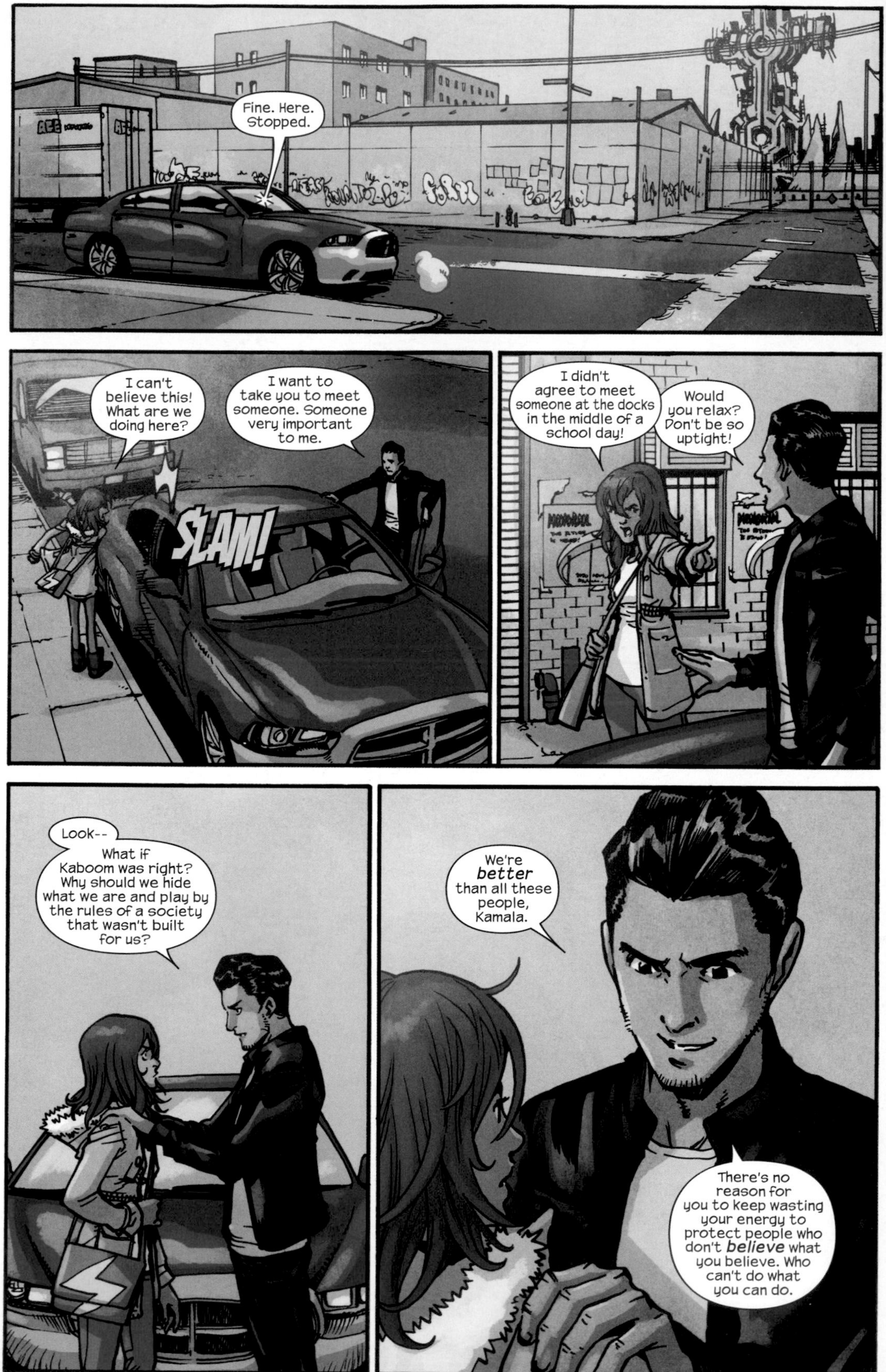

Fine. Here. Stopped.
I can't believe this! What are we doing here?
I want to take you to meet someone. Someone very important to me.
SLAM!
I didn't agree to meet someone at the docks in the middle of a school day!
Would you relax? Don't be so uptight!
Look--
What if Kaboom was right? Why should we hide what we are and play by the rules of a society that wasn't built for us?
We're *better* than all these people, Kamala.
There's no reason for you to keep wasting your energy to protect people who don't *believe* what you believe. Who can't do what you can do.

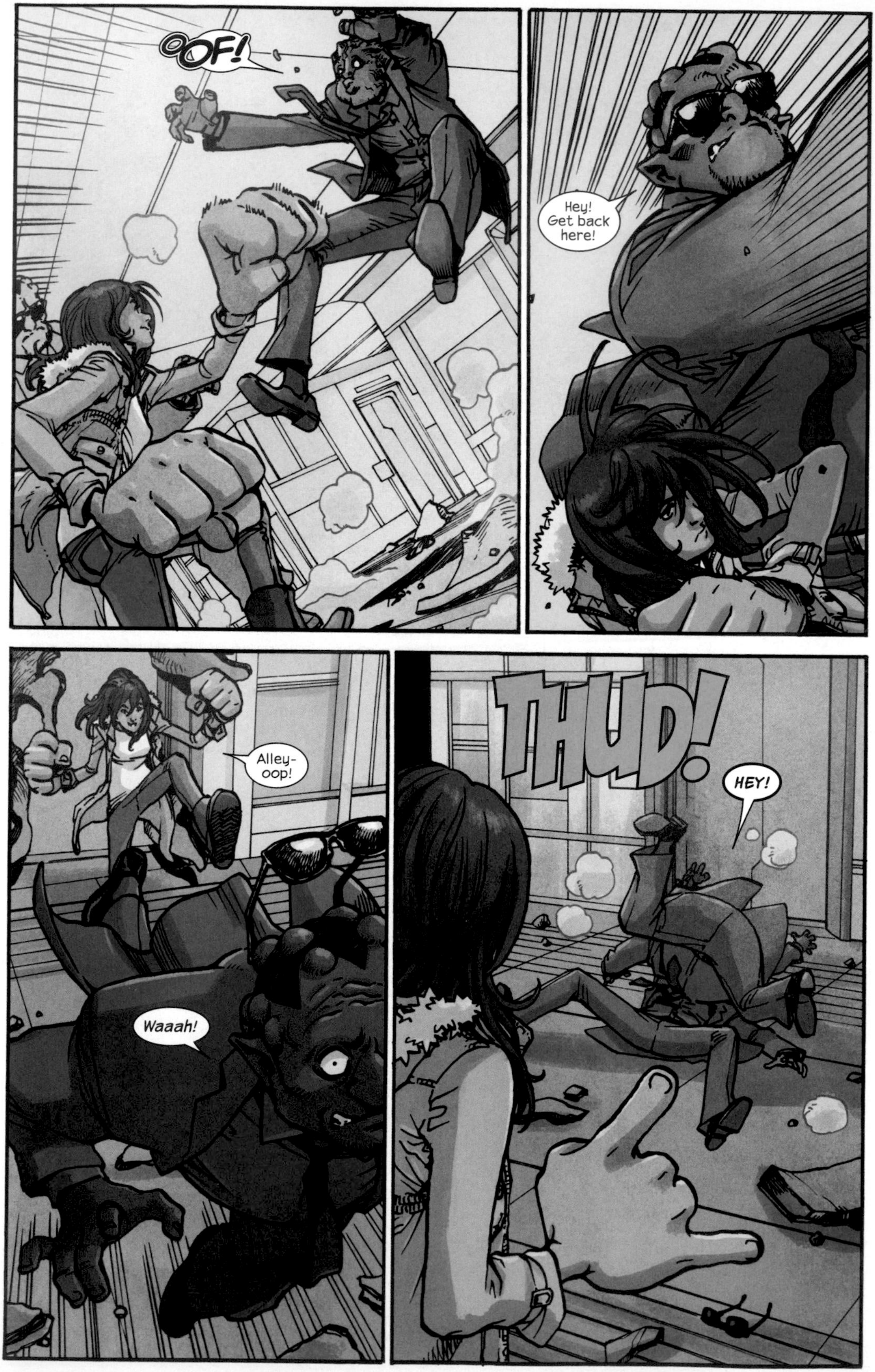
OOF!
Hey! Get back here!
Alley-oop!
Waaah!
THUD!
HEY!

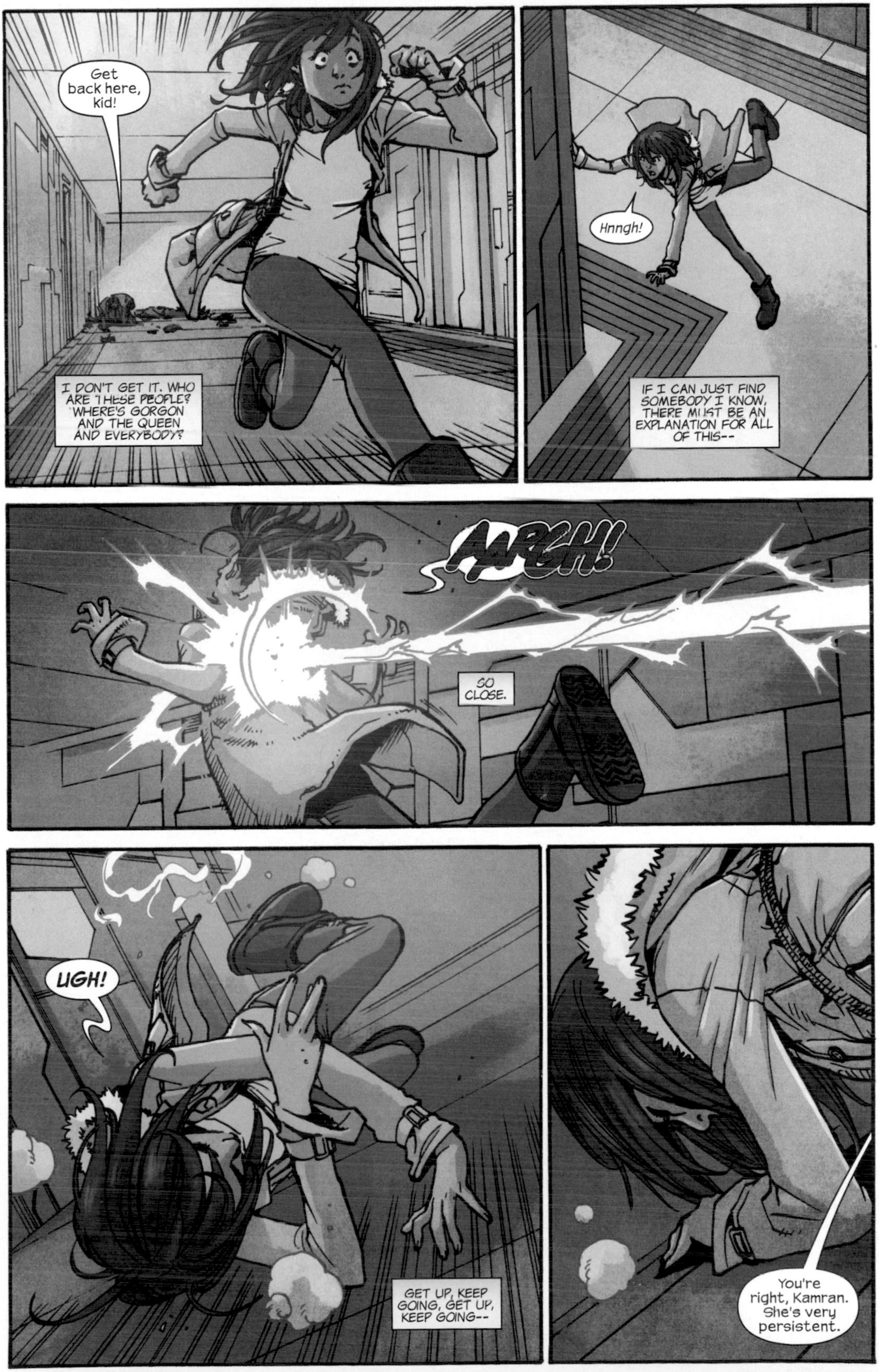
Get back here, kid!
I DON'T GET IT. WHO ARE THESE PEOPLE? WHERE'S GORGON AND THE QUEEN AND EVERYBODY?
Hnngh!
IF I CAN JUST FIND SOMEBODY I KNOW, THERE MUST BE AN EXPLANATION FOR ALL OF THIS--
AARGH!
SO CLOSE.
UGH!
GET UP, KEEP GOING, GET UP, KEEP GOING--
You're right, Kamran. She's very persistent.

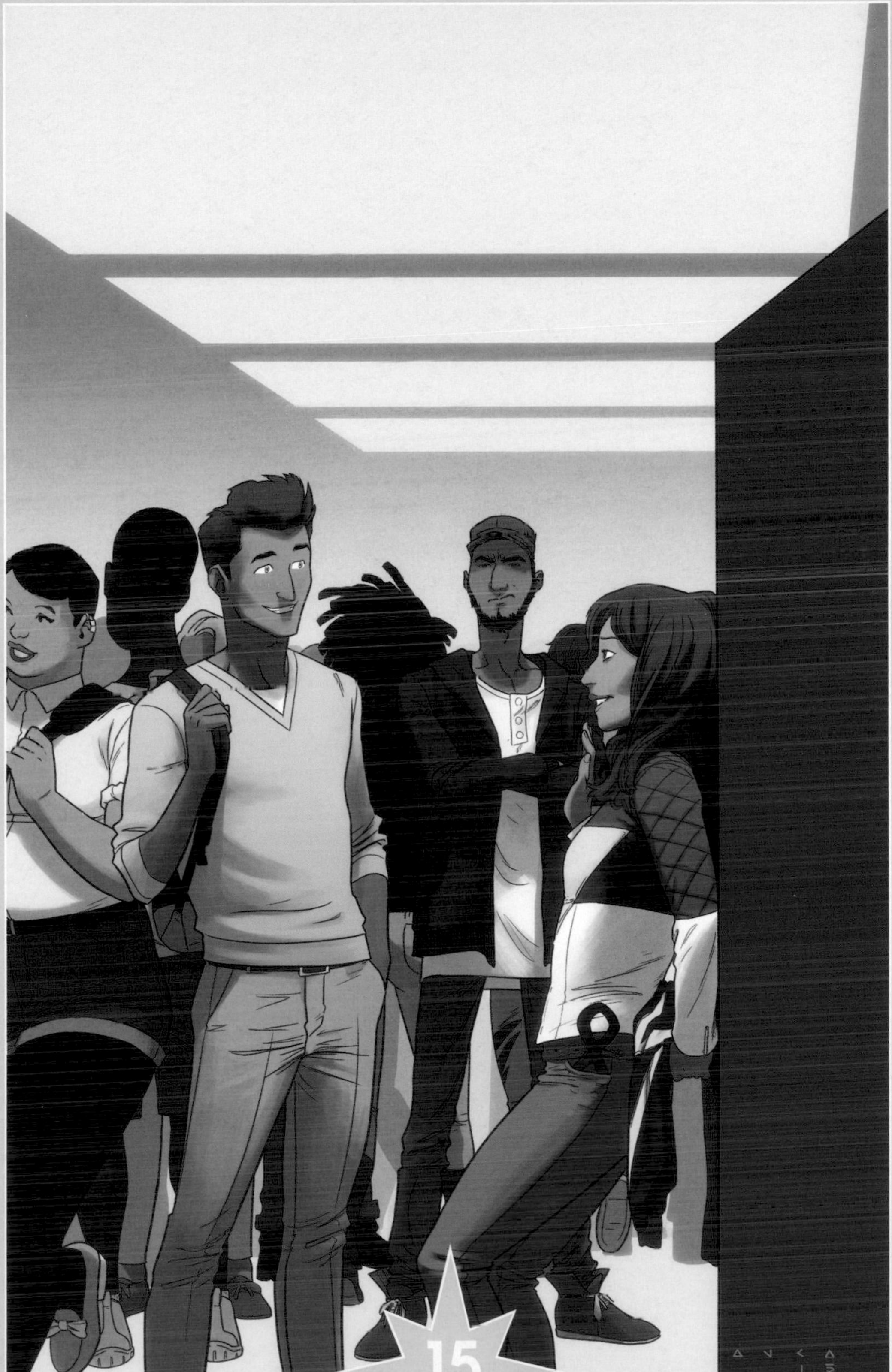
15

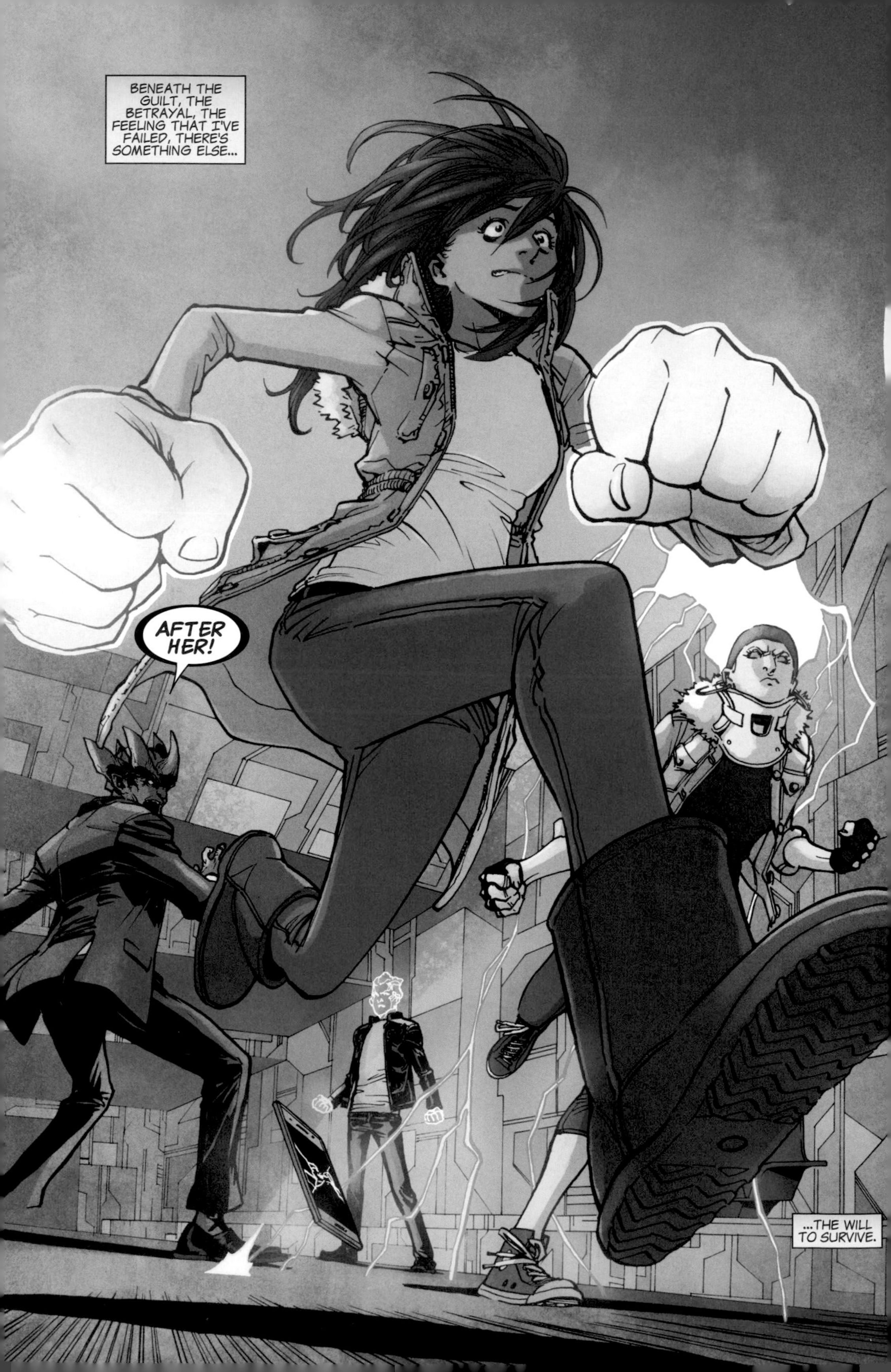
BENEATH THE GUILT, THE BETRAYAL, THE FEELING THAT I'VE FAILED, THERE'S SOMETHING ELSE...
AFTER HER!
...THE WILL TO SURVIVE.

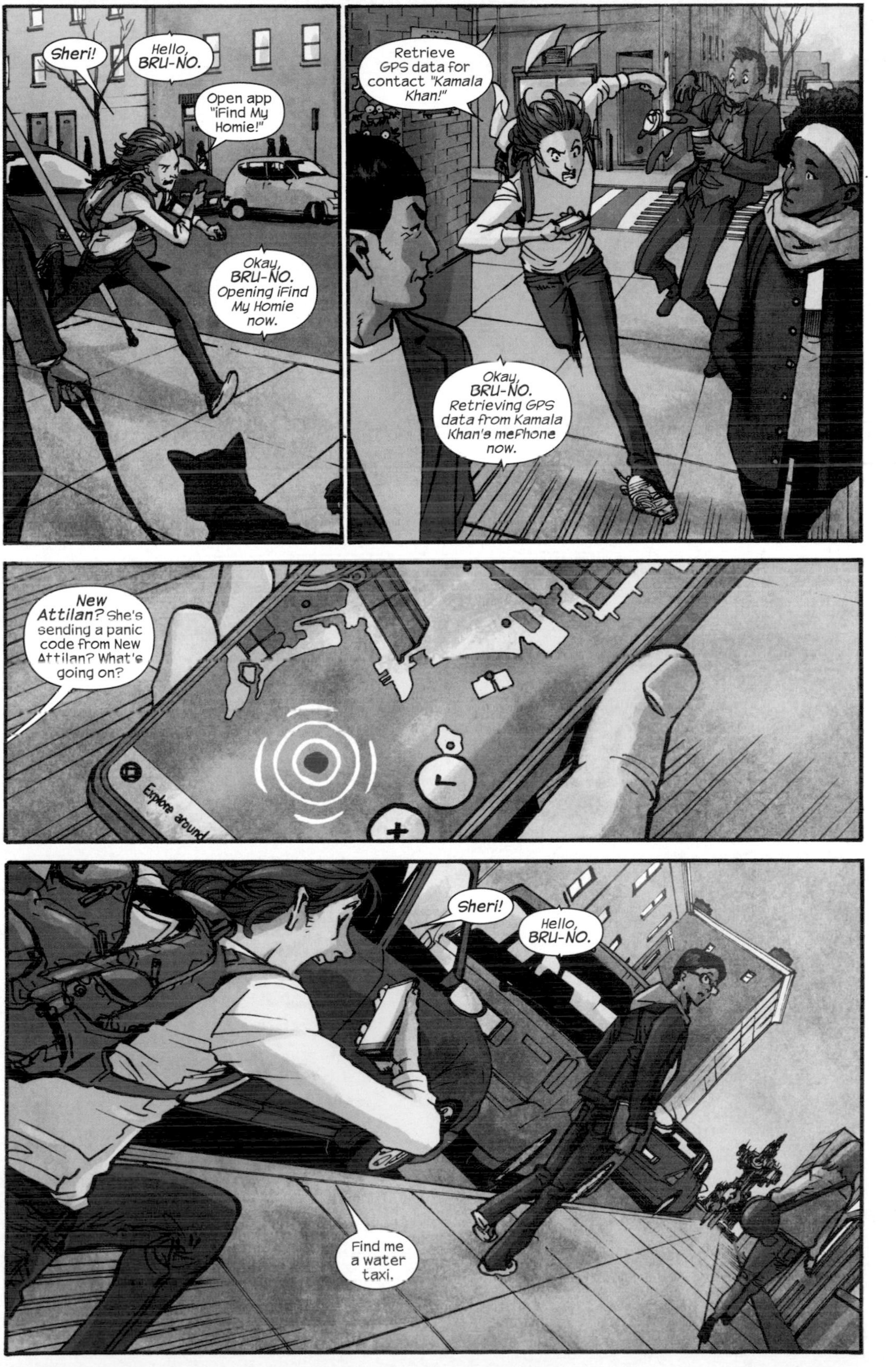
Sheri!
Hello, BRU-NO.
Open app "iFind My Homie!"
Okay, BRU-NO. Opening iFind My Homie now.
Retrieve GPS data for contact "Kamala Khan!"
Okay, BRU-NO. Retrieving GPS data from Kamala Khan's mePhone now.
New Attilan? She's sending a panic code from New Attilan? What's going on?
Explore around
Sheri!
Hello, BRU-NO.
Find me a water taxi.

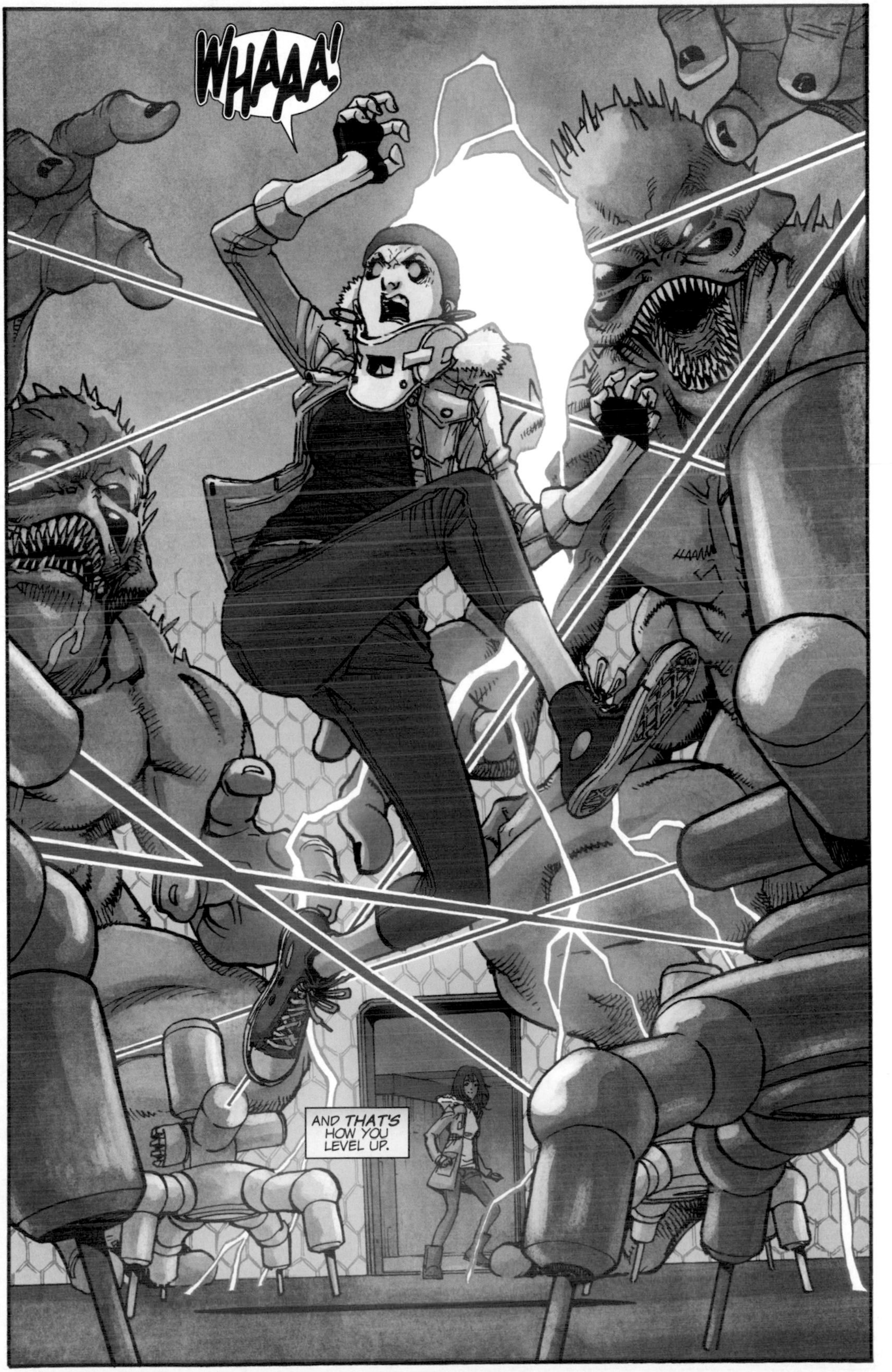
WHAAA!
AND THAT'S HOW YOU LEVEL UP.

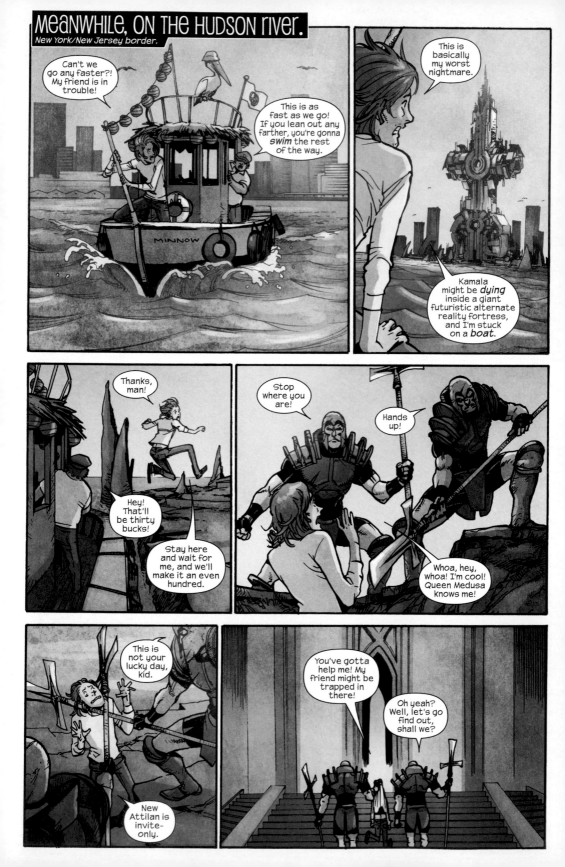

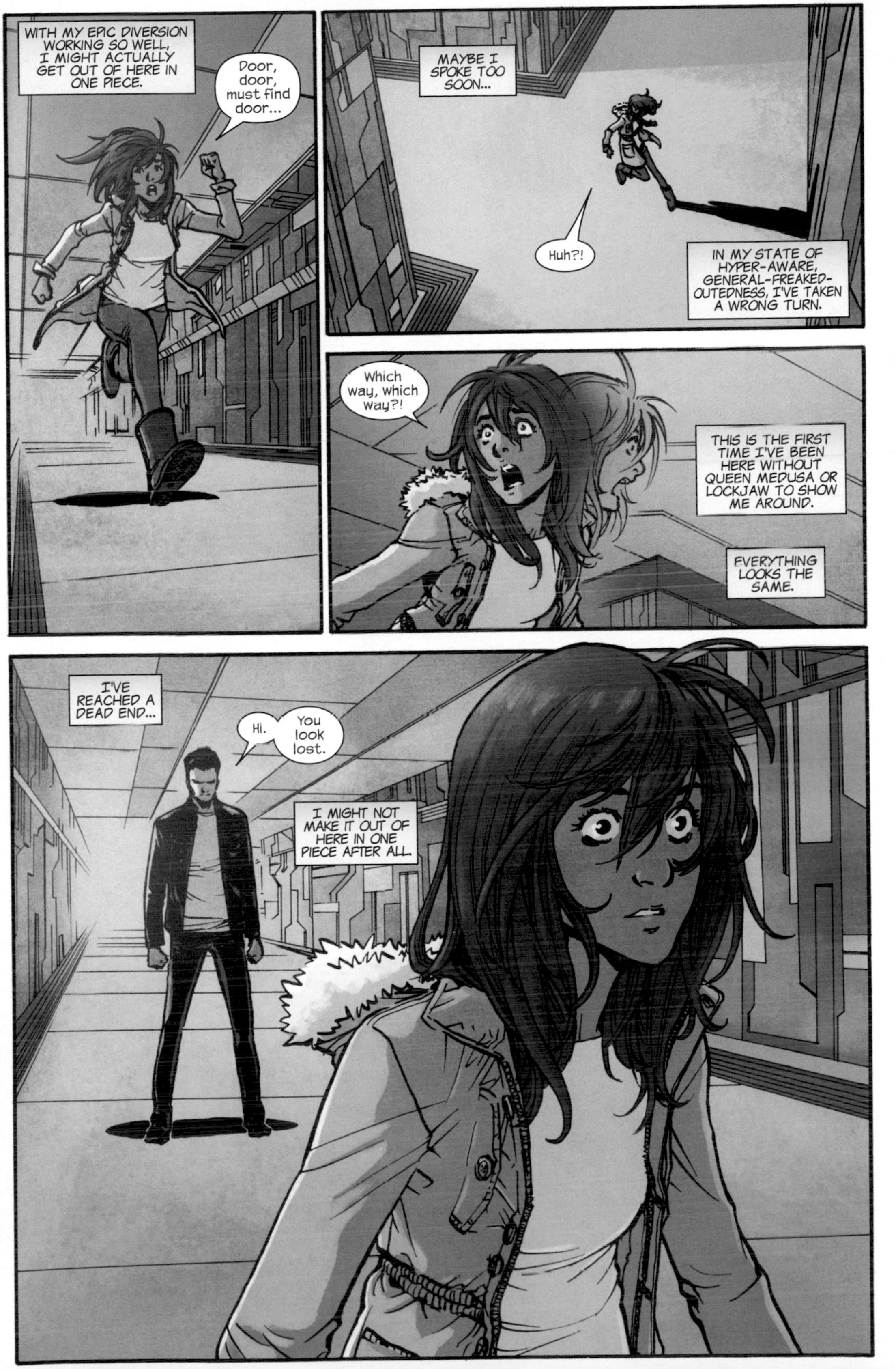
WITH MY EPIC DIVERSION WORKING SO WELL, I MIGHT ACTUALLY GET OUT OF HERE IN ONE PIECE.
Door, door, must find door...
MAYBE I SPOKE TOO SOON...
Huh?!
IN MY STATE OF HYPER-AWARE, GENERAL-FREAKED-OUTEDNESS, I'VE TAKEN A WRONG TURN.
Which way, which way?!
THIS IS THE FIRST TIME I'VE BEEN HERE WITHOUT QUEEN MEDUSA OR LOCKJAW TO SHOW ME AROUND.
EVERYTHING LOOKS THE SAME.
I'VE REACHED A DEAD END...
Hi.
You look lost.
I MIGHT NOT MAKE IT OUT OF HERE IN ONE PIECE AFTER ALL.

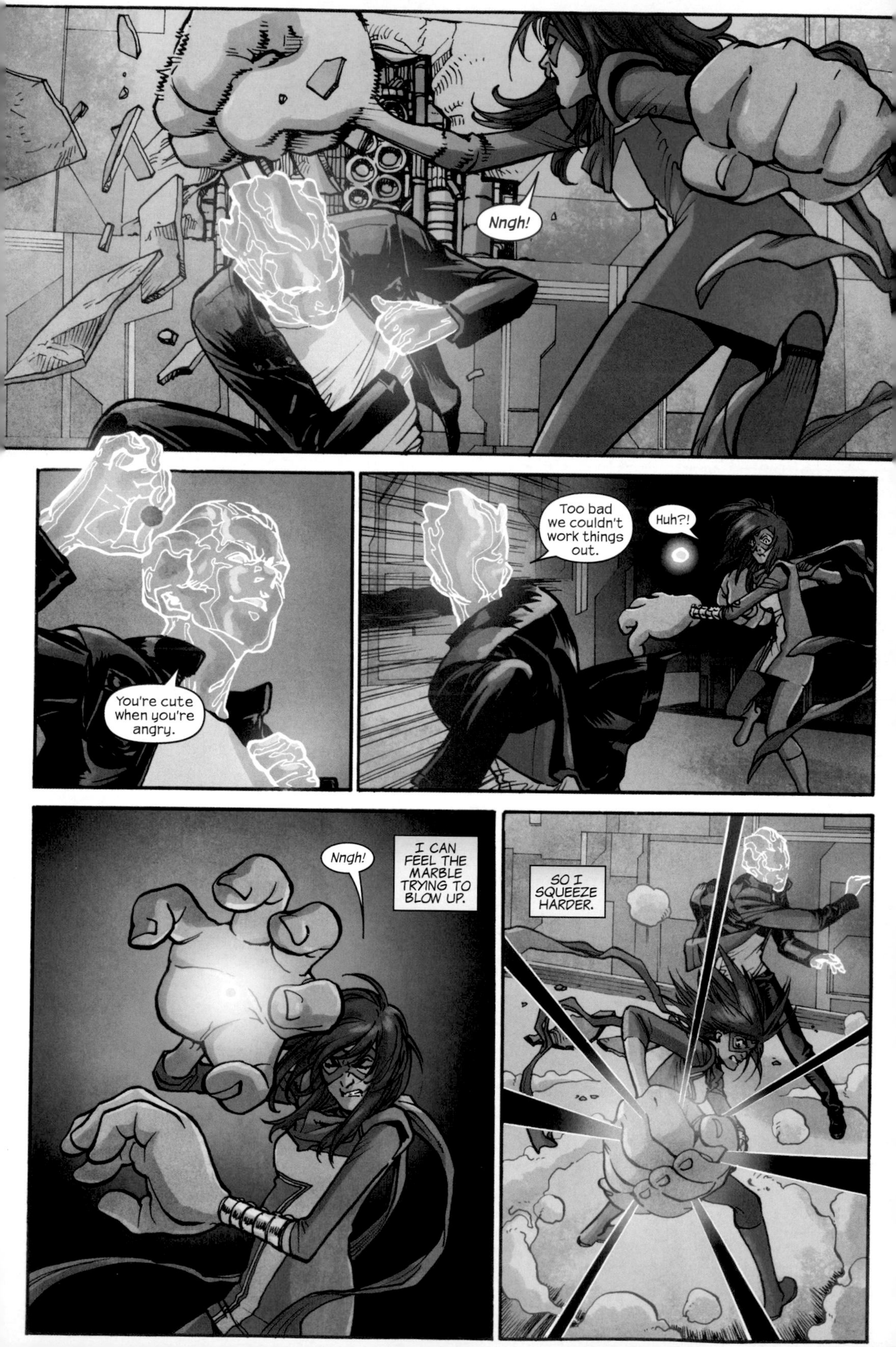
Nngh!
You're cute when you're angry.
Too bad we couldn't work things out.
Huh?!
Nngh!
I CAN FEEL THE MARBLE TRYING TO BLOW UP.
SO I SQUEEZE HARDER.

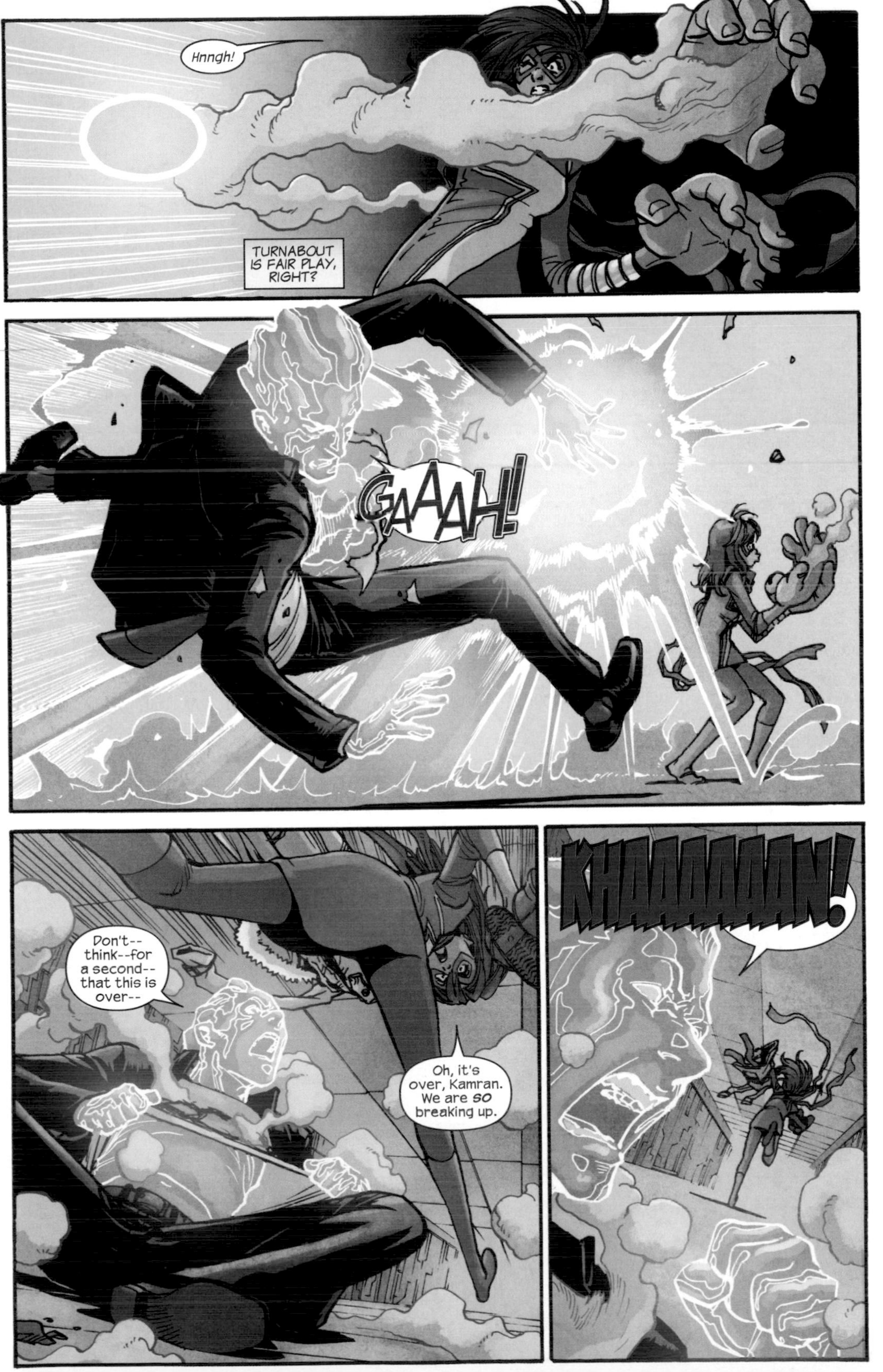
Hnngh!
TURNABOUT IS FAIR PLAY, RIGHT?
GAAAH!
Don't-- think--for a second-- that this is over--
Oh, it's over, Kamran. We are *SO* breaking up.
KHAAAAAAN!

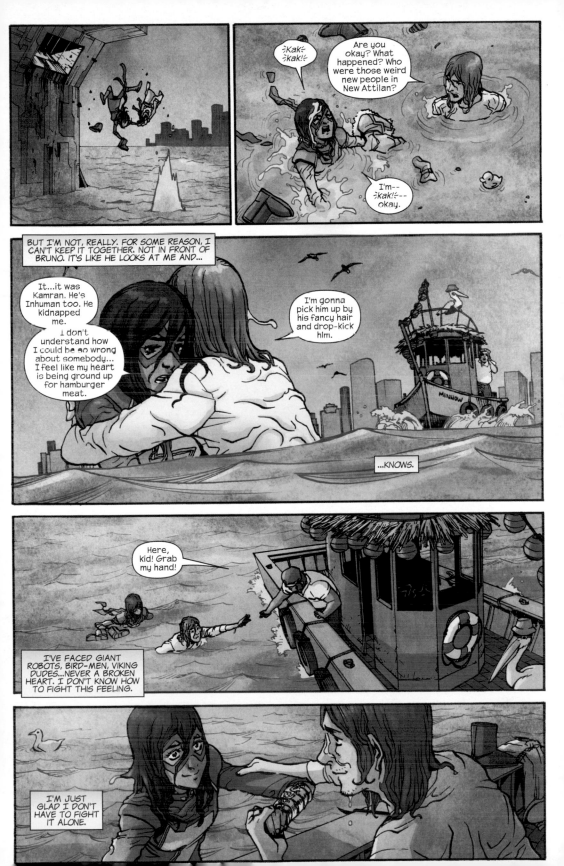

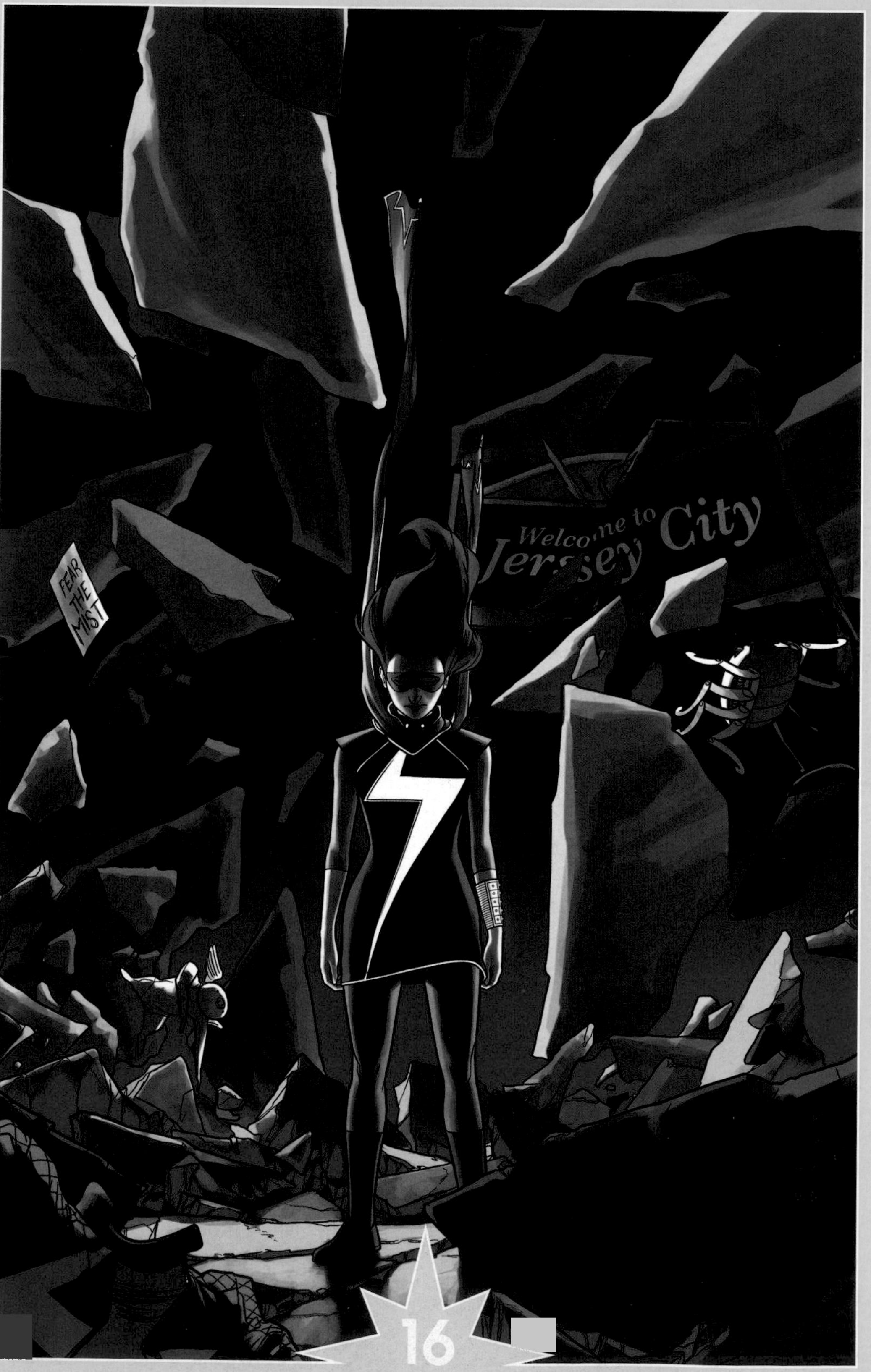
Welcome to Jersey City
FEAR THE MIST
16

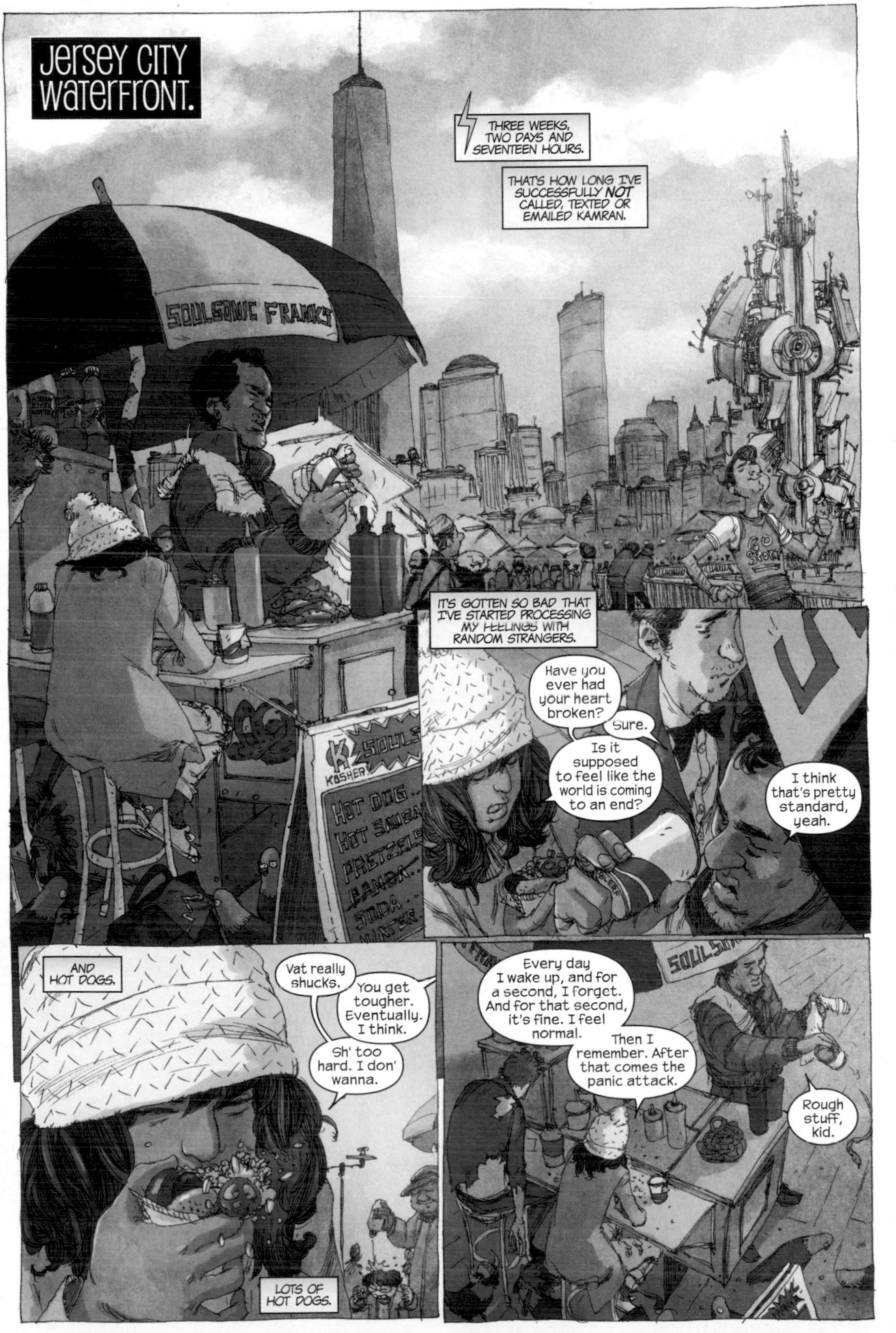
Jersey City Waterfront.
THREE WEEKS, TWO DAYS AND SEVENTEEN HOURS.
THAT'S HOW LONG I'VE SUCCESSFULLY NOT CALLED, TEXTED OR EMAILED KAMRAN.
SOULSONIC FRANKS
IT'S GOTTEN SO BAD THAT I'VE STARTED PROCESSING MY FEELINGS WITH RANDOM STRANGERS.
Have you ever had your heart broken?
Sure.
Is it supposed to feel like the world is coming to an end?
I think that's pretty standard, yeah.
KOSHER
HOT DOG
PRETZELS
SODA
AND HOT DOGS.
Vat really shucks.
You get tougher. Eventually. I think.
Sh' too hard. I don' wanna.
LOTS OF HOT DOGS.
Every day I wake up, and for a second, I forget. And for that second, it's fine. I feel normal.
Then I remember. After that comes the panic attack.
Rough stuff, kid.

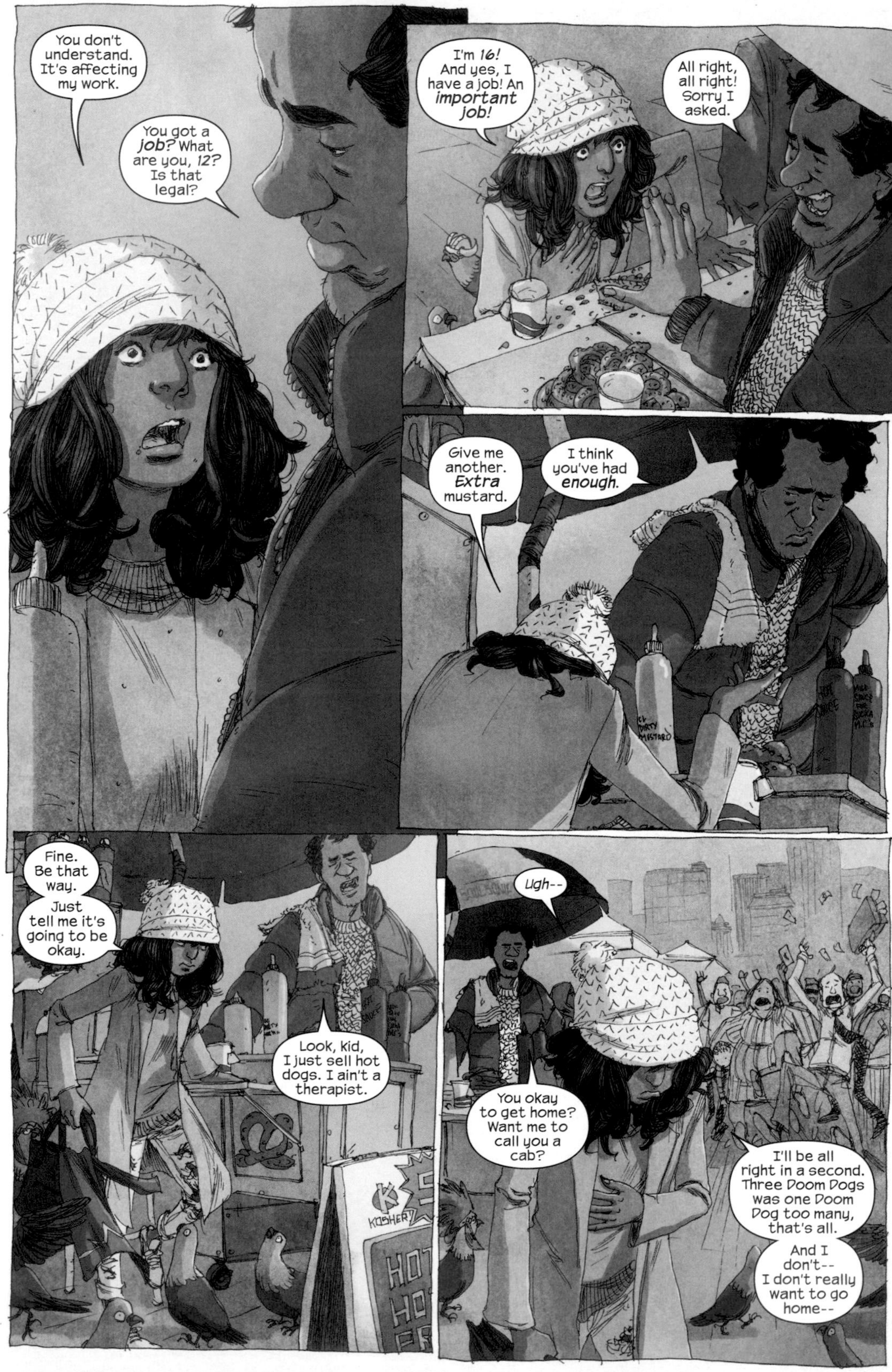
You don't understand. It's affecting my work.
You got a *job?* What are you, *12?* Is that legal?
I'm *16!* And yes, I have a job! An *important job!*
All right, all right! Sorry I asked.
Give me another. *Extra* mustard.
I think you've had *enough.*
Fine. Be that way.
Just tell me it's going to be okay.
Look, kid, I just sell hot dogs. I ain't a therapist.
KOSHER
Ugh--
You okay to get home? Want me to call you a cab?
I'll be all right in a second. Three Doom Dogs was one Doom Dog too many, that's all.
And I don't-- I don't really want to go home--

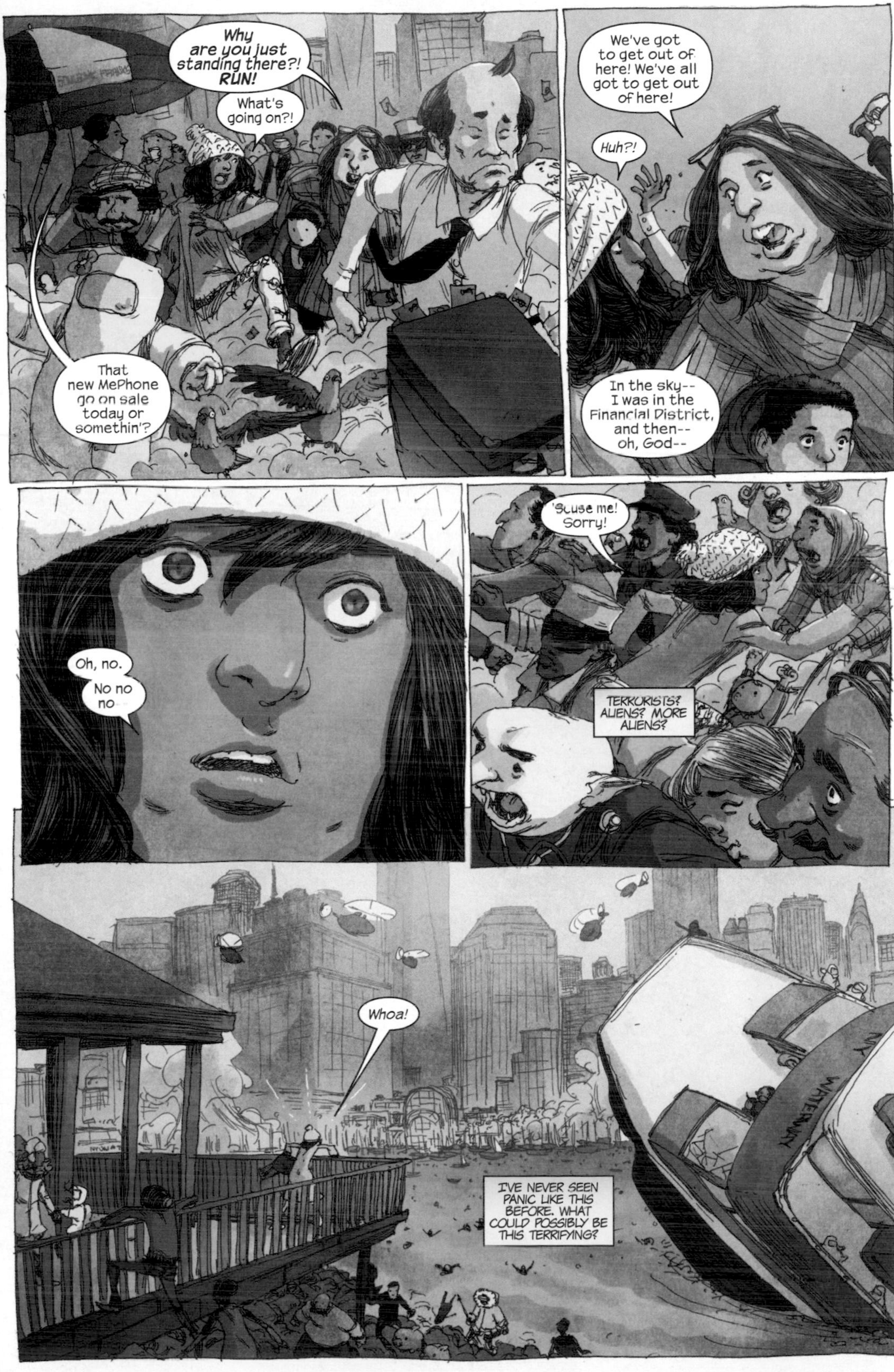
Why are you just standing there?! RUN!
What's going on?!
That new MePhone go on sale today or somethin'?
We've got to get out of here! We've all got to get out of here!
Huh?!
In the sky-- I was in the Financial District, and then-- oh, God--
Oh, no.
No no no--
'Scuse me! Sorry!
TERRORISTS? ALIENS? MORE ALIENS?
Whoa!
I'VE NEVER SEEN PANIC LIKE THIS BEFORE. WHAT COULD POSSIBLY BE THIS TERRIFYING?

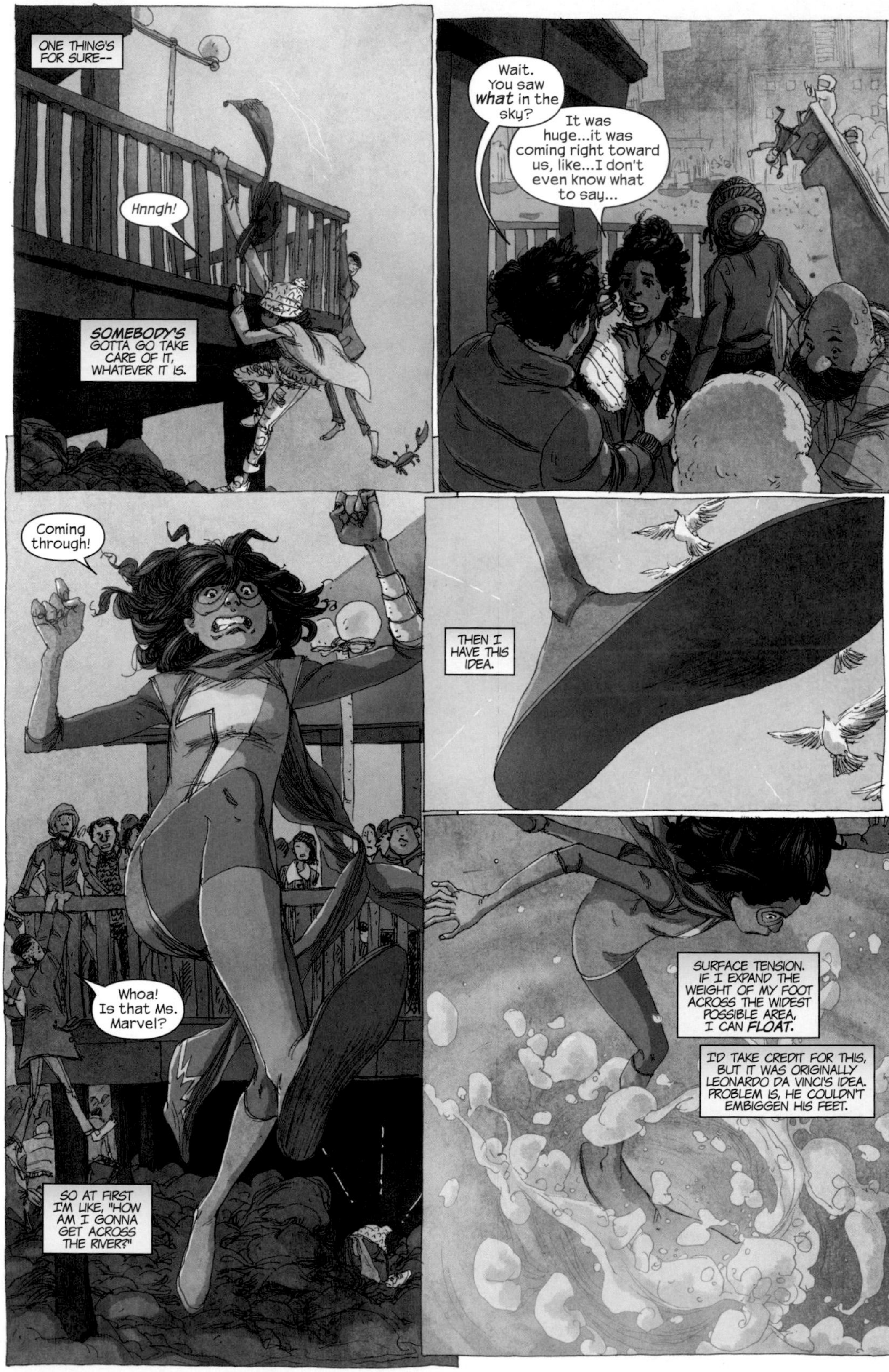
ONE THING'S FOR SURE--
Hnngh!
SOMEBODY'S GOTTA GO TAKE CARE OF IT, WHATEVER IT IS.
Wait. You saw what in the sky?
It was huge...it was coming right toward us, like...I don't even know what to say...
Coming through!
Whoa! Is that Ms. Marvel?
SO AT FIRST I'M LIKE, "HOW AM I GONNA GET ACROSS THE RIVER?"
THEN I HAVE THIS IDEA.
SURFACE TENSION. IF I EXPAND THE WEIGHT OF MY FOOT ACROSS THE WIDEST POSSIBLE AREA, I CAN FLOAT.
I'D TAKE CREDIT FOR THIS, BUT IT WAS ORIGINALLY LEONARDO DA VINCI'S IDEA. PROBLEM IS, HE COULDN'T EMBIGGEN HIS FEET.

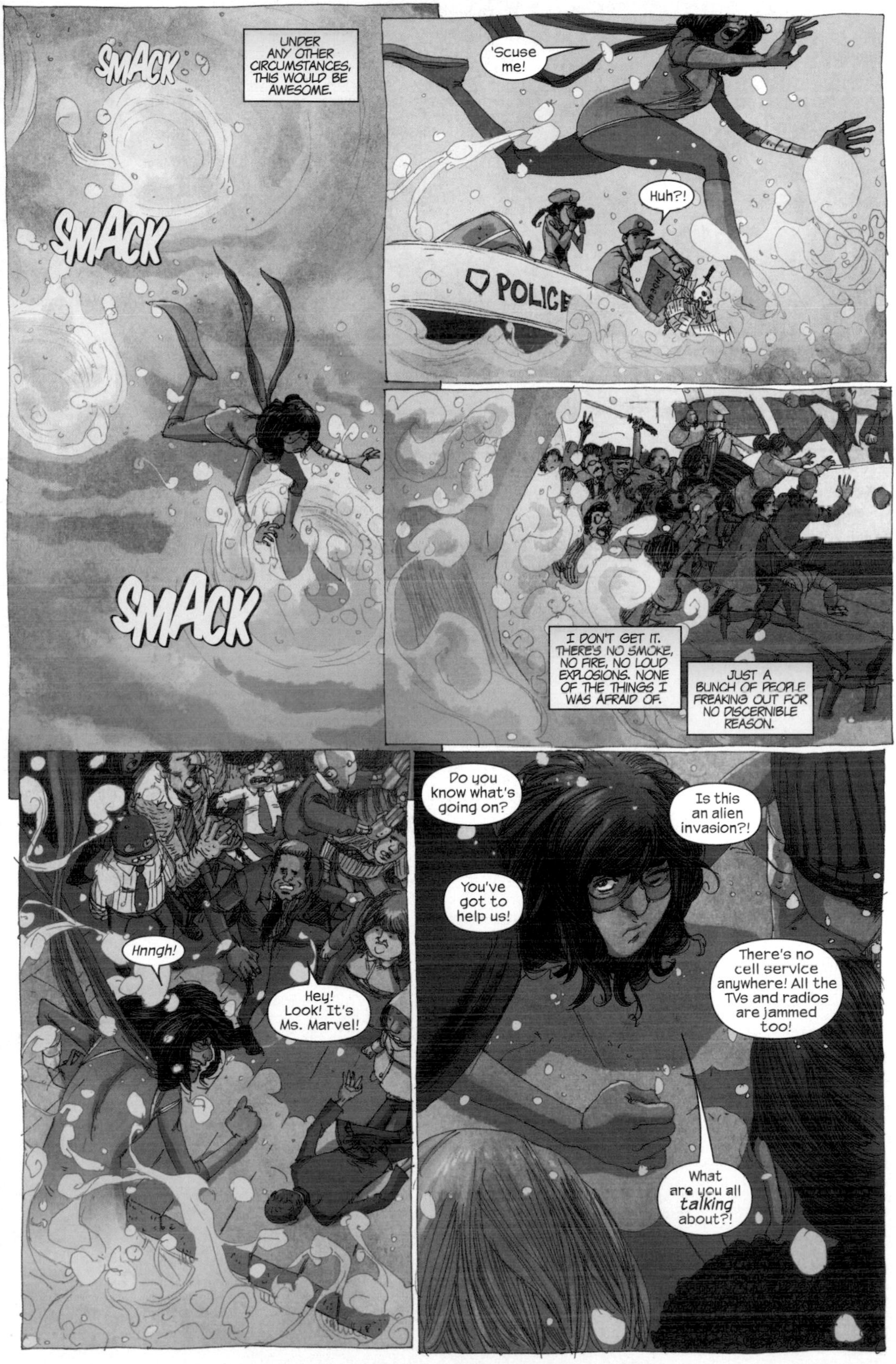
UNDER ANY OTHER CIRCUMSTANCES, THIS WOULD BE AWESOME.
SMACK
SMACK
SMACK
'Scuse me!
Huh?!
POLICE
I DON'T GET IT. THERE'S NO SMOKE, NO FIRE, NO LOUD EXPLOSIONS. NONE OF THE THINGS I WAS AFRAID OF.
JUST A BUNCH OF PEOPLE FREAKING OUT FOR NO DISCERNIBLE REASON.
Hnngh!
Hey! Look! It's Ms. Marvel!
Do you know what's going on?
Is this an alien invasion?!
You've got to help us!
There's no cell service anywhere! All the TVs and radios are jammed too!
What are you all *talking* about?!

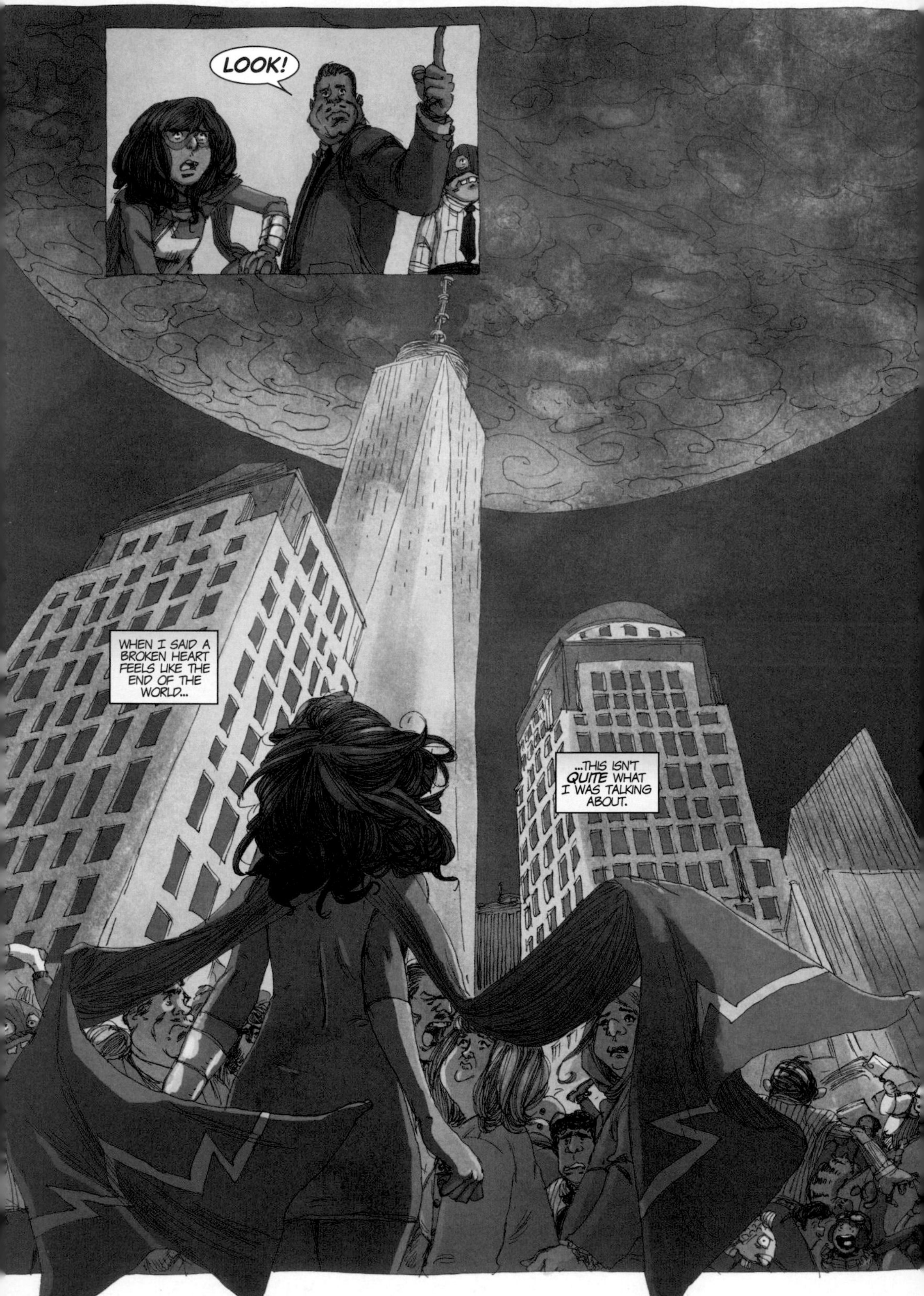
LOOK!
WHEN I SAID A BROKEN HEART FEELS LIKE THE END OF THE WORLD...
...THIS ISN'T QUITE WHAT I WAS TALKING ABOUT.

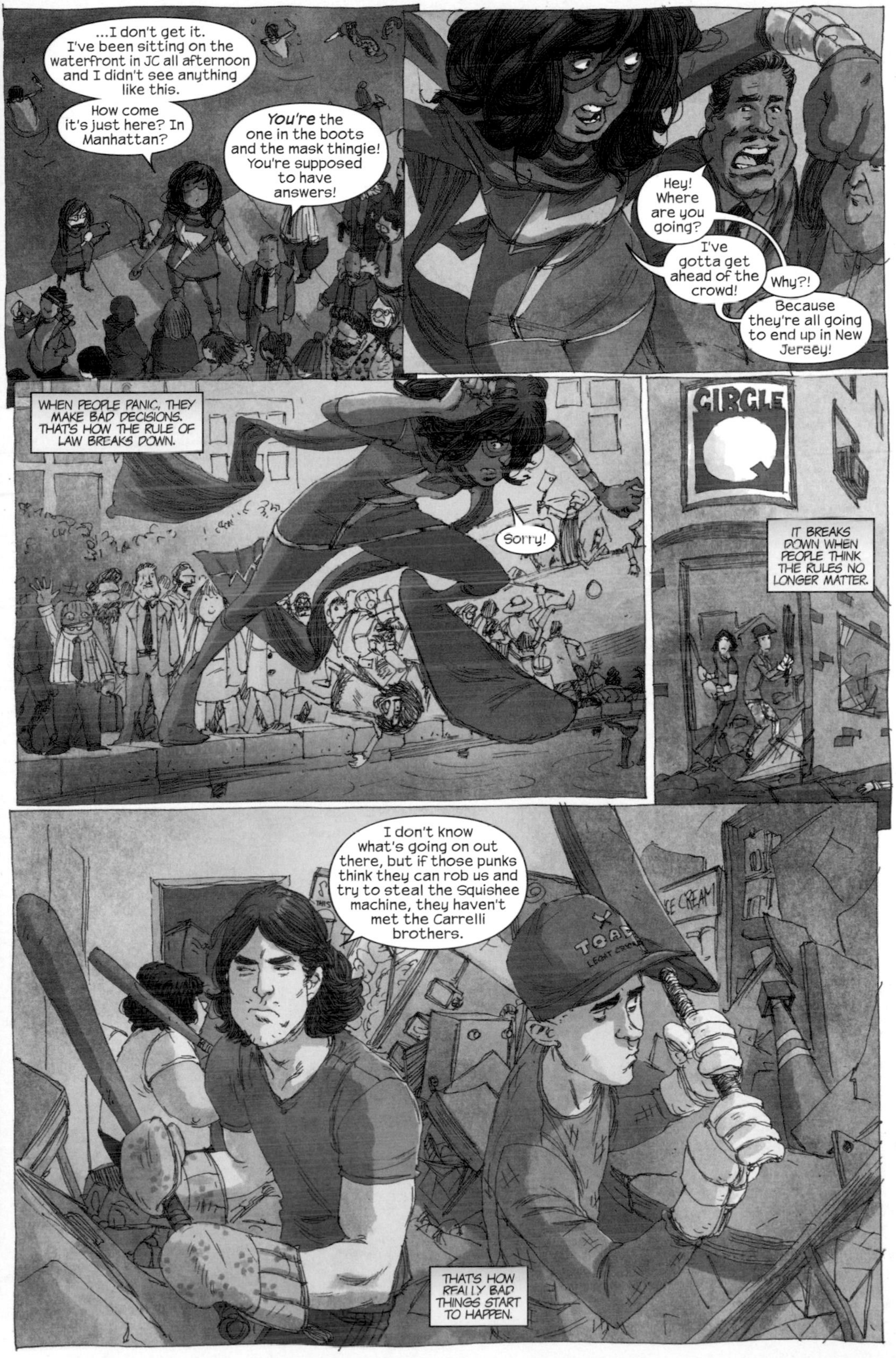

...I don't get it. I've been sitting on the waterfront in JC all afternoon and I didn't see anything like this.
How come it's just here? In Manhattan?
You're the one in the boots and the mask thingie! You're supposed to have answers!
Hey! Where are you going?
I've gotta get ahead of the crowd!
Why?!
Because they're all going to end up in New Jersey!
WHEN PEOPLE PANIC, THEY MAKE BAD DECISIONS. THAT'S HOW THE RULE OF LAW BREAKS DOWN.
Sorry!
CIRCLE
IT BREAKS DOWN WHEN PEOPLE THINK THE RULES NO LONGER MATTER.
I don't know what's going on out there, but if those punks think they can rob us and try to steal the Squishee machine, they haven't met the Carrelli brothers.
THAT'S HOW REALLY BAD THINGS START TO HAPPEN.

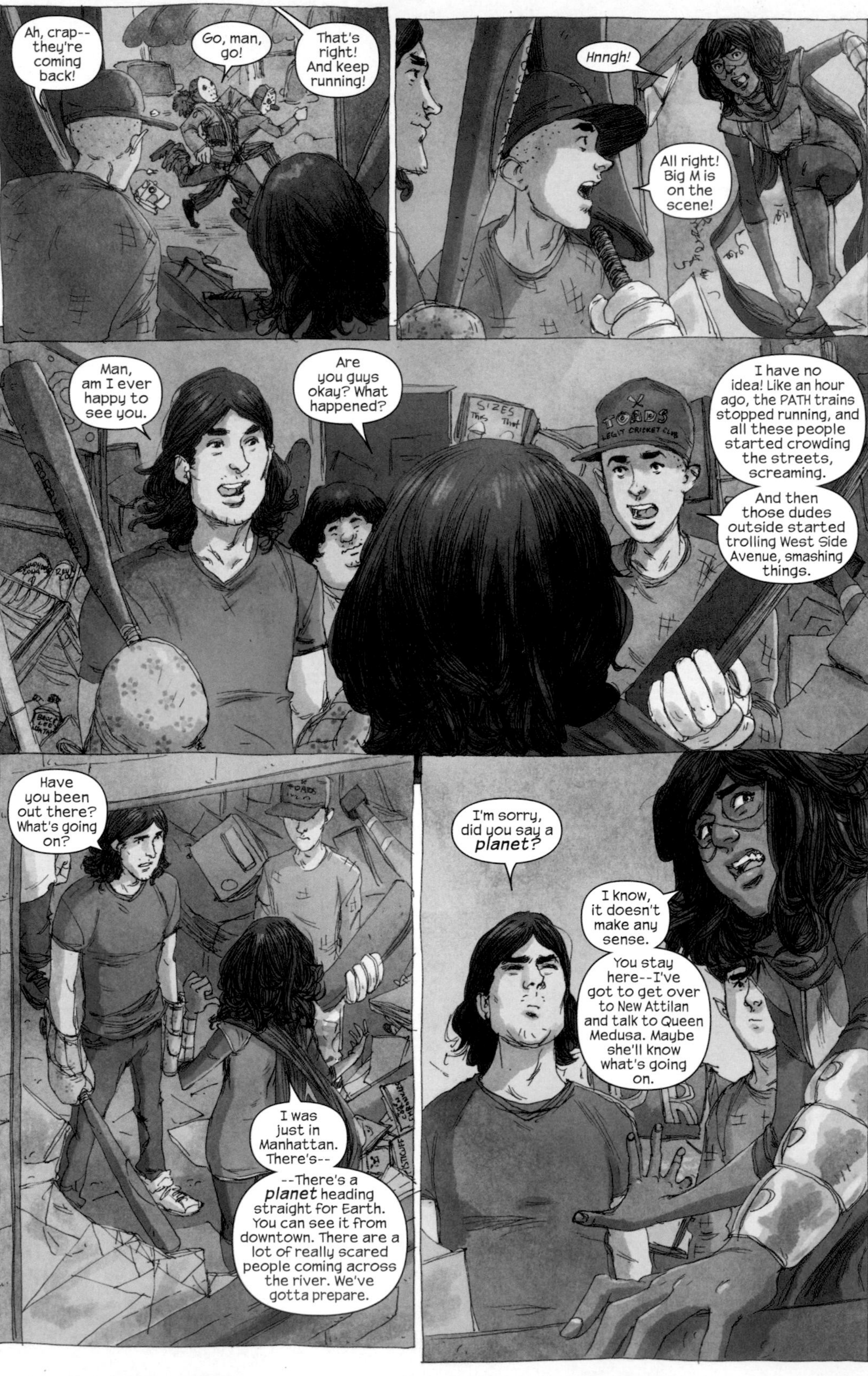
Ah, crap-- they're coming back!
Go, man, go!
That's right! And keep running!
Hnngh!
All right! Big M is on the scene!
Man, am I ever happy to see you.
Are you guys okay? What happened?
I have no idea! Like an hour ago, the PATH trains stopped running, and all these people started crowding the streets, screaming.
And then those dudes outside started trolling West Side Avenue, smashing things.
Have you been out there? What's going on?
I was just in Manhattan. There's--
--There's a *planet* heading straight for Earth. You can see it from downtown. There are a lot of really scared people coming across the river. We've gotta prepare.
I'm sorry, did you say a *planet*?
I know, it doesn't make any sense.
You stay here--I've got to get over to New Attilan and talk to Queen Medusa. Maybe she'll know what's going on.

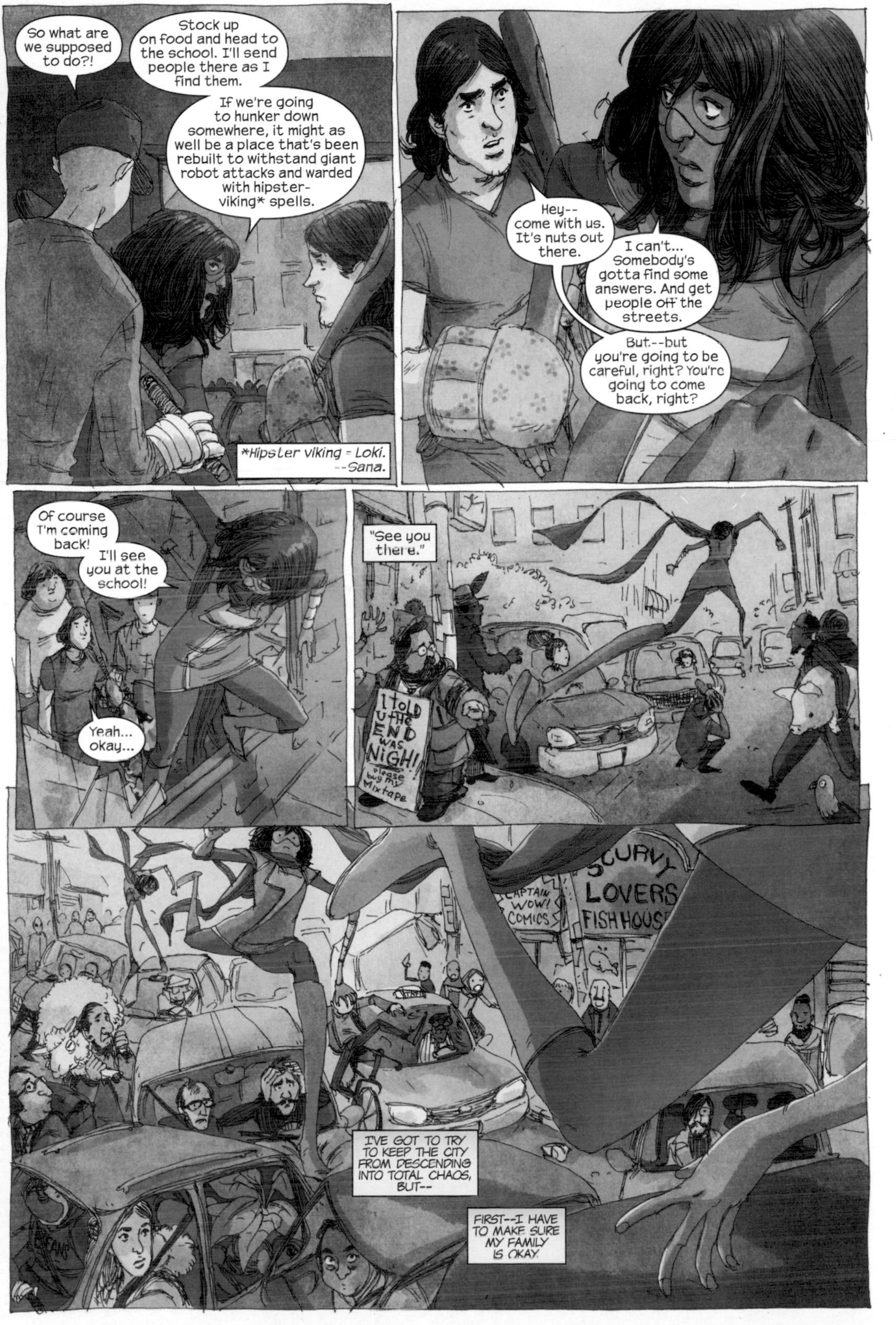
So what are we supposed to do?!
Stock up on food and head to the school. I'll send people there as I find them.
If we're going to hunker down somewhere, it might as well be a place that's been rebuilt to withstand giant robot attacks and warded with hipster-viking* spells.
*Hipster viking = Loki. --Sana.
Hey-- come with us. It's nuts out there.
I can't... Somebody's gotta find some answers. And get people off the streets.
But--but you're going to be careful, right? You're going to come back, right?
Of course I'm coming back!
I'll see you at the school!
Yeah... okay...
"See you there."
I TOLD U THE END WAS NIGH! please buy my Mixtape
SCURVY LOVERS FISH HOUSE
CAPTAIN WOW! COMICS
I'VE GOT TO TRY TO KEEP THE CITY FROM DESCENDING INTO TOTAL CHAOS, BUT--
FIRST--I HAVE TO MAKE SURE MY FAMILY IS OKAY.

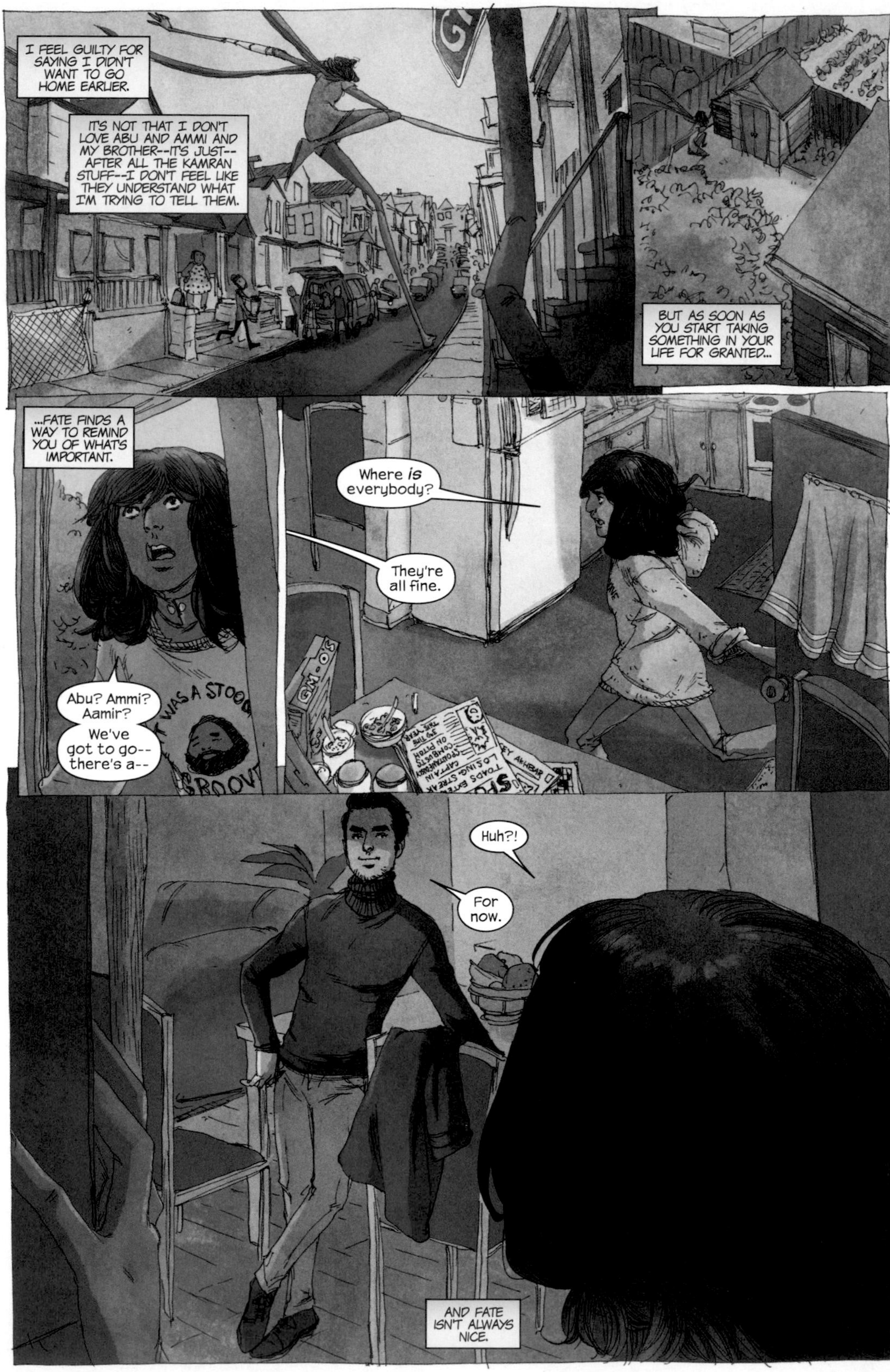
I FEEL GUILTY FOR SAYING I DIDN'T WANT TO GO HOME EARLIER.
IT'S NOT THAT I DON'T LOVE ABU AND AMMI AND MY BROTHER--IT'S JUST--AFTER ALL THE KAMRAN STUFF--I DON'T FEEL LIKE THEY UNDERSTAND WHAT I'M TRYING TO TELL THEM.
BUT AS SOON AS YOU START TAKING SOMETHING IN YOUR LIFE FOR GRANTED...
...FATE FINDS A WAY TO REMIND YOU OF WHAT'S IMPORTANT.
Abu? Ammi? Aamir?
We've got to go--there's a--
Where *is* everybody?
They're all fine.
Huh?!
For now.
AND FATE ISN'T ALWAYS NICE.

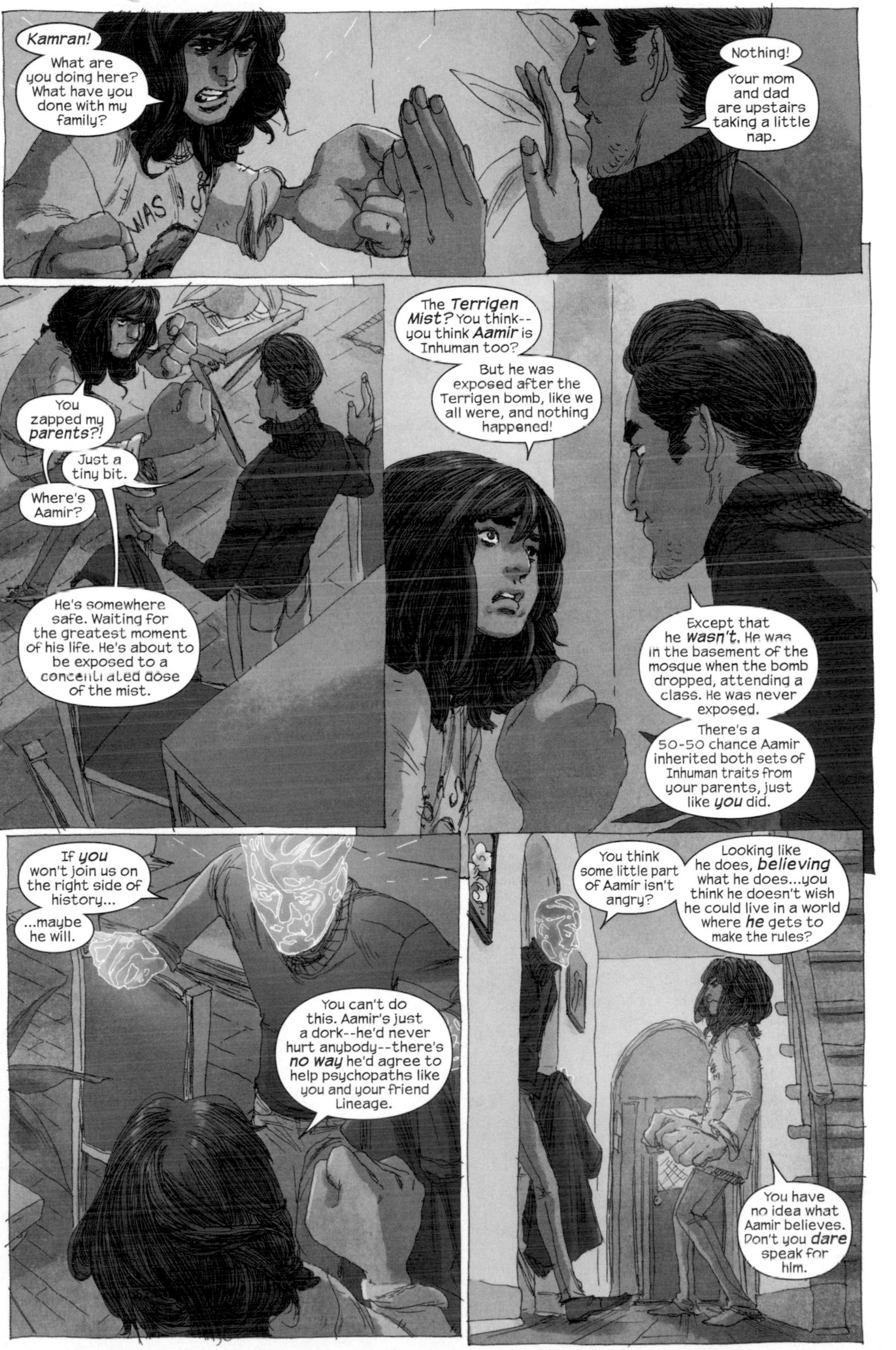
Kamran!
What are you doing here? What have you done with my family?
Nothing!
Your mom and dad are upstairs taking a little nap.
You zapped my parents?!
Just a tiny bit.
Where's Aamir?
He's somewhere safe. Waiting for the greatest moment of his life. He's about to be exposed to a concentrated dose of the mist.
The Terrigen Mist? You think--you think Aamir is Inhuman too?
But he was exposed after the Terrigen bomb, like we all were, and nothing happened!
Except that he wasn't. He was in the basement of the mosque when the bomb dropped, attending a class. He was never exposed.
There's a 50-50 chance Aamir inherited both sets of Inhuman traits from your parents, just like you did.
If you won't join us on the right side of history...
...maybe he will.
You can't do this. Aamir's just a dork--he'd never hurt anybody--there's no way he'd agree to help psychopaths like you and your friend Lineage.
You think some little part of Aamir isn't angry?
Looking like he does, believing what he does...you think he doesn't wish he could live in a world where he gets to make the rules?
You have no idea what Aamir believes. Don't you dare speak for him.

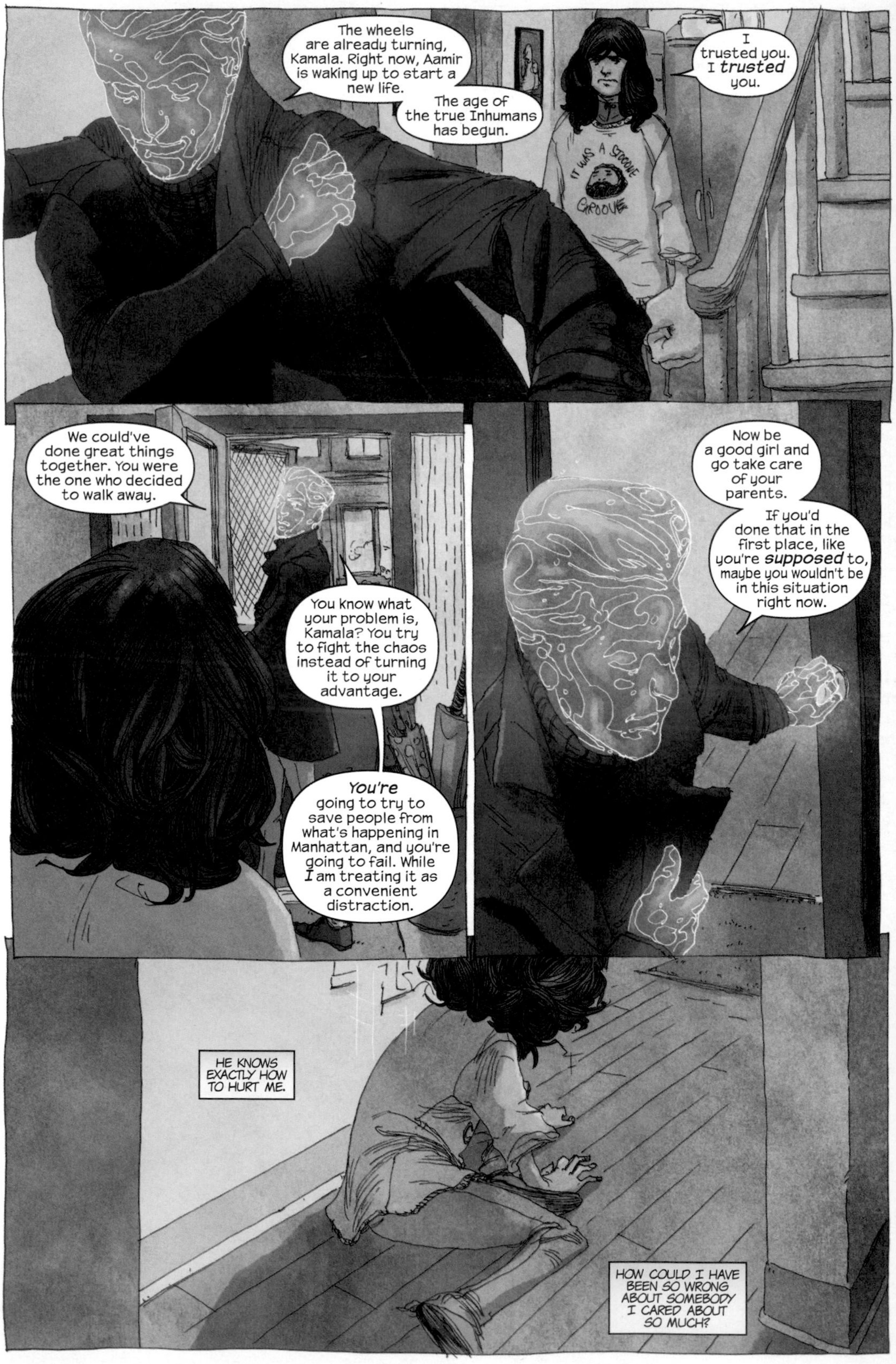
The wheels are already turning, Kamala. Right now, Aamir is waking up to start a new life.
The age of the true Inhumans has begun.
I trusted you. I *trusted* you.
We could've done great things together. You were the one who decided to walk away.
You know what your problem is, Kamala? You try to fight the chaos instead of turning it to your advantage.
You're going to try to save people from what's happening in Manhattan, and you're going to fail. While *I* am treating it as a convenient distraction.
Now be a good girl and go take care of your parents.
If you'd done that in the first place, like you're *supposed* to, maybe you wouldn't be in this situation right now.
HE KNOWS EXACTLY HOW TO HURT ME.
HOW COULD I HAVE BEEN SO WRONG ABOUT SOMEBODY I CARED ABOUT SO MUCH?

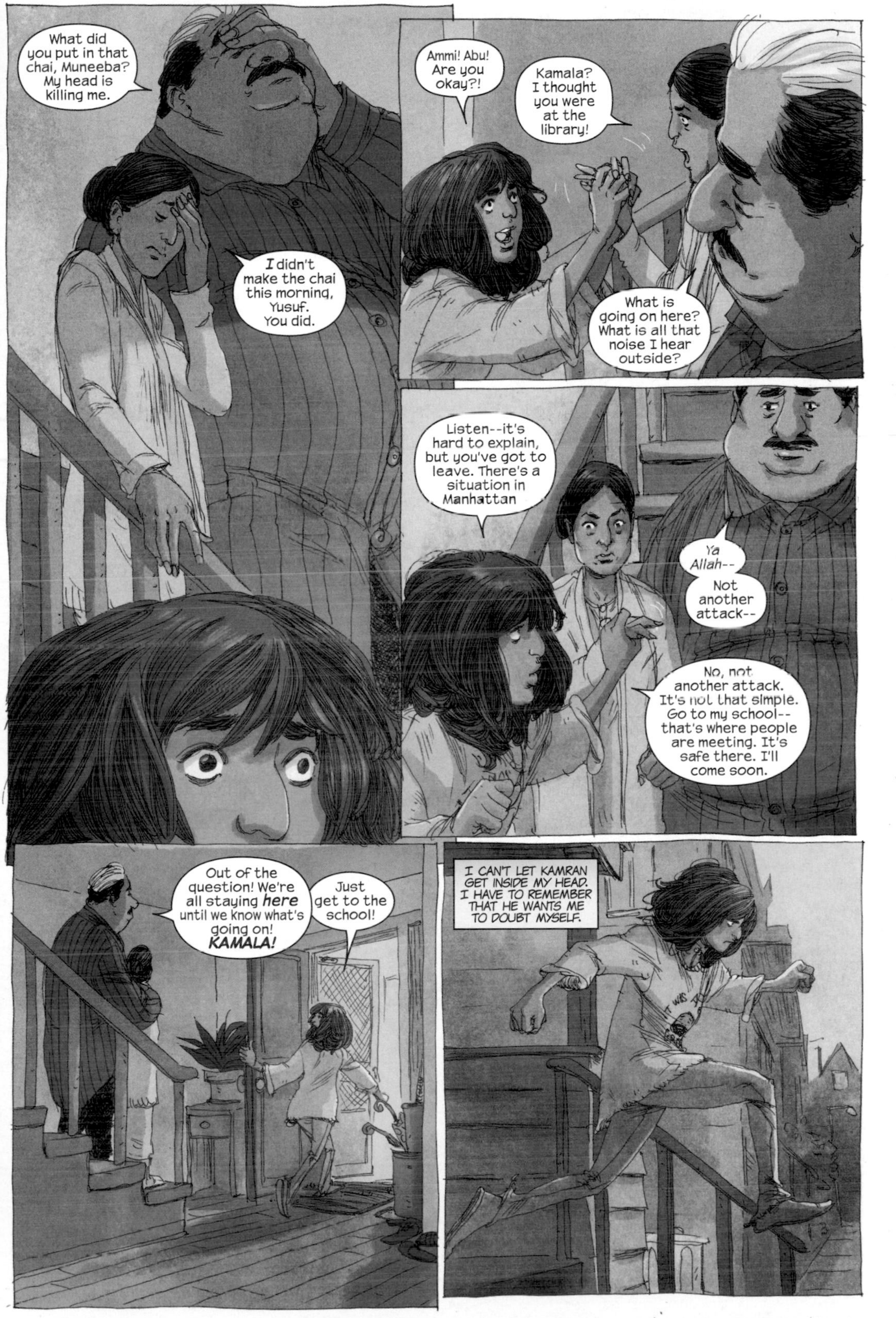
What did you put in that chai, Muneeba? My head is killing me.
I didn't make the chai this morning, Yusuf. You did.
Ammi! Abu! Are you okay?!
Kamala? I thought you were at the library!
What is going on here? What is all that noise I hear outside?
Listen--it's hard to explain, but you've got to leave. There's a situation in Manhattan
Ya Allah--
Not another attack--
No, not another attack. It's not that simple. Go to my school--that's where people are meeting. It's safe there. I'll come soon.
Out of the question! We're all staying here until we know what's going on! KAMALA!
Just get to the school!
I CAN'T LET KAMRAN GET INSIDE MY HEAD. I HAVE TO REMEMBER THAT HE WANTS ME TO DOUBT MYSELF.

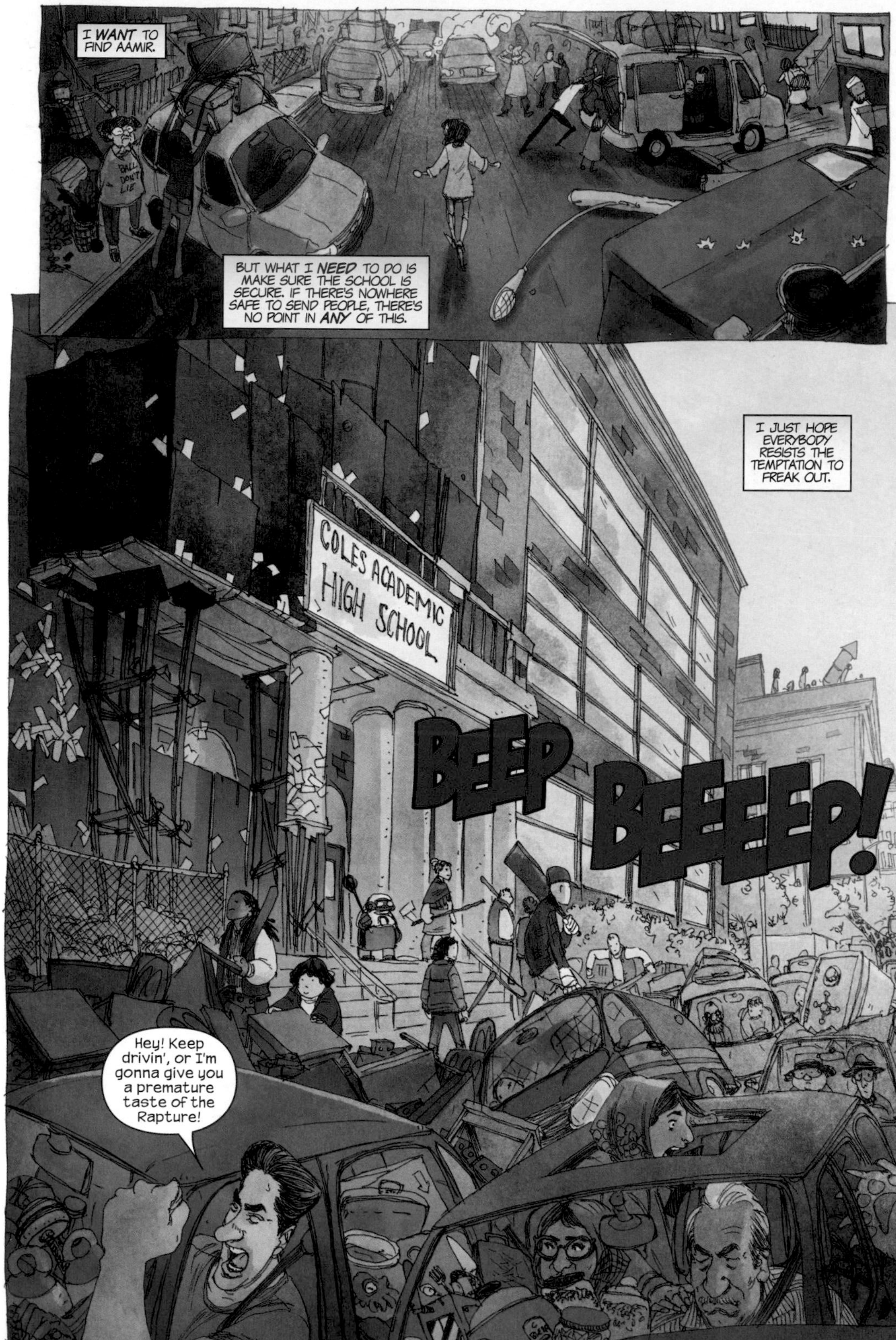
I *WANT* TO FIND AAMIR.
BALL DON'T LIE
BUT WHAT I *NEED* TO DO IS MAKE SURE THE SCHOOL IS SECURE. IF THERE'S NOWHERE SAFE TO SEND PEOPLE, THERE'S NO POINT IN *ANY* OF THIS.
COLES ACADEMIC HIGH SCHOOL
I JUST HOPE EVERYBODY RESISTS THE TEMPTATION TO FREAK OUT.
BEEP BEEEEP!
Hey! Keep drivin', or I'm gonna give you a premature taste of the Rapture!

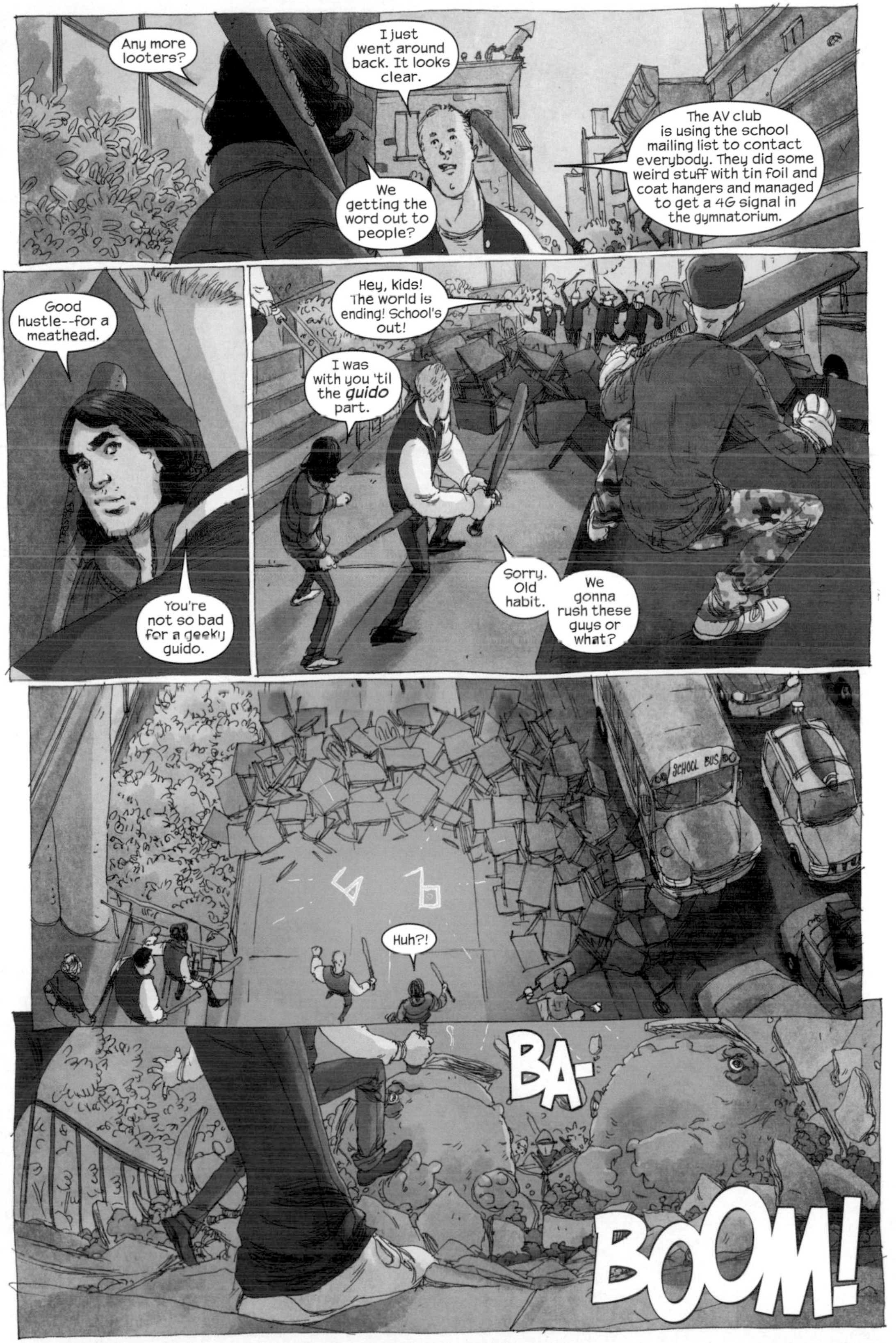
Any more looters?
I just went around back. It looks clear.
We getting the word out to people?
The AV club is using the school mailing list to contact everybody. They did some weird stuff with tin foil and coat hangers and managed to get a 4G signal in the gymnatorium.
Good hustle--for a meathead.
You're not so bad for a geeky guido.
Hey, kids! The world is ending! School's out!
I was with you 'til the *guido* part.
Sorry. Old habit.
We gonna rush these guys or what?
Huh?!
BA-
BOOM!

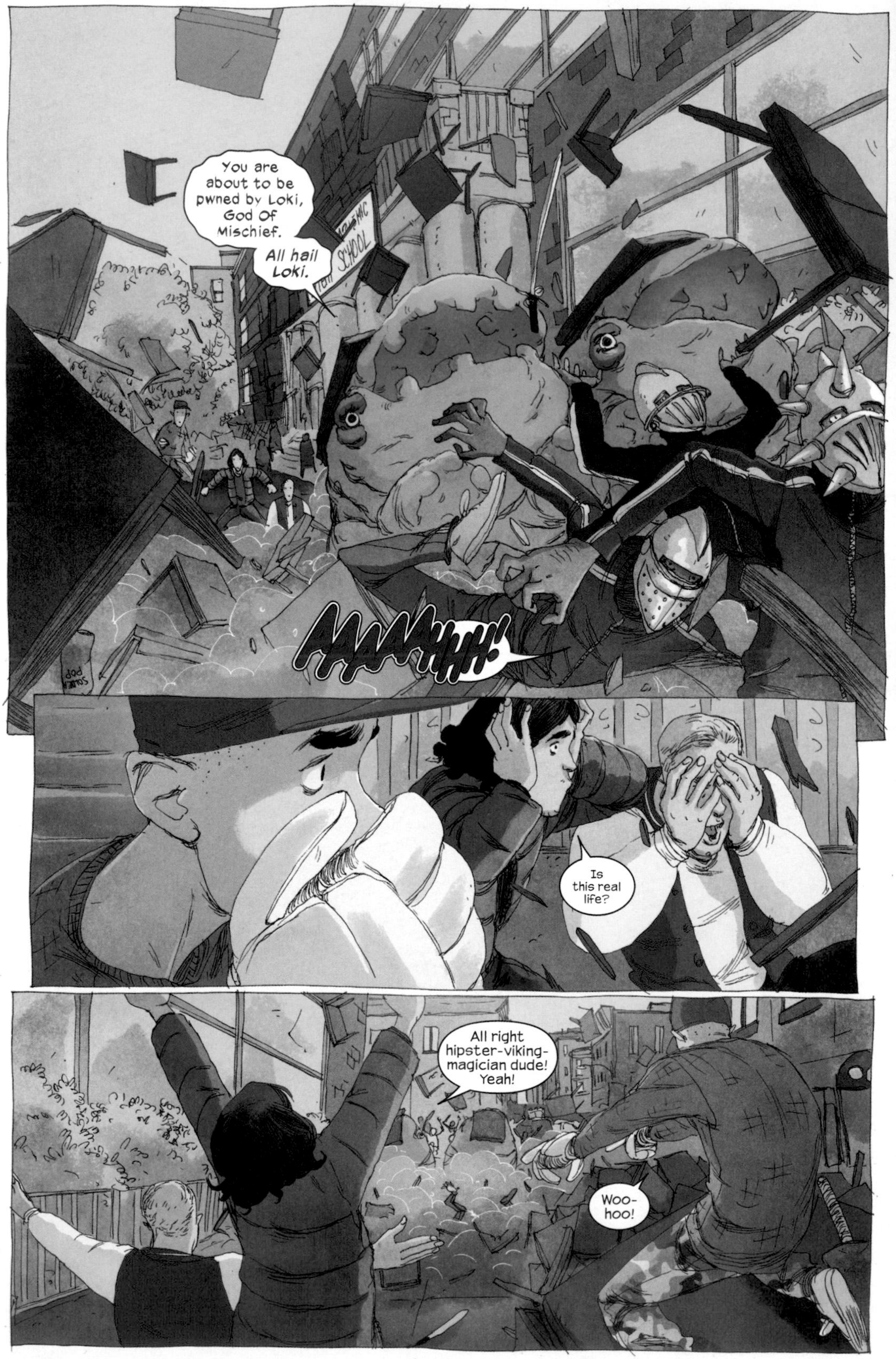
You are about to be pwned by Loki, God Of Mischief.
All hail Loki.
SCHOOL
AAAAHHHH!
Is this real life?
All right hipster-viking-magician dude! Yeah!
Woo-hoo!

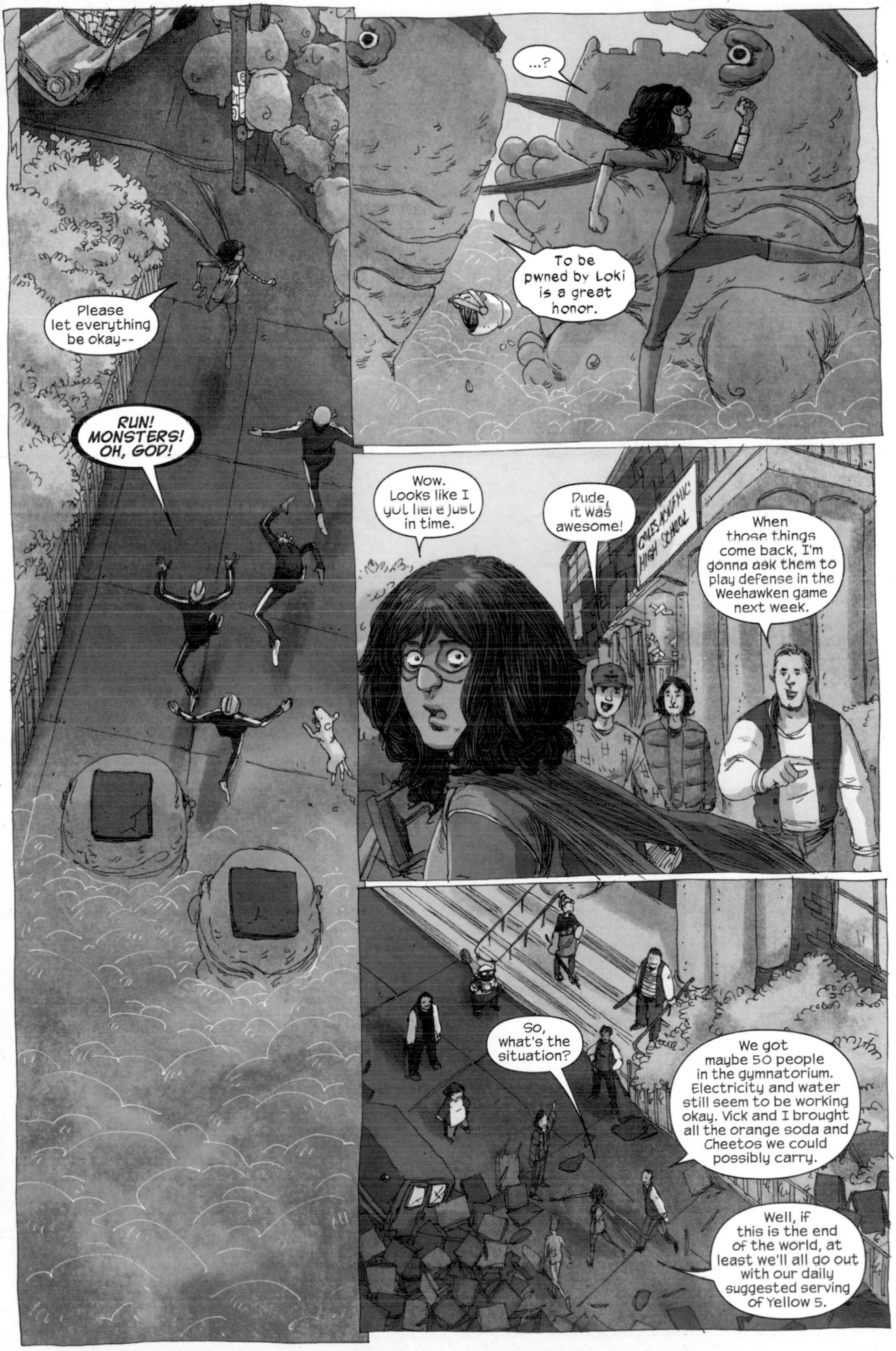
Please let everything be okay--
RUN! MONSTERS! OH, GOD!
...?
To be pwned by Loki is a great honor.
Wow. Looks like I got here just in time.
Dude, it was awesome!
When those things come back, I'm gonna ask them to play defense in the Weehawken game next week.
So, what's the situation?
We got maybe 50 people in the gymnatorium. Electricity and water still seem to be working okay. Vick and I brought all the orange soda and Cheetos we could possibly carry.
Well, if this is the end of the world, at least we'll all go out with our daily suggested serving of Yellow 5.

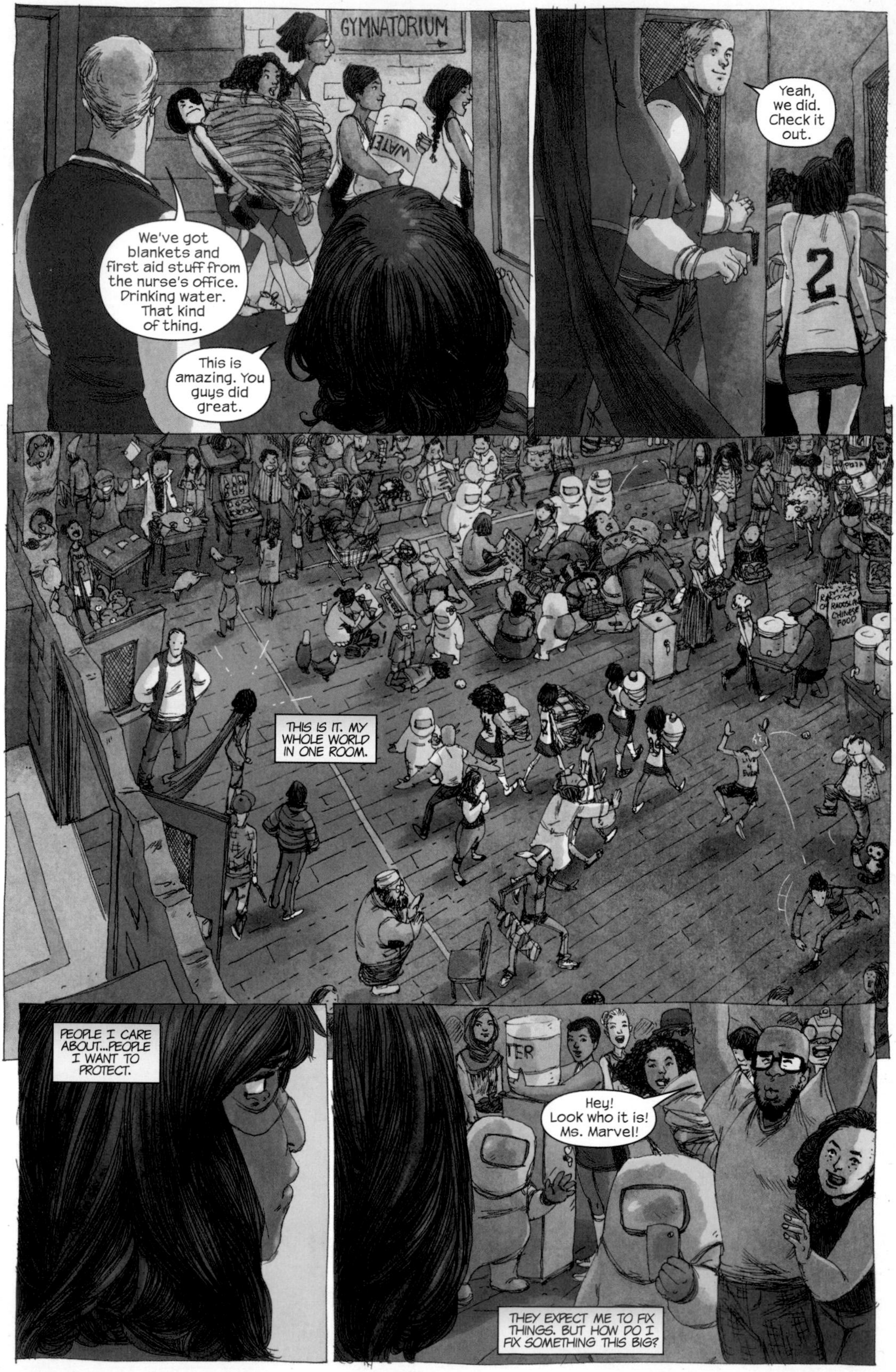

GYMNATORIUM
WATER
We've got blankets and first aid stuff from the nurse's office. Drinking water. That kind of thing.
This is amazing. You guys did great.
Yeah, we did. Check it out.
THIS IS IT. MY WHOLE WORLD IN ONE ROOM.
CHINESE FOOD
PEOPLE I CARE ABOUT...PEOPLE I WANT TO PROTECT.
Hey! Look who it is! Ms. Marvel!
THEY EXPECT ME TO FIX THINGS. BUT HOW DO I FIX SOMETHING THIS BIG?

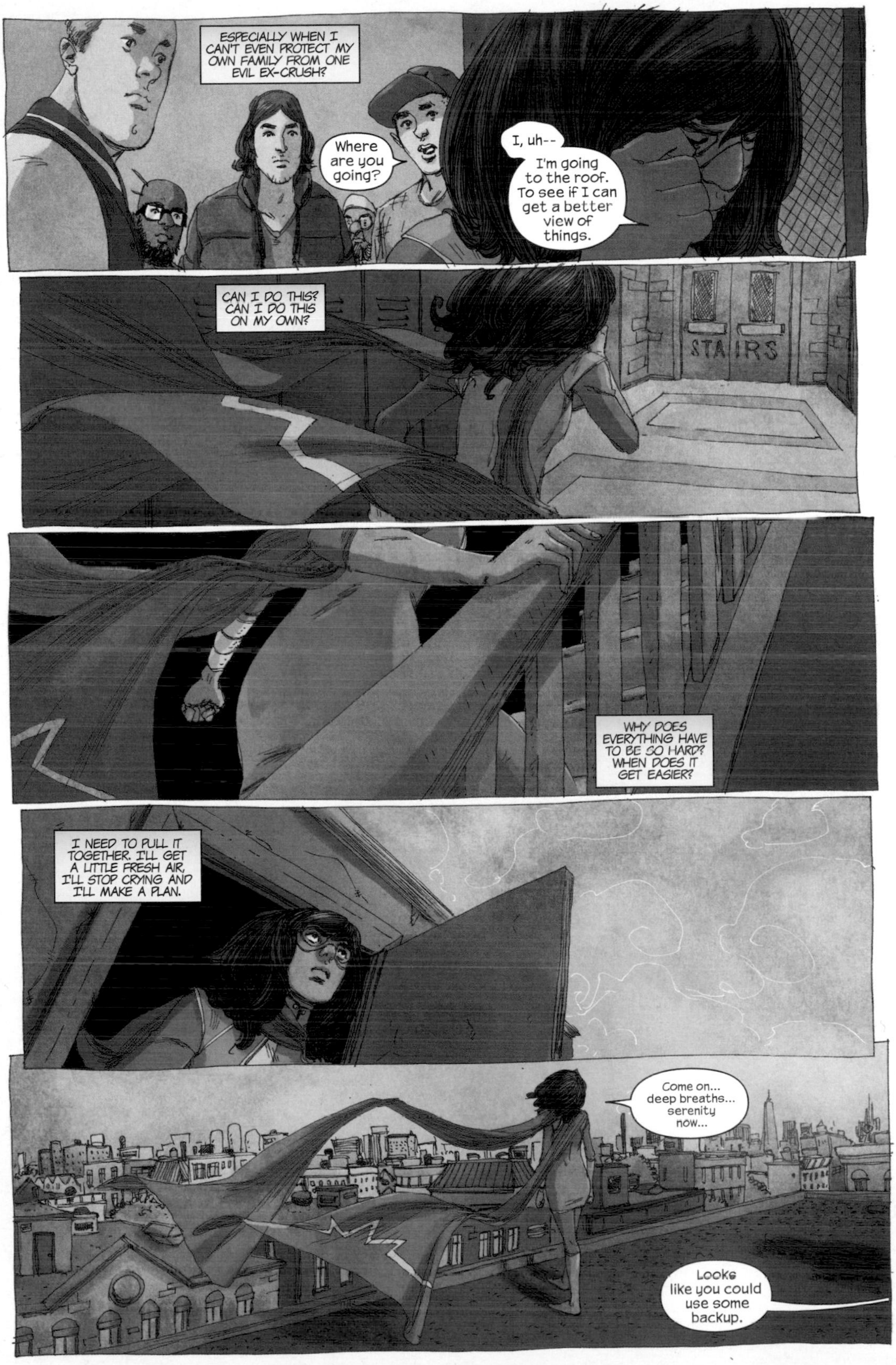

ESPECIALLY WHEN I CAN'T EVEN PROTECT MY OWN FAMILY FROM ONE EVIL EX-CRUSH?
Where are you going?
I, uh--
I'm going to the roof. To see if I can get a better view of things.
CAN I DO THIS? CAN I DO THIS ON MY OWN?
STAIRS
WHY DOES EVERYTHING HAVE TO BE SO HARD? WHEN DOES IT GET EASIER?
I NEED TO PULL IT TOGETHER. I'LL GET A LITTLE FRESH AIR, I'LL STOP CRYING AND I'LL MAKE A PLAN.
Come on... deep breaths... serenity now...
Looks like you could use some backup.

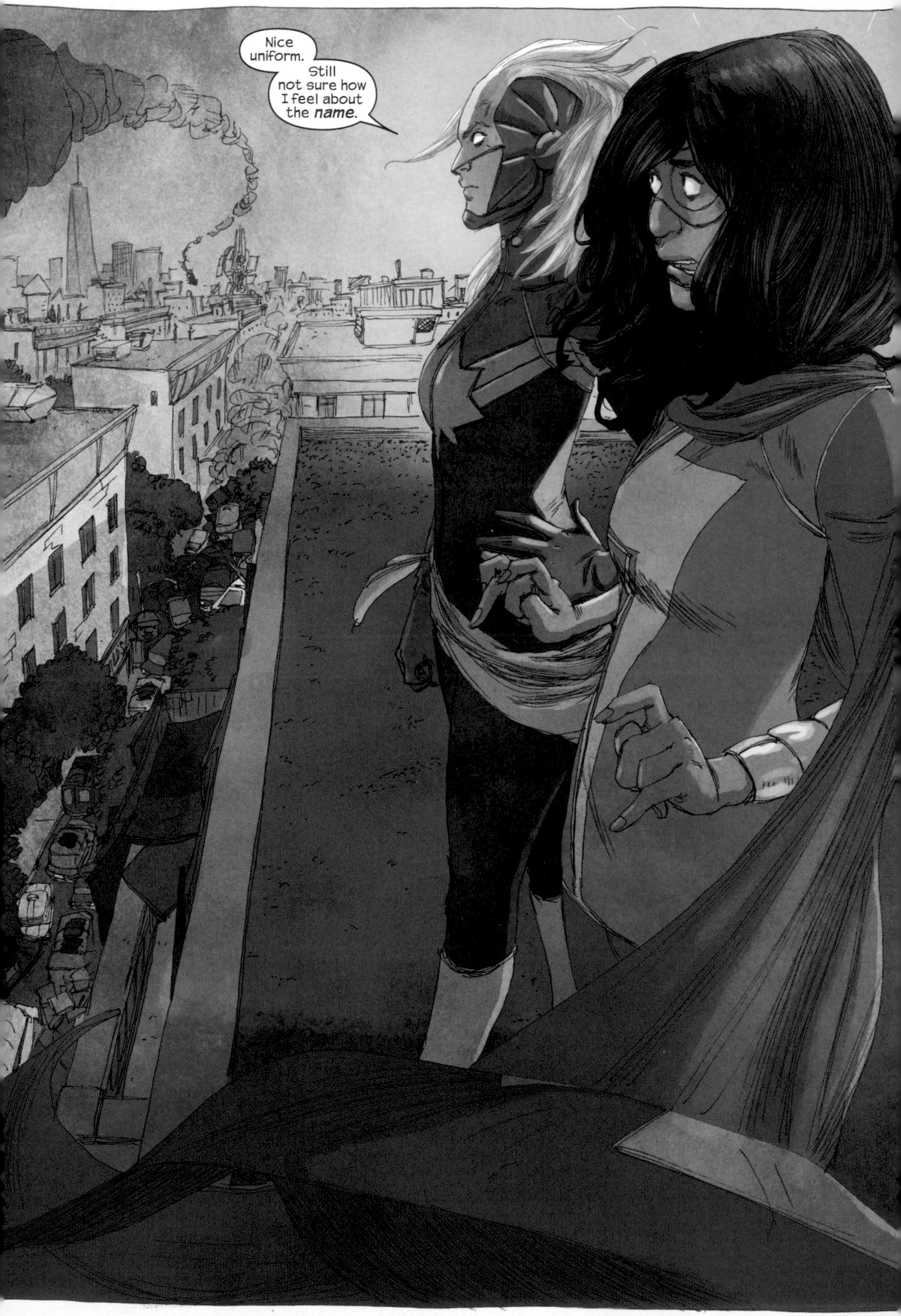
Nice uniform.
Still not sure how I feel about the *name*.

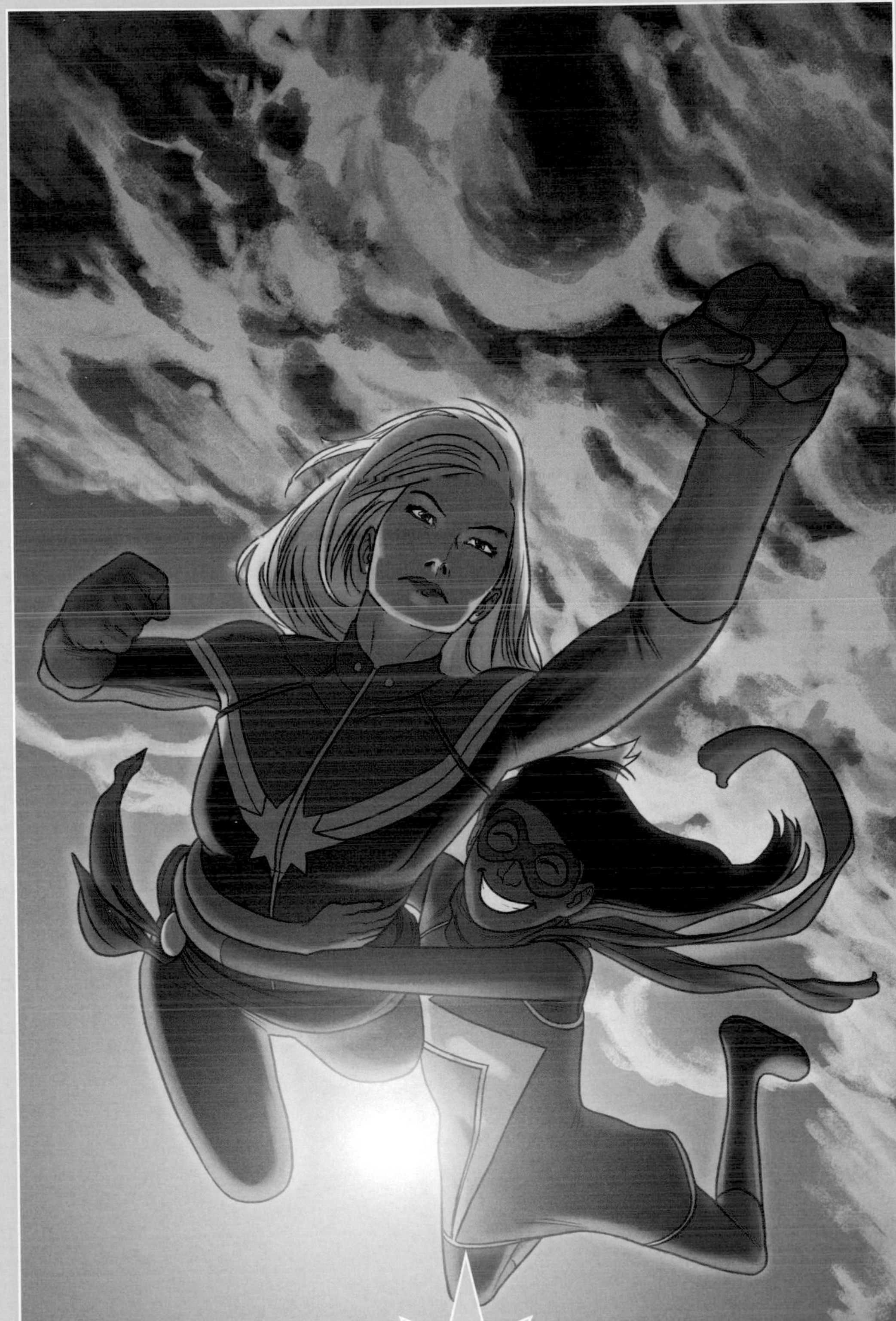
17

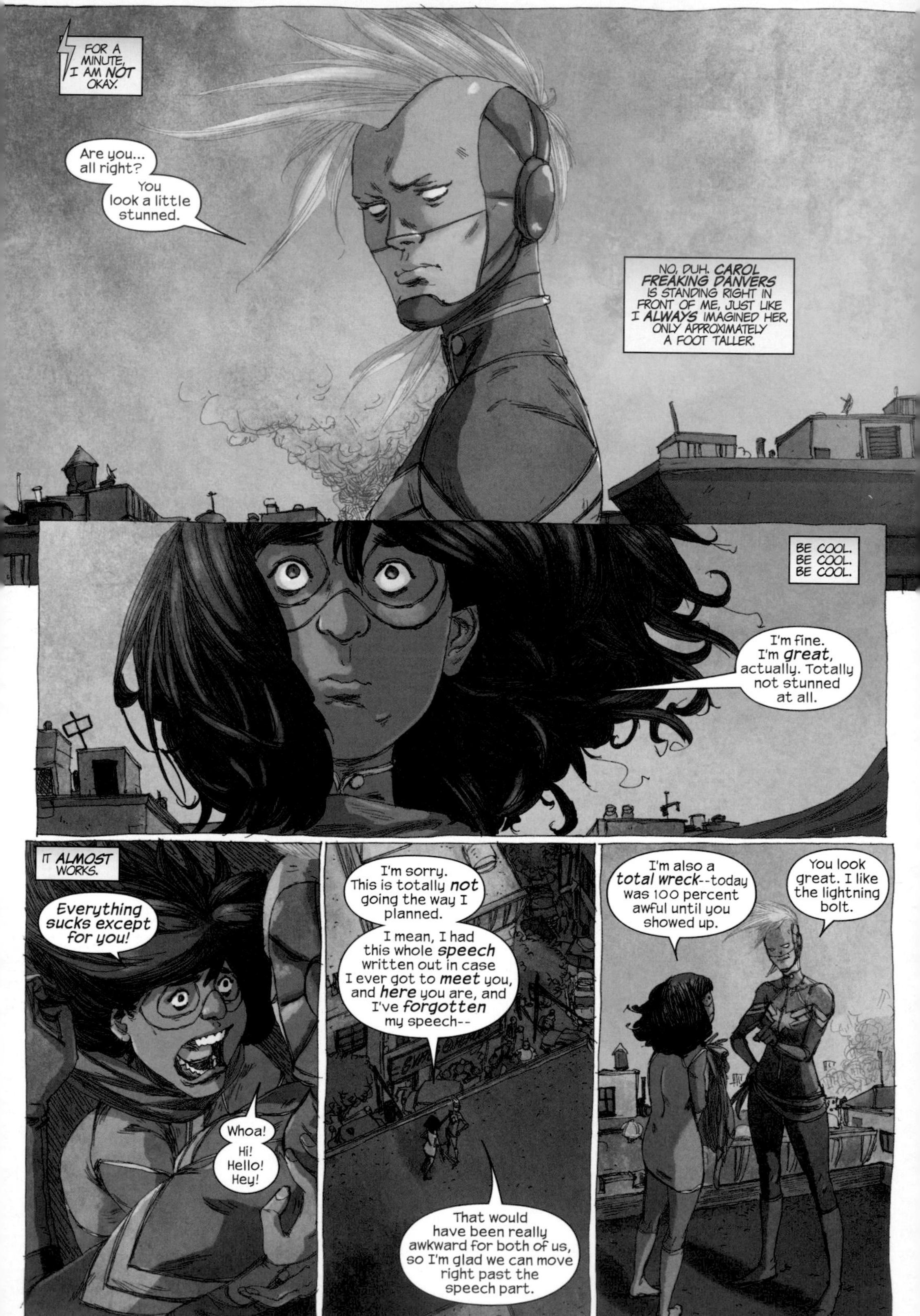
FOR A MINUTE, I AM NOT OKAY.
Are you... all right?
You look a little stunned.
NO, DUH. CAROL FREAKING DANVERS IS STANDING RIGHT IN FRONT OF ME, JUST LIKE I ALWAYS IMAGINED HER, ONLY APPROXIMATELY A FOOT TALLER.
BE COOL. BE COOL. BE COOL.
I'm fine. I'm great, actually. Totally not stunned at all.
IT ALMOST WORKS.
Everything sucks except for you!
Whoa! Hi! Hello! Hey!
I'm sorry. This is totally not going the way I planned.
I mean, I had this whole speech written out in case I ever got to meet you, and here you are, and I've forgotten my speech--
That would have been really awkward for both of us, so I'm glad we can move right past the speech part.
I'm also a total wreck--today was 100 percent awful until you showed up.
You look great. I like the lightning bolt.

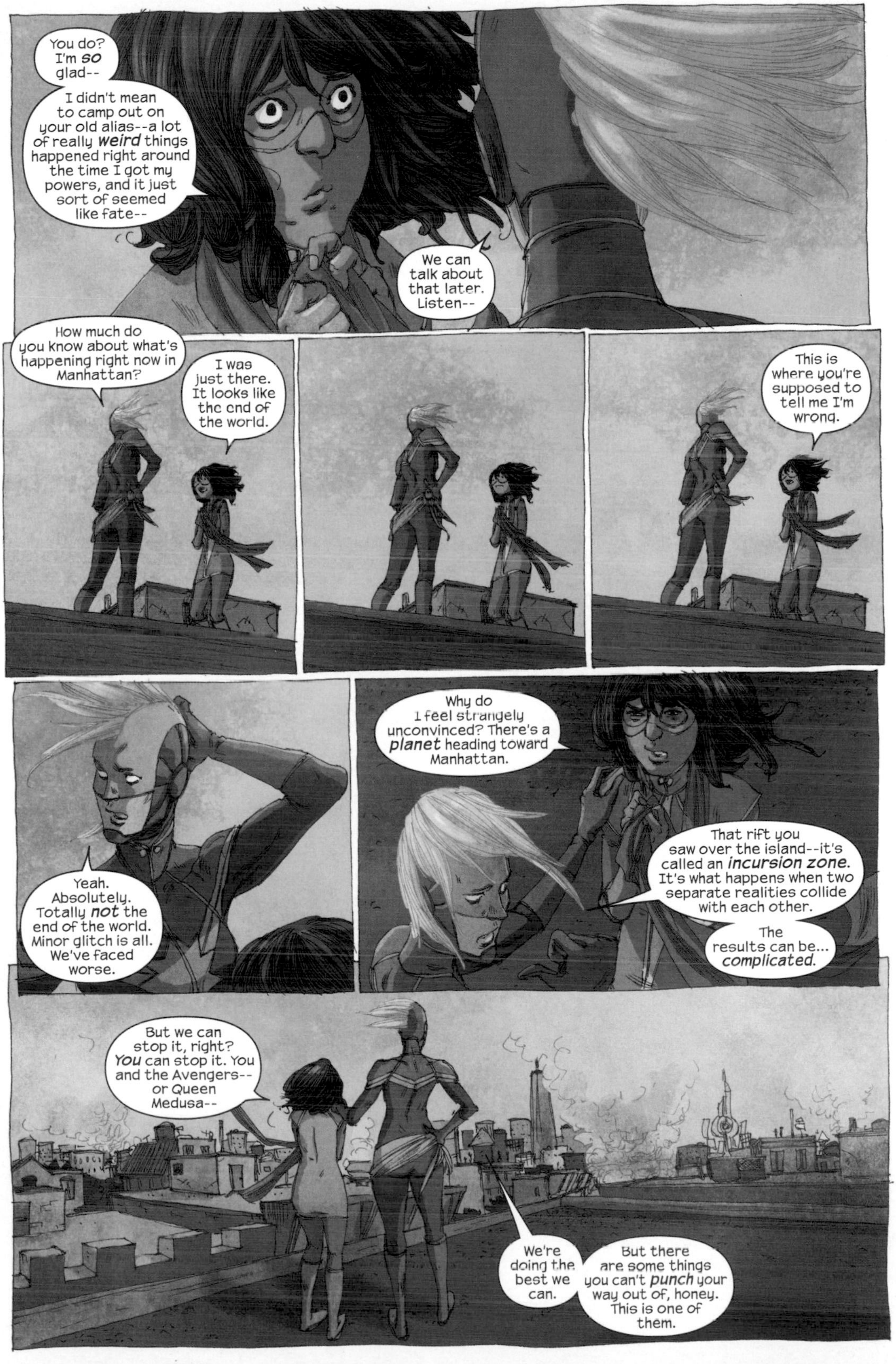
You do? I'm SO glad--
I didn't mean to camp out on your old alias--a lot of really weird things happened right around the time I got my powers, and it just sort of seemed like fate--
We can talk about that later. Listen--
How much do you know about what's happening right now in Manhattan?
I was just there. It looks like the end of the world.
This is where you're supposed to tell me I'm wrong.
Yeah. Absolutely. Totally not the end of the world. Minor glitch is all. We've faced worse.
Why do I feel strangely unconvinced? There's a planet heading toward Manhattan.
That rift you saw over the island--it's called an incursion zone. It's what happens when two separate realities collide with each other.
The results can be... complicated.
But we can stop it, right? YOU can stop it. You and the Avengers--or Queen Medusa--
We're doing the best we can.
But there are some things you can't punch your way out of, honey. This is one of them.

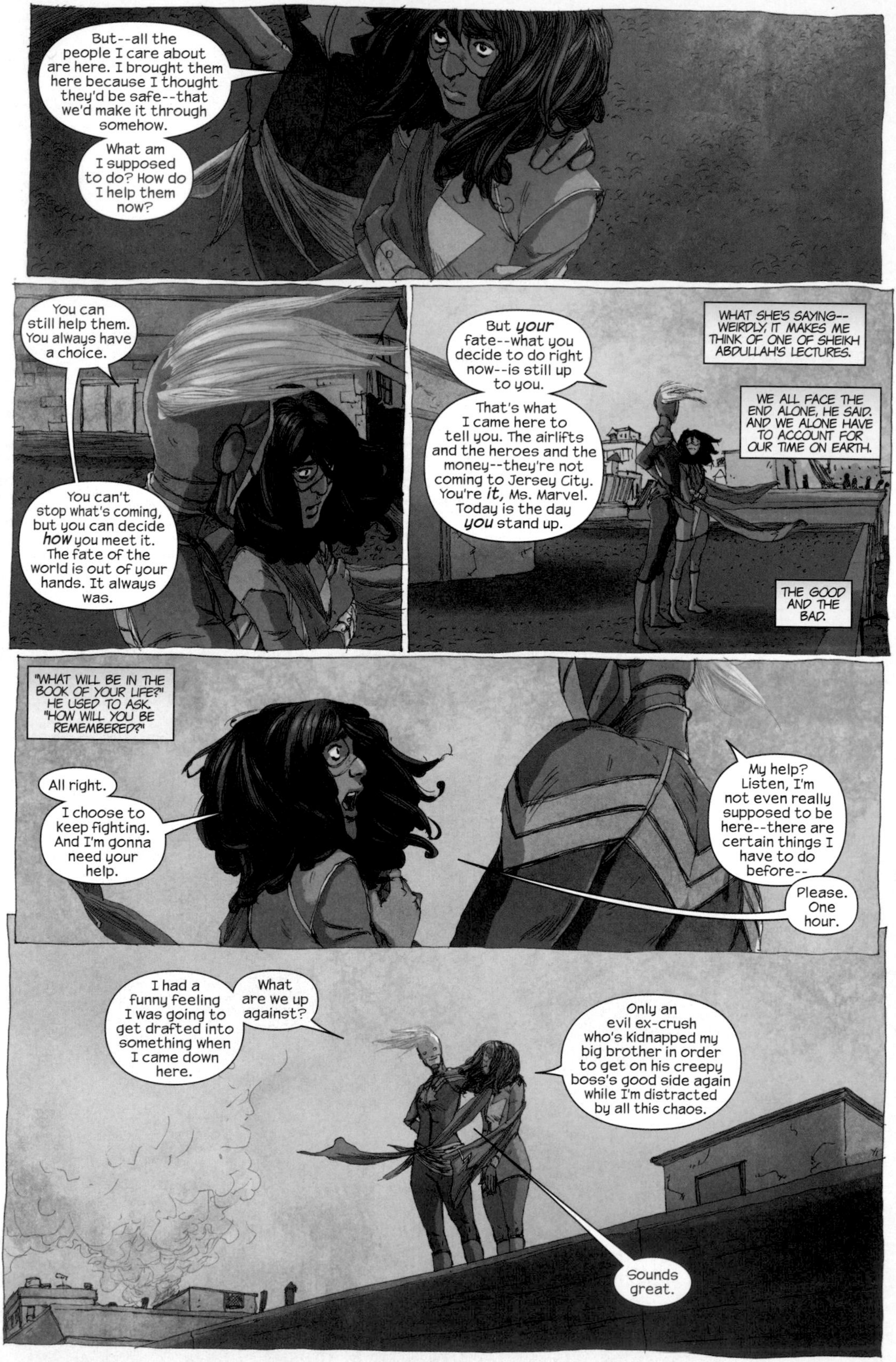
But--all the people I care about are here. I brought them here because I thought they'd be safe--that we'd make it through somehow.
What am I supposed to do? How do I help them now?
You can still help them. You always have a choice.
You can't stop what's coming, but you can decide *how* you meet it. The fate of the world is out of your hands. It always was.
But *your* fate--what you decide to do right now--is still up to you.
That's what I came here to tell you. The airlifts and the heroes and the money--they're not coming to Jersey City. You're *it,* Ms. Marvel. Today is the day *you* stand up.
WHAT SHE'S SAYING--WEIRDLY, IT MAKES ME THINK OF ONE OF SHEIKH ABDULLAH'S LECTURES.
WE ALL FACE THE END ALONE, HE SAID. AND WE ALONE HAVE TO ACCOUNT FOR OUR TIME ON EARTH.
THE GOOD AND THE BAD.
"WHAT WILL BE IN THE BOOK OF YOUR LIFE?" HE USED TO ASK. "HOW WILL YOU BE REMEMBERED?"
All right.
I choose to keep fighting. And I'm gonna need your help.
My help? Listen, I'm not even really supposed to be here--there are certain things I have to do before--
Please. One hour.
I had a funny feeling I was going to get drafted into something when I came down here.
What are we up against?
Only an evil ex-crush who's kidnapped my big brother in order to get on his creepy boss's good side again while I'm distracted by all this chaos.
Sounds great.

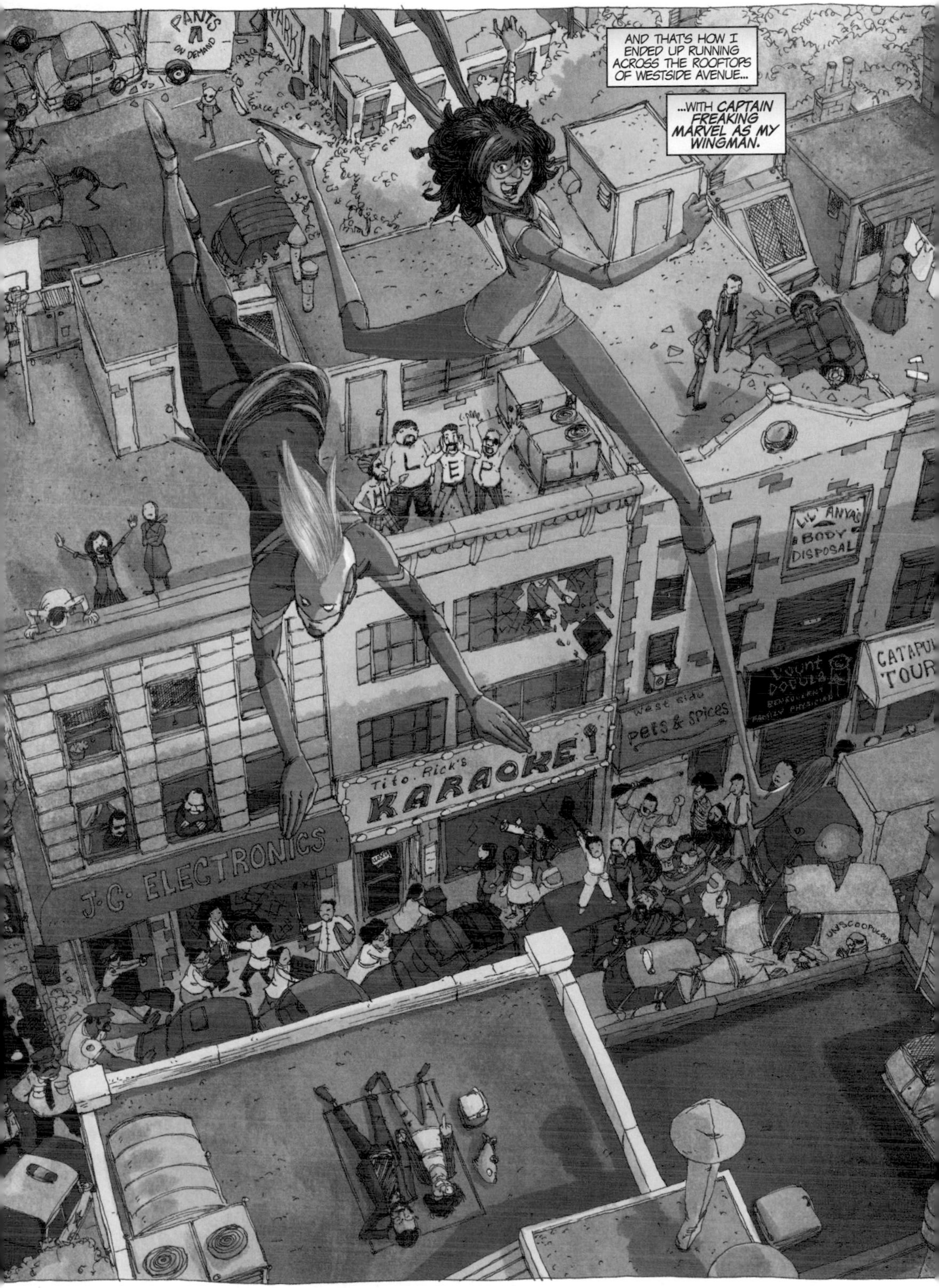
AND THAT'S HOW I ENDED UP RUNNING ACROSS THE ROOFTOPS OF WESTSIDE AVENUE...
...WITH CAPTAIN FREAKING MARVEL AS MY WINGMAN.
PANTS ON DEMAND
LIL' ANYA'S BODY DISPOSAL
West side pets & spices
Tito Rick's KARAOKE!
J.C. ELECTRONICS

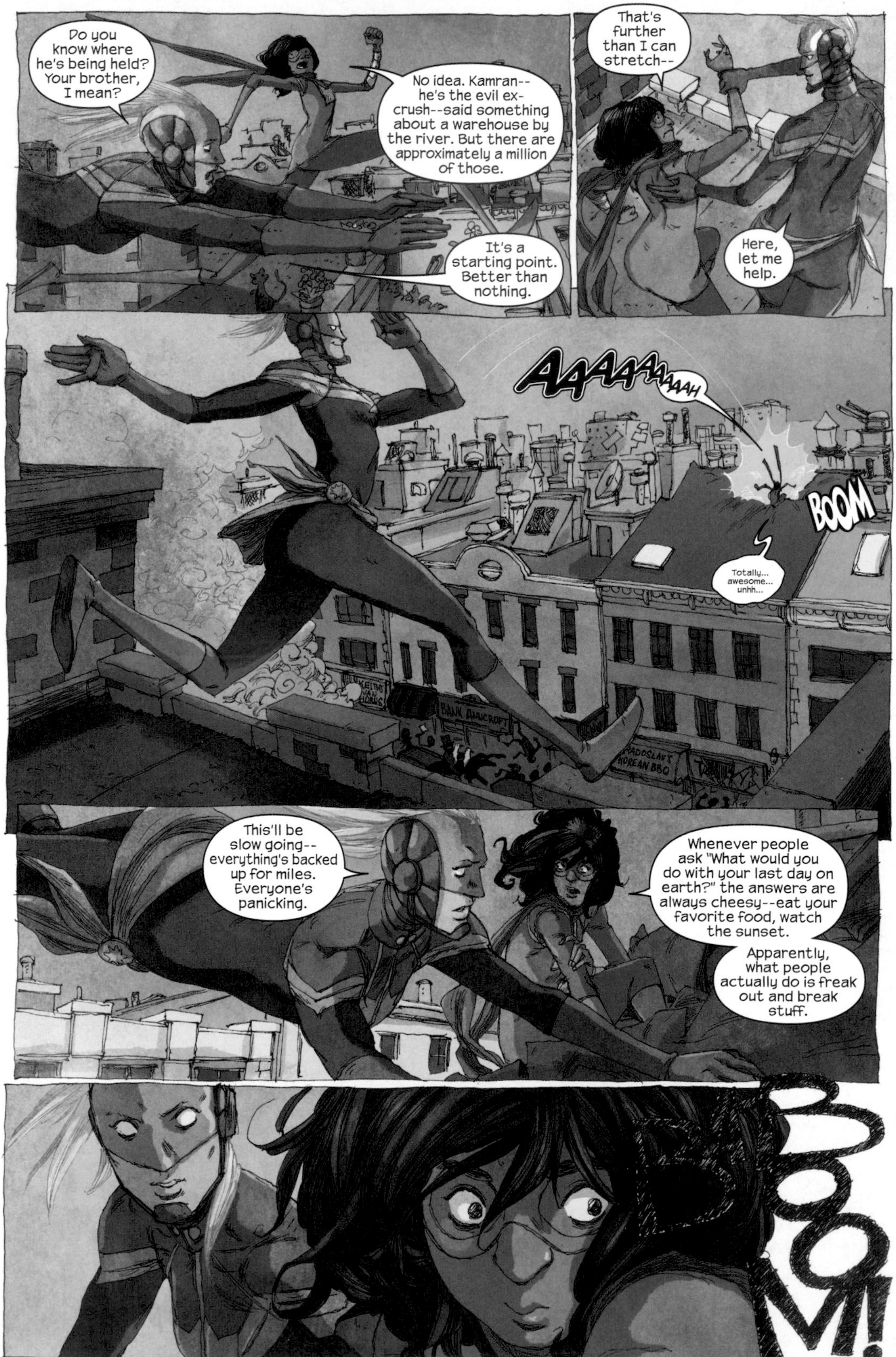

Do you know where he's being held? Your brother, I mean?
No idea. Kamran-- he's the evil ex-crush--said something about a warehouse by the river. But there are approximately a million of those.
It's a starting point. Better than nothing.
That's further than I can stretch--
Here, let me help.
AAAAAAAAAAH
BOOM
Totally... awesome... unhh...
RADOSLAV'S KOREAN BBQ
This'll be slow going-- everything's backed up for miles. Everyone's panicking.
Whenever people ask "What would you do with your last day on earth?" the answers are always cheesy--eat your favorite food, watch the sunset.
Apparently, what people actually do is freak out and break stuff.
BOOOM!

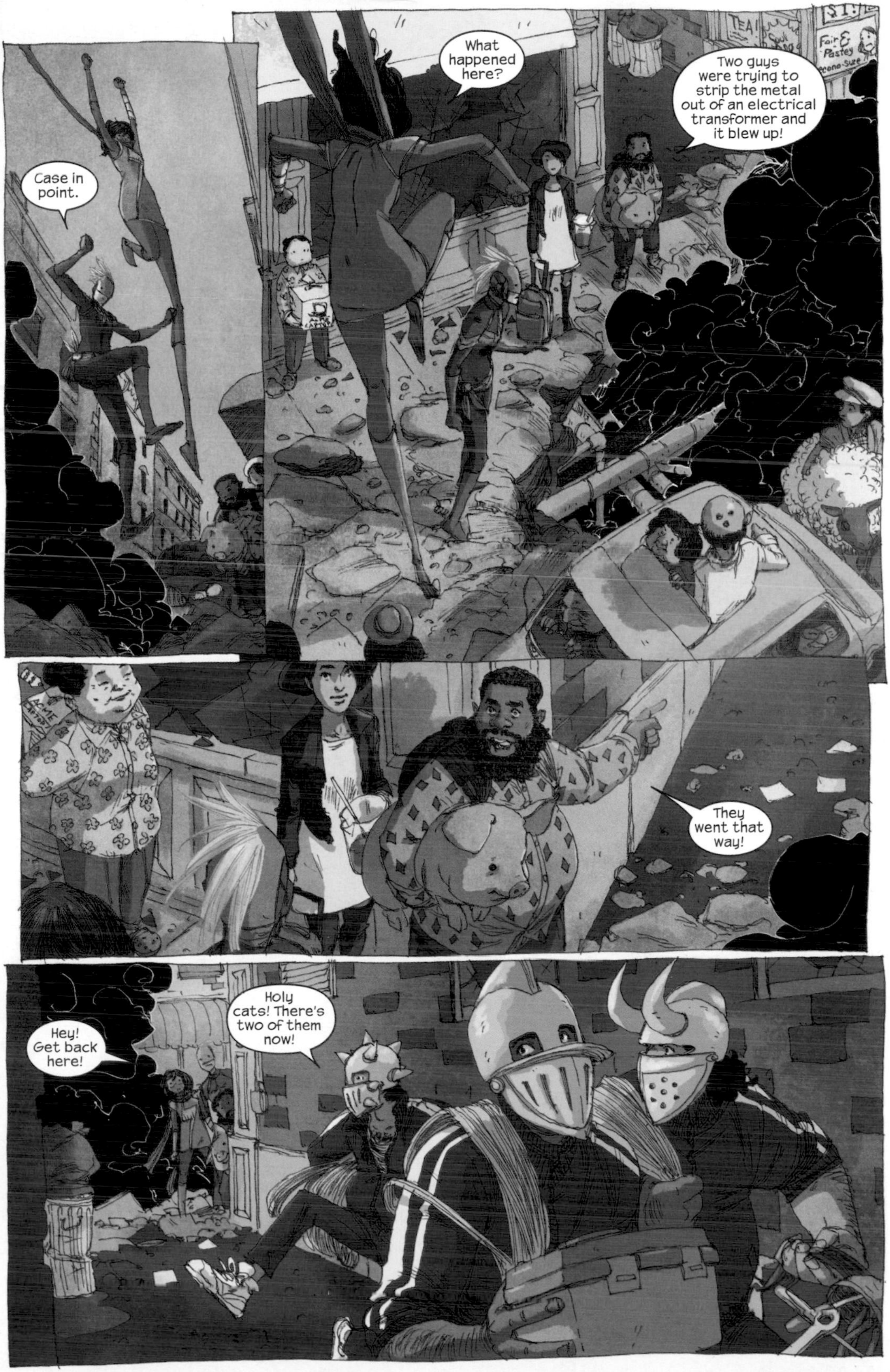
Case in point.
What happened here?
Two guys were trying to strip the metal out of an electrical transformer and it blew up!
TEA!
They went that way!
Hey! Get back here!
Holy cats! There's two of them now!

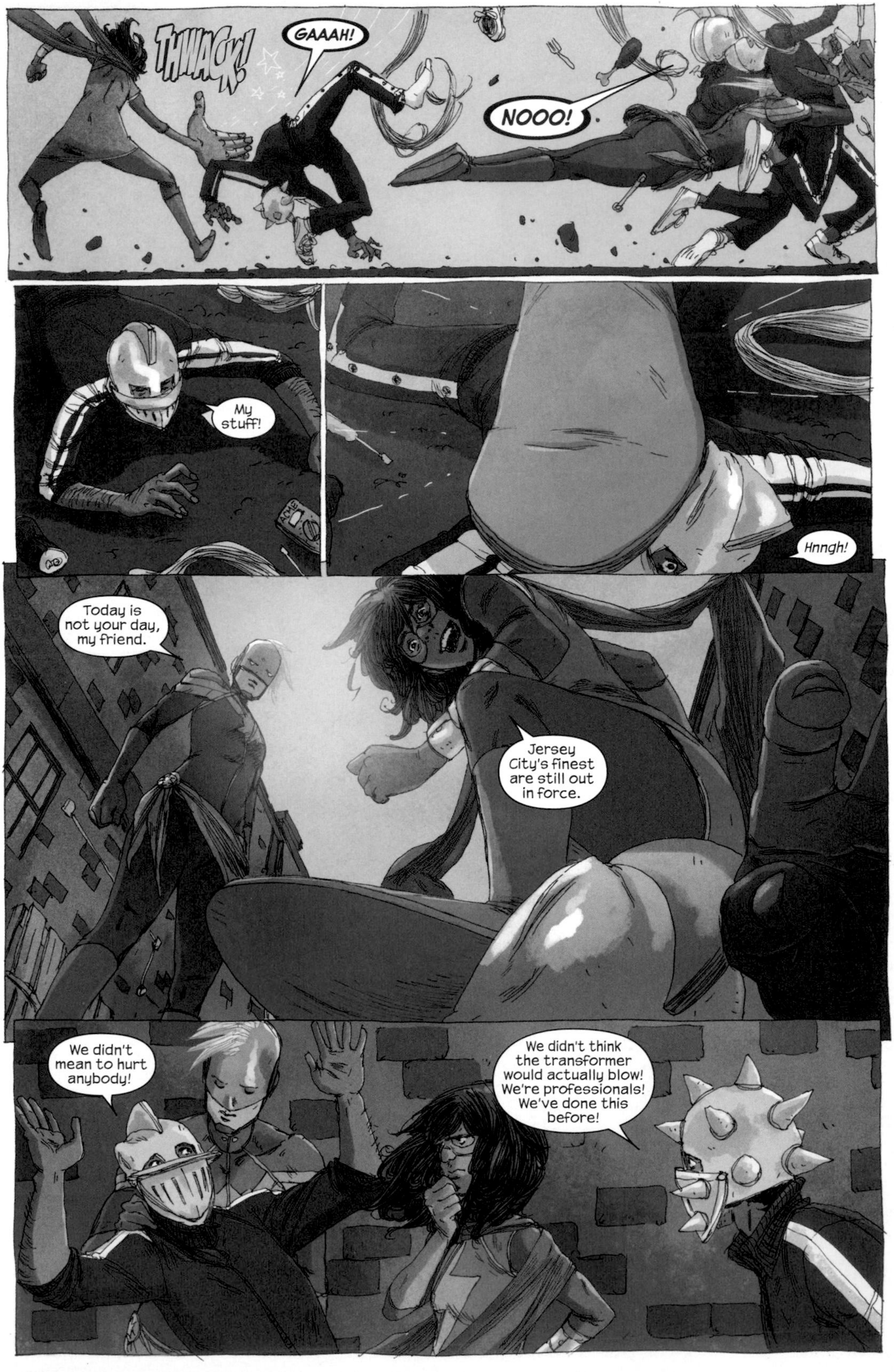

THWACK!
GAAAH!
NOOO!
My stuff!
Hnngh!
Today is not your day, my friend.
Jersey City's finest are still out in force.
We didn't mean to hurt anybody!
We didn't think the transformer would actually blow! We're professionals! We've done this before!

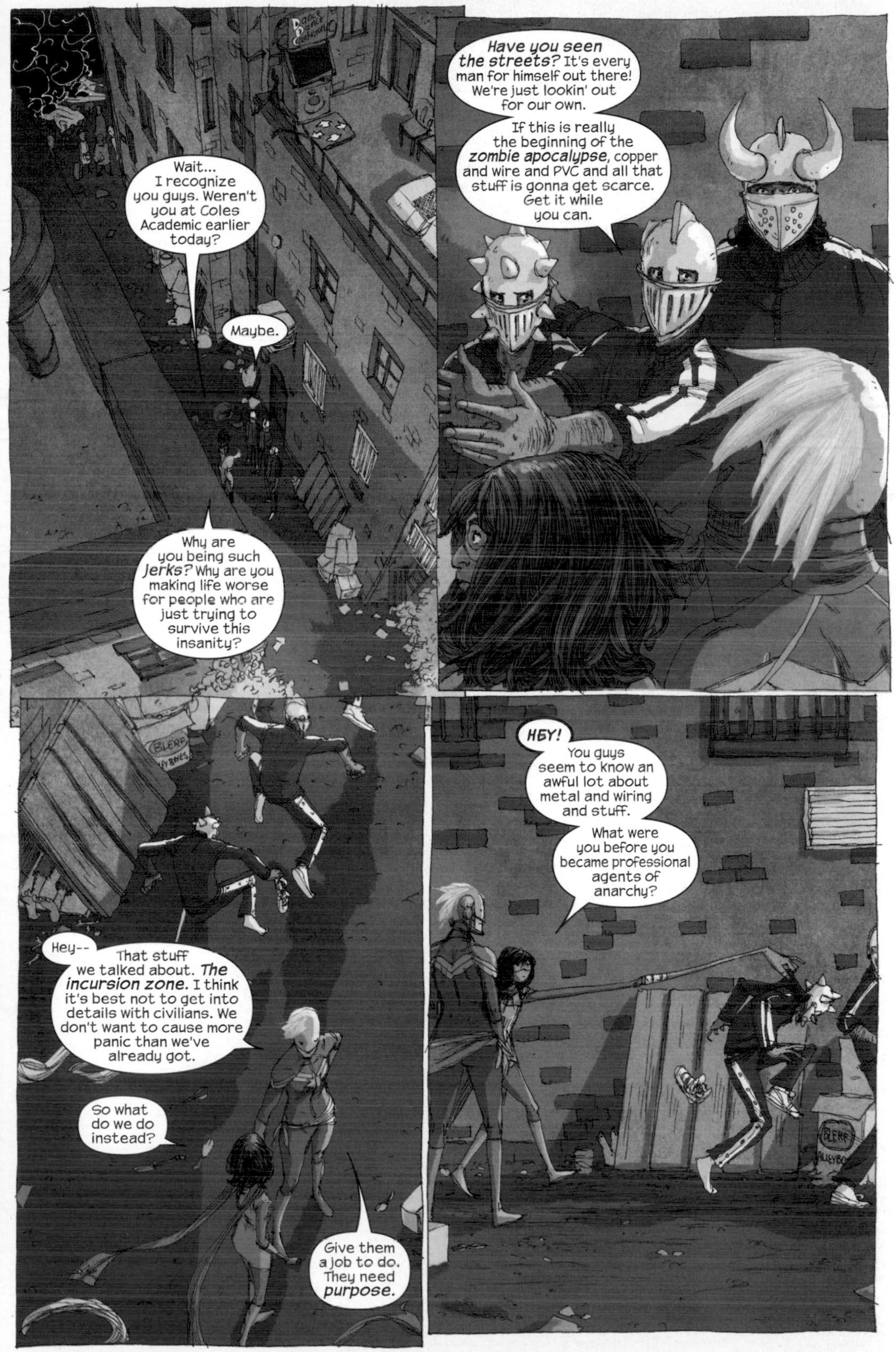
Dance Dance Cantonese
Wait... I recognize you guys. Weren't you at Coles Academic earlier today?
Maybe.
Why are you being such Jerks? Why are you making life worse for people who are just trying to survive this insanity?
Have you seen the streets? It's every man for himself out there! We're just lookin' out for our own.
If this is really the beginning of the zombie apocalypse, copper and wire and PVC and all that stuff is gonna get scarce. Get it while you can.
BLERB
ALLYBONES
Hey--
That stuff we talked about. The incursion zone. I think it's best not to get into details with civilians. We don't want to cause more panic than we've already got.
So what do we do instead?
Give them a job to do. They need purpose.
HEY!
You guys seem to know an awful lot about metal and wiring and stuff.
What were you before you became professional agents of anarchy?
BLERB
ALLEYBO

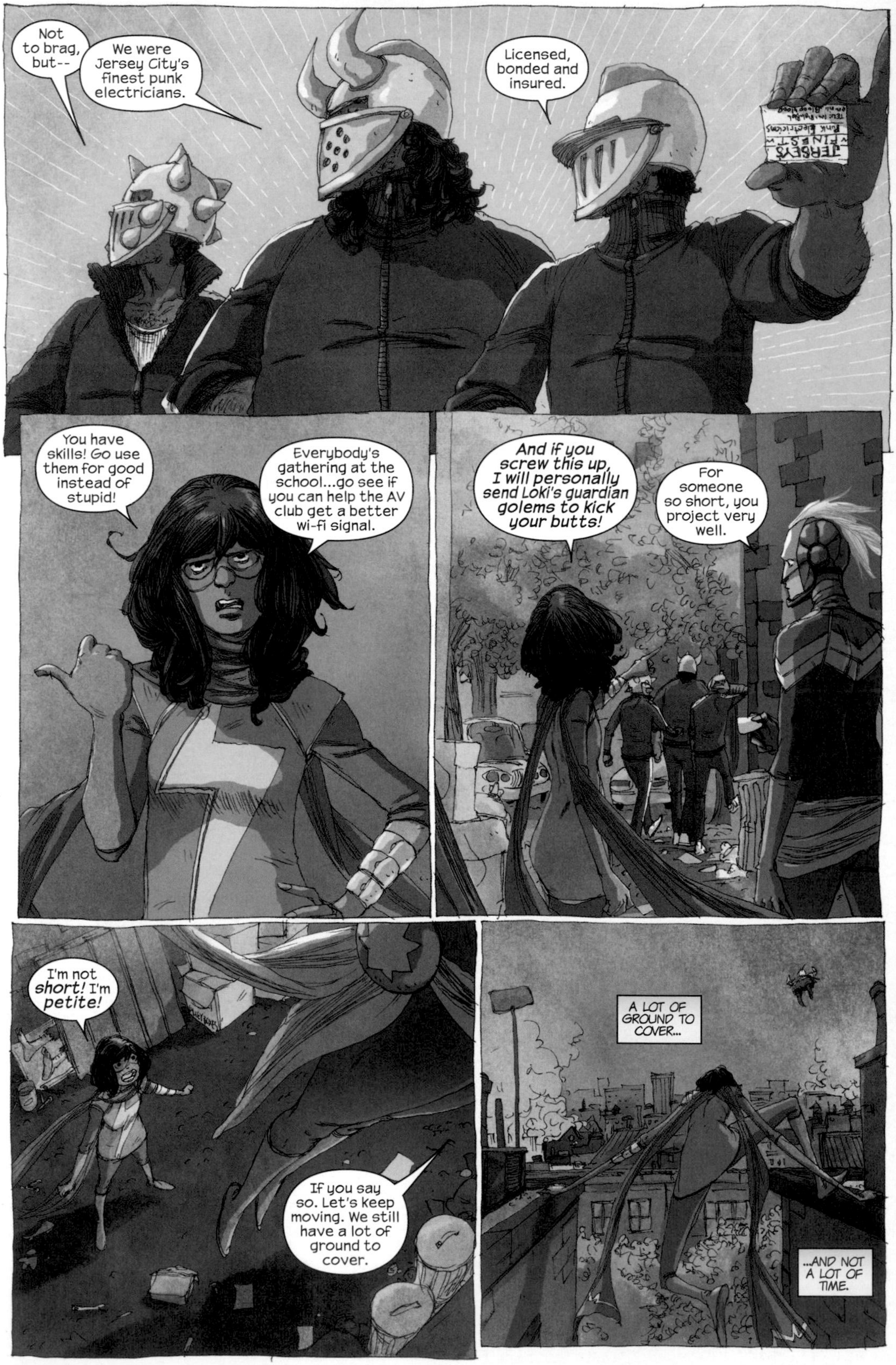
Not to brag, but--
We were Jersey City's finest punk electricians.
Licensed, bonded and insured.
You have skills! Go use them for good instead of stupid!
Everybody's gathering at the school...go see if you can help the AV club get a better wi-fi signal.
And if you screw this up, I will personally send Loki's guardian golems to kick your butts!
For someone so short, you project very well.
I'm not *short!* I'm *petite!*
If you say so. Let's keep moving. We still have a lot of ground to cover.
A LOT OF GROUND TO COVER...
...AND NOT A LOT OF TIME.

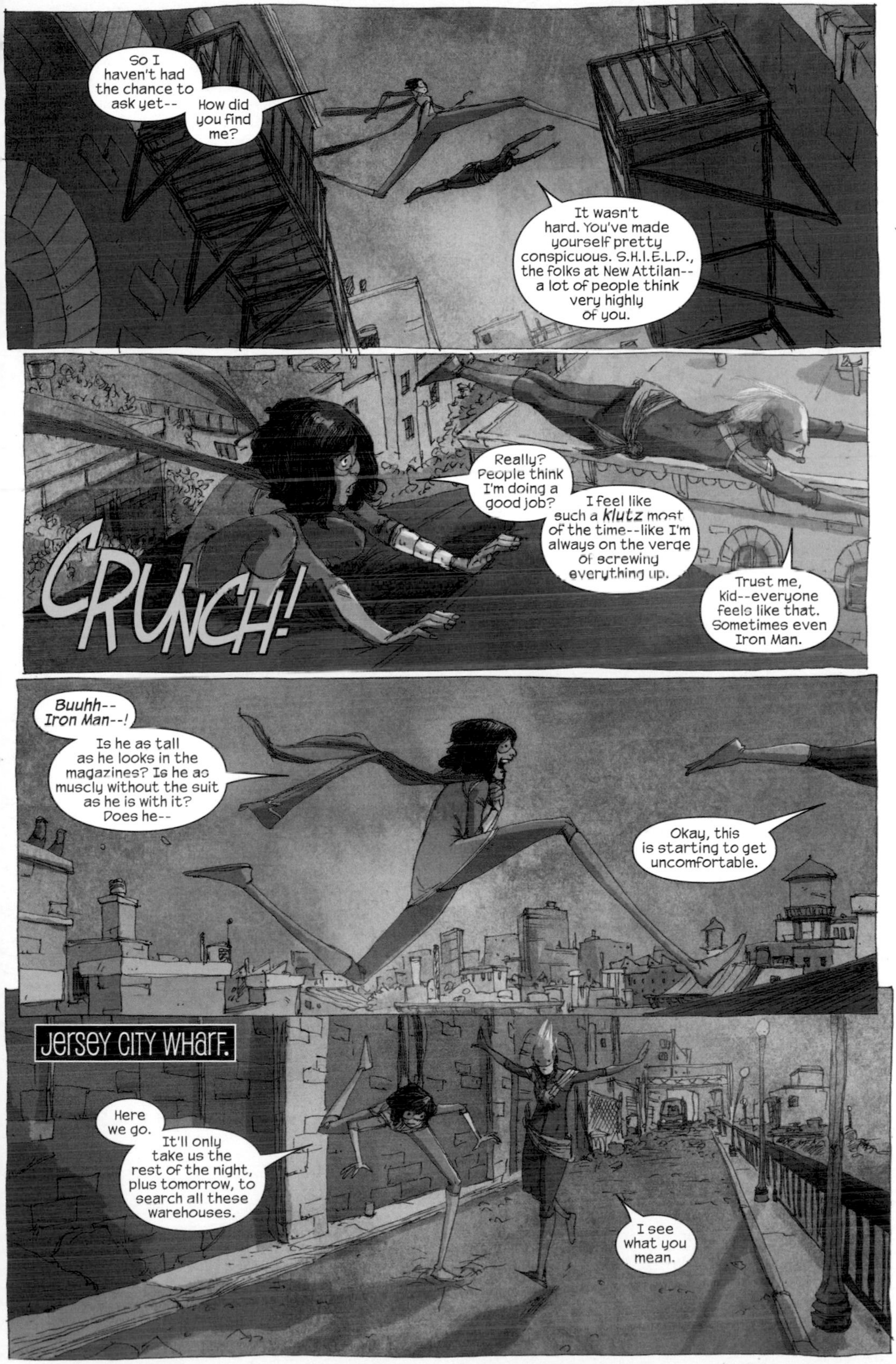
So I haven't had the chance to ask yet--
How did you find me?
It wasn't hard. You've made yourself pretty conspicuous. S.H.I.E.L.D., the folks at New Attilan-- a lot of people think very highly of you.
CRUNCH!
Really? People think I'm doing a good job?
I feel like such a klutz most of the time--like I'm always on the verge of screwing everything up.
Trust me, kid--everyone feels like that. Sometimes even Iron Man.
Buuhh-- Iron Man--!
Is he as tall as he looks in the magazines? Is he as muscly without the suit as he is with it? Does he--
Okay, this is starting to get uncomfortable.
Jersey City Wharf.
Here we go.
It'll only take us the rest of the night, plus tomorrow, to search all these warehouses.
I see what you mean.

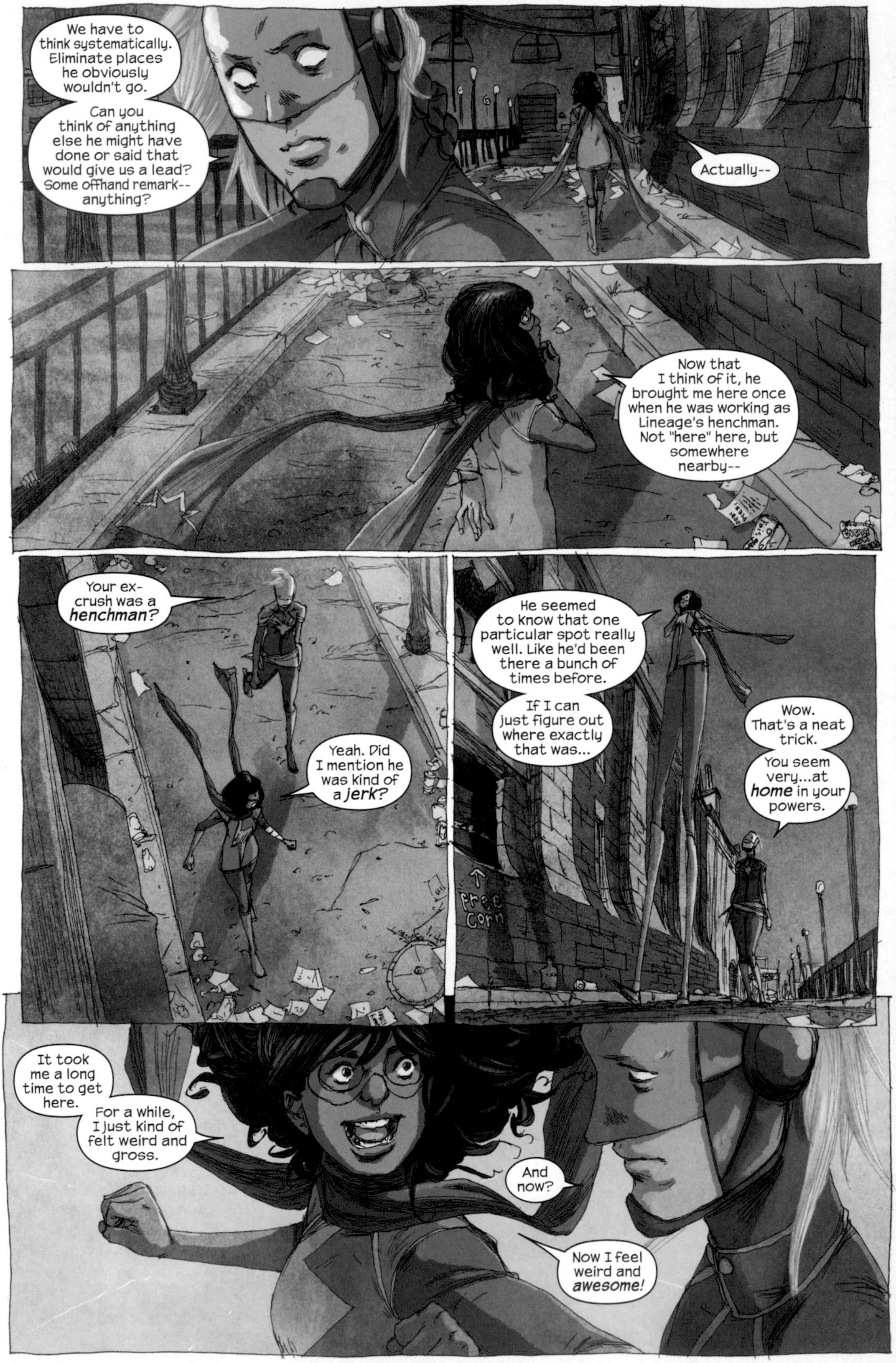

We have to think systematically. Eliminate places he obviously wouldn't go.
Can you think of anything else he might have done or said that would give us a lead? Some offhand remark-- anything?
Actually--
Now that I think of it, he brought me here once when he was working as Lineage's henchman. Not "here" here, but somewhere nearby--
Your ex-crush was a *henchman?*
Yeah. Did I mention he was kind of a *jerk?*
He seemed to know that one particular spot really well. Like he'd been there a bunch of times before.
If I can just figure out where exactly that was...
Wow. That's a neat trick.
You seem very...at *home* in your powers.
free corn
It took me a long time to get here.
For a while, I just kind of felt weird and gross.
And now?
Now I feel weird and *awesome!*

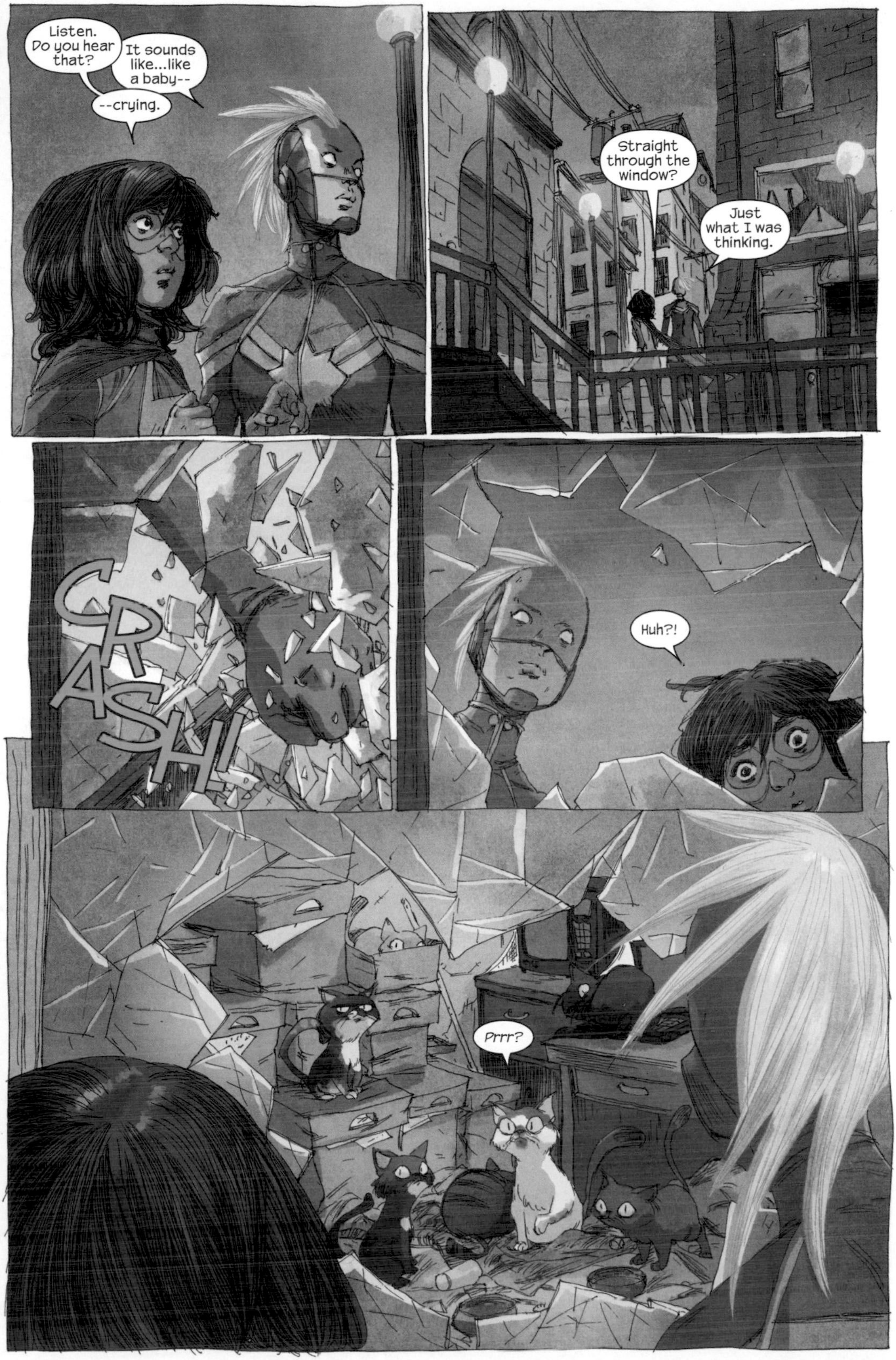
Listen. Do you hear that?
It sounds like...like a baby--
--crying.
Straight through the window?
Just what I was thinking.
CRASH!
Huh?!
Prrr?

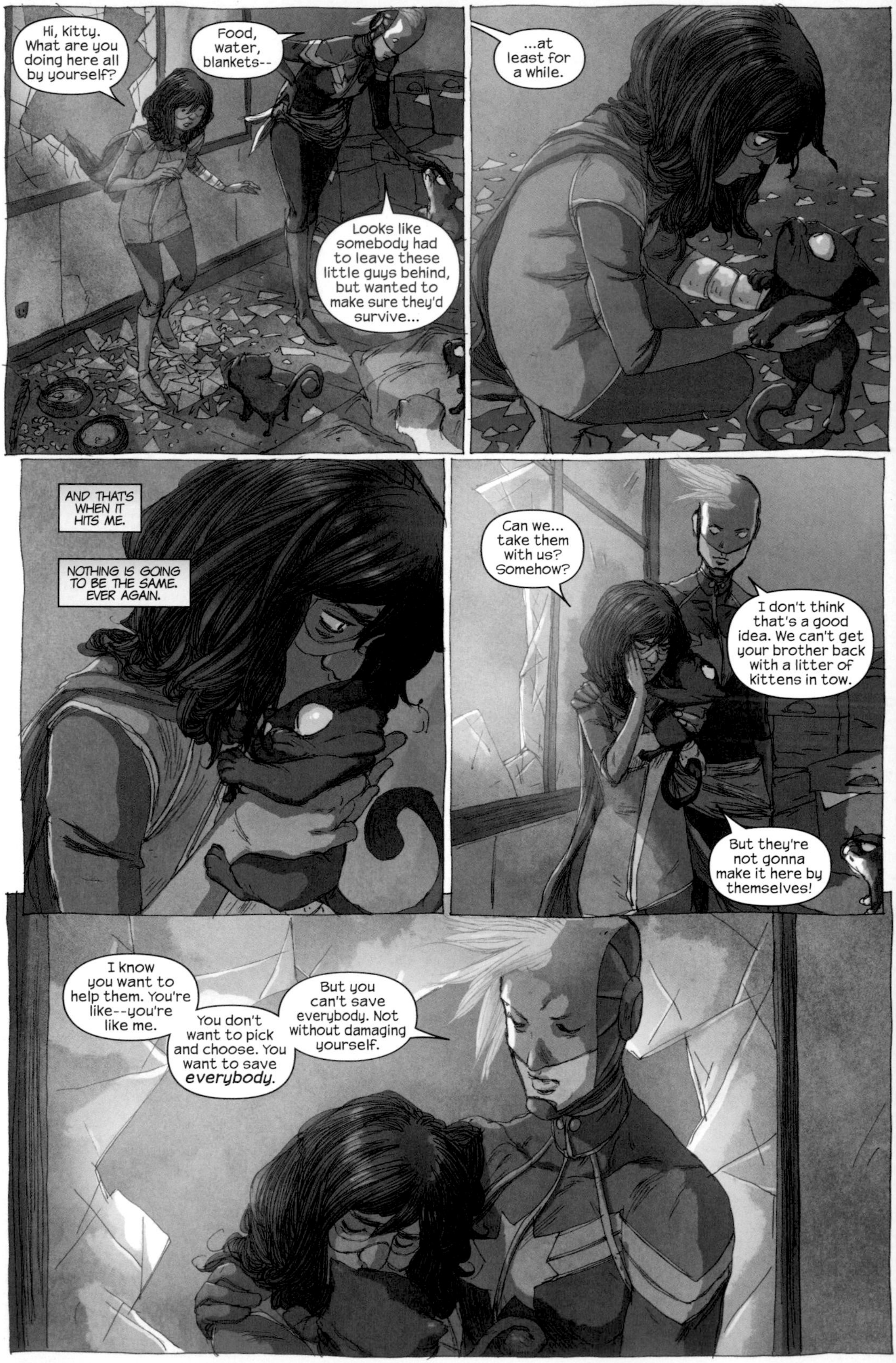

Hi, kitty. What are you doing here all by yourself?
Food, water, blankets--
Looks like somebody had to leave these little guys behind, but wanted to make sure they'd survive...
...at least for a while.
AND THAT'S WHEN IT HITS ME.
NOTHING IS GOING TO BE THE SAME. EVER AGAIN.
Can we... take them with us? Somehow?
I don't think that's a good idea. We can't get your brother back with a litter of kittens in tow.
But they're not gonna make it here by themselves!
I know you want to help them. You're like--you're like me.
You don't want to pick and choose. You want to save *everybody*.
But you can't save everybody. Not without damaging yourself.

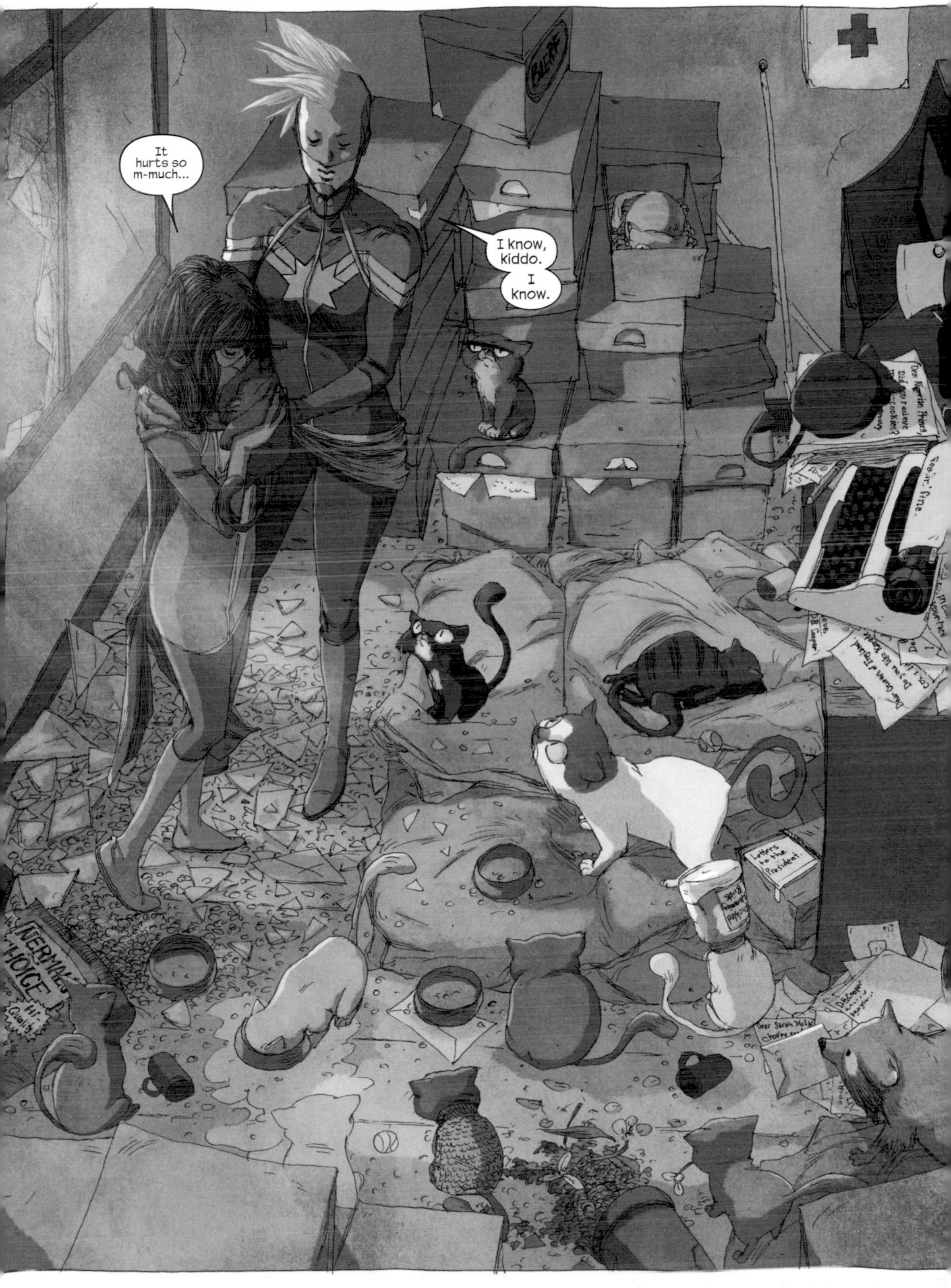
It hurts so m-much...
I know, kiddo.
I know.
Letters to the President.

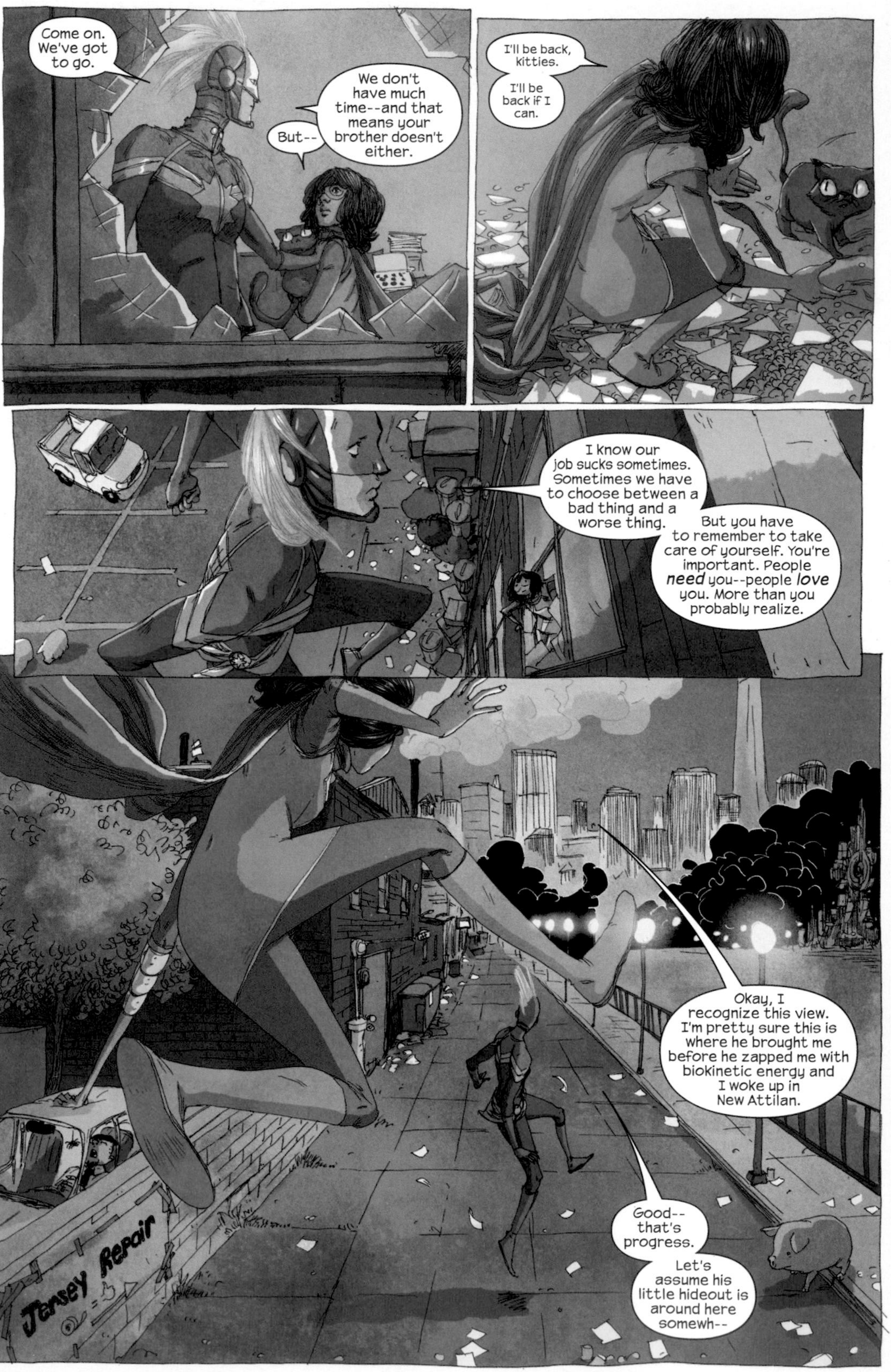
Come on. We've got to go.
But--
We don't have much time--and that means your brother doesn't either.
I'll be back, kitties.
I'll be back if I can.
I know our job sucks sometimes. Sometimes we have to choose between a bad thing and a worse thing.
But you have to remember to take care of yourself. You're important. People *need* you--people *love* you. More than you probably realize.
Okay, I recognize this view. I'm pretty sure this is where he brought me before he zapped me with biokinetic energy and I woke up in New Attilan.
Good--that's progress.
Let's assume his little hideout is around here somewh--
Jersey Repair

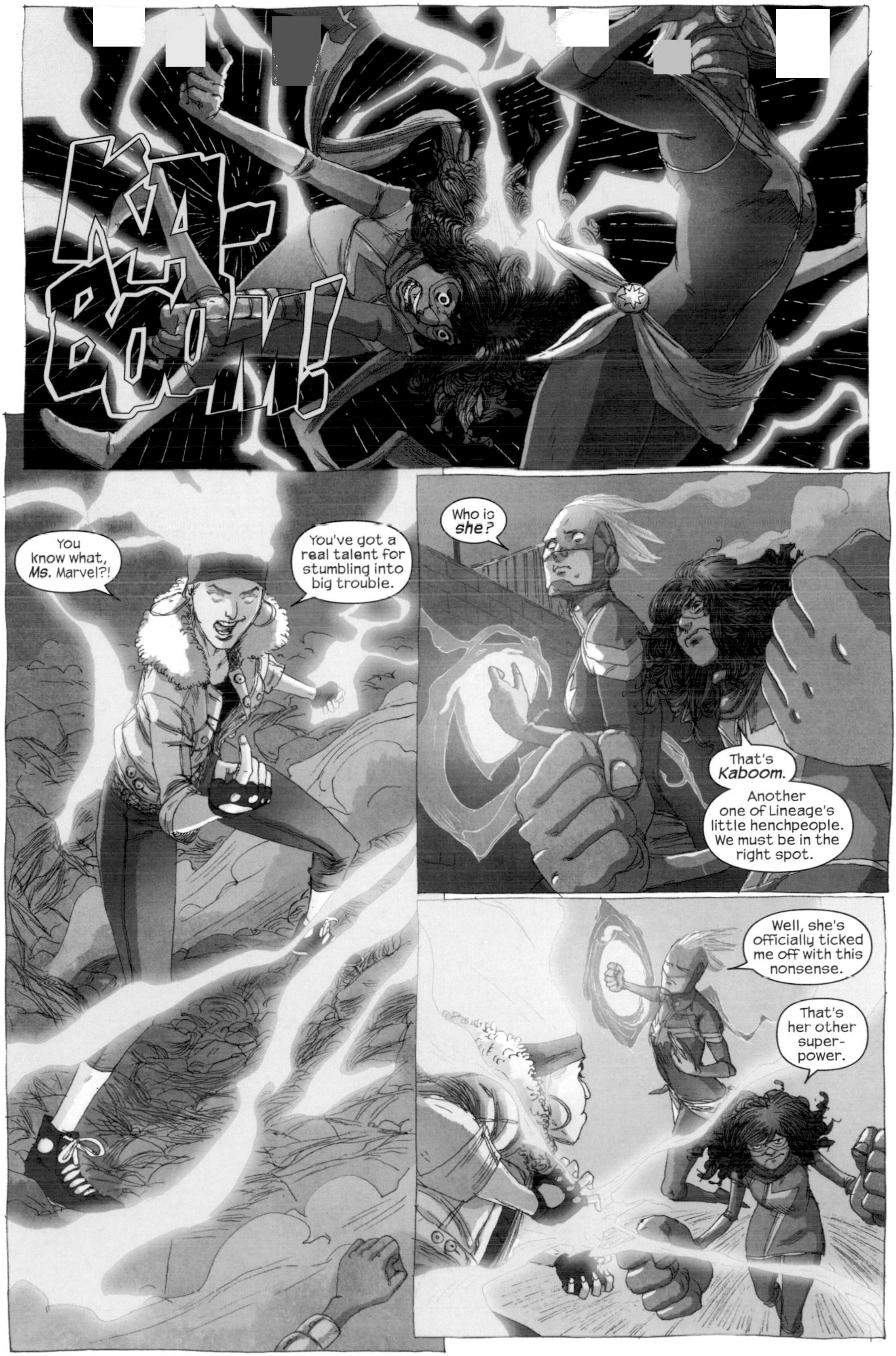
KABOOM!
You know what, *Ms.* Marvel?!
You've got a real talent for stumbling into big trouble.
Who is *she?*
That's *Kaboom.* Another one of Lineage's little henchpeople. We must be in the right spot.
Well, she's officially ticked me off with this nonsense.
That's her other super-power.

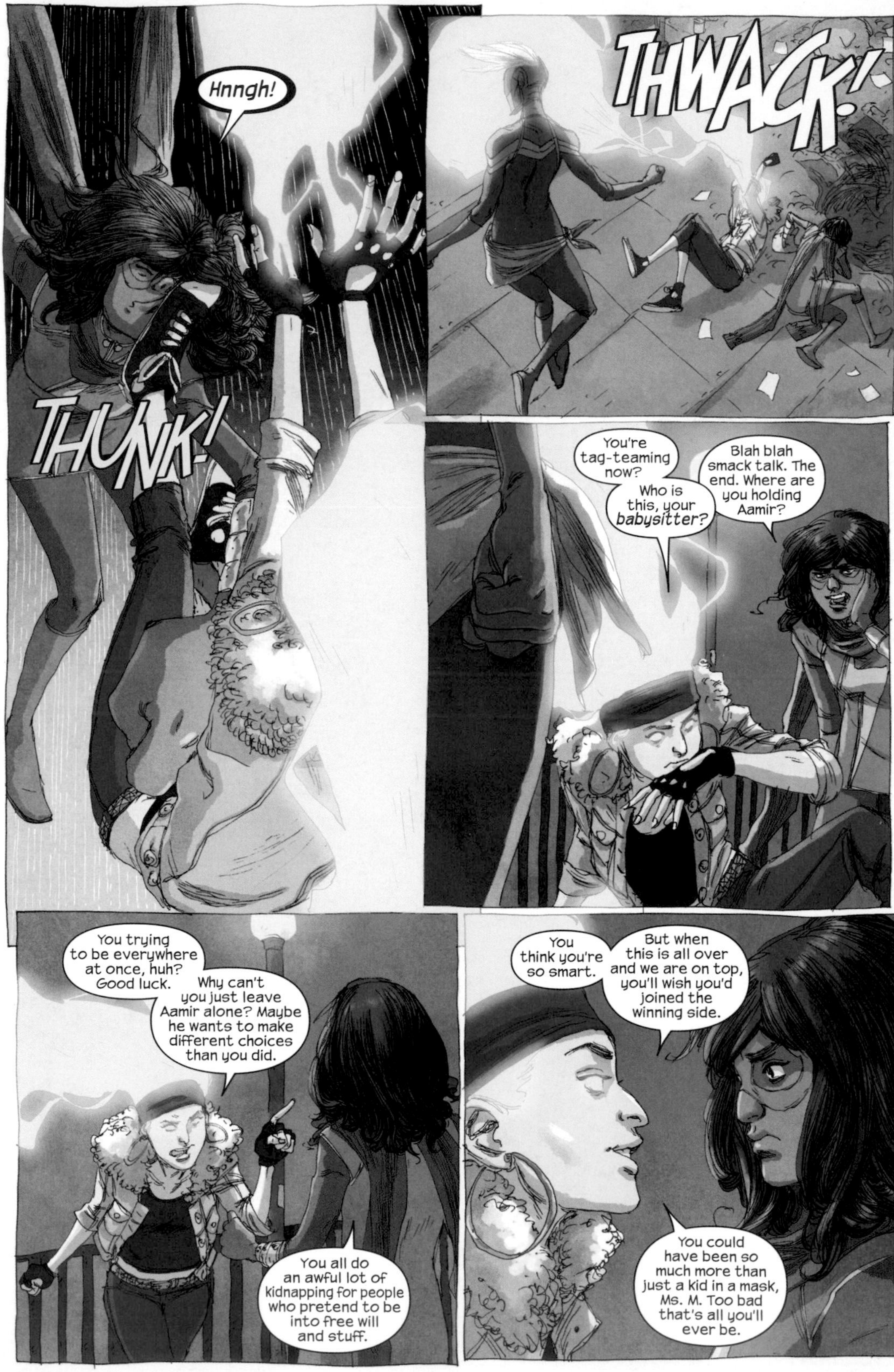
Hnngh!
THUNK!
THWACK!
You're tag-teaming now?
Who is this, your *babysitter?*
Blah blah smack talk. The end. Where are you holding Aamir?
You trying to be everywhere at once, huh? Good luck.
Why can't you just leave Aamir alone? Maybe he wants to make different choices than you did.
You all do an awful lot of kidnapping for people who pretend to be into free will and stuff.
You think you're so smart.
But when this is all over and we are on top, you'll wish you'd joined the winning side.
You could have been so much more than just a kid in a mask, Ms. M. Too bad that's all you'll ever be.

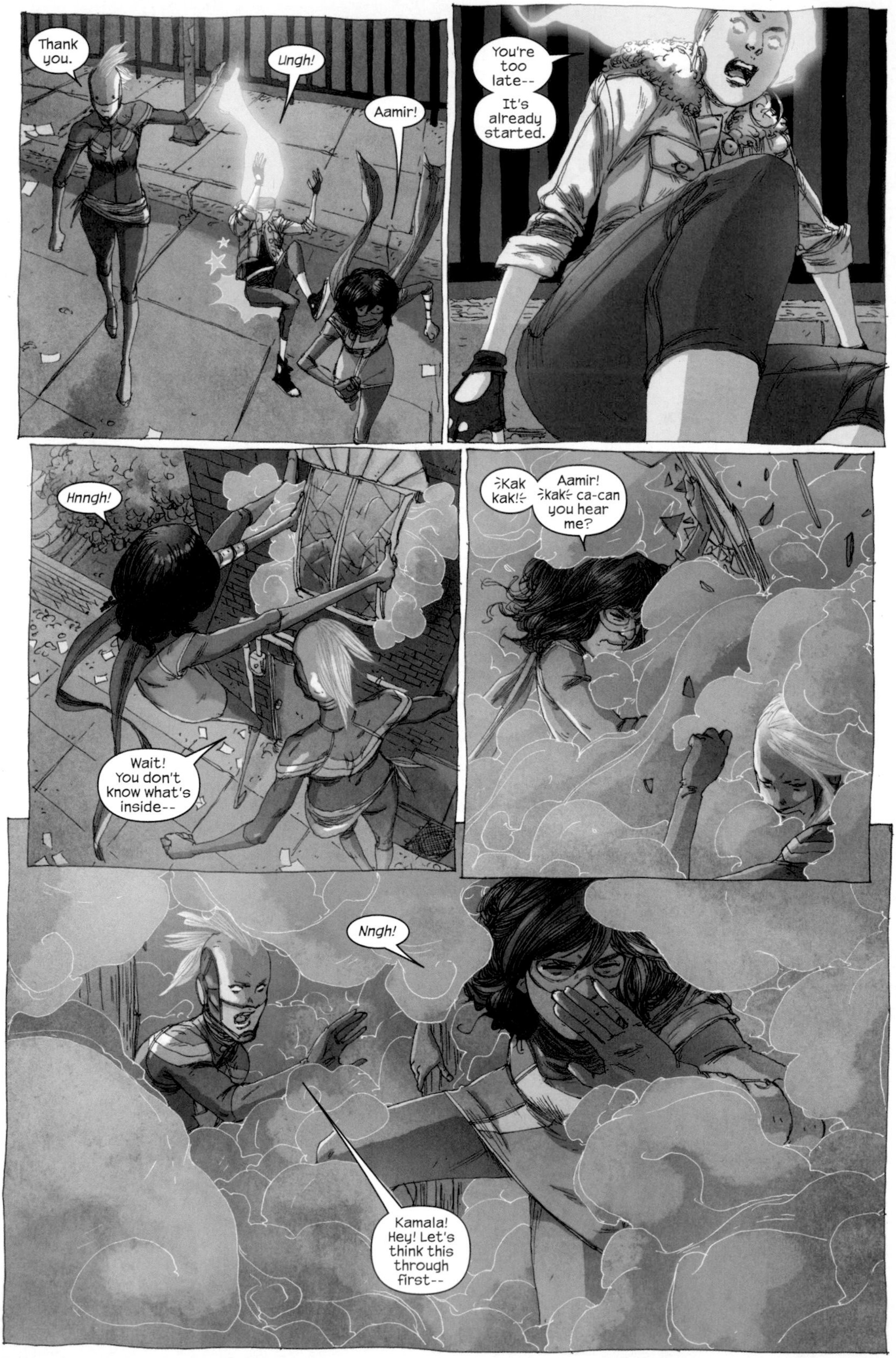
Thank you.
Ungh!
Aamir!
You're too late--
It's already started.
Hnngh!
Wait! You don't know what's inside--
Kak kak!
Aamir! kak ca-can you hear me?
Nngh!
Kamala! Hey! Let's think this through first--

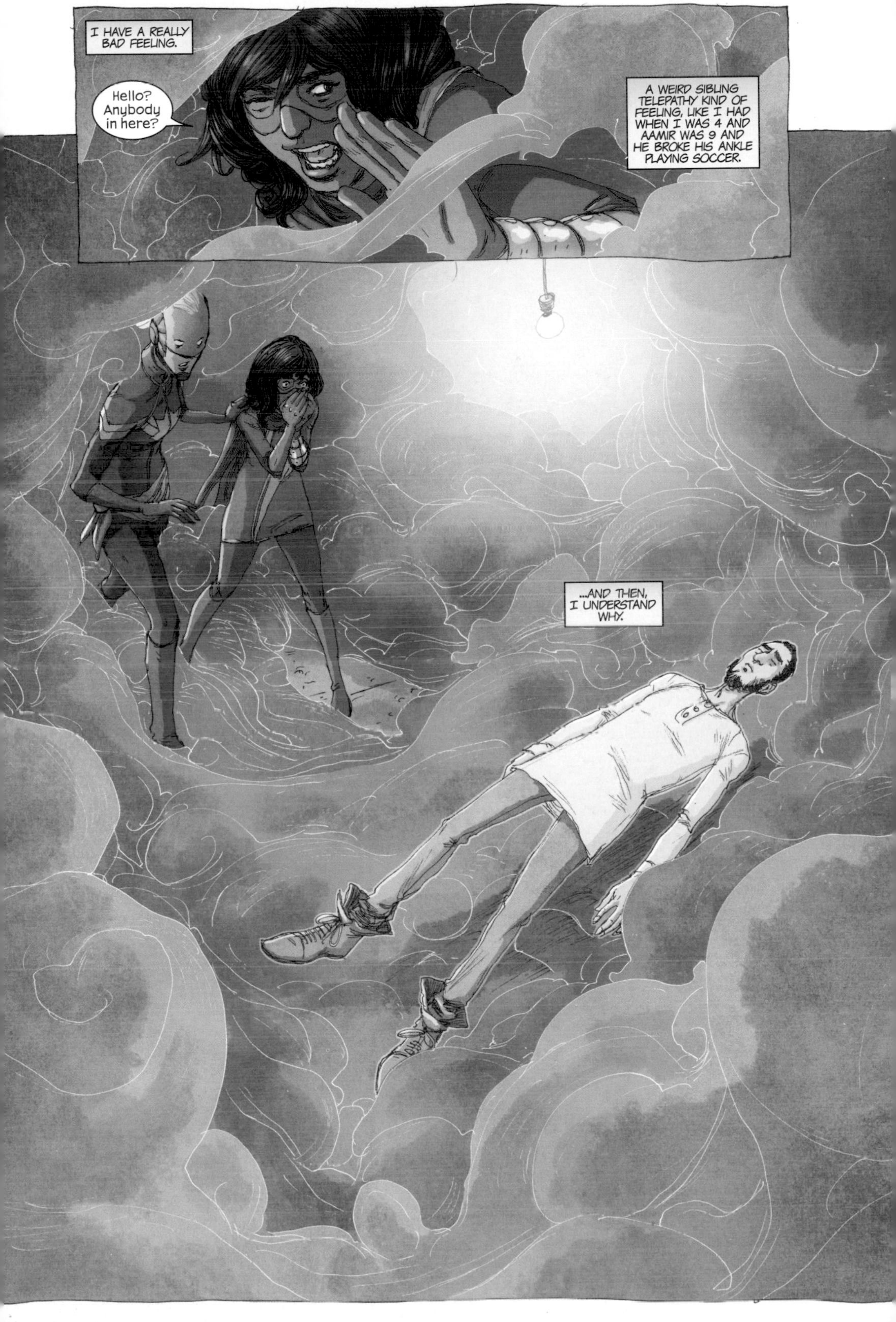
I HAVE A REALLY BAD FEELING.
Hello? Anybody in here?
A WEIRD SIBLING TELEPATHY KIND OF FEELING, LIKE I HAD WHEN I WAS 4 AND AAMIR WAS 9 AND HE BROKE HIS ANKLE PLAYING SOCCER.
...AND THEN, I UNDERSTAND WHY.

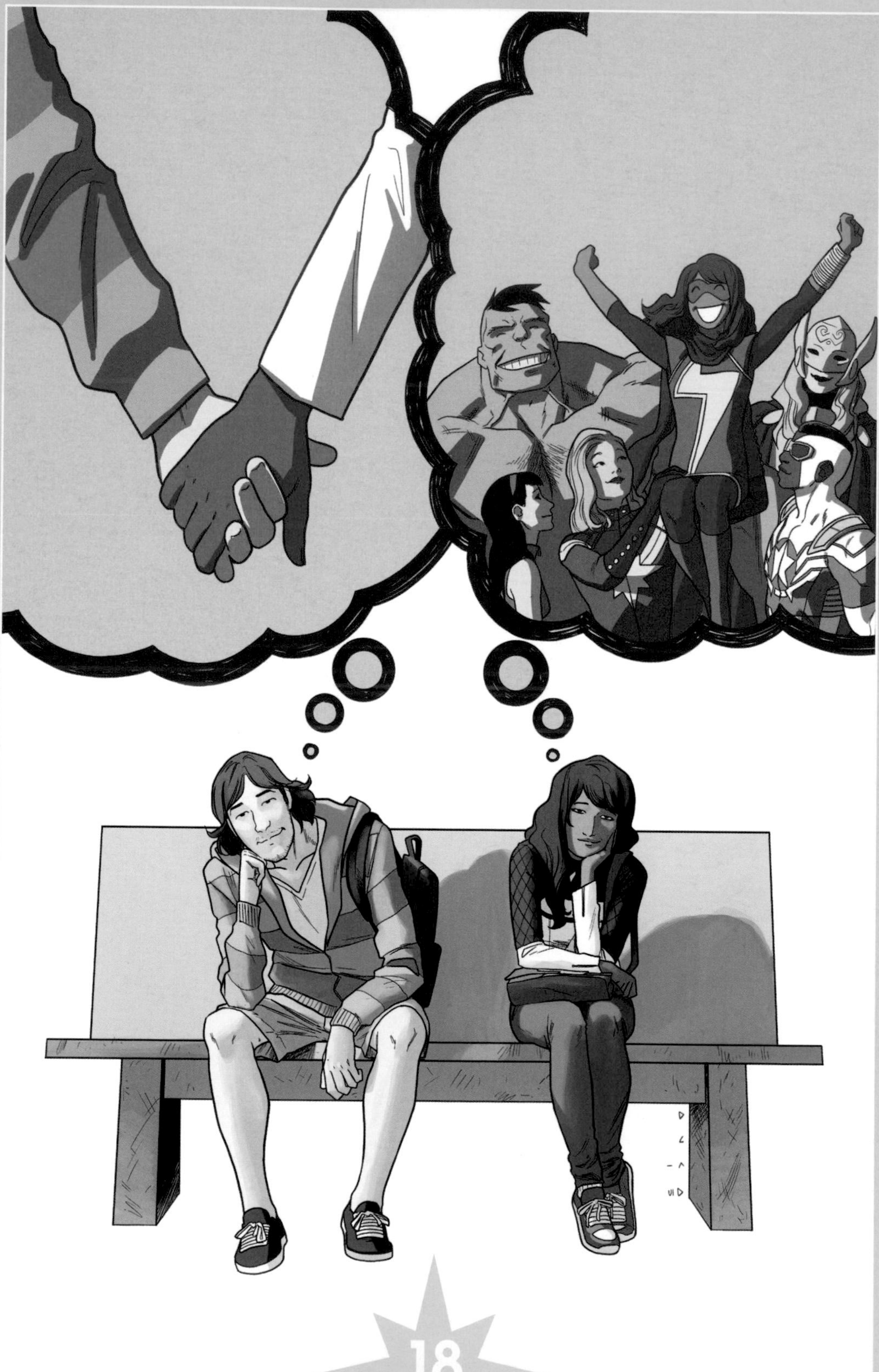

18

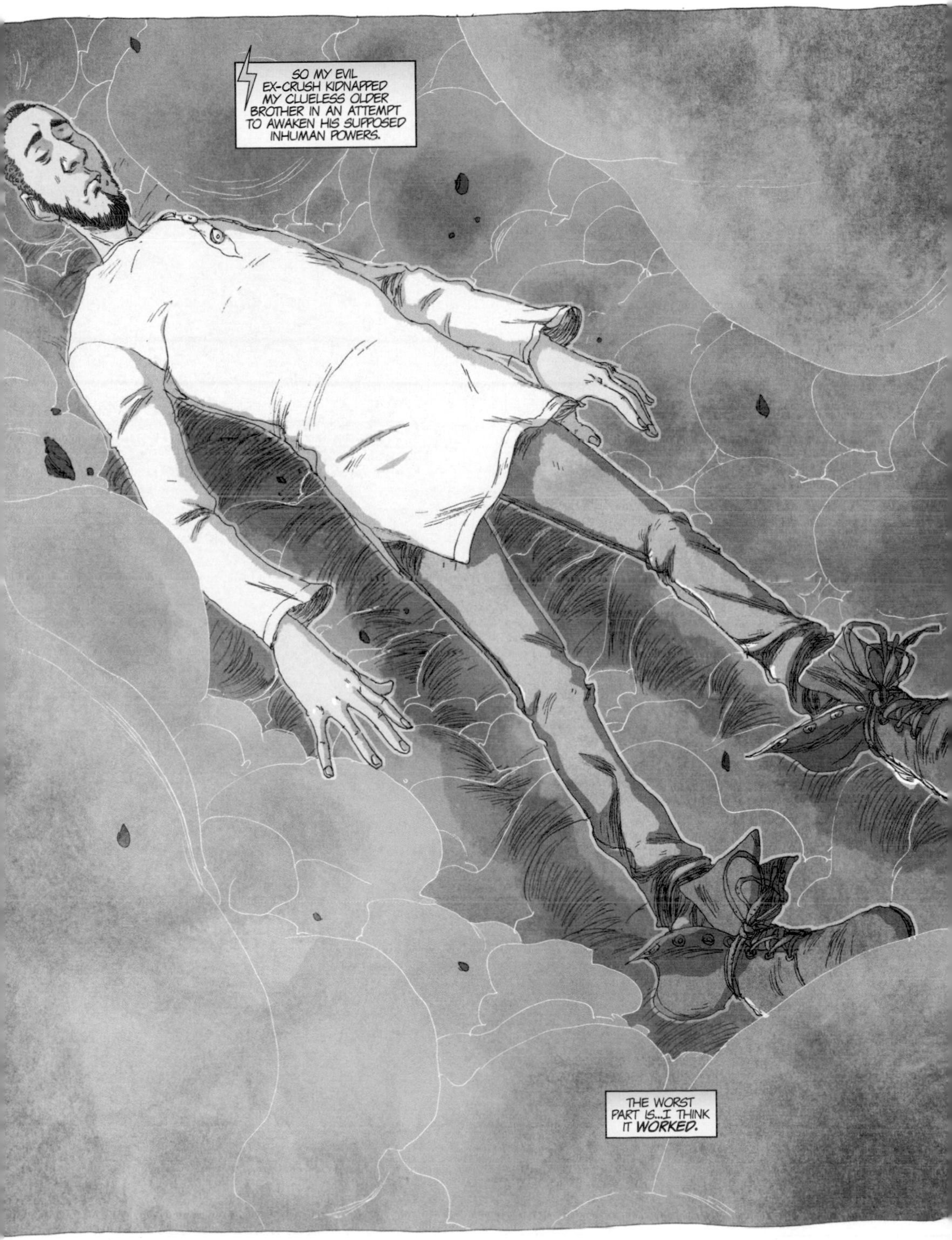
SO MY EVIL EX-CRUSH KIDNAPPED MY CLUELESS OLDER BROTHER IN AN ATTEMPT TO AWAKEN HIS SUPPOSED INHUMAN POWERS.
THE WORST PART IS...I THINK IT *WORKED.*

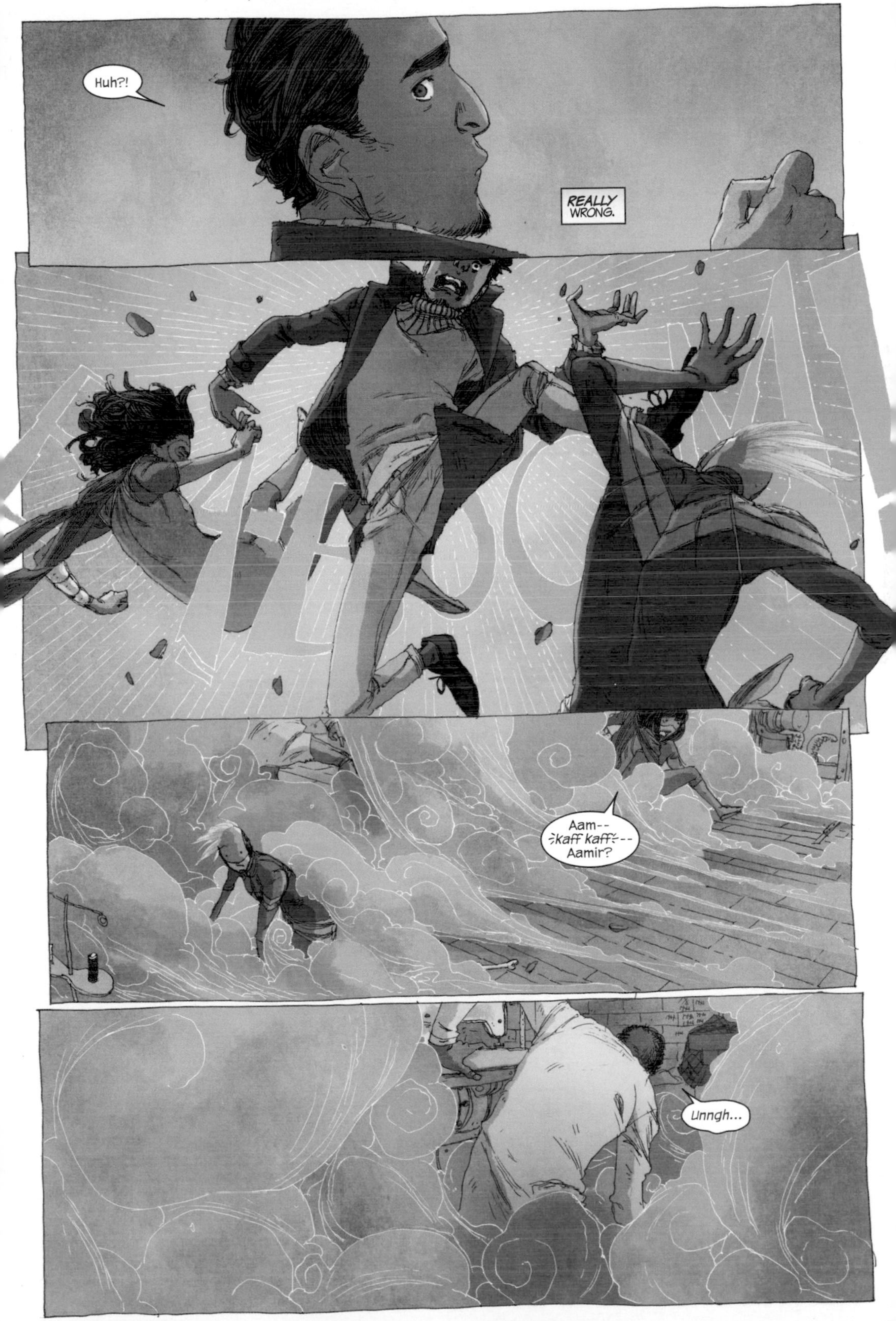
Huh?!
REALLY WRONG.
Aam-- kaff kaff -- Aamir?
Unngh...

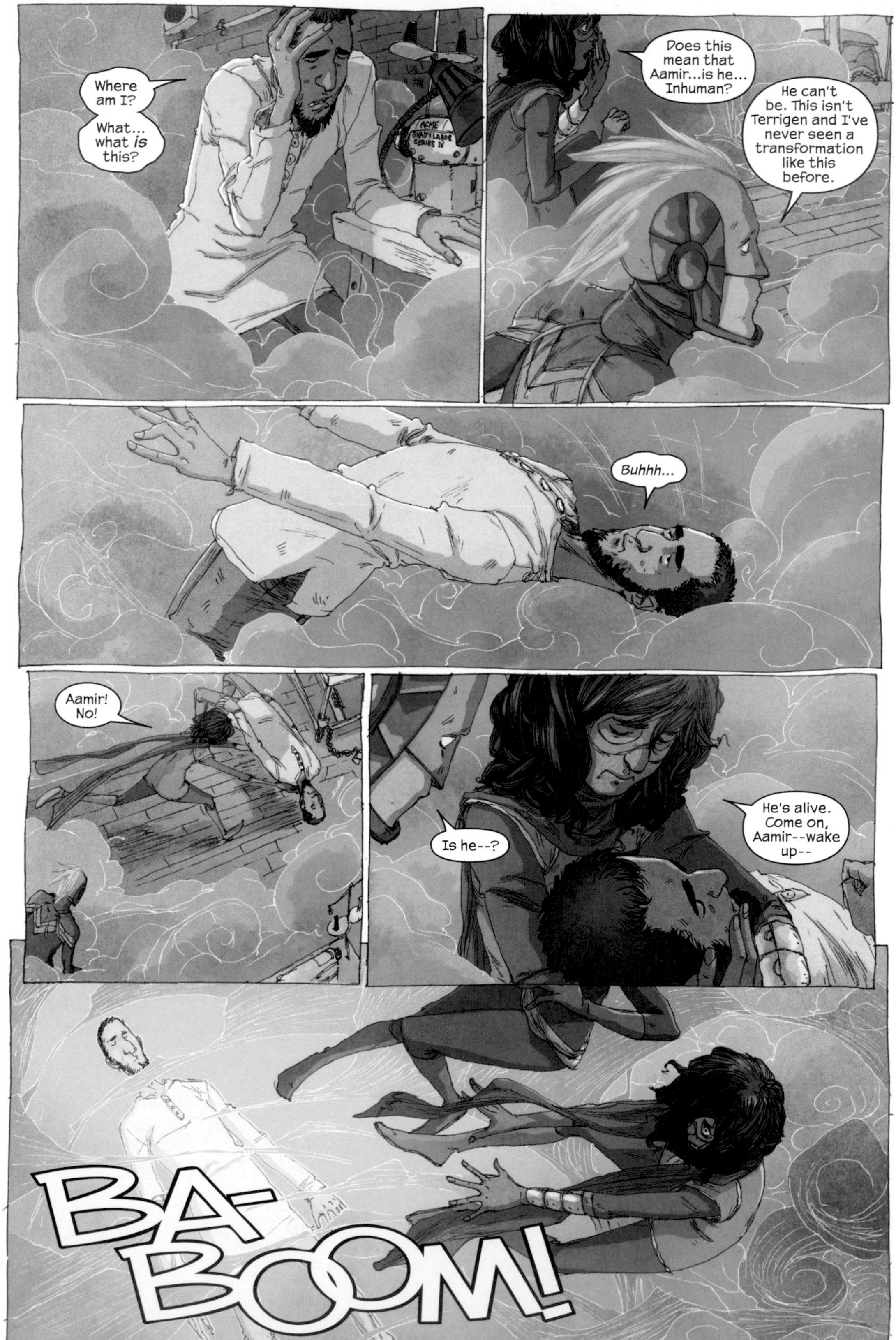
Where am I?
What... what *is* this?
ACME SHADY LABOR SERIES IV
Does this mean that Aamir...is he... Inhuman?
He can't be. This isn't Terrigen and I've never seen a transformation like this before.
Buhhh...
Aamir! No!
Is he--?
He's alive. Come on, Aamir--wake up--
BA-BOOM!

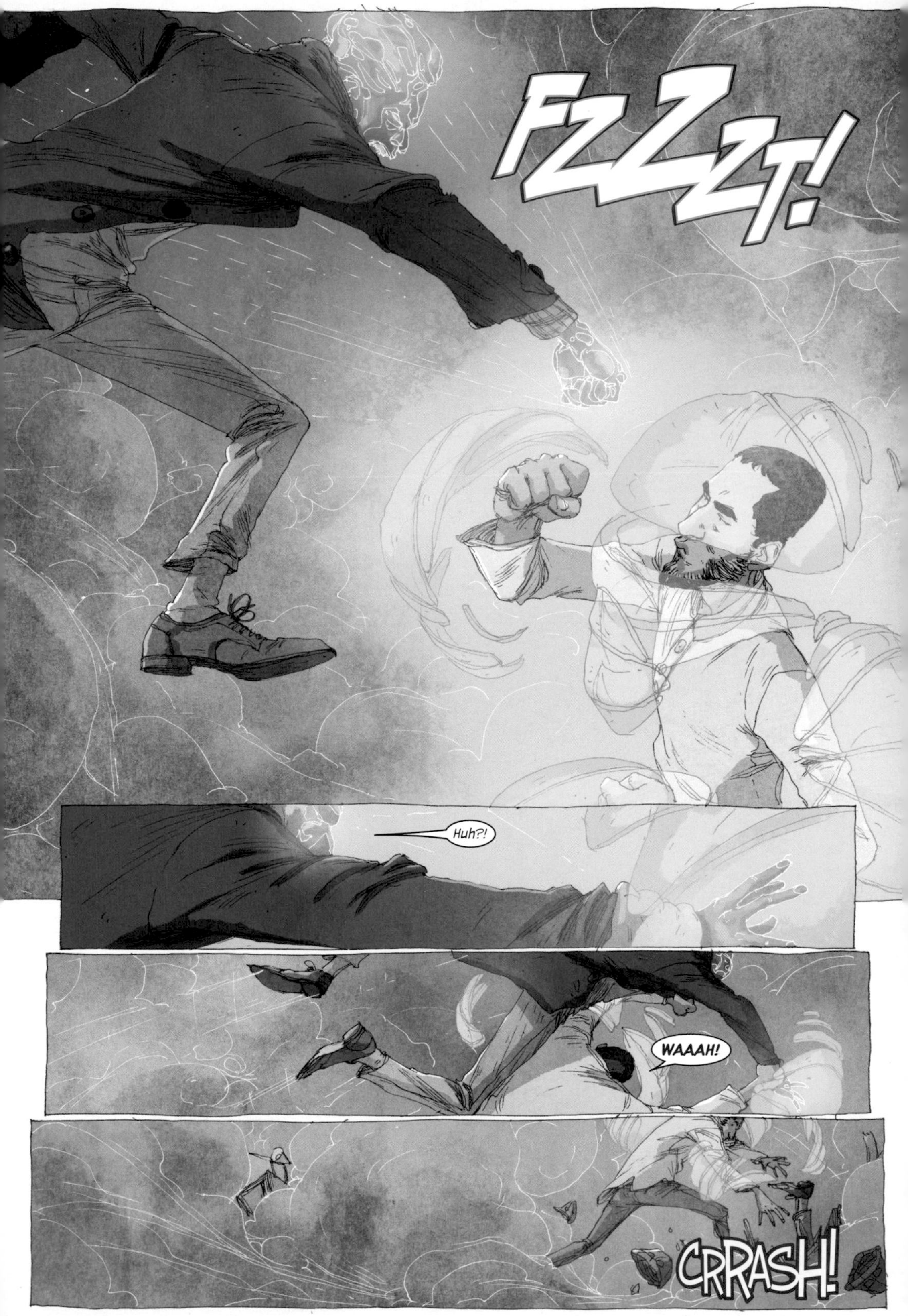

FZZZZT!
Huh?!
WAAAH!
CRRASH!

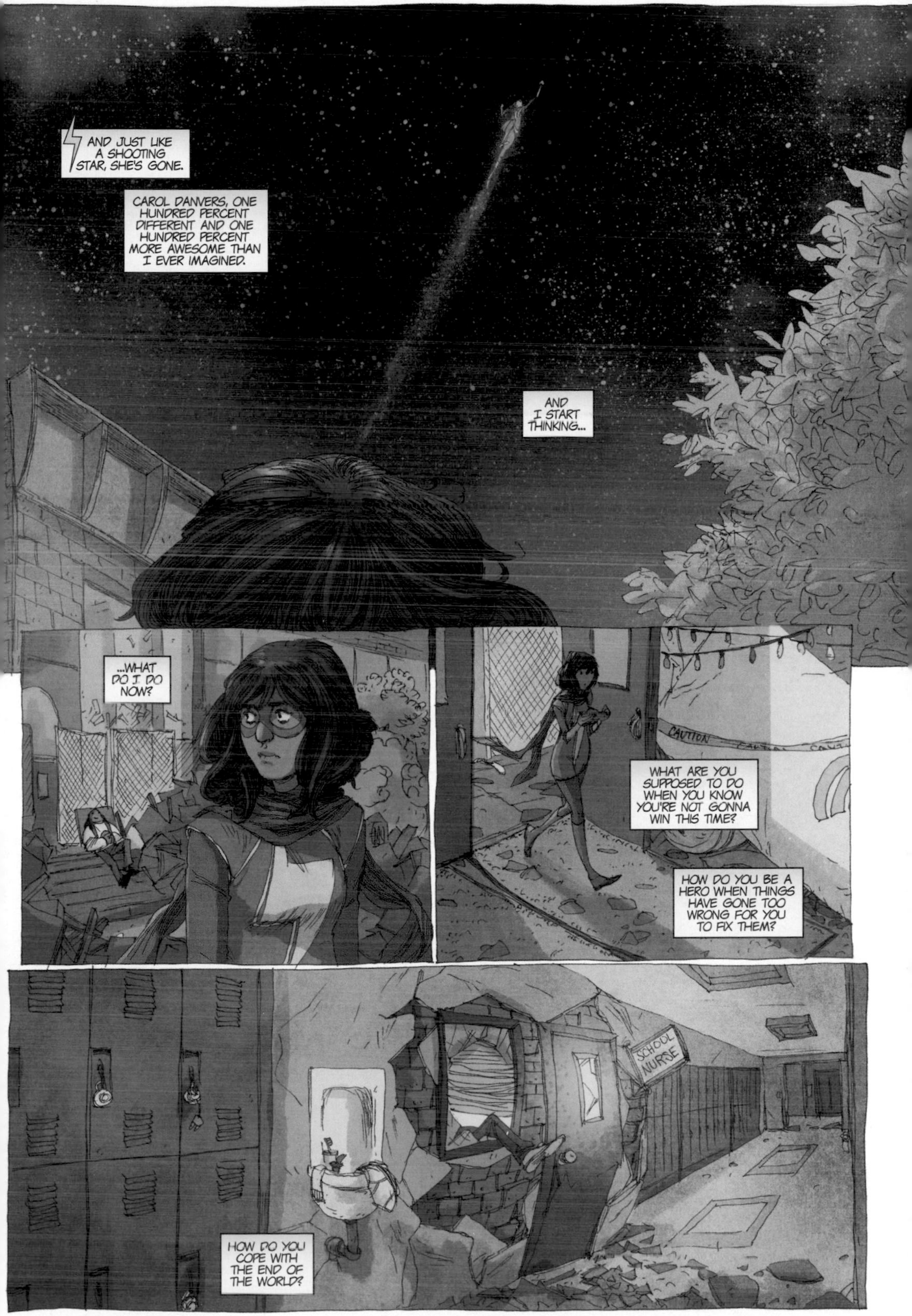
AND JUST LIKE A SHOOTING STAR, SHE'S GONE.
CAROL DANVERS, ONE HUNDRED PERCENT DIFFERENT AND ONE HUNDRED PERCENT MORE AWESOME THAN I EVER IMAGINED.
AND I START THINKING...
...WHAT DO I DO NOW?
WHAT ARE YOU SUPPOSED TO DO WHEN YOU KNOW YOU'RE NOT GONNA WIN THIS TIME?
HOW DO YOU BE A HERO WHEN THINGS HAVE GONE TOO WRONG FOR YOU TO FIX THEM?
SCHOOL NURSE
HOW DO YOU COPE WITH THE END OF THE WORLD?

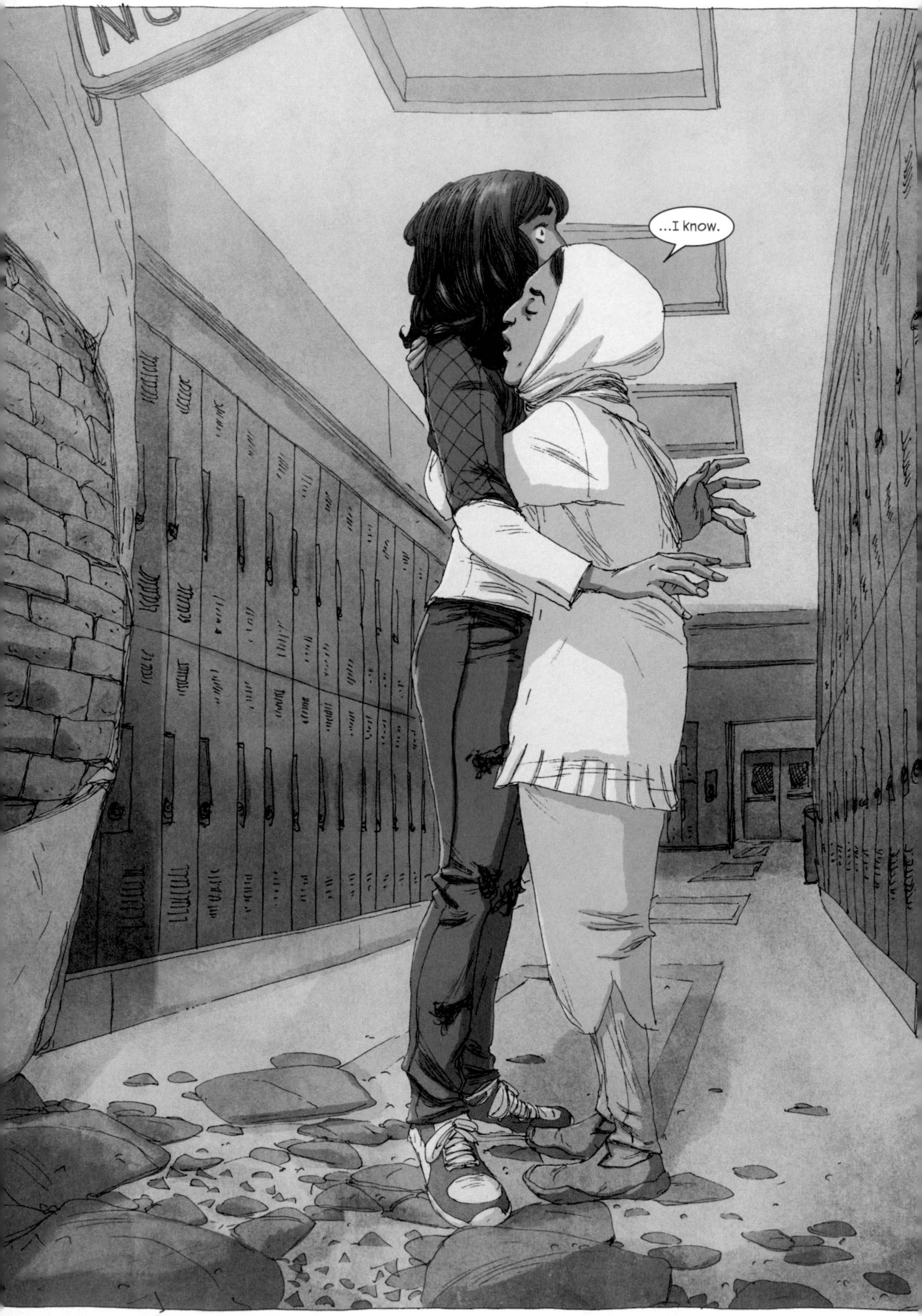
...I know.

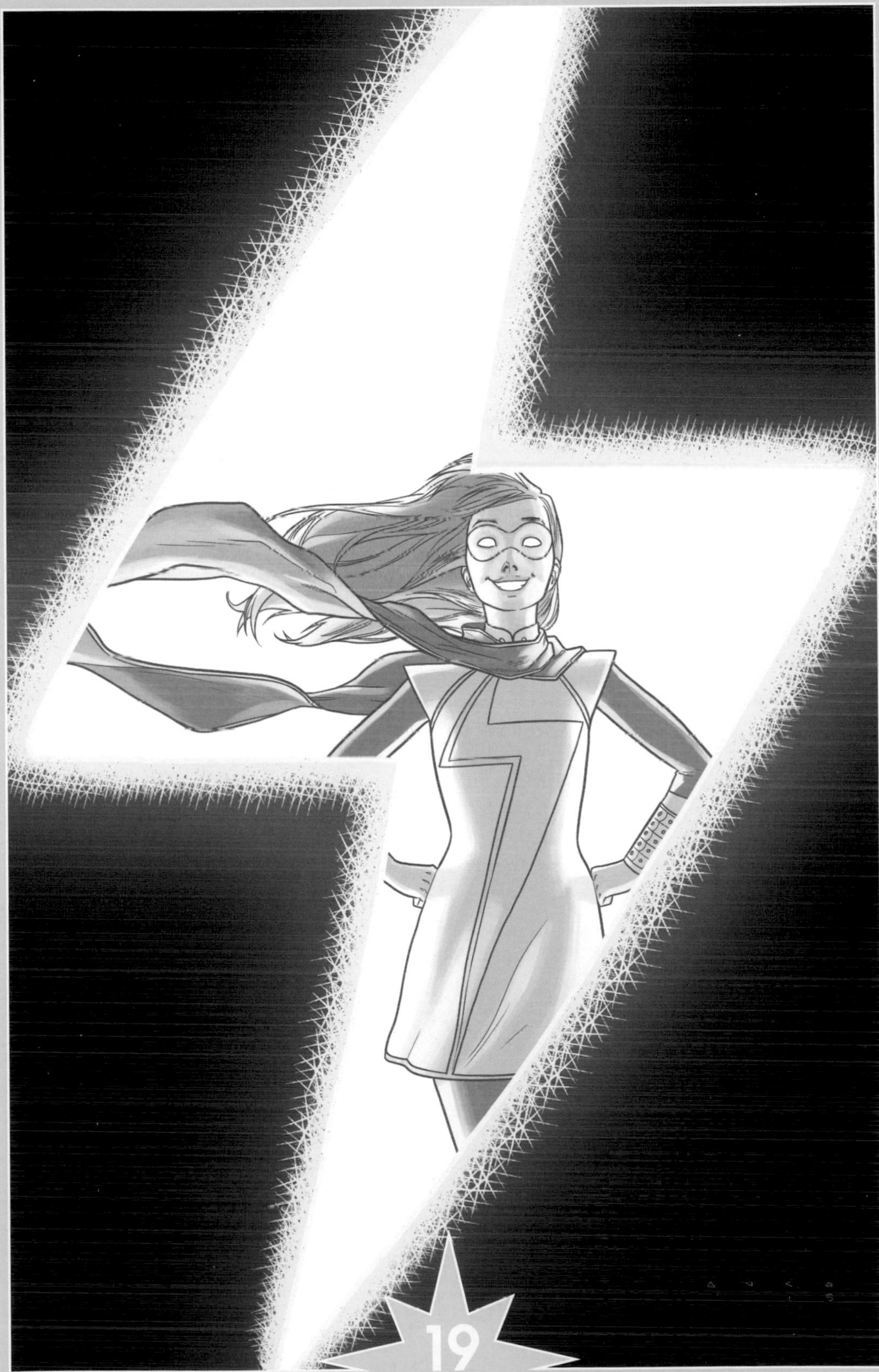
19

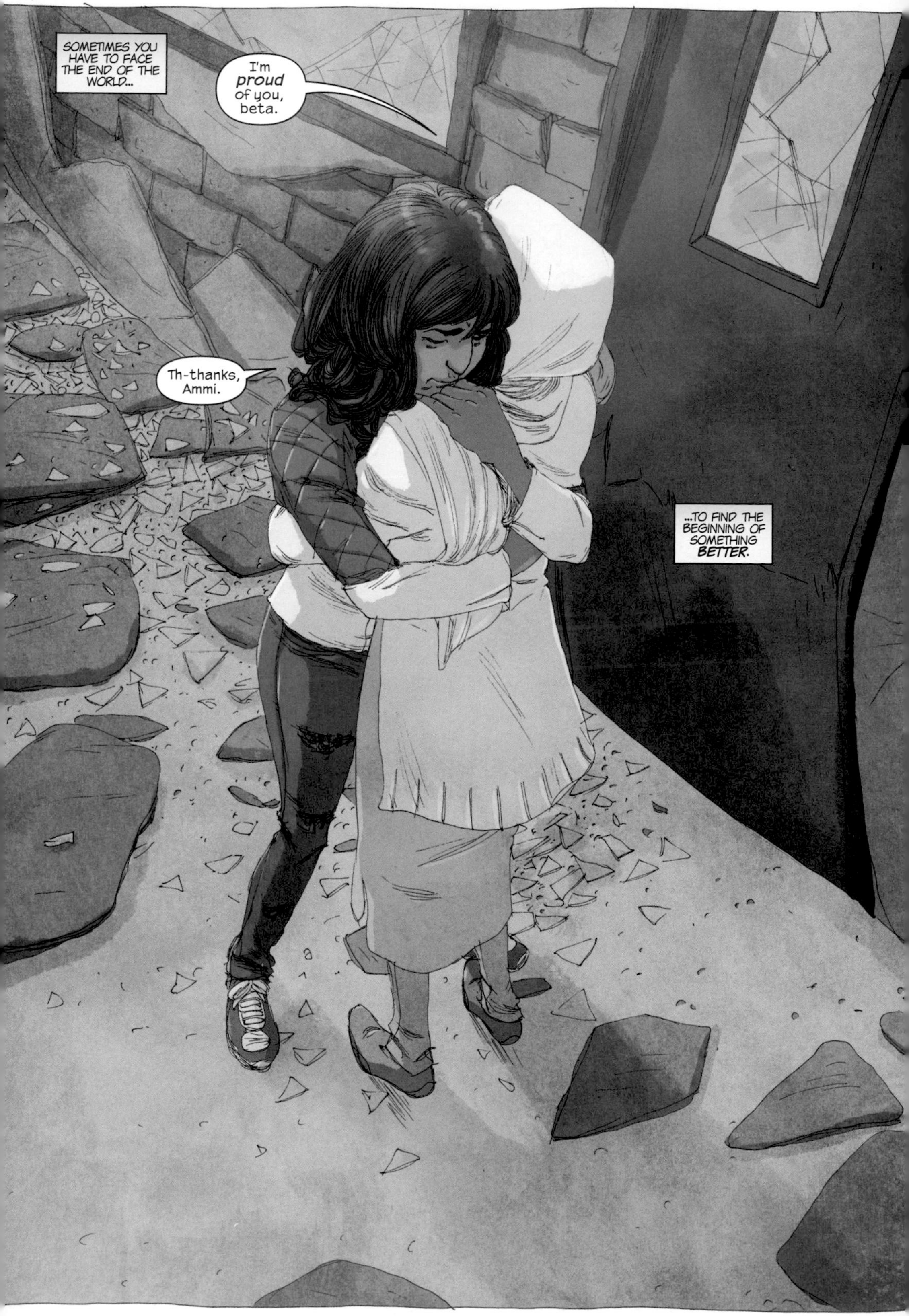
SOMETIMES YOU HAVE TO FACE THE END OF THE WORLD...
I'm *proud* of you, beta.
Th-thanks, Ammi.
...TO FIND THE BEGINNING OF SOMETHING **BETTER**.

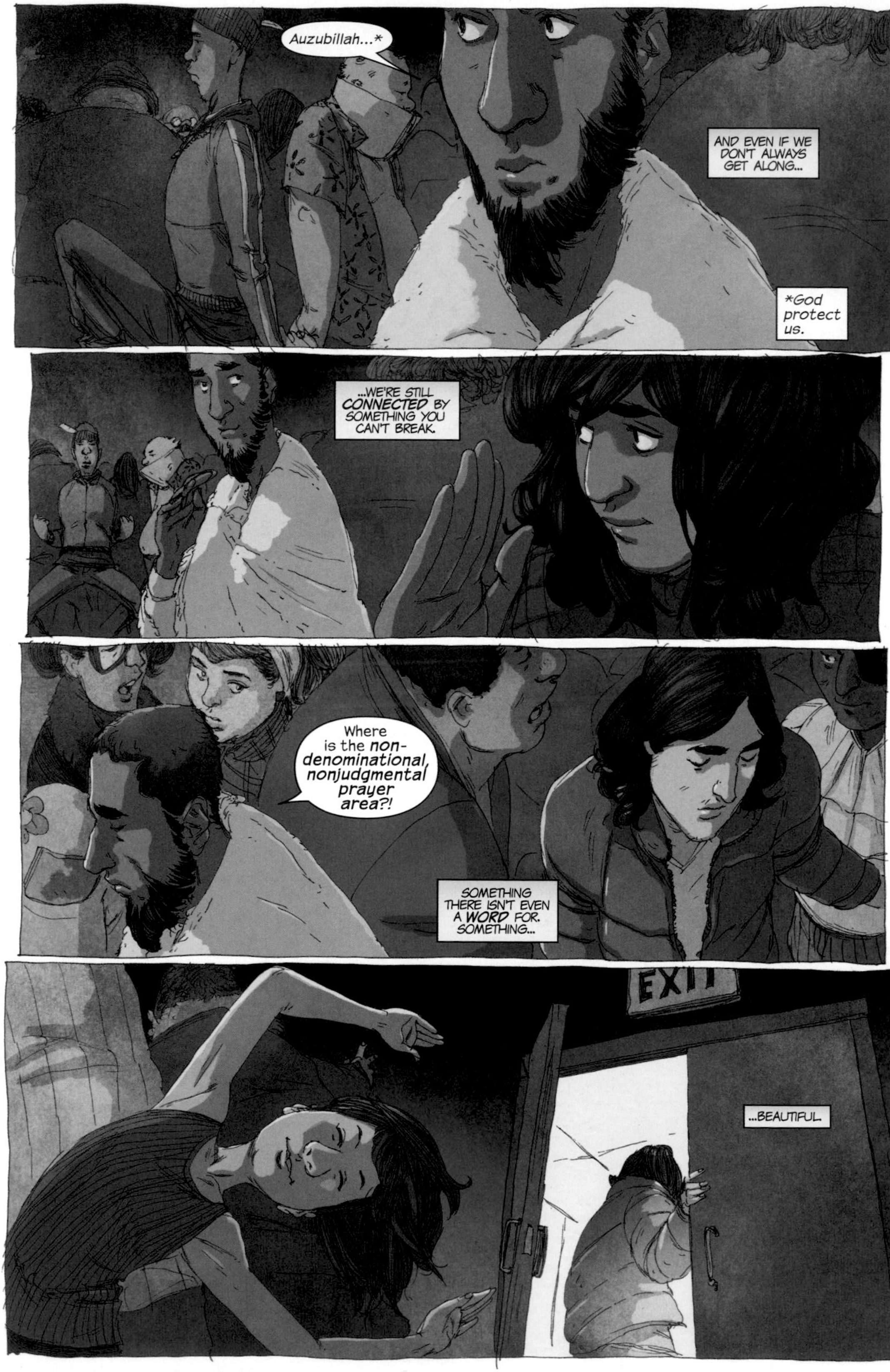
Auzubillah...*
AND EVEN IF WE DON'T ALWAYS GET ALONG...
*God protect us.
...WE'RE STILL CONNECTED BY SOMETHING YOU CAN'T BREAK.
Where is the non-denominational, nonjudgmental prayer area?!
SOMETHING THERE ISN'T EVEN A WORD FOR. SOMETHING...
EXIT
...BEAUTIFUL.

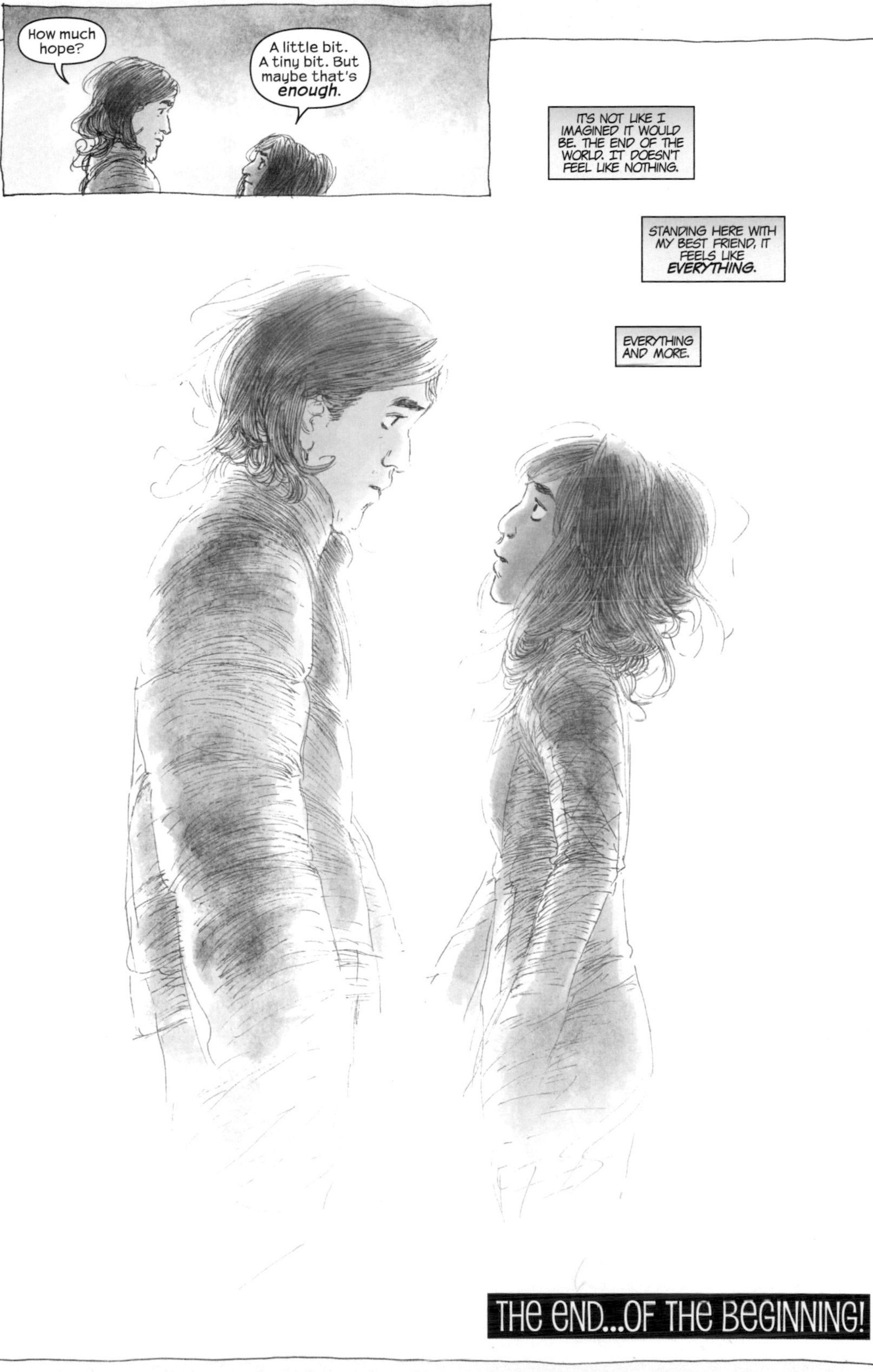
How much hope?
A little bit. A tiny bit. But maybe that's *enough*.
IT'S NOT LIKE I IMAGINED IT WOULD BE. THE END OF THE WORLD. IT DOESN'T FEEL LIKE NOTHING.
STANDING HERE WITH MY BEST FRIEND, IT FEELS LIKE *EVERYTHING*.
EVERYTHING AND MORE.
THE END...OF THE BEGINNING!

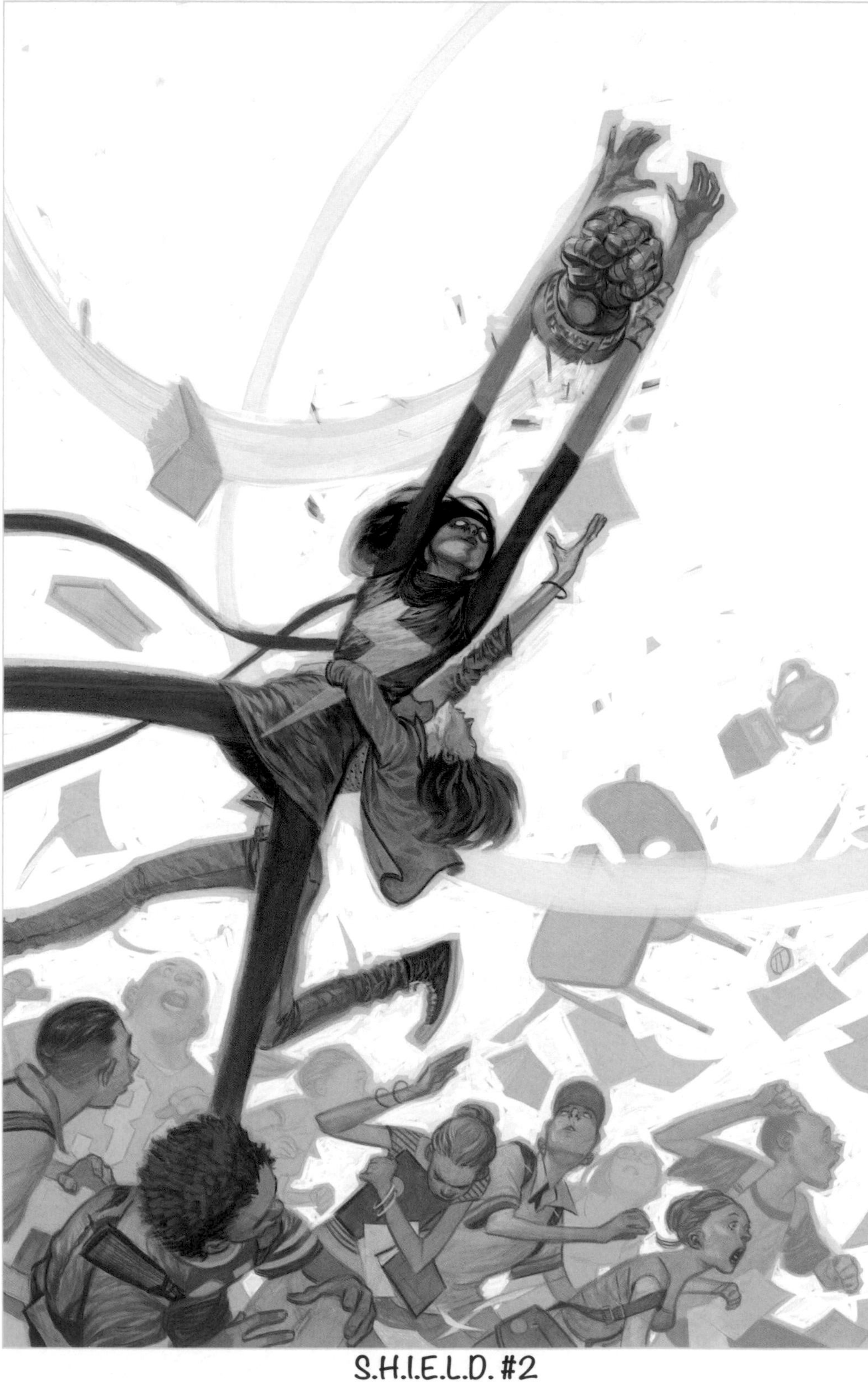

S.H.I.E.L.D. #2

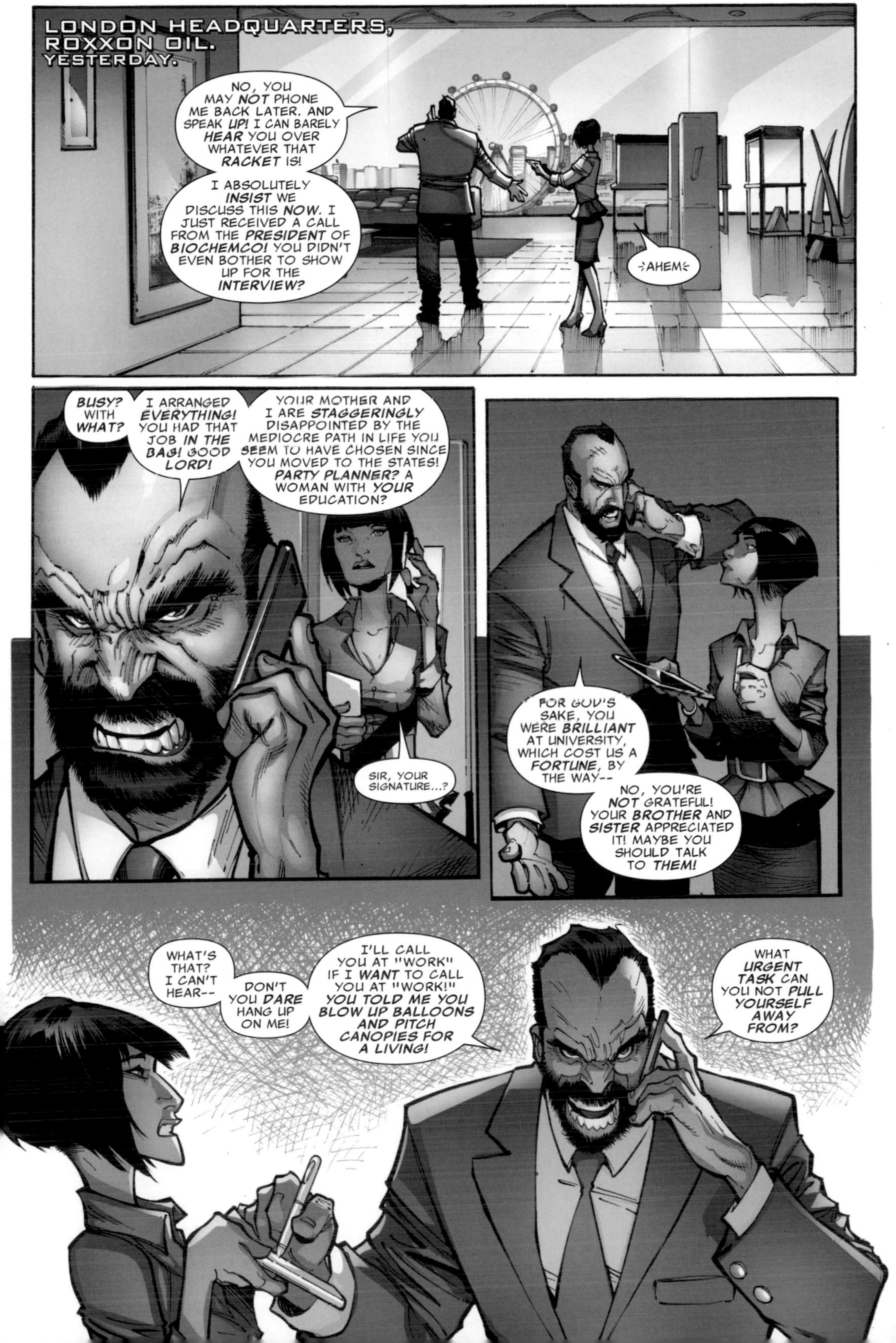
LONDON HEADQUARTERS, ROXXON OIL. YESTERDAY.
NO, YOU MAY NOT PHONE ME BACK LATER. AND SPEAK UP! I CAN BARELY HEAR YOU OVER WHATEVER THAT RACKET IS!
I ABSOLUTELY INSIST WE DISCUSS THIS NOW. I JUST RECEIVED A CALL FROM THE PRESIDENT OF BIOCHEMCO! YOU DIDN'T EVEN BOTHER TO SHOW UP FOR THE INTERVIEW?
AHEM
BUSY? WITH WHAT?
I ARRANGED EVERYTHING! YOU HAD THAT JOB IN THE BAG! GOOD LORD!
YOUR MOTHER AND I ARE STAGGERINGLY DISAPPOINTED BY THE MEDIOCRE PATH IN LIFE YOU SEEM TO HAVE CHOSEN SINCE YOU MOVED TO THE STATES! PARTY PLANNER? A WOMAN WITH YOUR EDUCATION?
SIR, YOUR SIGNATURE...?
FOR GOD'S SAKE, YOU WERE BRILLIANT AT UNIVERSITY, WHICH COST US A FORTUNE, BY THE WAY--
NO, YOU'RE NOT GRATEFUL! YOUR BROTHER AND SISTER APPRECIATED IT! MAYBE YOU SHOULD TALK TO THEM!
WHAT'S THAT? I CAN'T HEAR--
DON'T YOU DARE HANG UP ON ME!
I'LL CALL YOU AT "WORK" IF I WANT TO CALL YOU AT "WORK!" YOU TOLD ME YOU BLOW UP BALLOONS AND PITCH CANOPIES FOR A LIVING!
WHAT URGENT TASK CAN YOU NOT PULL YOURSELF AWAY FROM?

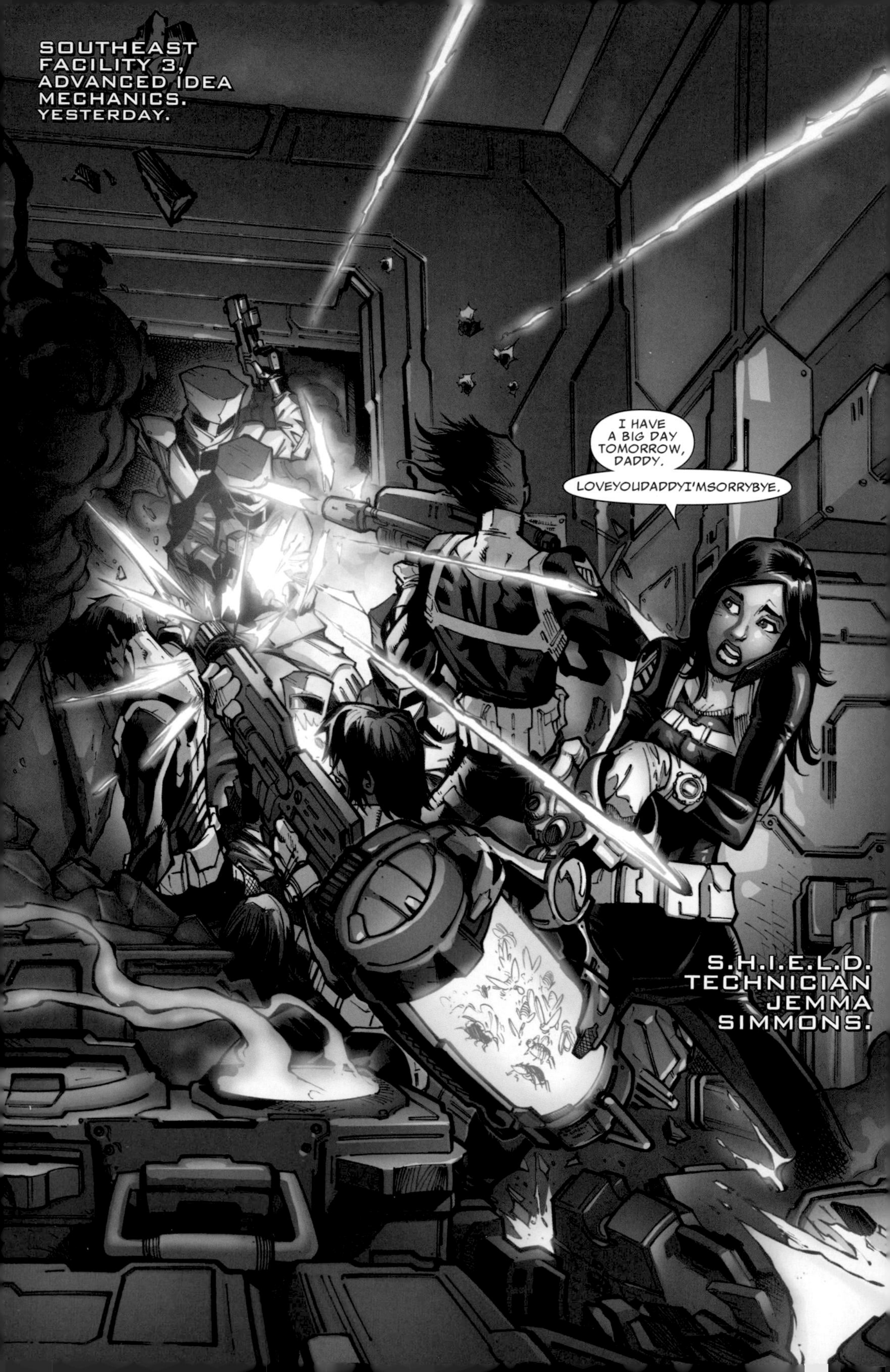
SOUTHEAST FACILITY 3, ADVANCED IDEA MECHANICS. YESTERDAY.
I HAVE A BIG DAY TOMORROW, DADDY.
LOVEYOUDADDYI'MSORRYBYE.
S.H.I.E.L.D. TECHNICIAN JEMMA SIMMONS.

ACCESS GRANTED...

STRATEGIC HOMELAND INTERVENTION ENFORCEMENT LOGISTICS DIVISION

S.H.I.E.L.D.

ACTIVE MISSION: THE ANIMATOR

PAST MISSION:

S.H.I.E.L.D., the Strategic Homeland Intervention, Enforcement and Logistics Division, mitigates and confronts threats to the security of the Earth and its people. Its highly trained agents detect and defend against any menace that might rear its ugly head against us. Among these agents are Phil Coulson—cool-headed, mild-mannered, and singularly dedicated to his work—and xenobiologist Jemma Simmons, calmly collected, wildly intelligent, and surprisingly sentimental. Coulson, Simmons, and their fellow S.H.I.E.L.D. agents encounter mutants, monsters, villains, gods, and the best and worst of humanity on a daily basis as they endeavor to carry out S.H.I.E.L.D.'s mission.

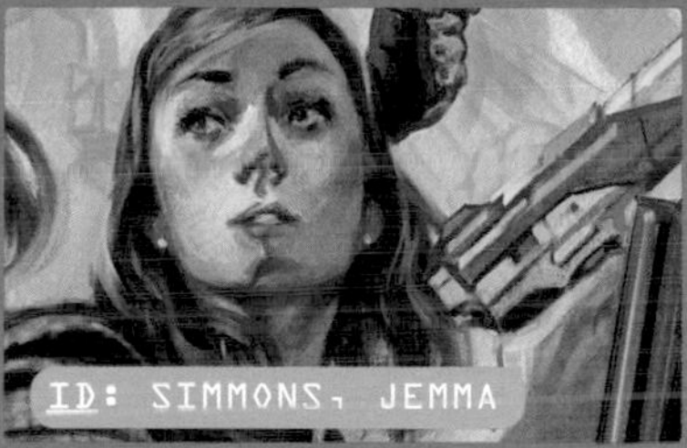
ID: SIMMONS, JEMMA

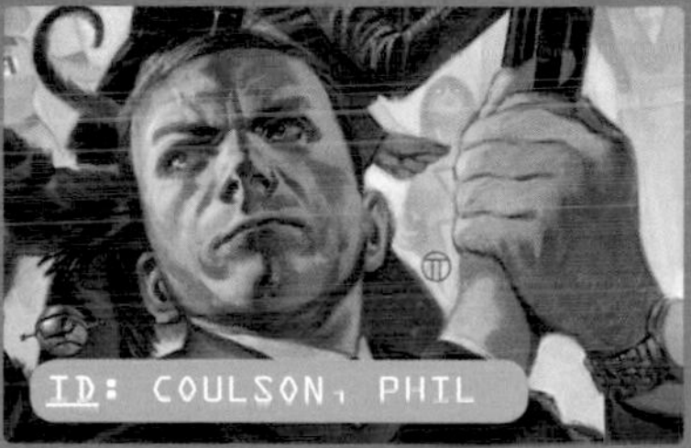
ID: COULSON, PHIL

KNOWN AGENTS:

MARK WAID
WRITER

HUMBERTO RAMOS
PENCILER

VICTOR OLAZABA
INKER

EDGAR DELGADO
COLORIST

VC'S JOE CARAMAGNA
LETTERER

JESSICA PIZARRO
DESIGNER

JULIAN TOTINO TEDESCO
COVER ARTIST

HUMBERTO RAMOS & EDGAR DELGADO; SALVADOR LARROCA & ISRAEL SILVA
VARIANT COVER ARTISTS

JON MOISAN
ASSISTANT EDITOR

TOM BREVOORT WITH ELLIE PYLE (K.I.A.)
EDITORS

AXEL ALONSO
EDITOR IN CHIEF

JOE QUESADA
CHIEF CREATIVE OFFICER

DAN BUCKLEY
PUBLISHER

ALAN FINE
EXECUTIVE PRODUCER

FITZ AND H.E.N.R.Y. STRIPS BY JOE QUESADA
S.H.I.E.L.D. CREATED BY STAN LEE AND JACK KIRBY

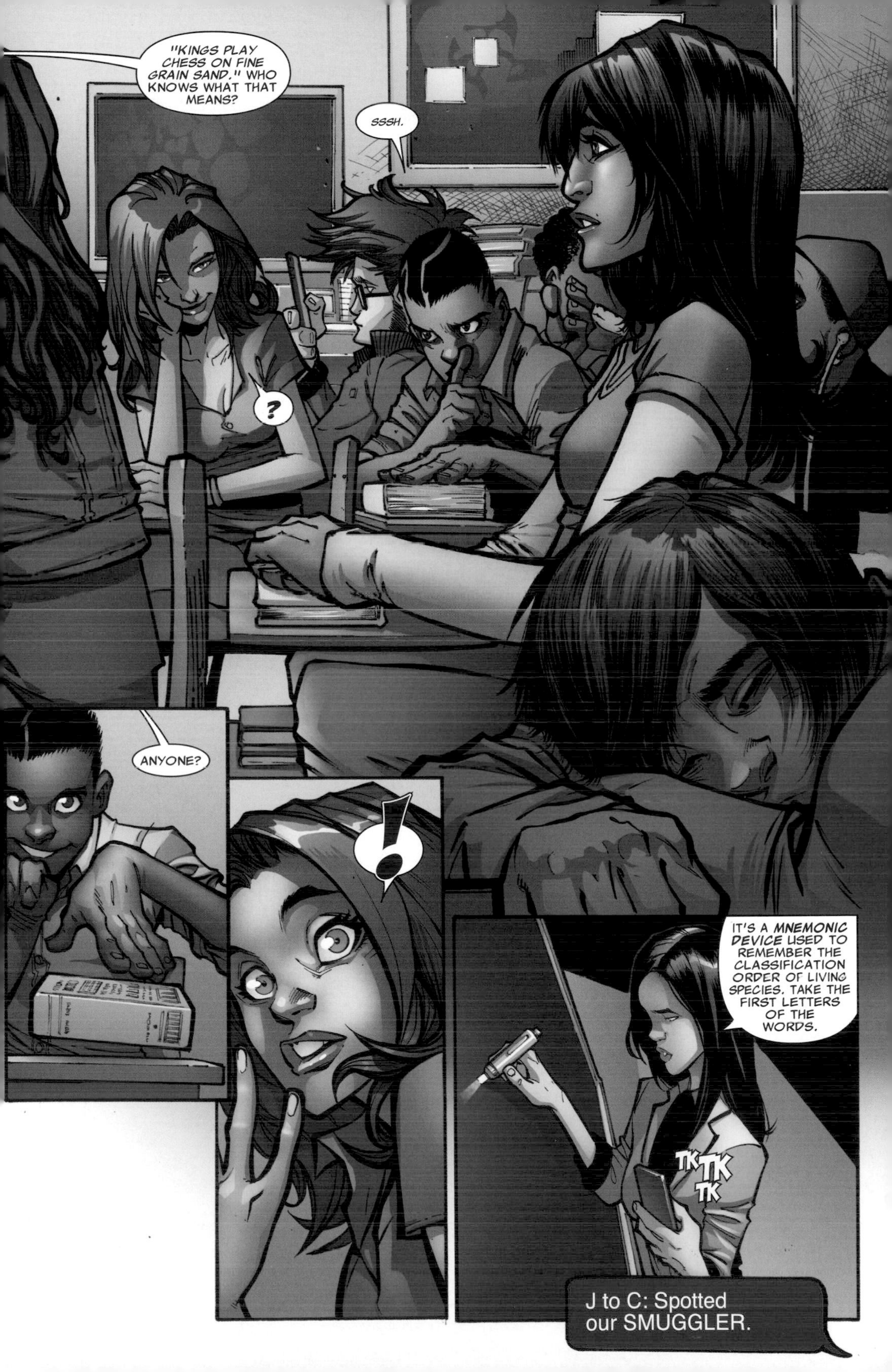
"KINGS PLAY CHESS ON FINE GRAIN SAND." WHO KNOWS WHAT THAT MEANS?
SSSH.
?
ANYONE?
!
IT'S A MNEMONIC DEVICE USED TO REMEMBER THE CLASSIFICATION ORDER OF LIVING SPECIES. TAKE THE FIRST LETTERS OF THE WORDS.
TK TK TK
J to C: Spotted our SMUGGLER.

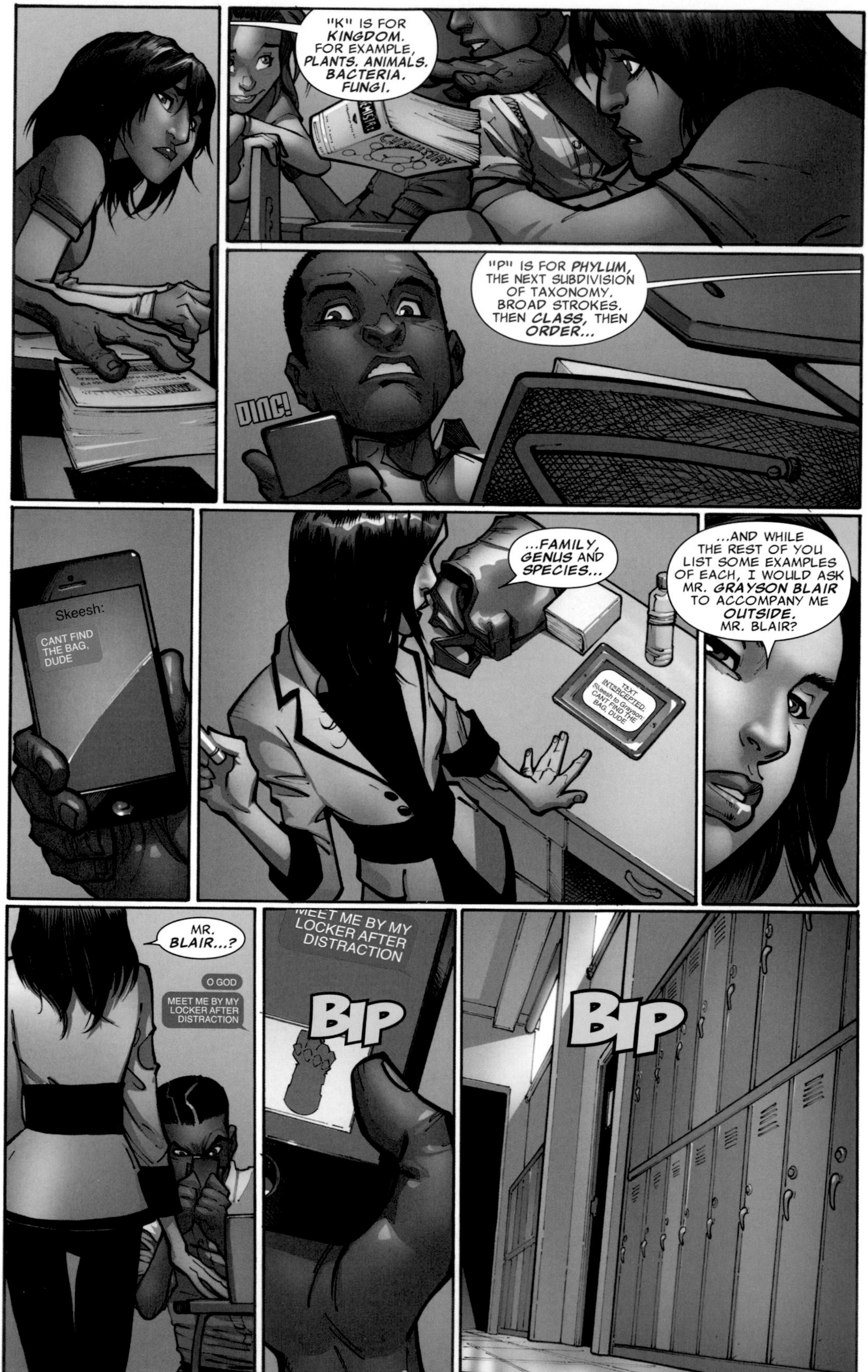
"K" IS FOR KINGDOM. FOR EXAMPLE, PLANTS. ANIMALS. BACTERIA. FUNGI.
CHEMISTRY
"P" IS FOR PHYLUM, THE NEXT SUBDIVISION OF TAXONOMY. BROAD STROKES. THEN CLASS, THEN ORDER...
DING!
Skeesh:
CANT FIND THE BAG, DUDE
...FAMILY, GENUS AND SPECIES...
TEXT INTERCEPTED: Skeesh to Grayson: CANT FIND THE BAG, DUDE
...AND WHILE THE REST OF YOU LIST SOME EXAMPLES OF EACH, I WOULD ASK MR. GRAYSON BLAIR TO ACCOMPANY ME OUTSIDE. MR. BLAIR?
MR. BLAIR...?
O GOD
MEET ME BY MY LOCKER AFTER DISTRACTION
MEET ME BY MY LOCKER AFTER DISTRACTION
BIP
BIP

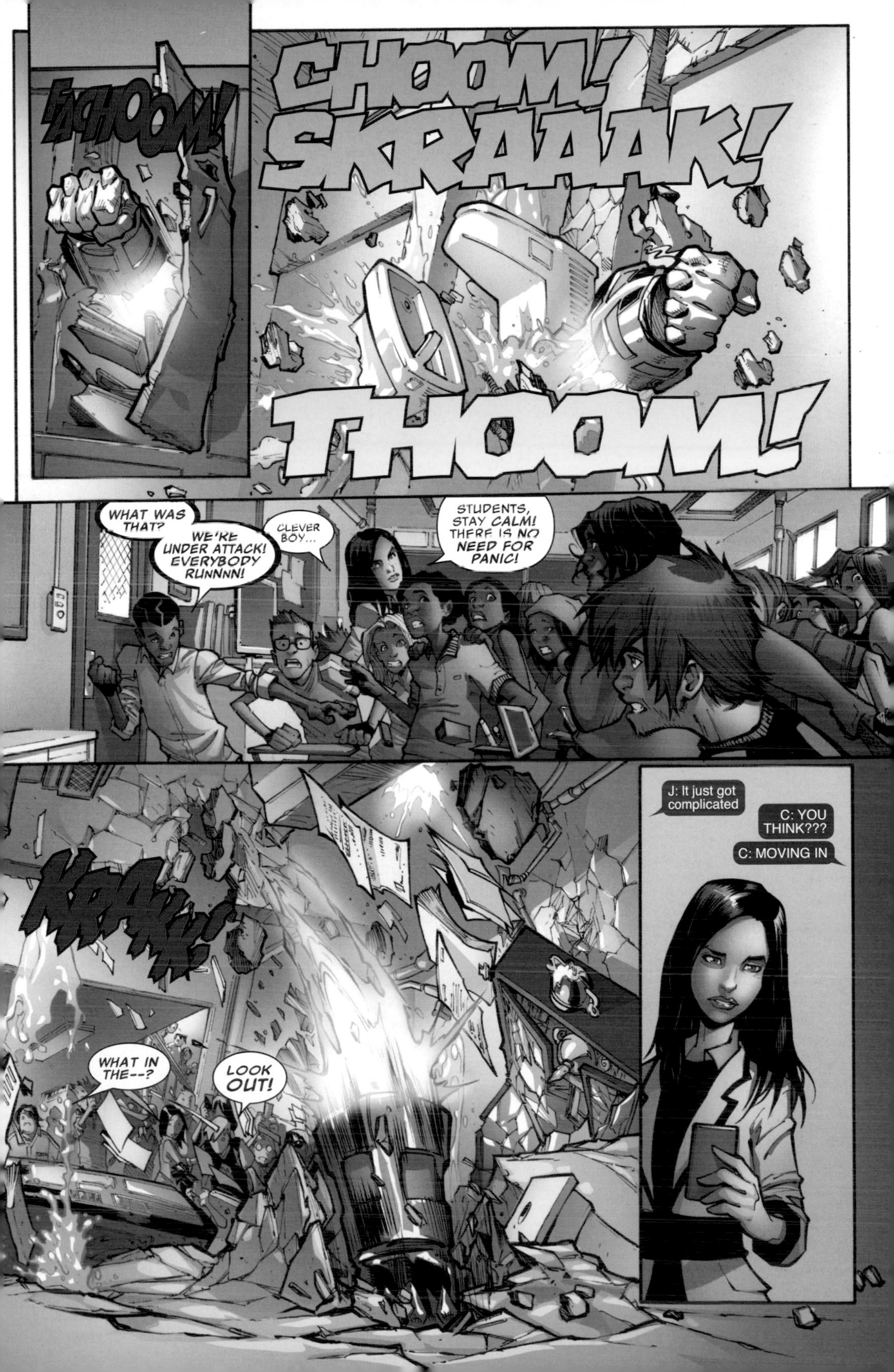
FAPHOOM!
CHOOM!
SKRAAAK!
THOOM!
WHAT WAS THAT?
WE'RE UNDER ATTACK! EVERYBODY RUNNNN!
CLEVER BOY...
STUDENTS, STAY CALM! THERE IS NO NEED FOR PANIC!
J: It just got complicated
C: YOU THINK???
C: MOVING IN
KRAAK!
WHAT IN THE--?
LOOK OUT!

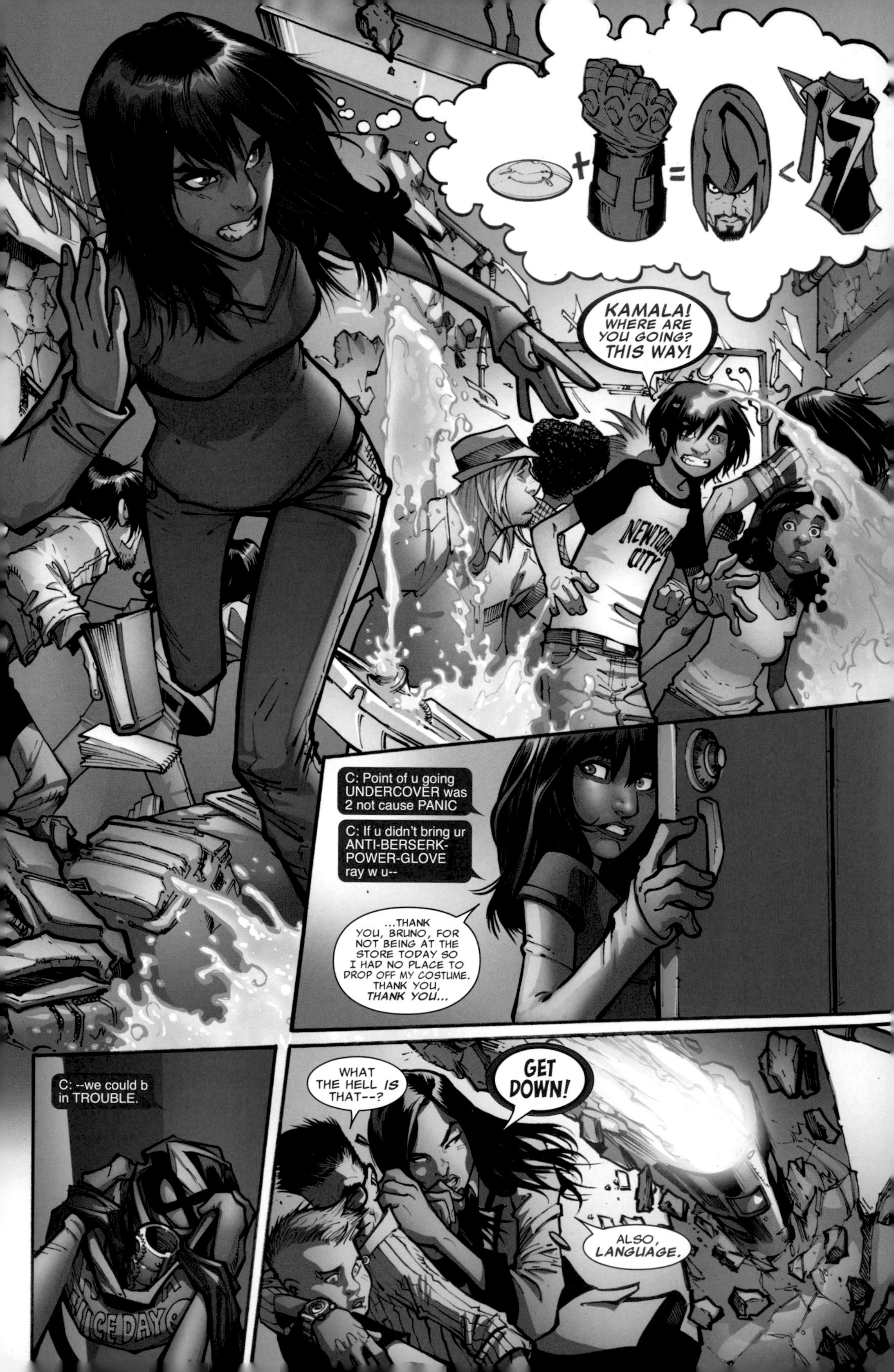
KAMALA! WHERE ARE YOU GOING? THIS WAY!
NEW YORK CITY
C: Point of u going UNDERCOVER was 2 not cause PANIC
C: If u didn't bring ur ANTI-BERSERK-POWER-GLOVE ray w u--
...THANK YOU, BRUNO, FOR NOT BEING AT THE STORE TODAY SO I HAD NO PLACE TO DROP OFF MY COSTUME. THANK YOU, THANK YOU...
C: --we could b in TROUBLE.
WHAT THE HELL IS THAT--?
GET DOWN!
ALSO, LANGUAGE.

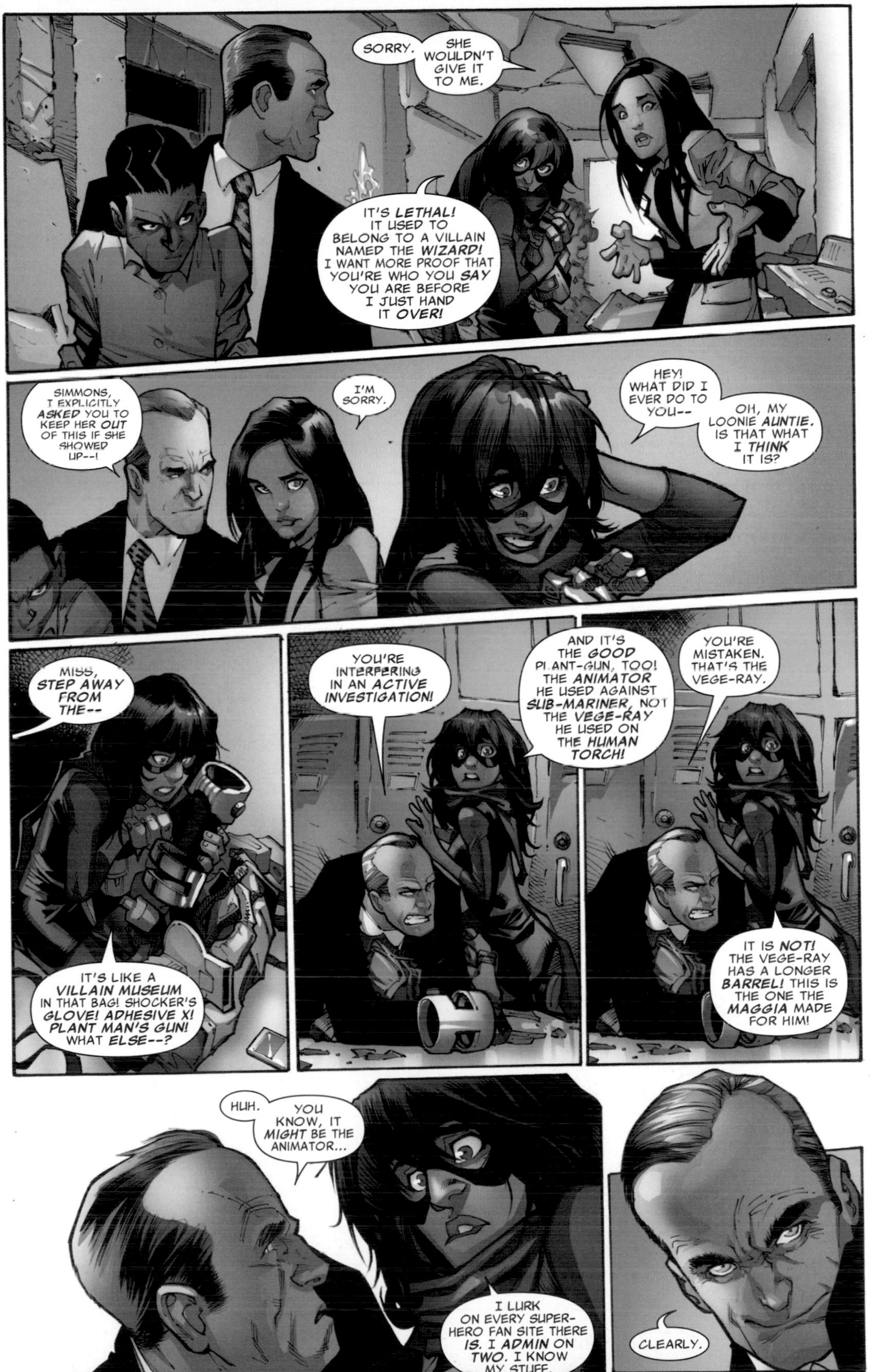
SORRY.
SHE WOULDN'T GIVE IT TO ME.
IT'S LETHAL! IT USED TO BELONG TO A VILLAIN NAMED THE WIZARD! I WANT MORE PROOF THAT YOU'RE WHO YOU SAY YOU ARE BEFORE I JUST HAND IT OVER!
SIMMONS, I EXPLICITLY ASKED YOU TO KEEP HER OUT OF THIS IF SHE SHOWED UP--!
I'M SORRY.
HEY! WHAT DID I EVER DO TO YOU--
OH, MY LOONIE AUNTIE. IS THAT WHAT I THINK IT IS?
MISS, STEP AWAY FROM THE--
IT'S LIKE A VILLAIN MUSEUM IN THAT BAG! SHOCKER'S GLOVE! ADHESIVE X! PLANT MAN'S GUN! WHAT ELSE--?
YOU'RE INTERFERING IN AN ACTIVE INVESTIGATION!
AND IT'S THE GOOD PLANT-GUN, TOO! THE ANIMATOR HE USED AGAINST SUB-MARINER, NOT THE VEGE-RAY HE USED ON THE HUMAN TORCH!
YOU'RE MISTAKEN. THAT'S THE VEGE-RAY.
IT IS NOT! THE VEGE-RAY HAS A LONGER BARREL! THIS IS THE ONE THE MAGGIA MADE FOR HIM!
HUH.
YOU KNOW, IT MIGHT BE THE ANIMATOR...
I LURK ON EVERY SUPER-HERO FAN SITE THERE IS. I ADMIN ON TWO. I KNOW MY STUFF.
CLEARLY.

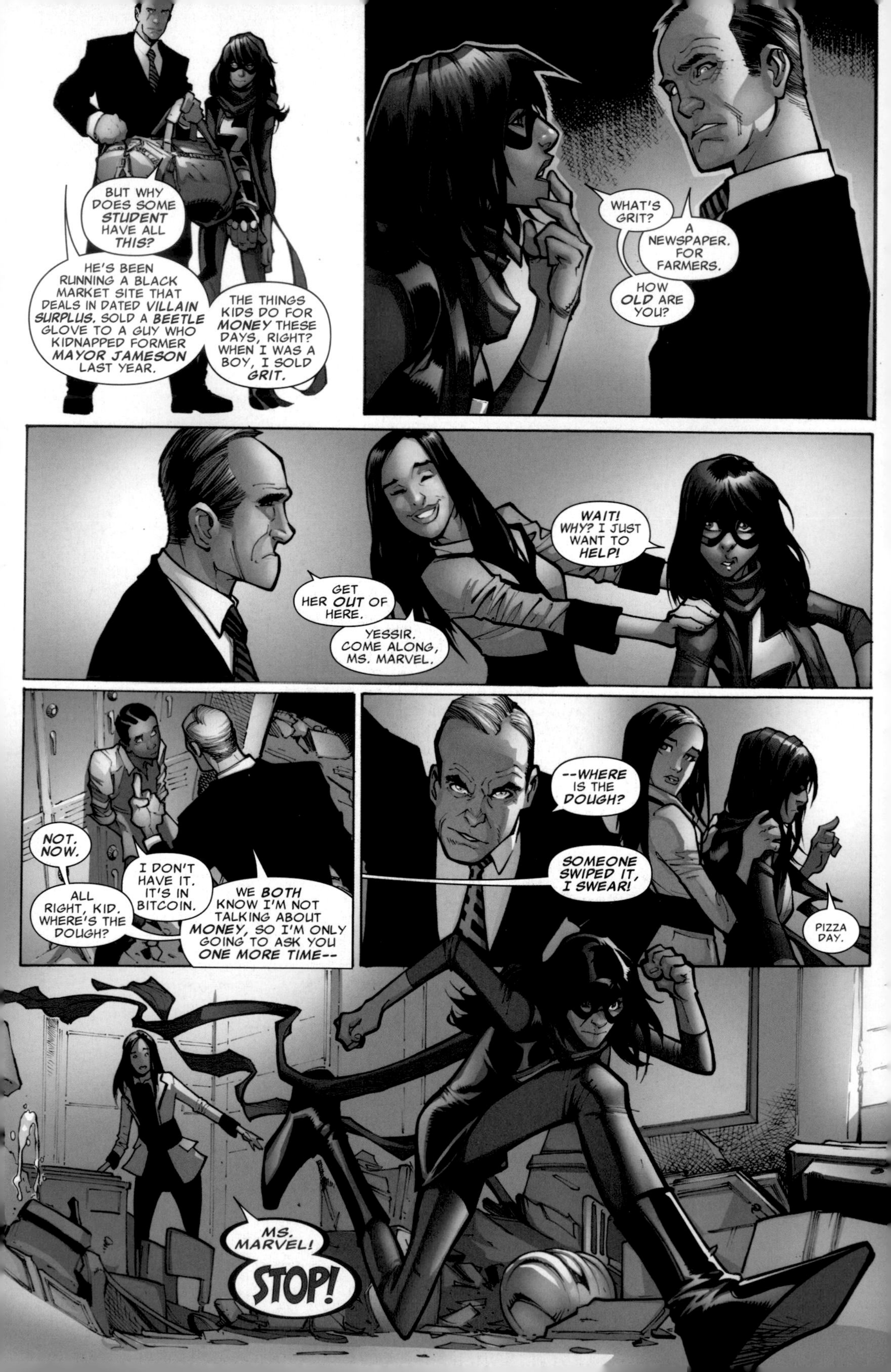
BUT WHY DOES SOME STUDENT HAVE ALL THIS?
HE'S BEEN RUNNING A BLACK MARKET SITE THAT DEALS IN DATED VILLAIN SURPLUS. SOLD A BEETLE GLOVE TO A GUY WHO KIDNAPPED FORMER MAYOR JAMESON LAST YEAR.
THE THINGS KIDS DO FOR MONEY THESE DAYS, RIGHT? WHEN I WAS A BOY, I SOLD GRIT.
WHAT'S GRIT?
A NEWSPAPER. FOR FARMERS.
HOW OLD ARE YOU?
GET HER OUT OF HERE.
YESSIR. COME ALONG, MS. MARVEL.
WAIT! WHY? I JUST WANT TO HELP!
NOT. NOW.
ALL RIGHT, KID. WHERE'S THE DOUGH?
I DON'T HAVE IT. IT'S IN BITCOIN.
WE BOTH KNOW I'M NOT TALKING ABOUT MONEY, SO I'M ONLY GOING TO ASK YOU ONE MORE TIME--
--WHERE IS THE DOUGH?
SOMEONE SWIPED IT, I SWEAR!
PIZZA DAY.
MS. MARVEL!
STOP!

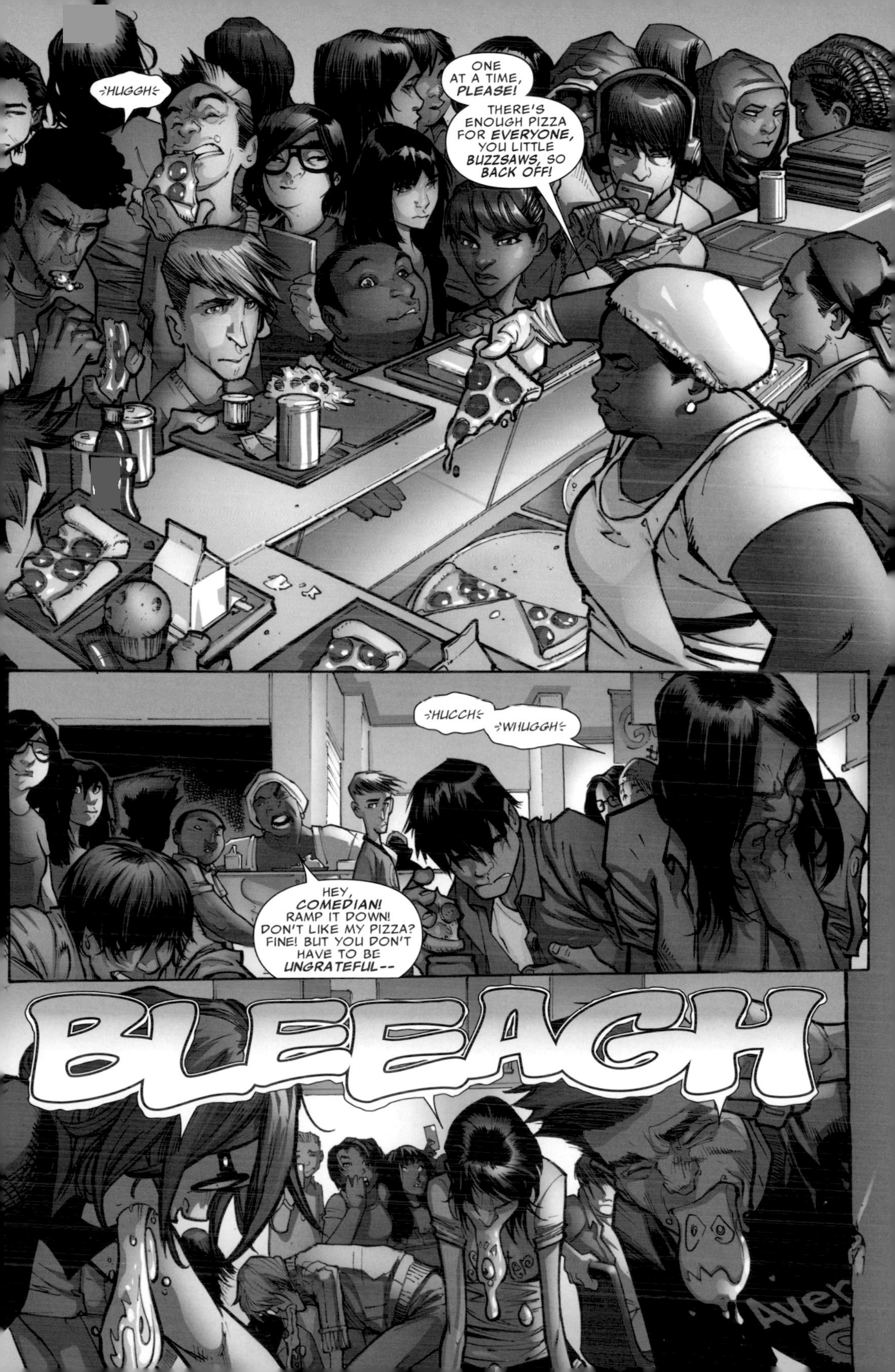
HUGGH
ONE AT A TIME, PLEASE! THERE'S ENOUGH PIZZA FOR EVERYONE, YOU LITTLE BUZZSAWS, SO BACK OFF!
HUCCH
WHUGGH
HEY, COMEDIAN! RAMP IT DOWN! DON'T LIKE MY PIZZA? FINE! BUT YOU DON'T HAVE TO BE UNGRATEFUL--
BLEEACH

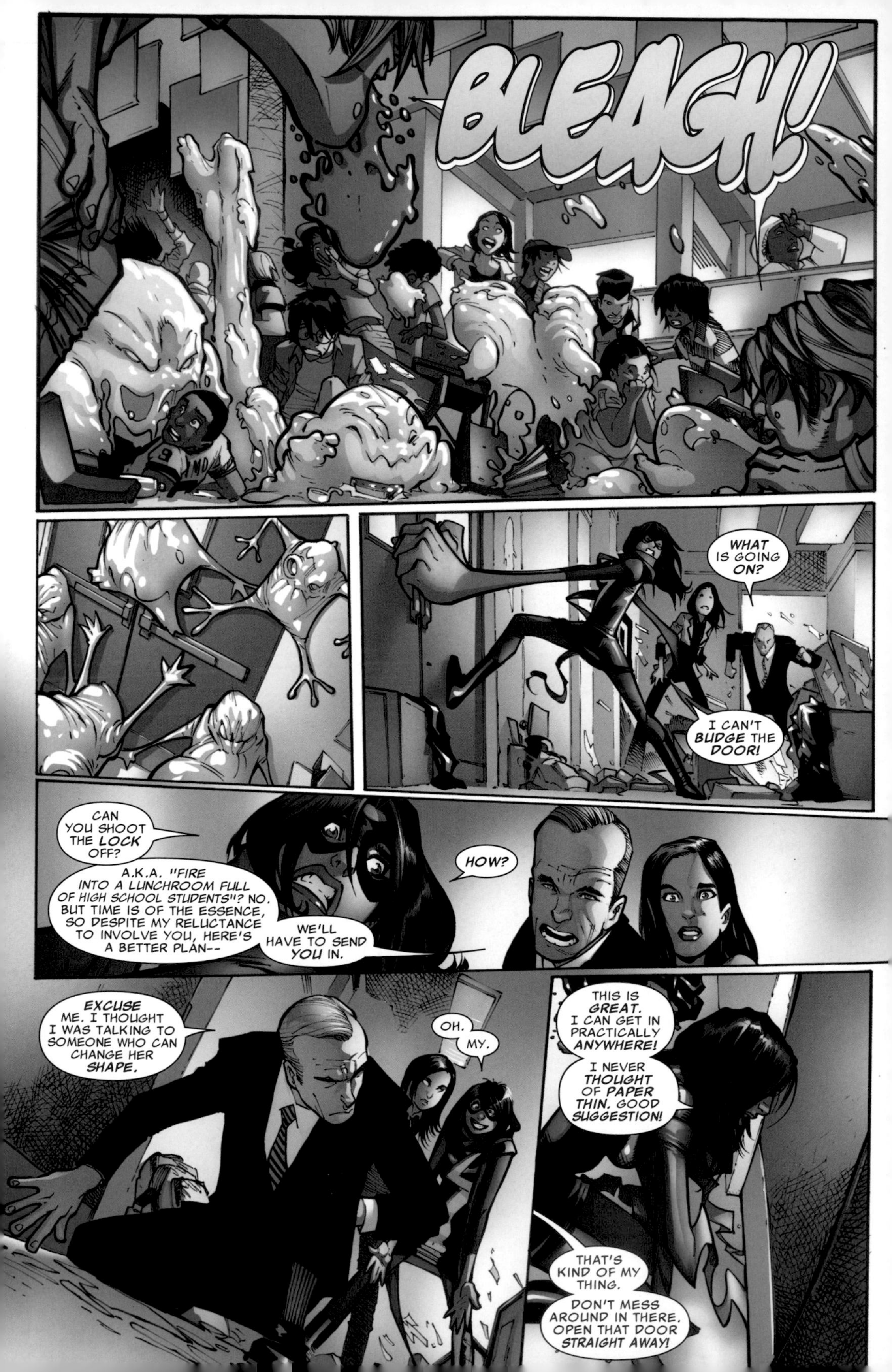
BLEACH!
WHAT IS GOING ON?
I CAN'T BUDGE THE DOOR!
CAN YOU SHOOT THE LOCK OFF?
A.K.A. "FIRE INTO A LUNCHROOM FULL OF HIGH SCHOOL STUDENTS"? NO. BUT TIME IS OF THE ESSENCE, SO DESPITE MY RELUCTANCE TO INVOLVE YOU, HERE'S A BETTER PLAN--
HOW?
WE'LL HAVE TO SEND YOU IN.
EXCUSE ME. I THOUGHT I WAS TALKING TO SOMEONE WHO CAN CHANGE HER SHAPE.
OH.
MY.
THIS IS GREAT. I CAN GET IN PRACTICALLY ANYWHERE!
I NEVER THOUGHT OF PAPER THIN. GOOD SUGGESTION!
THAT'S KIND OF MY THING.
DON'T MESS AROUND IN THERE. OPEN THAT DOOR STRAIGHT AWAY!

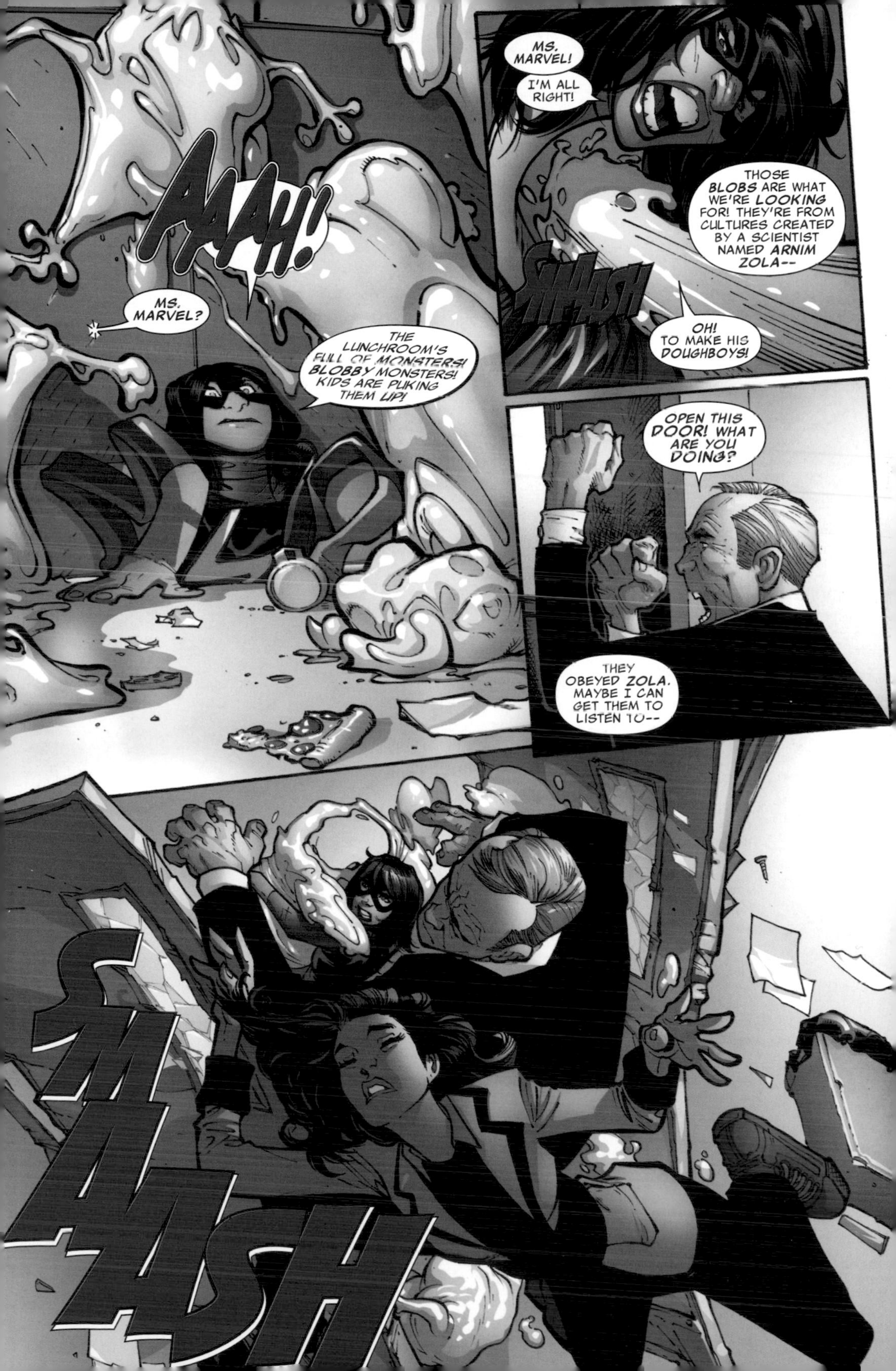
AAAH!
MS. MARVEL?
THE LUNCHROOM'S FULL OF MONSTERS! BLOBBY MONSTERS! KIDS ARE PUKING THEM UP!
MS. MARVEL!
I'M ALL RIGHT!
THOSE BLOBS ARE WHAT WE'RE LOOKING FOR! THEY'RE FROM CULTURES CREATED BY A SCIENTIST NAMED ARNIM ZOLA--
SMAASH
OH! TO MAKE HIS DOUGHBOYS!
OPEN THIS DOOR! WHAT ARE YOU DOING?
THEY OBEYED ZOLA. MAYBE I CAN GET THEM TO LISTEN TO--
SMAASH

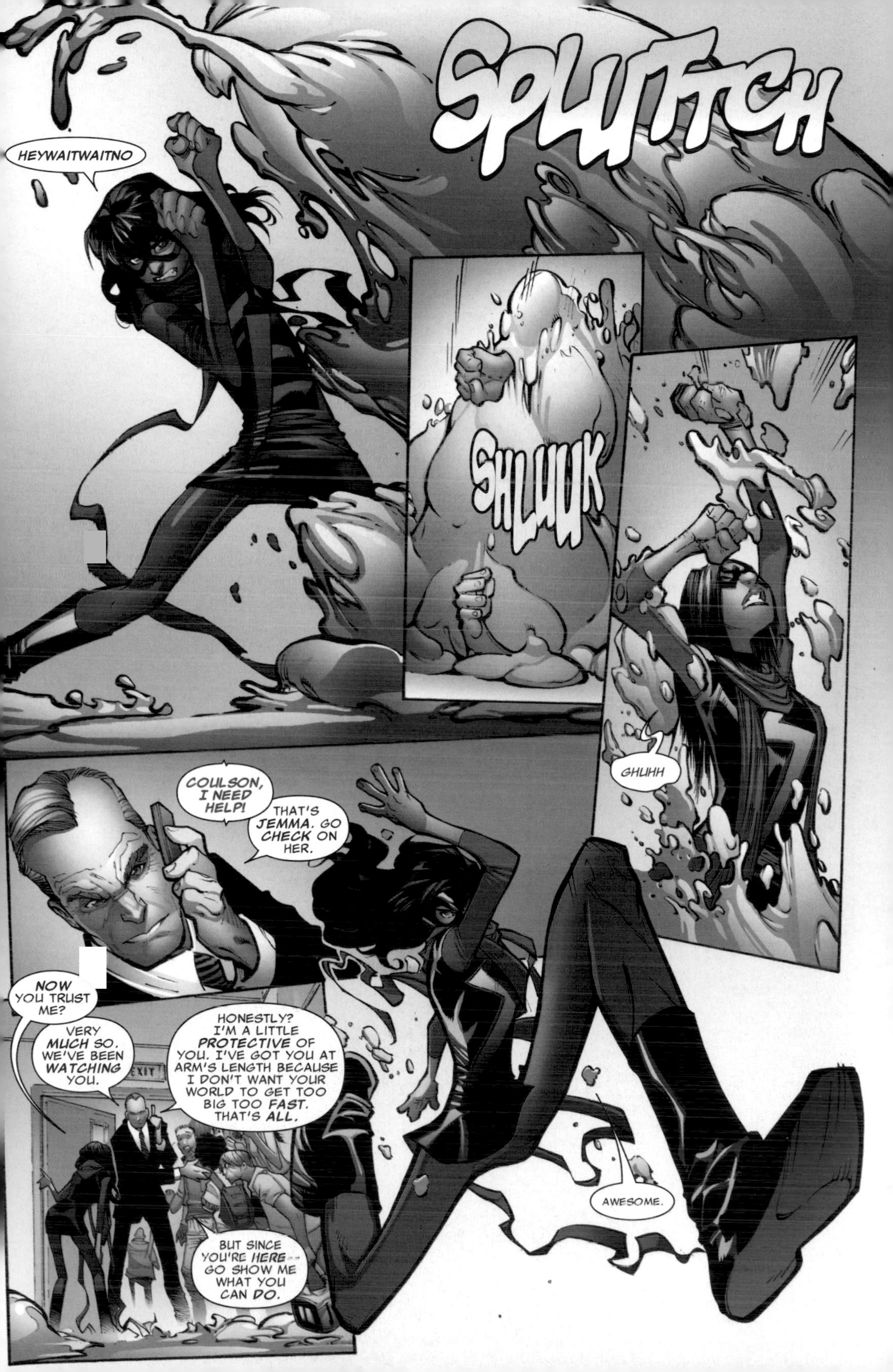
SPLUTCH
HEYWAITWAITNO
SHLUUK
GHUHH
COULSON, I NEED HELP!
THAT'S JEMMA. GO CHECK ON HER.
NOW YOU TRUST ME?
VERY MUCH SO. WE'VE BEEN WATCHING YOU.
HONESTLY? I'M A LITTLE PROTECTIVE OF YOU. I'VE GOT YOU AT ARM'S LENGTH BECAUSE I DON'T WANT YOUR WORLD TO GET TOO BIG TOO FAST. THAT'S ALL.
EXIT
BUT SINCE YOU'RE HERE-- GO SHOW ME WHAT YOU CAN DO.
AWESOME.

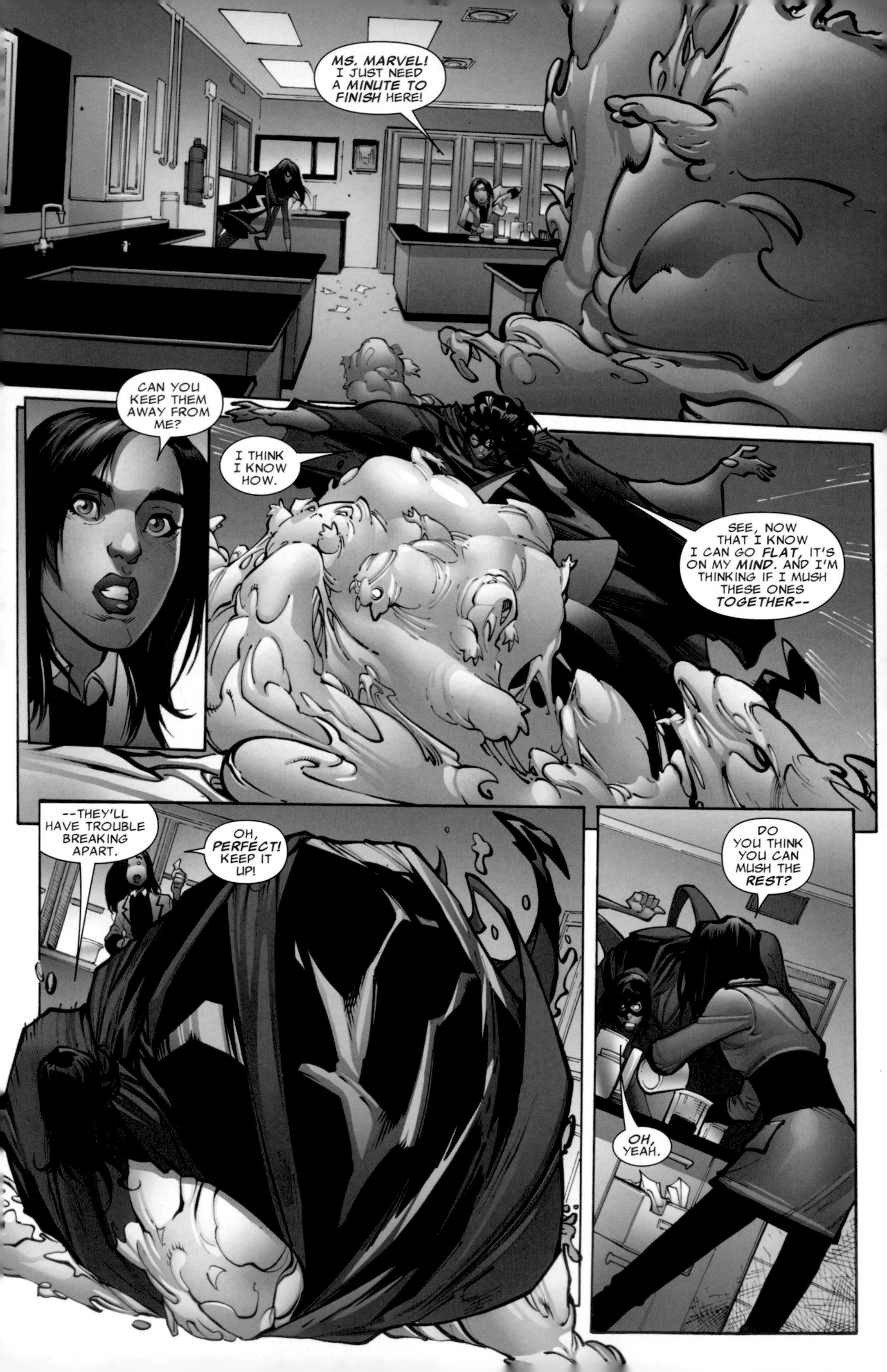

MS. MARVEL! I JUST NEED A MINUTE TO FINISH HERE!
CAN YOU KEEP THEM AWAY FROM ME?
I THINK I KNOW HOW.
SEE, NOW THAT I KNOW I CAN GO FLAT, IT'S ON MY MIND. AND I'M THINKING IF I MUSH THESE ONES TOGETHER--
--THEY'LL HAVE TROUBLE BREAKING APART.
OH, PERFECT! KEEP IT UP!
DO YOU THINK YOU CAN MUSH THE REST?
OH, YEAH.

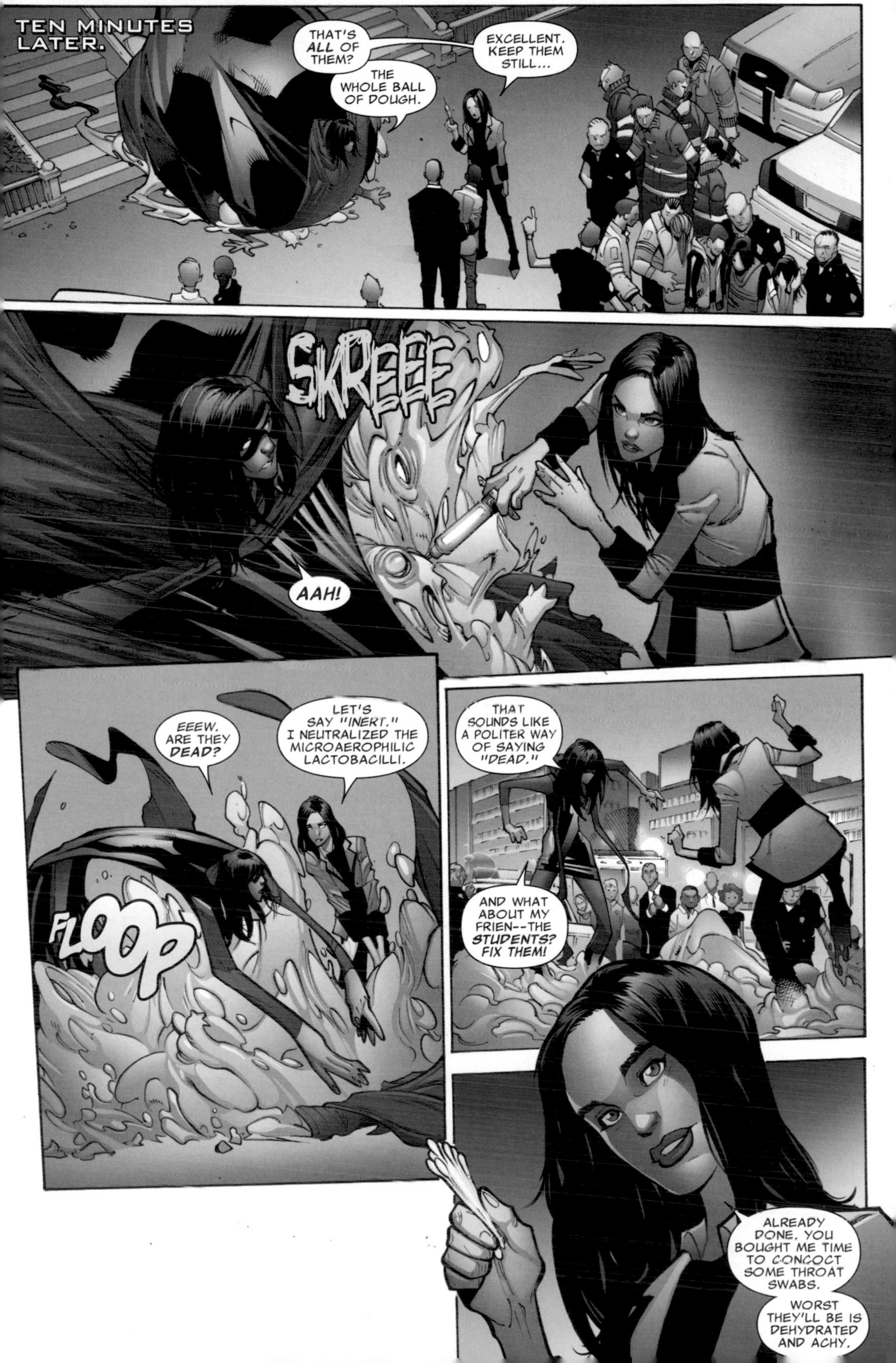
TEN MINUTES LATER.
THAT'S ALL OF THEM?
THE WHOLE BALL OF DOUGH.
EXCELLENT. KEEP THEM STILL...
SKREEE
AAH!
EEEW. ARE THEY DEAD?
LET'S SAY "INERT." I NEUTRALIZED THE MICROAEROPHILIC LACTOBACILLI.
FLOOP
THAT SOUNDS LIKE A POLITER WAY OF SAYING "DEAD."
AND WHAT ABOUT MY FRIEN--THE STUDENTS? FIX THEM!
ALREADY DONE. YOU BOUGHT ME TIME TO CONCOCT SOME THROAT SWABS.
WORST THEY'LL BE IS DEHYDRATED AND ACHY.

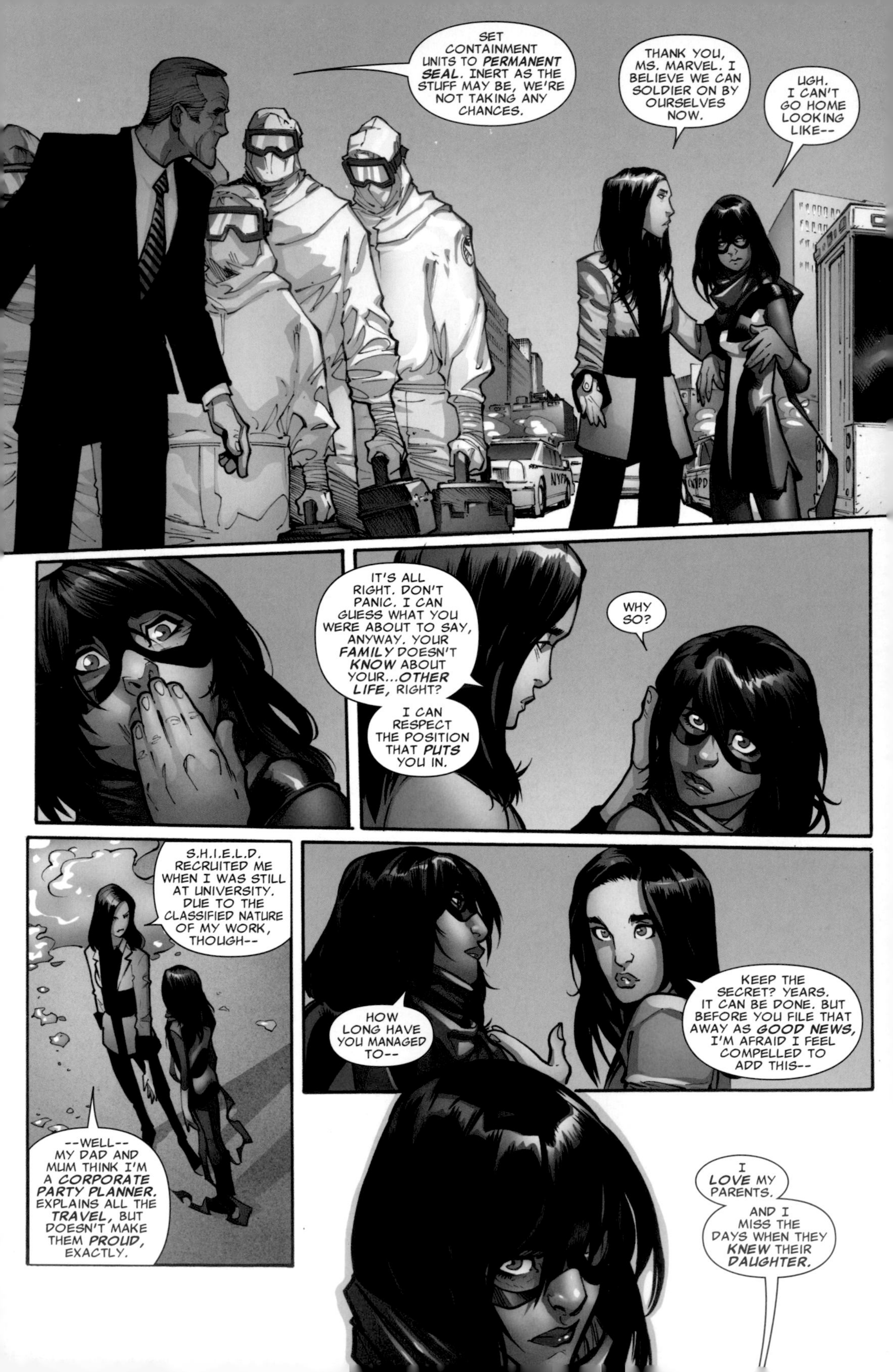

SET CONTAINMENT UNITS TO PERMANENT SEAL. INERT AS THE STUFF MAY BE, WE'RE NOT TAKING ANY CHANCES.
THANK YOU, MS. MARVEL. I BELIEVE WE CAN SOLDIER ON BY OURSELVES NOW.
UGH. I CAN'T GO HOME LOOKING LIKE--
IT'S ALL RIGHT. DON'T PANIC. I CAN GUESS WHAT YOU WERE ABOUT TO SAY, ANYWAY. YOUR FAMILY DOESN'T KNOW ABOUT YOUR...OTHER LIFE, RIGHT?
I CAN RESPECT THE POSITION THAT PUTS YOU IN.
WHY SO?
S.H.I.E.L.D. RECRUITED ME WHEN I WAS STILL AT UNIVERSITY. DUE TO THE CLASSIFIED NATURE OF MY WORK, THOUGH--
--WELL-- MY DAD AND MUM THINK I'M A CORPORATE PARTY PLANNER. EXPLAINS ALL THE TRAVEL, BUT DOESN'T MAKE THEM PROUD, EXACTLY.
HOW LONG HAVE YOU MANAGED TO--
KEEP THE SECRET? YEARS. IT CAN BE DONE. BUT BEFORE YOU FILE THAT AWAY AS GOOD NEWS, I'M AFRAID I FEEL COMPELLED TO ADD THIS--
I LOVE MY PARENTS.
AND I MISS THE DAYS WHEN THEY KNEW THEIR DAUGHTER.

CONTINUED IN *S.H.I.E.L.D. VOL. 1: PERFECT BULLETS.*

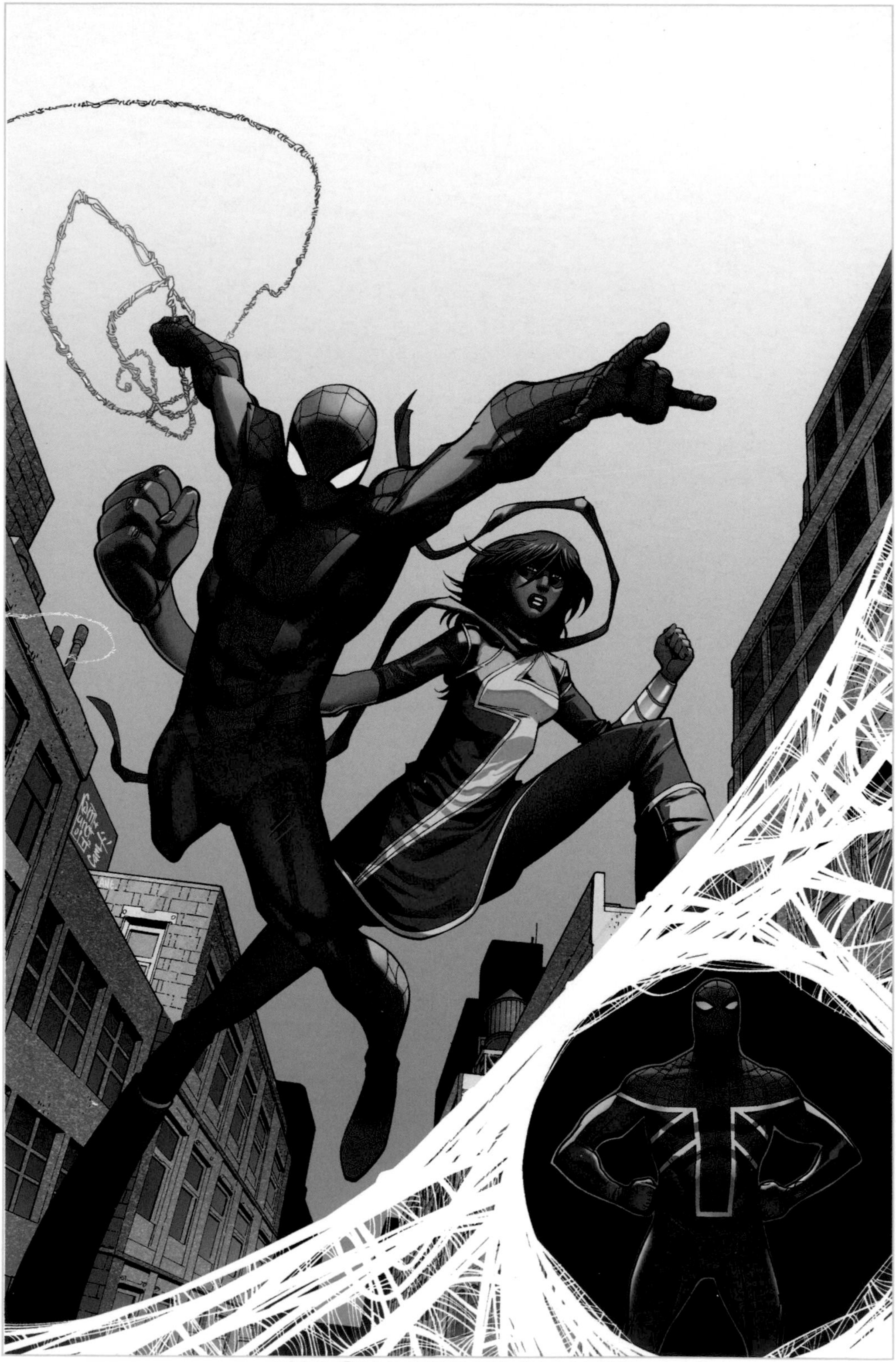

AMAZING SPIDER-MAN #7

Years ago, high school student PETER PARKER was bitten by a radioactive spider and gained the speed, agility, and proportional strength of a spider as well as the ability to stick to walls and a spider-sense that warned him of imminent danger. After learning that with great power there must also come great responsibility, he became the crime-fighting super hero...

the AMAZING SPIDER-MAN

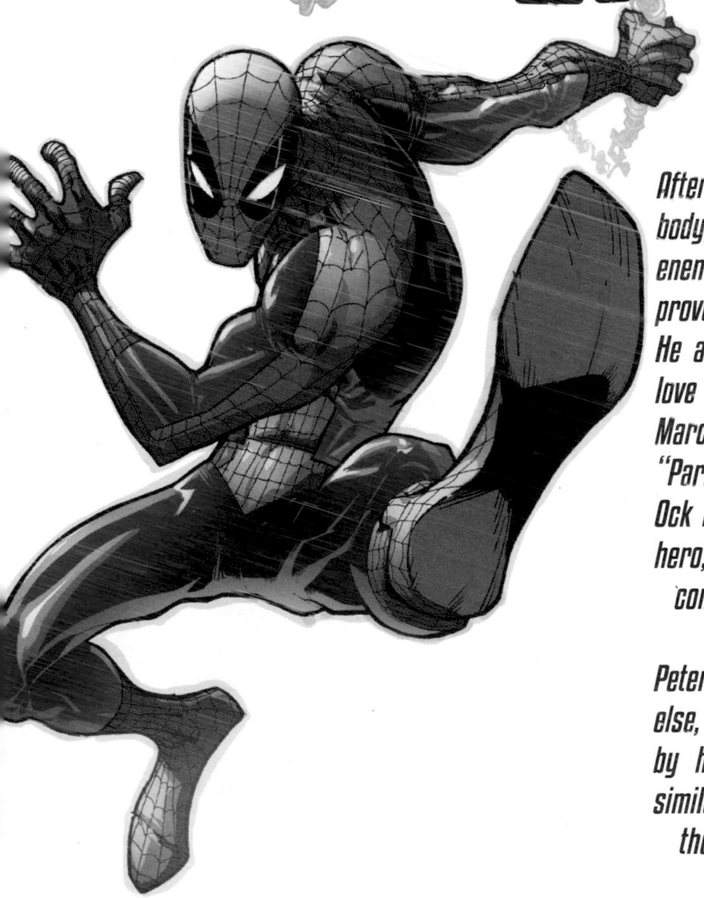

After swapping his mind into Peter's body, one of Spider-Man's greatest enemies, DOCTOR OCTOPUS, set out to prove himself the SUPERIOR SPIDER-MAN. He also completed Peter's PhD, fell in love with a woman named Anna Maria Marconi, and started his own company, "Parker Industries." But in the end Doc Ock realized that in order to be a true hero, he had to sacrifice himself and give control of Peter's body back to Peter.

Peter recently found out that someone else, Cindy Moon A.K.A. SILK, was bitten by his radioactive spider giving her similar powers to Peter. And that's not the only thing they have in common.

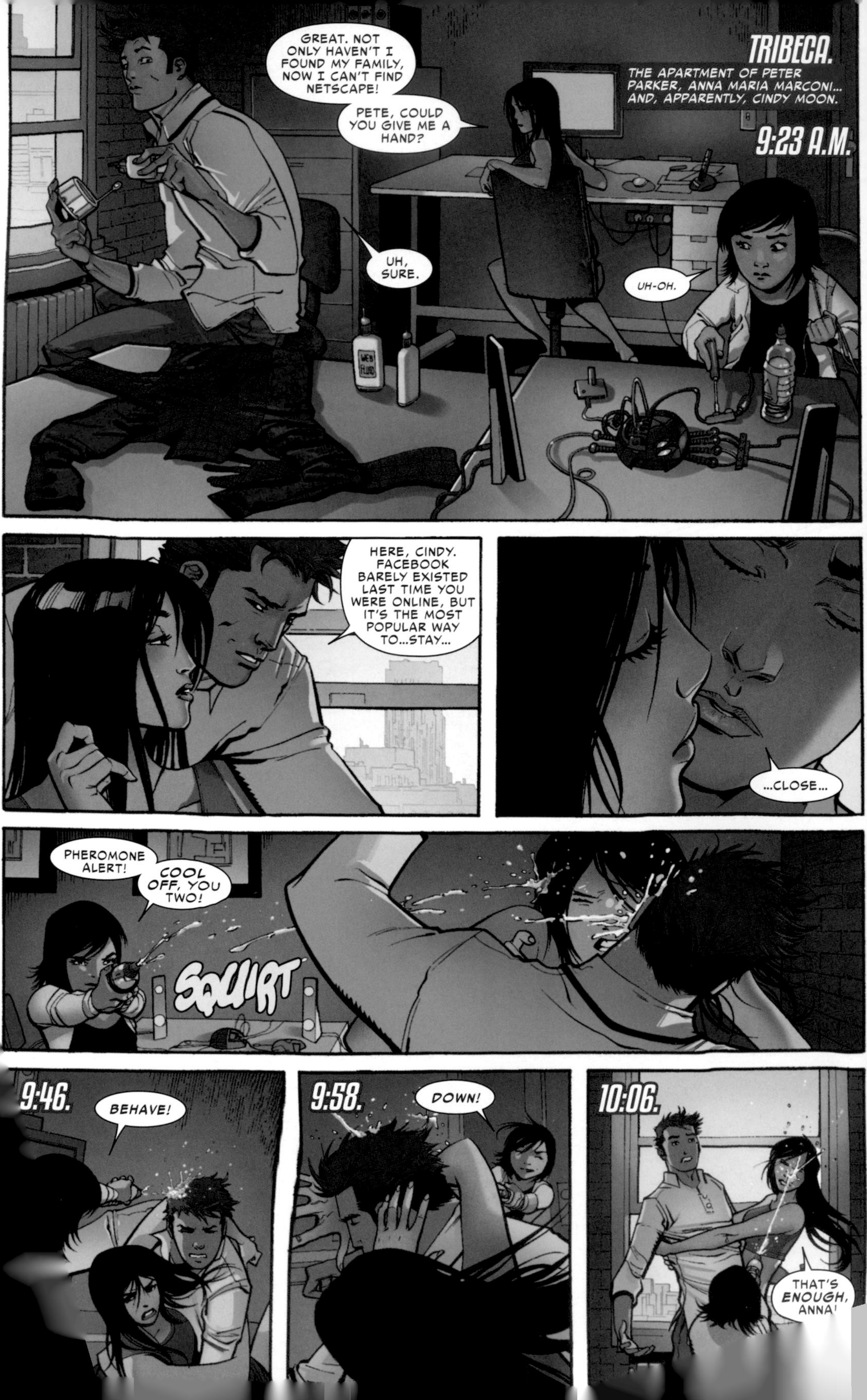
TRIBECA.
THE APARTMENT OF PETER PARKER, ANNA MARIA MARCONI... AND, APPARENTLY, CINDY MOON.
9:23 A.M.
GREAT. NOT ONLY HAVEN'T I FOUND MY FAMILY, NOW I CAN'T FIND NETSCAPE!
PETE, COULD YOU GIVE ME A HAND?
UH, SURE.
UH-OH.
WEB FLUID
HERE, CINDY. FACEBOOK BARELY EXISTED LAST TIME YOU WERE ONLINE, BUT IT'S THE MOST POPULAR WAY TO...STAY...
...CLOSE...
PHEROMONE ALERT!
COOL OFF, YOU TWO!
SQUIRT
9:46.
BEHAVE!
9:58.
DOWN!
10:06.
THAT'S ENOUGH, ANNA!

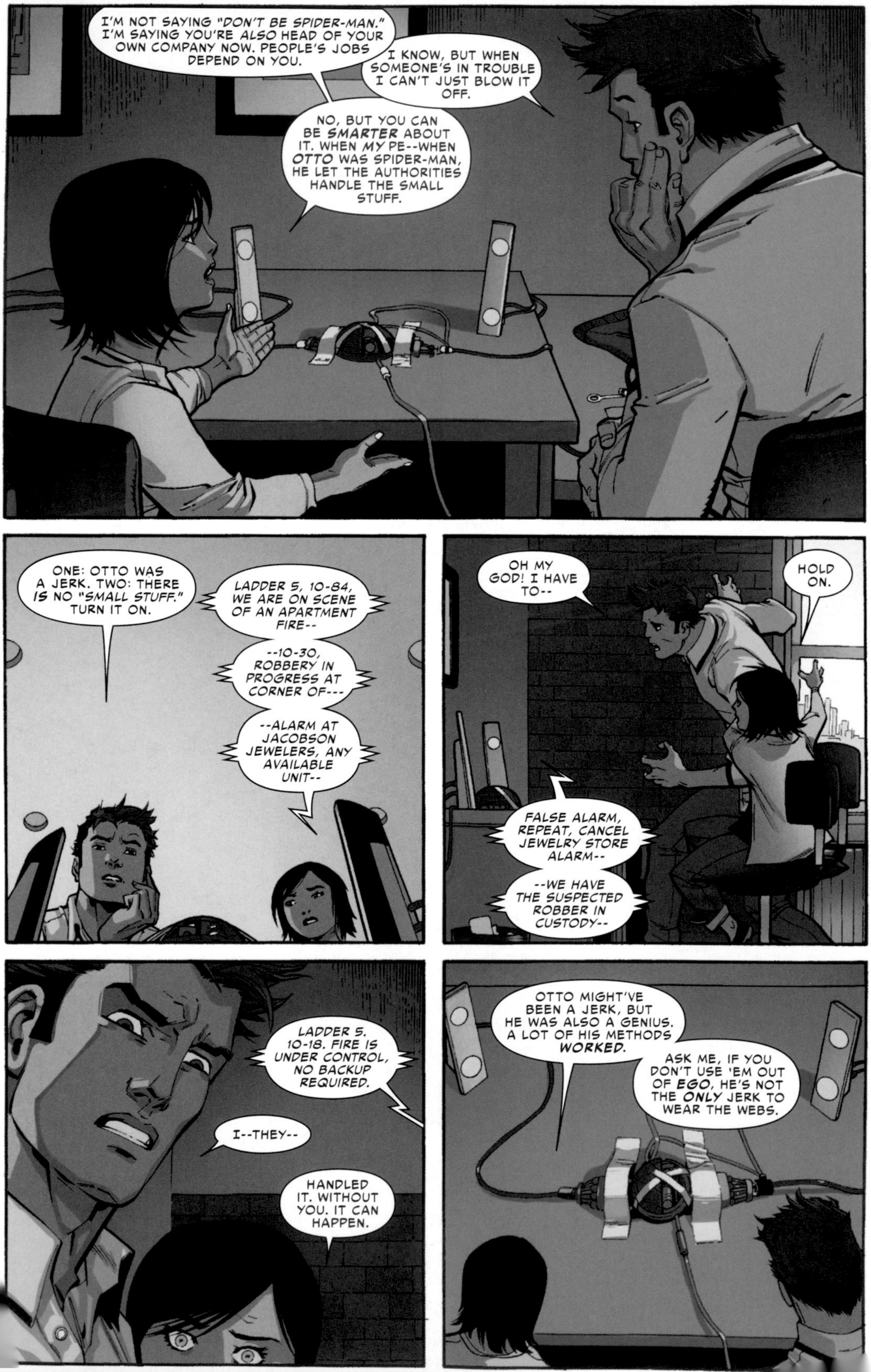

I'M NOT SAYING "DON'T BE SPIDER-MAN." I'M SAYING YOU'RE ALSO HEAD OF YOUR OWN COMPANY NOW. PEOPLE'S JOBS DEPEND ON YOU.
I KNOW, BUT WHEN SOMEONE'S IN TROUBLE I CAN'T JUST BLOW IT OFF.
NO, BUT YOU CAN BE SMARTER ABOUT IT. WHEN MY PE--WHEN OTTO WAS SPIDER-MAN, HE LET THE AUTHORITIES HANDLE THE SMALL STUFF.
ONE: OTTO WAS A JERK. TWO: THERE IS NO "SMALL STUFF." TURN IT ON.
LADDER 5, 10-84, WE ARE ON SCENE OF AN APARTMENT FIRE--
--10-30, ROBBERY IN PROGRESS AT CORNER OF---
--ALARM AT JACOBSON JEWELERS, ANY AVAILABLE UNIT--
OH MY GOD! I HAVE TO--
HOLD ON.
FALSE ALARM, REPEAT, CANCEL JEWELRY STORE ALARM--
--WE HAVE THE SUSPECTED ROBBER IN CUSTODY--
LADDER 5. 10-18. FIRE IS UNDER CONTROL, NO BACKUP REQUIRED.
I--THEY--
HANDLED IT. WITHOUT YOU. IT CAN HAPPEN.
OTTO MIGHT'VE BEEN A JERK, BUT HE WAS ALSO A GENIUS. A LOT OF HIS METHODS WORKED.
ASK ME, IF YOU DON'T USE 'EM OUT OF EGO, HE'S NOT THE ONLY JERK TO WEAR THE WEBS.

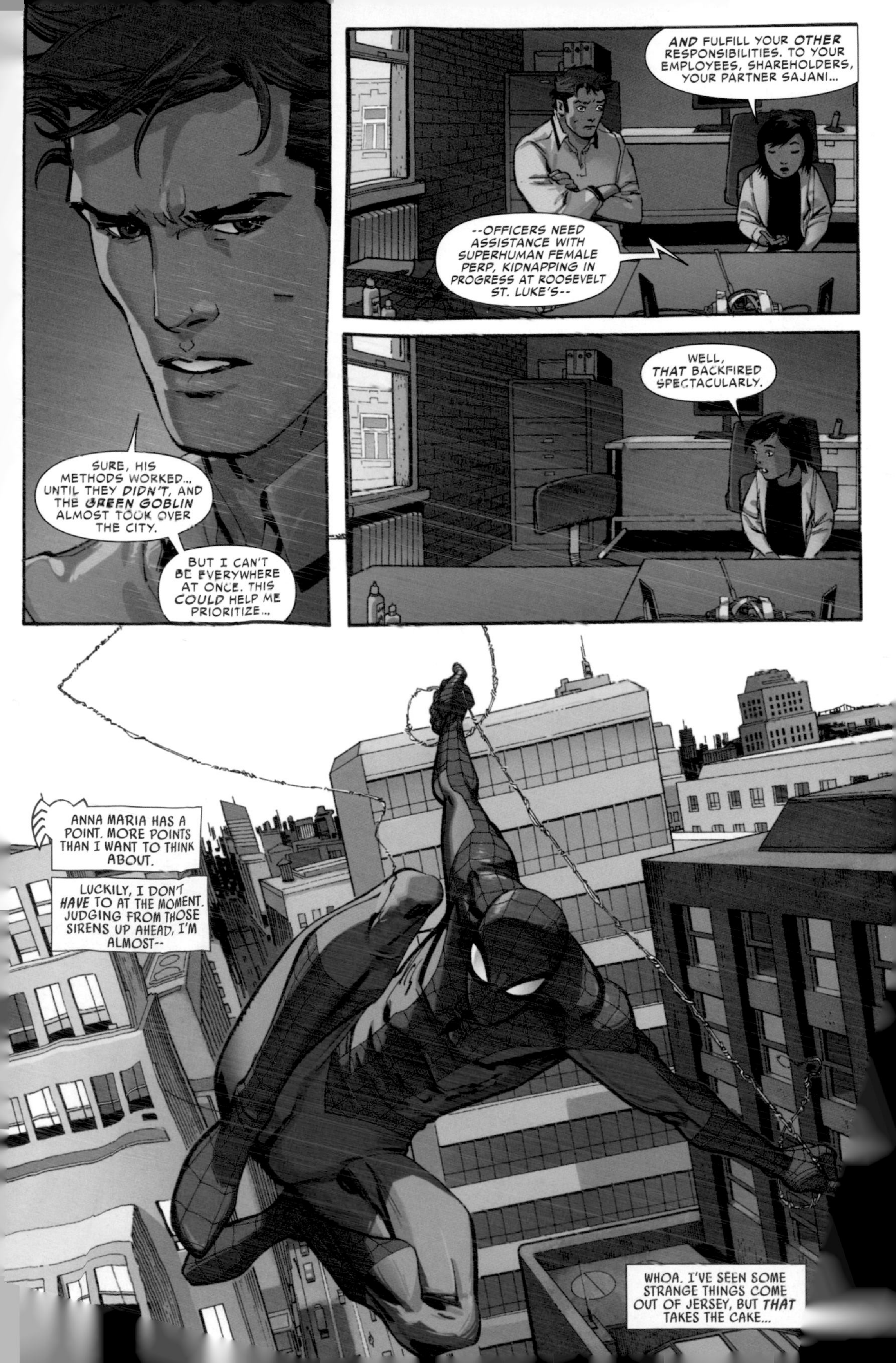
AND FULFILL YOUR OTHER RESPONSIBILITIES. TO YOUR EMPLOYEES, SHAREHOLDERS, YOUR PARTNER SAJANI...
--OFFICERS NEED ASSISTANCE WITH SUPERHUMAN FEMALE PERP, KIDNAPPING IN PROGRESS AT ROOSEVELT ST. LUKE'S--
SURE, HIS METHODS WORKED... UNTIL THEY DIDN'T, AND THE GREEN GOBLIN ALMOST TOOK OVER THE CITY.
BUT I CAN'T BE EVERYWHERE AT ONCE. THIS COULD HELP ME PRIORITIZE...
WELL, THAT BACKFIRED SPECTACULARLY.
ANNA MARIA HAS A POINT. MORE POINTS THAN I WANT TO THINK ABOUT.
LUCKILY, I DON'T HAVE TO AT THE MOMENT. JUDGING FROM THOSE SIRENS UP AHEAD, I'M ALMOST--
WHOA. I'VE SEEN SOME STRANGE THINGS COME OUT OF JERSEY, BUT THAT TAKES THE CAKE...

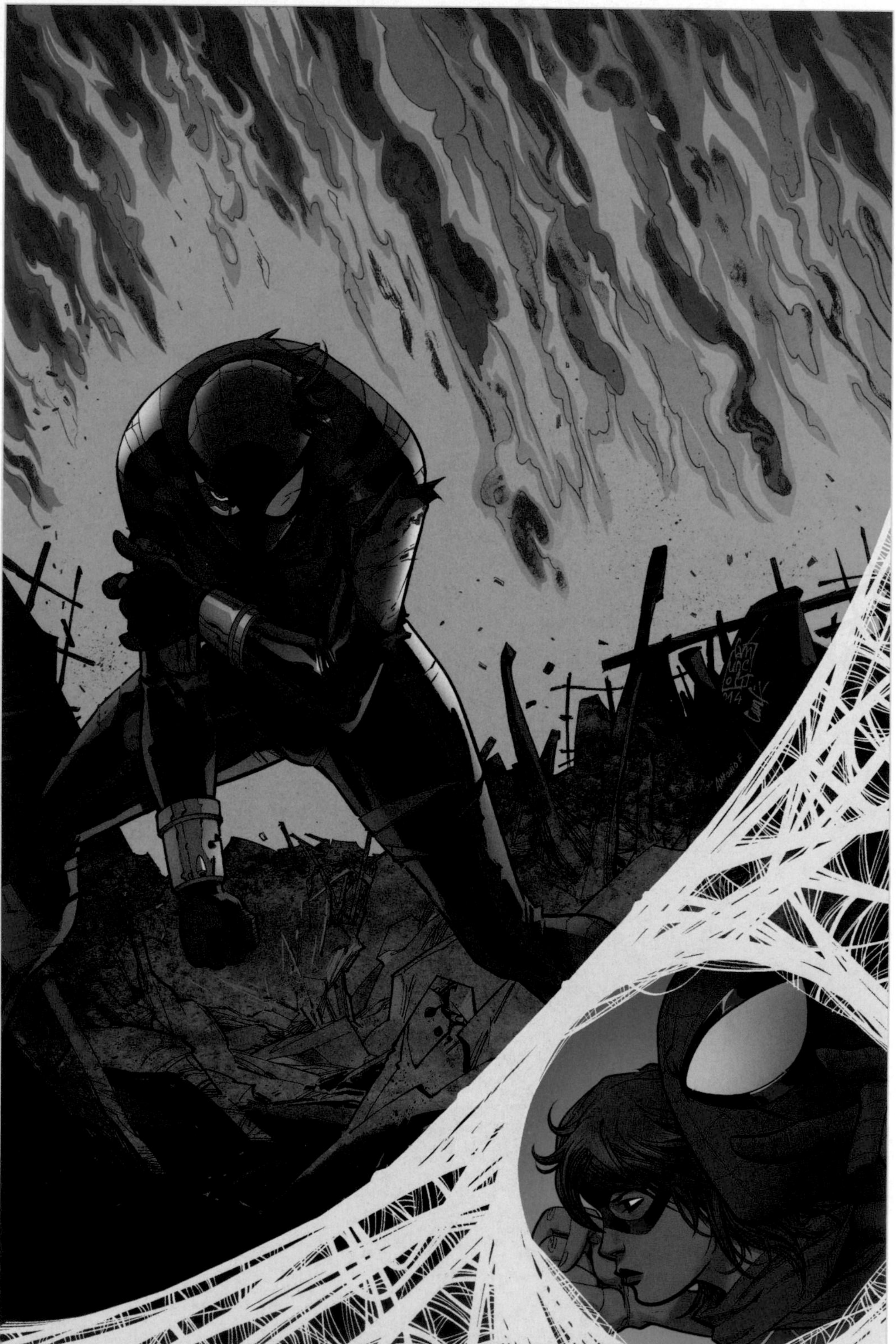

AMAZING SPIDER-MAN #8

THE FACT CHANNEL STUDIOS.

...RENT IN THIS CITY'S GONE *NUTS!* BUT STAYING WITH PETER IS *NOT* AN OPTION. NOT WHEN EVERY TIME WE'RE TOGETHER WE ACT LIKE TEENAGERS ON PROM NIGHT.

YOU'RE NATALIE LONG'S INTERN. CINDY MOON, RIGHT? SHE'S BEEN ASKING FOR YOU...

...AND SHE'S IN A *MOOD.* YOU BETTER GET OVER TO THE EDITING BAY. STAT.

SORRY I'M LATE, MS. LONG. EVERYTHING OKAY?

IT'S THE FIGHT BETWEEN *SILK* AND *ELECTRO.* I'D LOVE TO MAKE HER *OURS,* LIKE THE *DAILY BUGLE* DOES WITH SPIDER-MAN.

BUT SHE'S COMING OFF *TERRIBLY.*

UM, HER MOVES LOOK PRETTY SLICK...

MOVES ARE FINE. IT'S THE *OUTFIT.* LOOKS LIKE SHE JUST WEBBED IT ON. *SO* TACKY, RIGHT?

NATALIE, WE GOT TWO MASK CRIMES IN PROGRESS. SPIDER-MAN'S HANDLING ONE. THE OTHER'S IN THE DIAMOND DISTRICT.

WE'VE GOT ENOUGH SPIDEY FOOTAGE. I'LL TAKE THE OTHER ONE.

C'MON, CINDY. IF WE'RE LUCKY MAYBE ANOTHER HERO WILL...

CINDY?

SWIPP
SWIPP

"TACKY," HUH? EVERYONE'S A CRITIC. BET SPIDER-WOMAN DOESN'T HAVE TO PUT UP WITH THIS.

FINE! LET'S TAKE ANOTHER SHOT AT IT. LOOKS LIKE SILK'S ABOUT TO GET A *MAKEOVER.*

"THIS NOT PRE

THANK YOU. WE WERE SO WORRIED. YOU'RE A REAL HERO!

I'M TRYING.

DON'T GO ANYWHERE.

THEY DON'T KNOW WHAT POWERS THE BABY HAS. I JUST HOPE WHEN THEY FIND OUT, THEY STILL--

THEY LOVE HER. DOESN'T SOLVE EVERY PROBLEM, BUT IT'S A GOOD START.

I'VE GOTTA HEAD TO AVENGERS HQ...PUT OUT AN APB ON DR. MINERVA. AND YOU--

ST. LUKE'S-ROOSEVELT HOSPITAL.

OH! MY! GOSH! ARE YOU TAKING ME TO *AVENGERS TOWER?* THAT WOULD BE SO UNBELIEVABLY, INCREDIBLY--

NO.

IT'S A *SCHOOL DAY,* AND I'M GUESSING YOU'VE MISSED AT LEAST TWO CLASSES ALREADY.

OII. YEAH. *HEH.* UM, I ACTUALLY NEVER DITCH--

RELAX, KIDDO. YOU'LL BE FINE.

AS A SUPER HERO? OR THE WHOLE INHUMAN THING?

AS A TEENAGER. YOU REMIND ME OF A WEB-HEADED WHIPPERSNAPPER WHO ALWAYS WONDERED HOW *HE* WAS DOING.

AND HE THINKS *YOU'RE* DOING GREAT.

SEE YA, SPIDEY!

NOW WHAT TO DO ABOUT *YOU*...

LISTEN, I KNOW I MESSED UP, BUT IF MY PAROLE OFFICER HEARS I'VE BEEN HENCHING AGAIN...

I SWEAR, I'VE TRIED TO FIND A LEGIT JOB, BUT NO ONE WANTS TO HIRE A GUY WITH A RECORD GOING BACK TO JUVIE...

EVER SINCE I WEBBED YOU UP IN THE SCHOOLYARD... RIGHT, *"CLASH"*?

BEARD FOOLED ME AT FIRST. BUT ONLY *CLAYTON COLE* COULD'VE WHIPPED UP A SONIC CANNON THAT FAST. YOU'RE GOOD.

SURE. MAD SCIENTIST SUPER VILLAIN AT FIFTEEN. LOOKS GREAT ON A RESUME.

YOU-- RECOGNIZED ME?*

*DO YOU? SEE ASM: LEARNING TO CRAWL. -NICK

IT MIGHT TO *THIS* GUY. HE BELIEVES IN SECOND CHANCES.

JUST TELL PARKER I SENT YOU.

PARKER INDUSTRIES.

I CAN'T TELL YOU HOW MUCH I APPRECIATE THIS, MR. PARKER.

PETE. NICE TO HAVE YOU ON BOARD, CLAYTON.

I'VE BEEN WORKING ON CURING SUPER-CRIMINALS *AND* REFORMING THEM. TIME TO PUT MY MONEY WHERE MY MOUTH IS.

RUNNING THIS COMPANY GIVES ME GREAT POWER... AND GREAT RESPONSIBILITY. AND I KNOW BETTER THAN ANYONE, HEROES CAN COME FROM THE *UNLIKELIEST* PLACES.

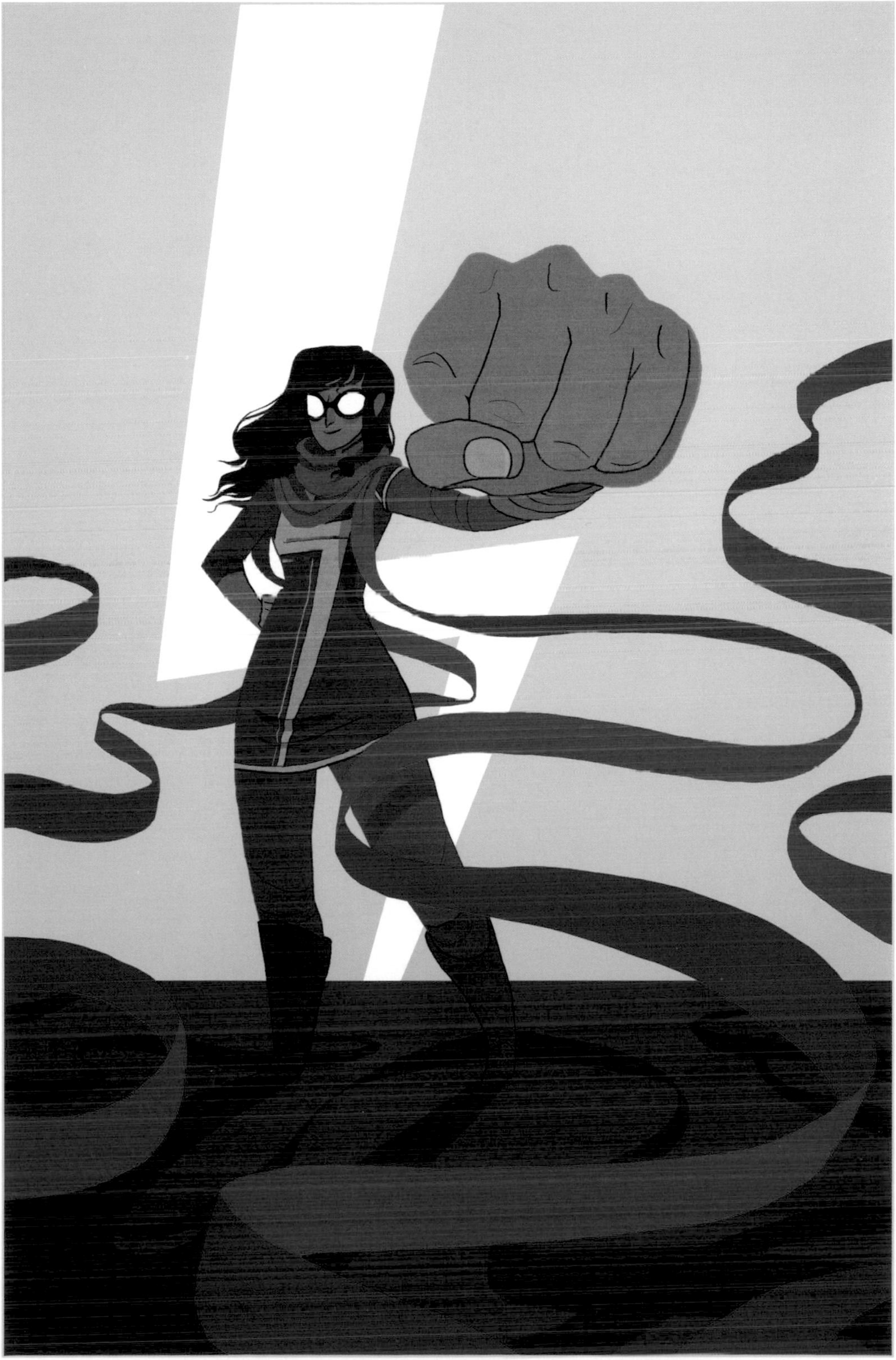

MS. MARVEL #13 WOMEN OF MARVEL VARIANT
BY NOELLE STEVENSON

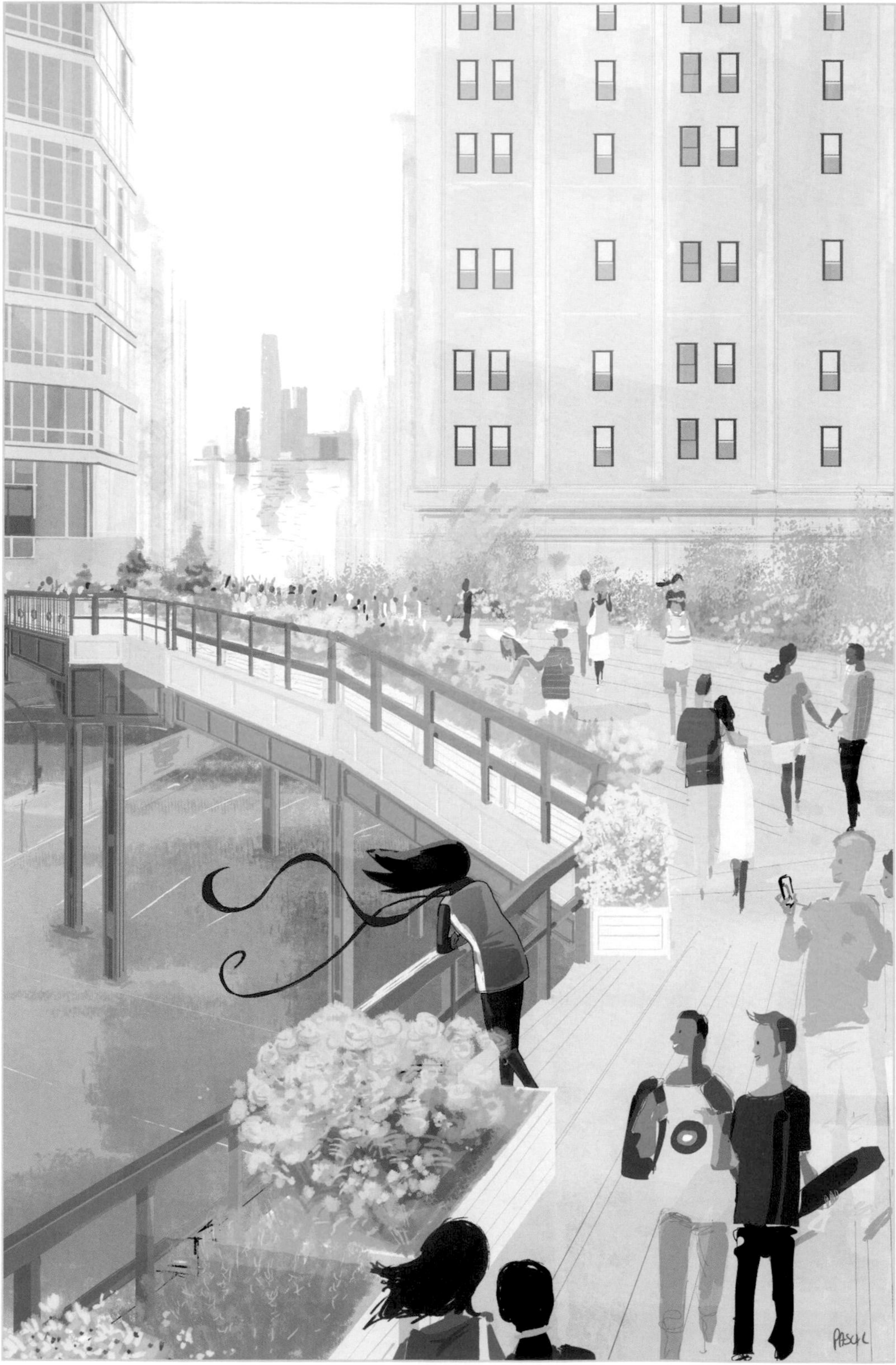

MS. MARVEL #15 NYCC VARIANT
BY PASCAL CAMPION

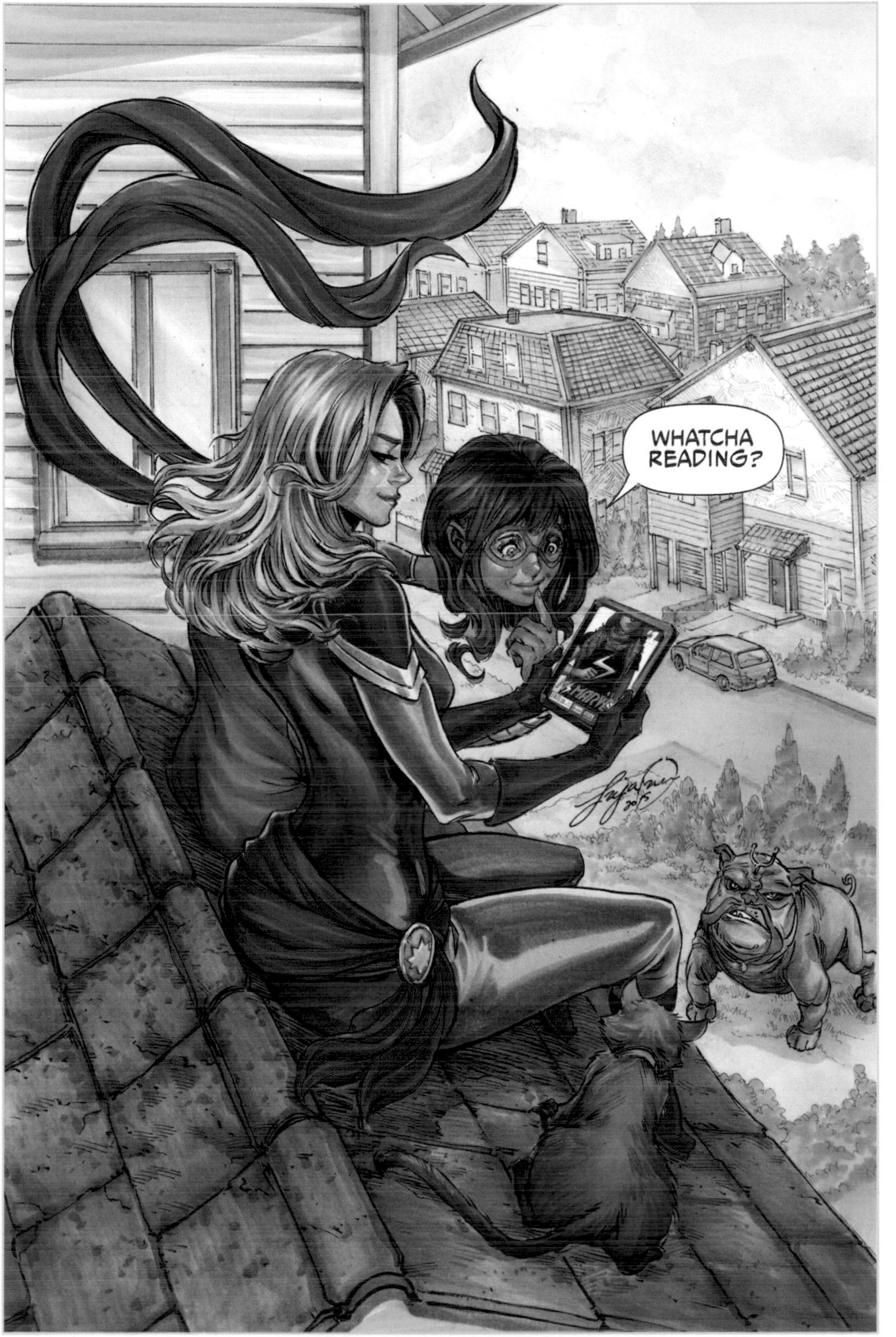
WHATCHA READING?

MS. MARVEL #17 VARIANT
BY SIYA OUM

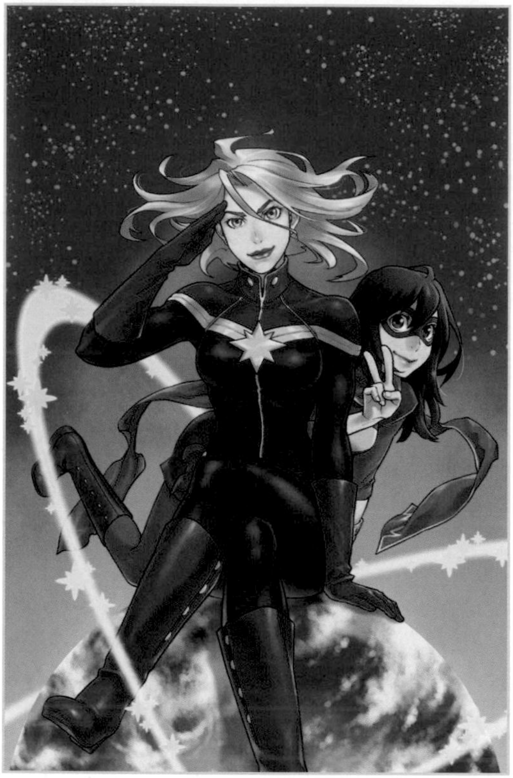

MS. MARVEL #18 MANGA VARIANT
BY RETSU TATEO

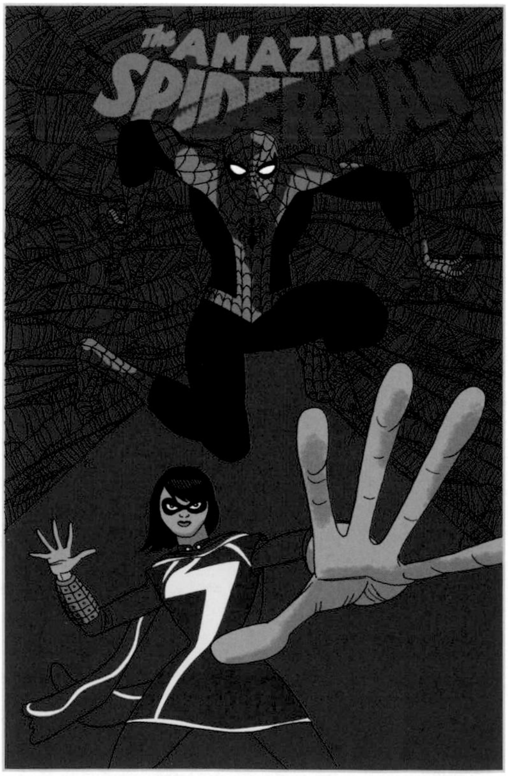
The AMAZING SPIDER-MAN

AMAZING SPIDER-MAN #7 VARIANT
BY JAVIER PULIDO

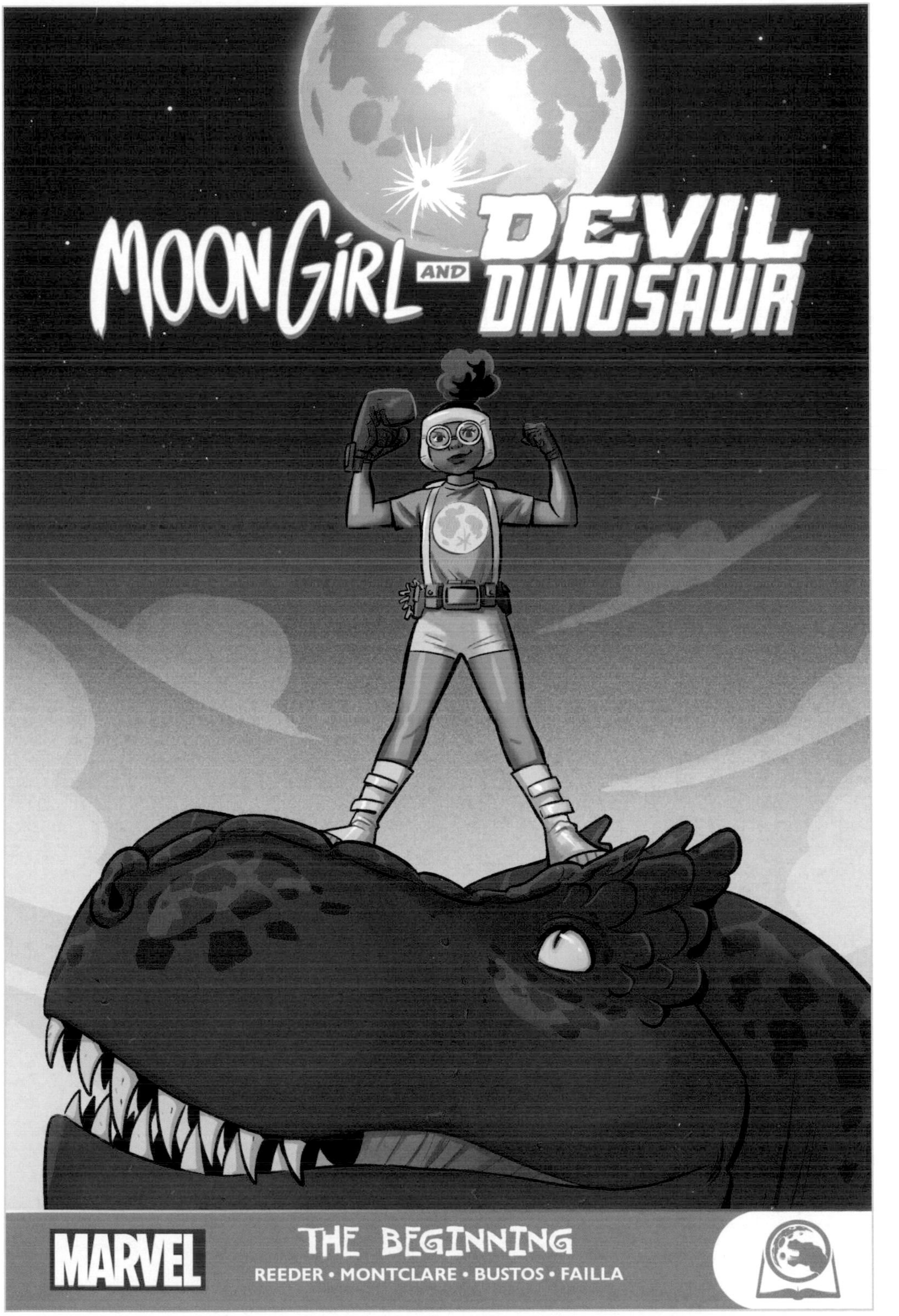
MOON GIRL AND DEVIL DINOSAUR
MARVEL
THE BEGINNING
REEDER • MONTCLARE • BUSTOS • FAILLA

MOON GIRL AND DEVIL DINOSAUR: THE BEGINNING GN-TPB BONUS PREVIEW!

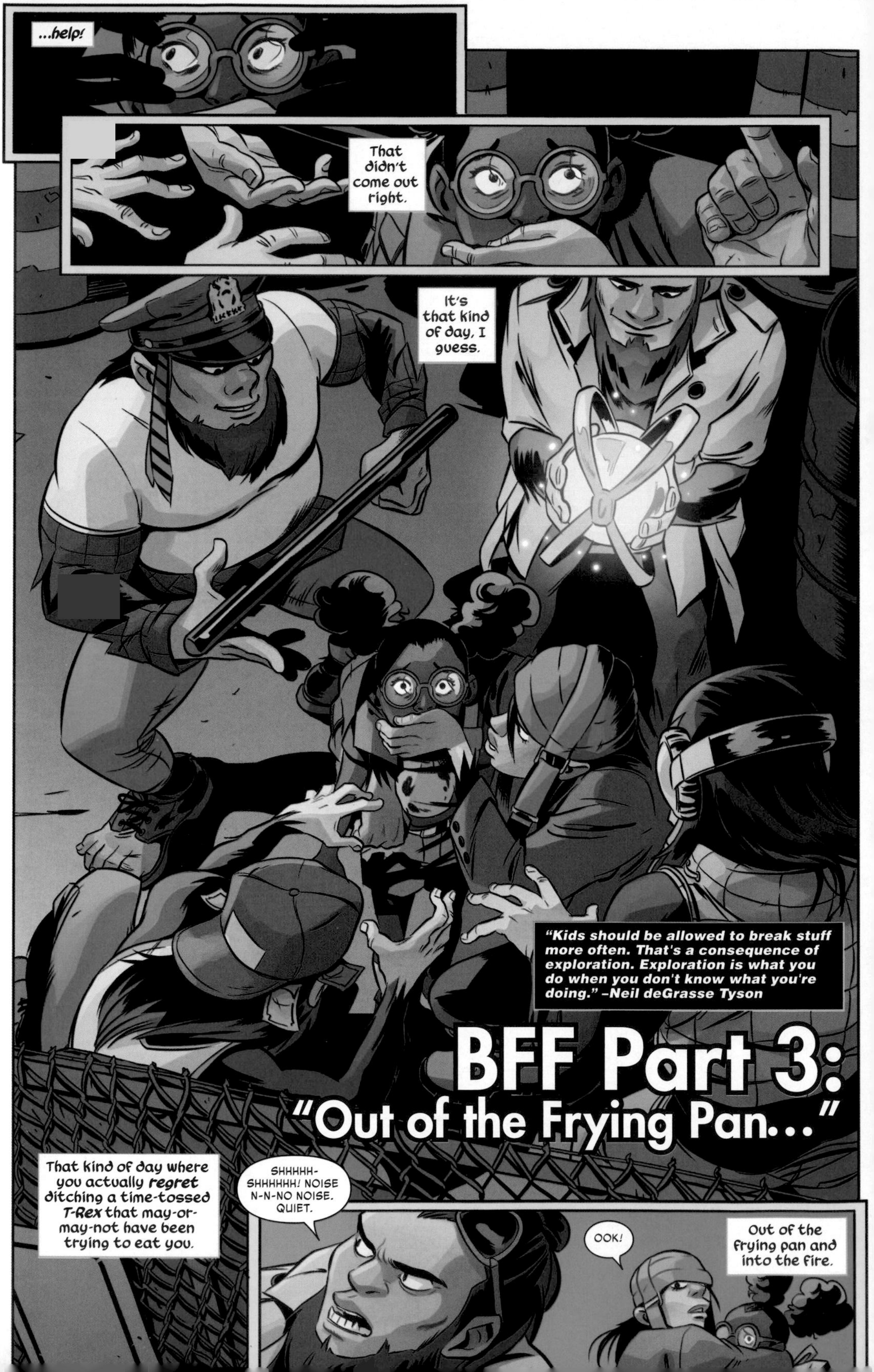
...help!
That didn't come out right.
It's that kind of day, I guess.
"Kids should be allowed to break stuff more often. That's a consequence of exploration. Exploration is what you do when you don't know what you're doing." –Neil deGrasse Tyson
BFF Part 3:
"Out of the Frying Pan..."
That kind of day where you actually regret ditching a time-tossed T-Rex that may-or-may-not have been trying to eat you.
SHHHHH-SHHHHHH! NOISE N-N-NO NOISE. QUIET.
OOK!
Out of the frying pan and into the fire.

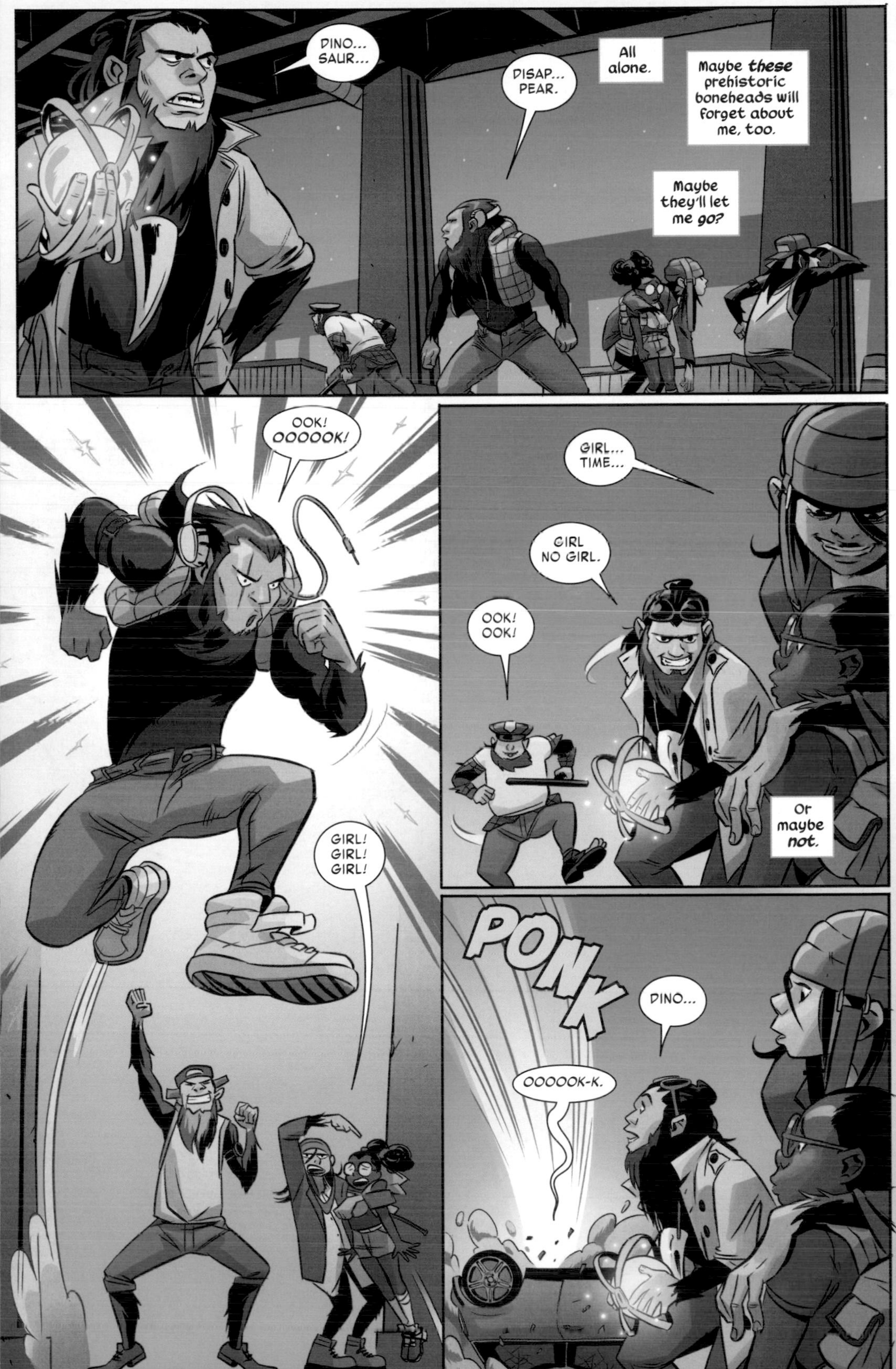
DINO... SAUR...
DISAP... PEAR.
All alone.
Maybe *these* prehistoric boneheads will forget about me, too.
Maybe they'll let me *go?*
OOK! *OOOOOK!*
GIRL! GIRL! GIRL!
GIRL... TIME...
GIRL NO GIRL.
OOK! OOK!
Or maybe *not.*
PONK
DINO...
OOOOOK-K.

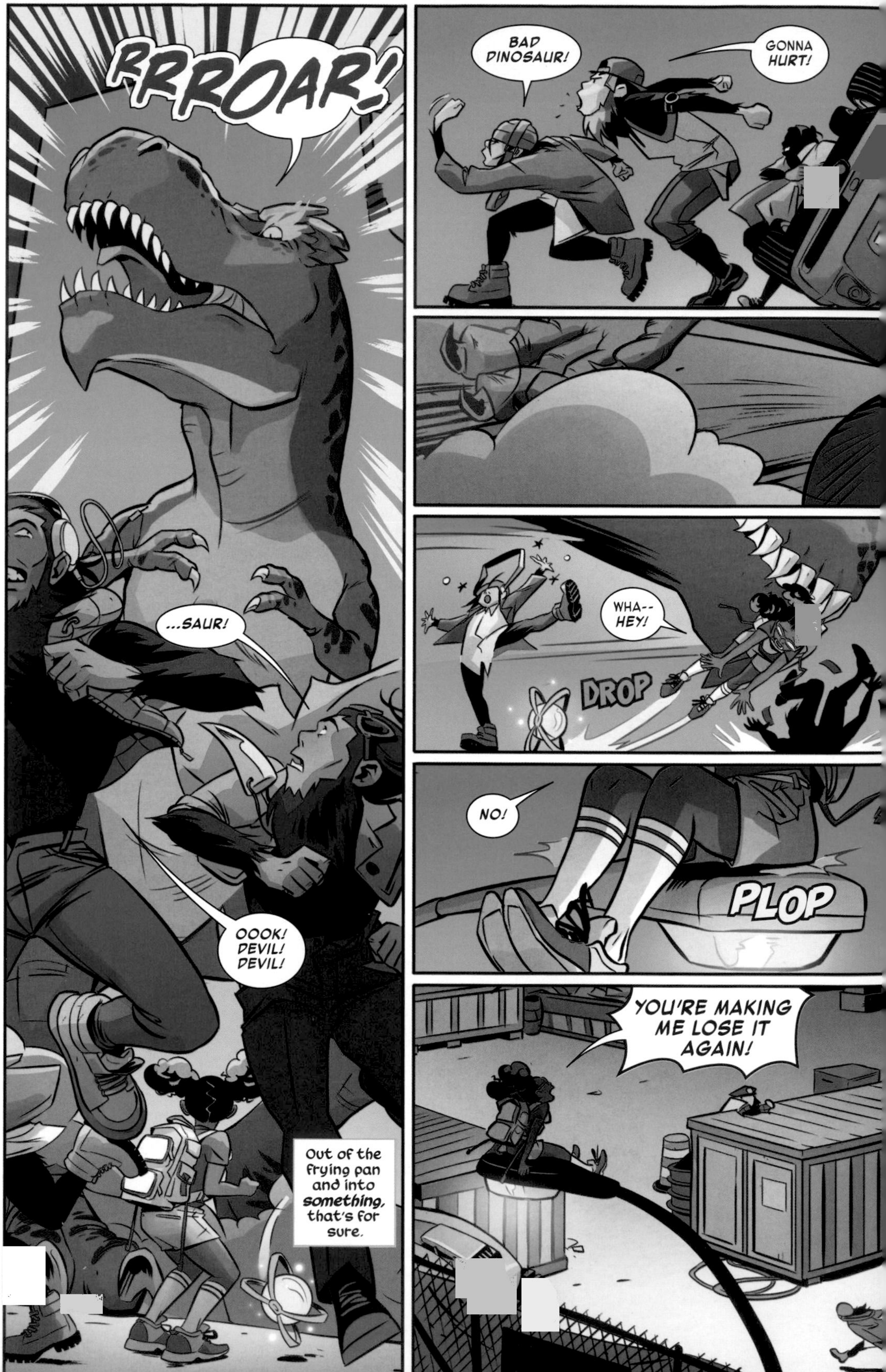
RRRROAR!
...SAUR!
OOOK! DEVIL! DEVIL!
Out of the frying pan and into *something*, that's for sure.
BAD DINOSAUR!
GONNA HURT!
WHA-- HEY!
DROP
NO!
PLOP
YOU'RE MAKING ME LOSE IT AGAIN!

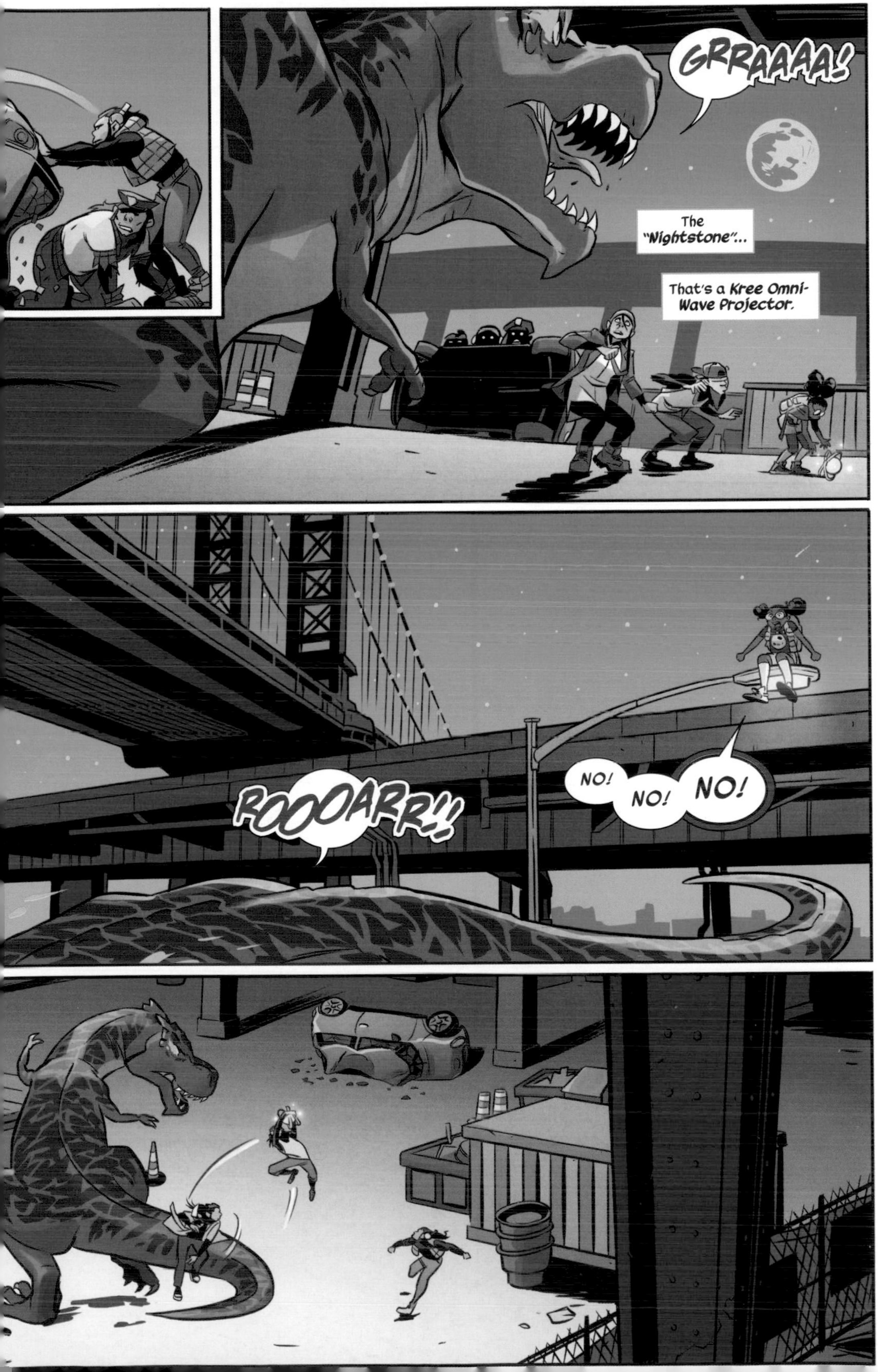
GRRAAAA!
The "Nightstone"...
That's a Kree Omni-Wave Projector.
ROOOARR!!
NO!
NO!
NO!

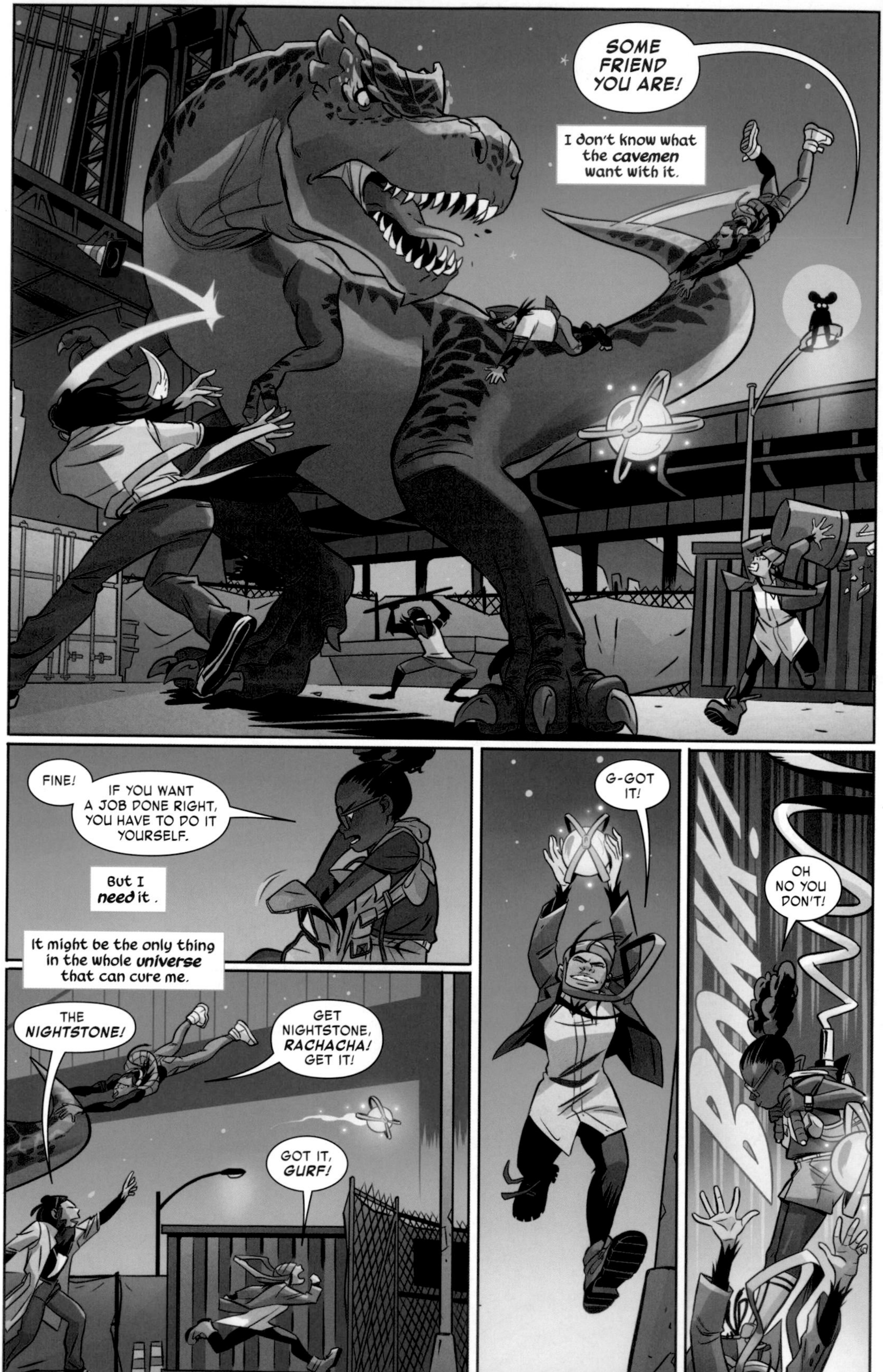
SOME FRIEND YOU ARE!
I don't know what the *cavemen* want with it.
FINE!
IF YOU WANT A JOB DONE RIGHT, YOU HAVE TO DO IT YOURSELF.
But I *need* it.
It might be the only thing in the whole *universe* that can cure me.
THE *NIGHTSTONE!*
GET NIGHTSTONE, *RACHACHA!* GET IT!
GOT IT, *GURF!*
G-GOT IT!
OH NO YOU DON'T!

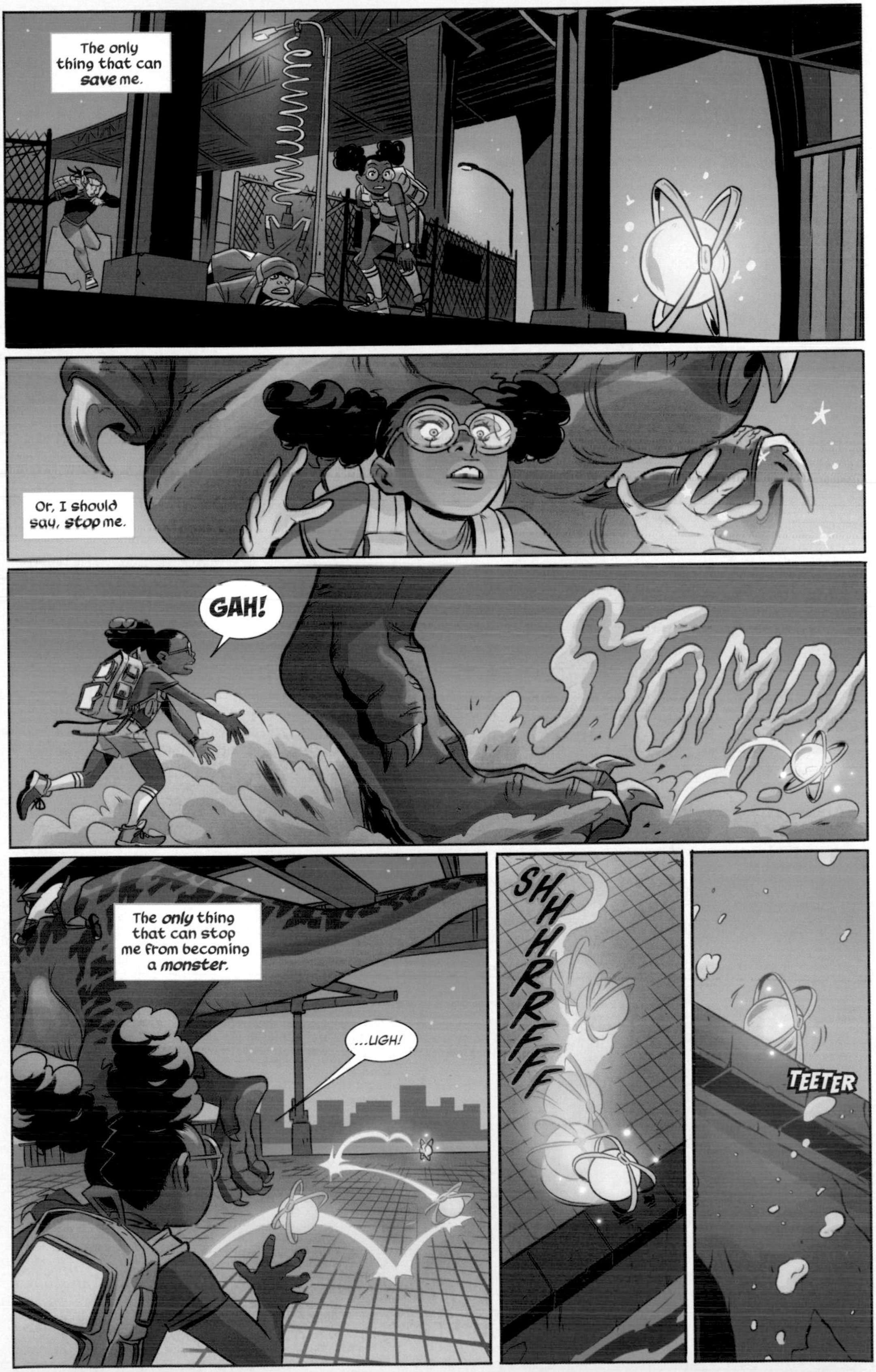
The only thing that can save me.
Or, I should say, stop me.
GAH!
STOMP!
The only thing that can stop me from becoming a monster.
...UGH!
SHHHRRFFFF
TEETER

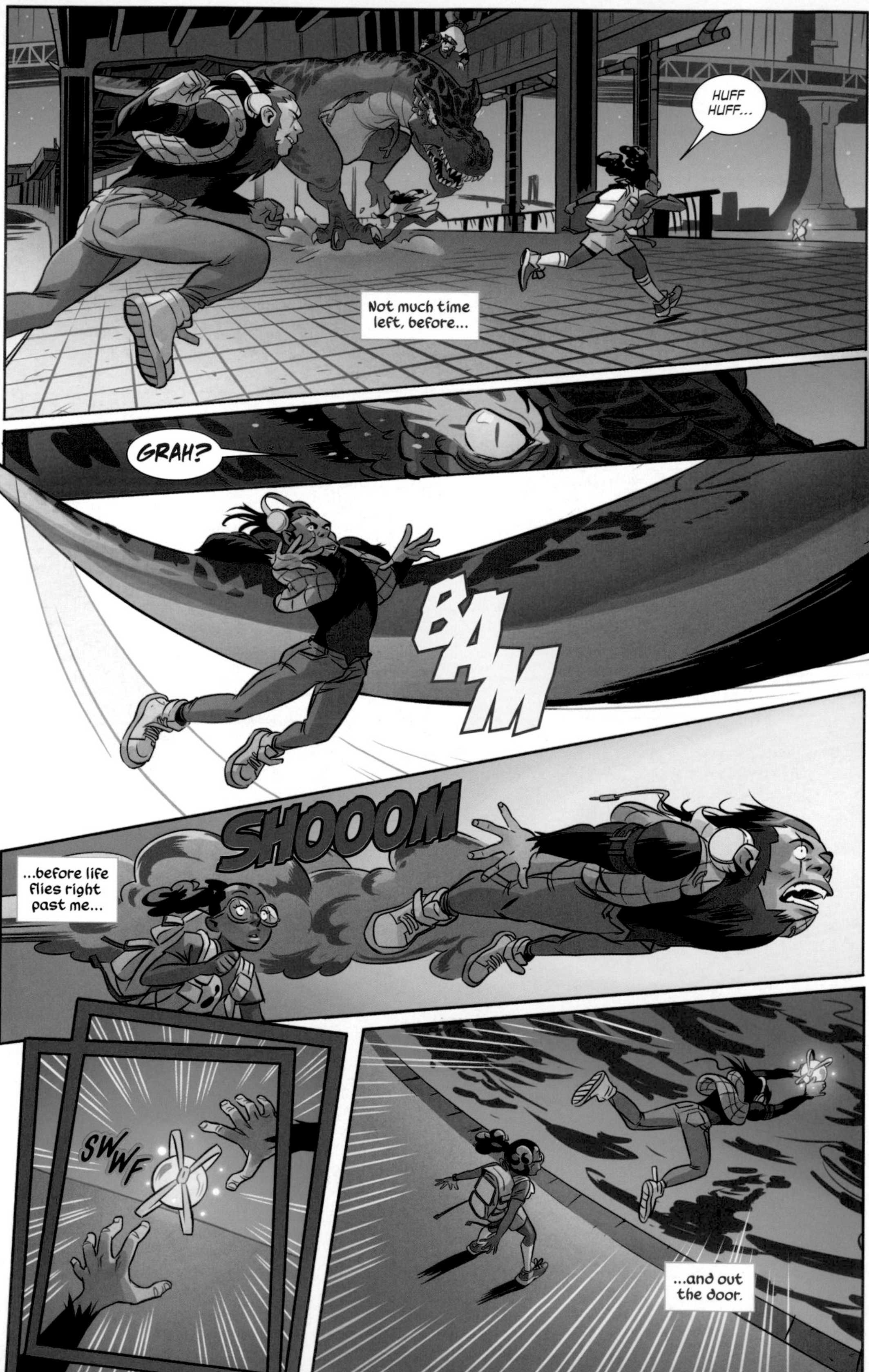
HUFF HUFF...
Not much time left, before...
GRAH?
BAM
SHOOOM
...before life flies right past me...
SWWF
...and out the door.

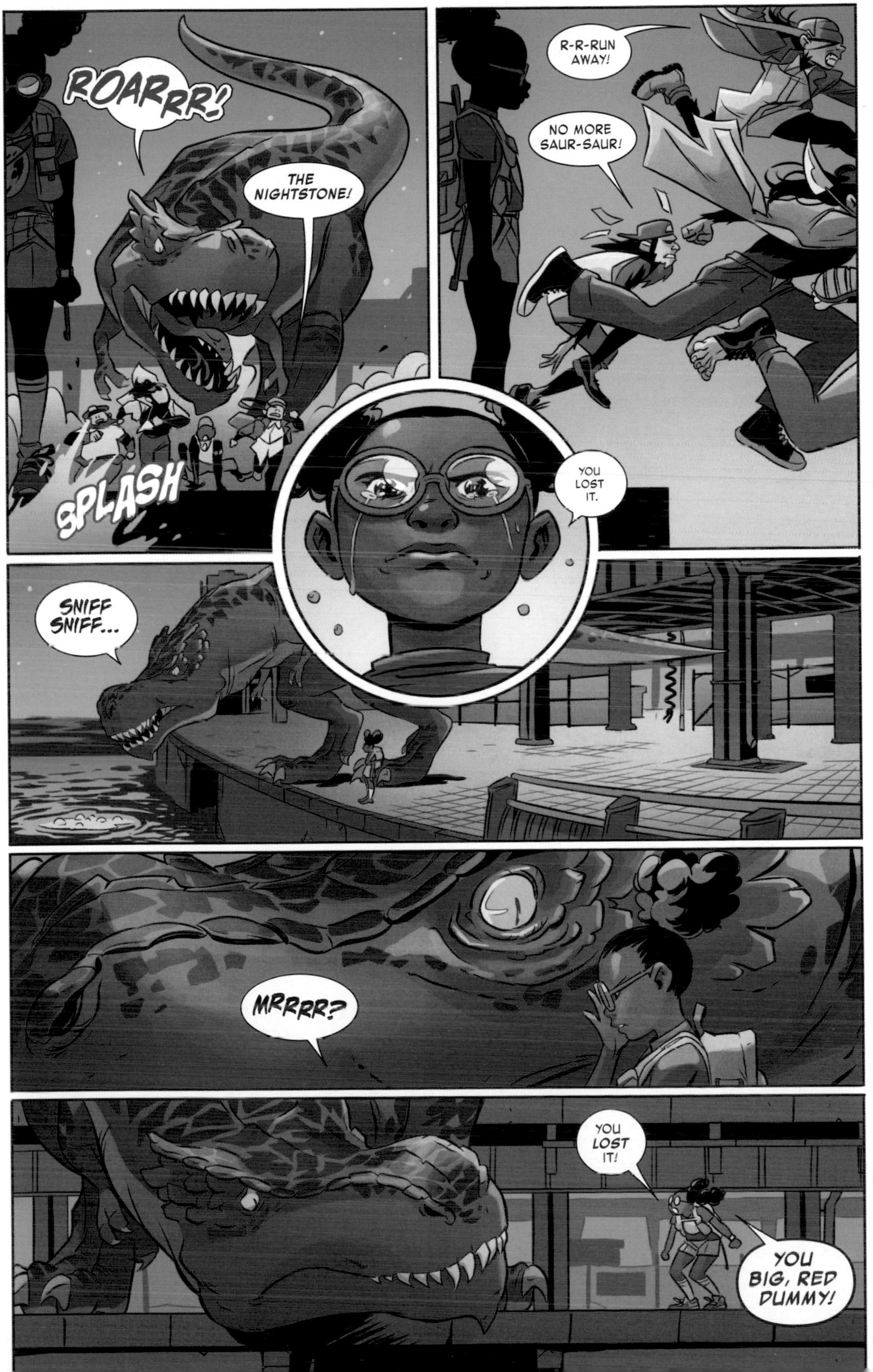
ROARRR!
THE NIGHTSTONE!
SPLASH
R-R-RUN AWAY!
NO MORE SAUR-SAUR!
YOU LOST IT.
SNIFF SNIFF...
MRRRR?
YOU LOST IT!
YOU BIG, RED DUMMY!

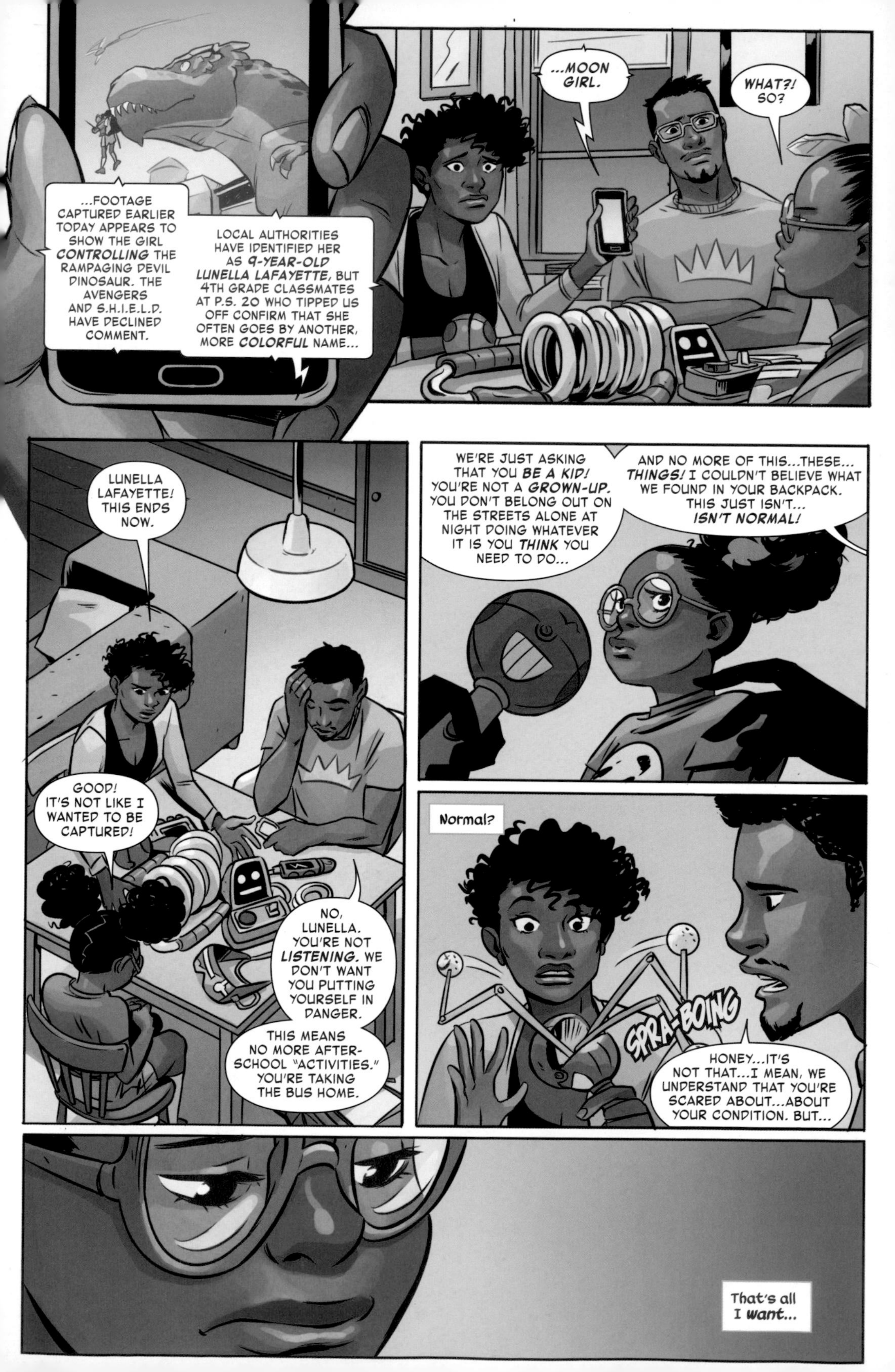
...FOOTAGE CAPTURED EARLIER TODAY APPEARS TO SHOW THE GIRL CONTROLLING THE RAMPAGING DEVIL DINOSAUR. THE AVENGERS AND S.H.I.E.L.D. HAVE DECLINED COMMENT.
LOCAL AUTHORITIES HAVE IDENTIFIED HER AS 9-YEAR-OLD LUNELLA LAFAYETTE, BUT 4TH GRADE CLASSMATES AT P.S. 20 WHO TIPPED US OFF CONFIRM THAT SHE OFTEN GOES BY ANOTHER, MORE COLORFUL NAME...
...MOON GIRL.
WHAT?! SO?
LUNELLA LAFAYETTE! THIS ENDS NOW.
GOOD! IT'S NOT LIKE I WANTED TO BE CAPTURED!
NO, LUNELLA. YOU'RE NOT LISTENING. WE DON'T WANT YOU PUTTING YOURSELF IN DANGER.
THIS MEANS NO MORE AFTER-SCHOOL "ACTIVITIES." YOU'RE TAKING THE BUS HOME.
WE'RE JUST ASKING THAT YOU BE A KID! YOU'RE NOT A GROWN-UP. YOU DON'T BELONG OUT ON THE STREETS ALONE AT NIGHT DOING WHATEVER IT IS YOU THINK YOU NEED TO DO...
AND NO MORE OF THIS...THESE... THINGS! I COULDN'T BELIEVE WHAT WE FOUND IN YOUR BACKPACK. THIS JUST ISN'T... ISN'T NORMAL!
Normal?
SPRA-BOING
HONEY...IT'S NOT THAT...I MEAN, WE UNDERSTAND THAT YOU'RE SCARED ABOUT...ABOUT YOUR CONDITION. BUT...
That's all I want...

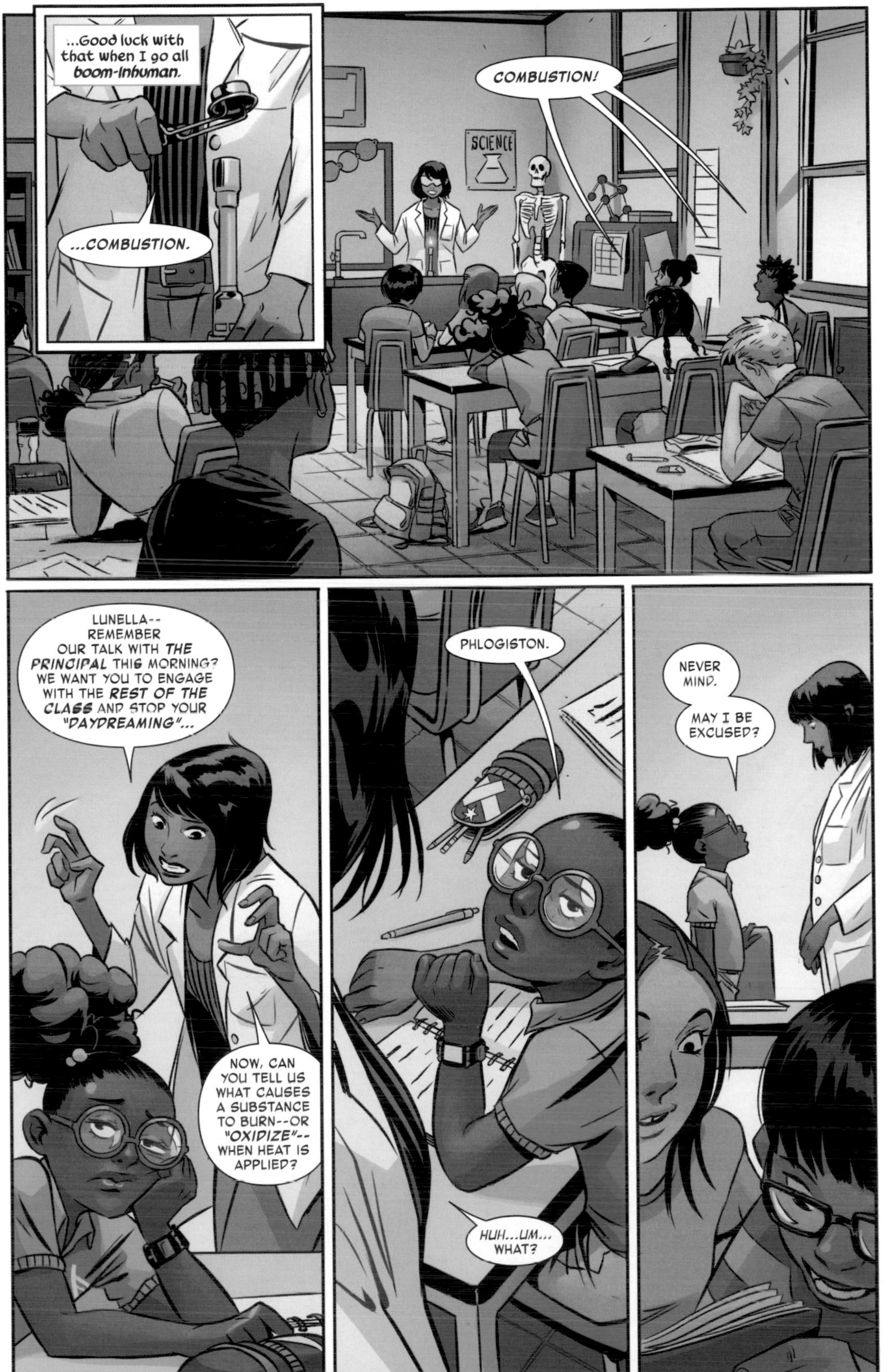
...Good luck with that when I go all *boom-Inhuman*.
...COMBUSTION.
COMBUSTION!
SCIENCE
LUNELLA-- REMEMBER OUR TALK WITH *THE PRINCIPAL* THIS MORNING? WE WANT YOU TO ENGAGE WITH THE *REST OF THE CLASS* AND STOP YOUR *"DAYDREAMING"*...
NOW, CAN YOU TELL US WHAT CAUSES A SUBSTANCE TO BURN--OR *"OXIDIZE"*-- WHEN HEAT IS APPLIED?
PHLOGISTON.
HUH...UM... WHAT?
NEVER MIND.
MAY I BE EXCUSED?

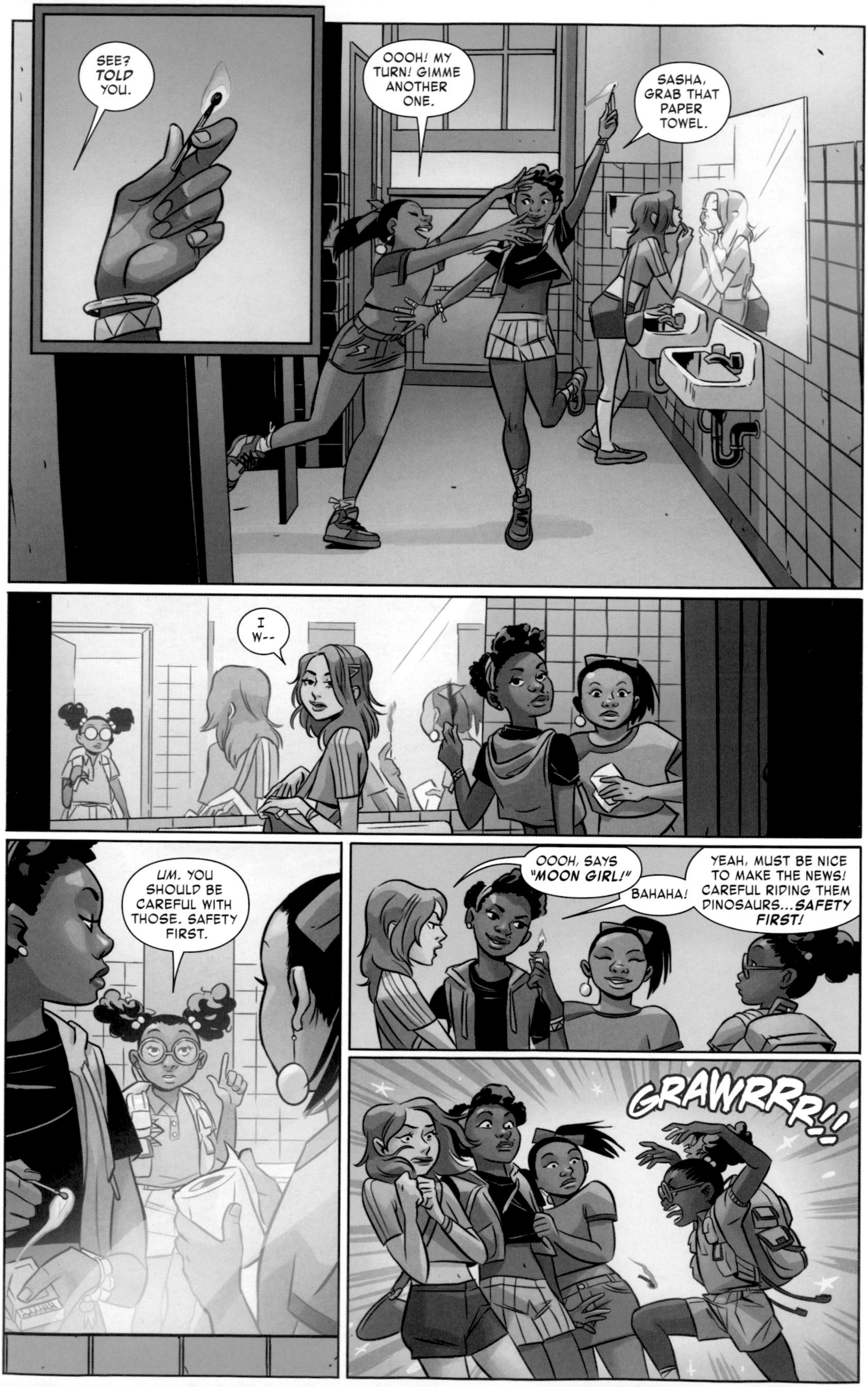
SEE? TOLD YOU.
OOOH! MY TURN! GIMME ANOTHER ONE.
SASHA, GRAB THAT PAPER TOWEL.
I W--
UM. YOU SHOULD BE CAREFUL WITH THOSE. SAFETY FIRST.
OOOH, SAYS "MOON GIRL!"
BAHAHA!
YEAH, MUST BE NICE TO MAKE THE NEWS! CAREFUL RIDING THEM DINOSAURS...SAFETY FIRST!
GRAWRRR!!

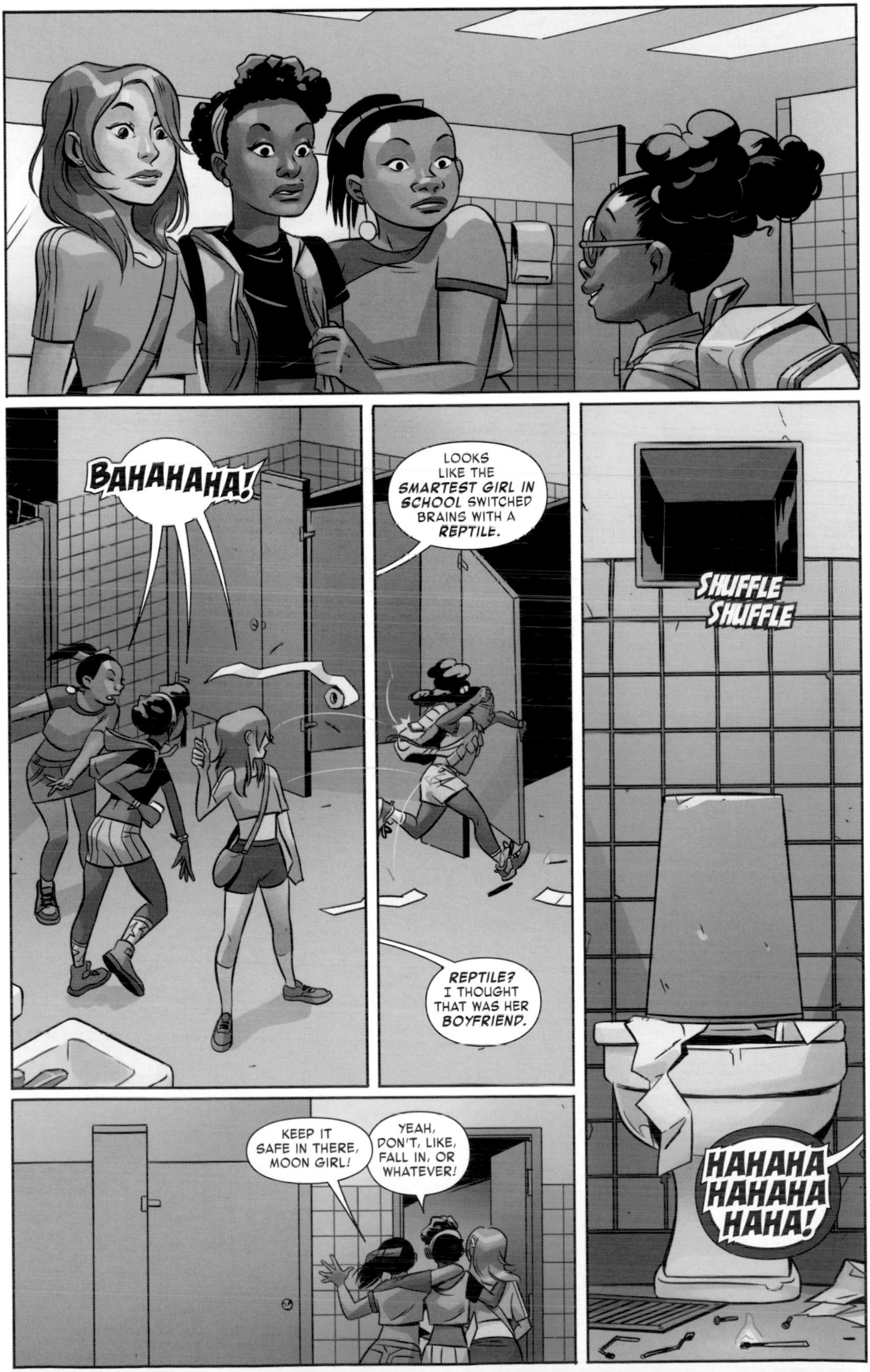
BAHAHAHA!
LOOKS LIKE THE SMARTEST GIRL IN SCHOOL SWITCHED BRAINS WITH A REPTILE.
REPTILE? I THOUGHT THAT WAS HER BOYFRIEND.
SHUFFLE SHUFFLE
KEEP IT SAFE IN THERE, MOON GIRL!
YEAH, DON'T, LIKE, FALL IN, OR WHATEVER!
HAHAHA HAHAHA HAHA!

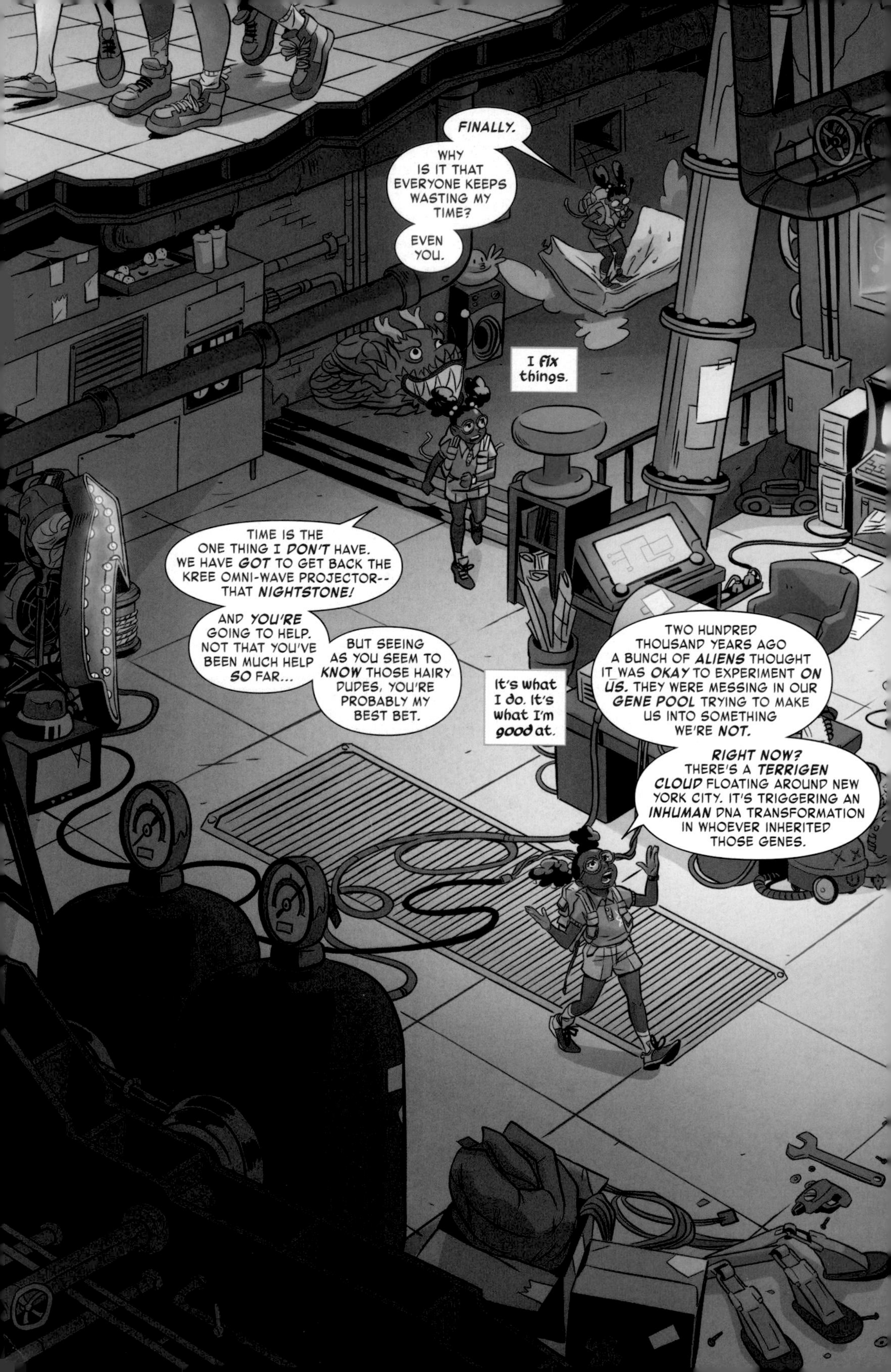
FINALLY.
WHY IS IT THAT EVERYONE KEEPS WASTING MY TIME?
EVEN YOU.
I fix things.
TIME IS THE ONE THING I DON'T HAVE. WE HAVE GOT TO GET BACK THE KREE OMNI-WAVE PROJECTOR-- THAT NIGHTSTONE!
AND YOU'RE GOING TO HELP. NOT THAT YOU'VE BEEN MUCH HELP SO FAR...
BUT SEEING AS YOU SEEM TO KNOW THOSE HAIRY DUDES, YOU'RE PROBABLY MY BEST BET.
It's what I do. It's what I'm good at.
TWO HUNDRED THOUSAND YEARS AGO A BUNCH OF ALIENS THOUGHT IT WAS OKAY TO EXPERIMENT ON US. THEY WERE MESSING IN OUR GENE POOL TRYING TO MAKE US INTO SOMETHING WE'RE NOT.
RIGHT NOW? THERE'S A TERRIGEN CLOUD FLOATING AROUND NEW YORK CITY. IT'S TRIGGERING AN INHUMAN DNA TRANSFORMATION IN WHOEVER INHERITED THOSE GENES.

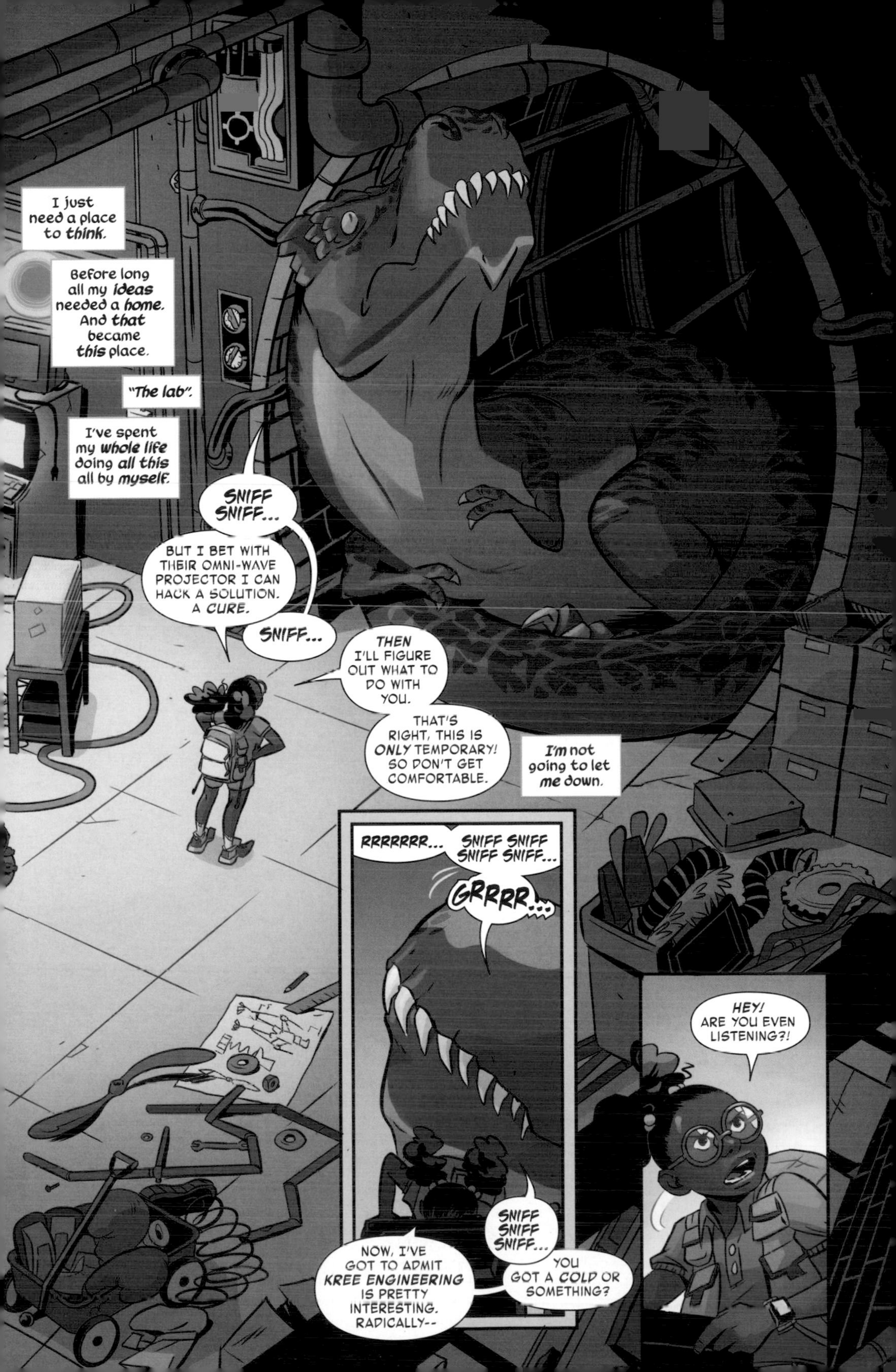

I just need a place to *think*.
Before long all my *ideas* needed a *home*. And *that* became *this* place.
"The lab".
I've spent my *whole life* doing *all this* all by *myself*.
SNIFF SNIFF...
BUT I BET WITH THEIR OMNI-WAVE PROJECTOR I CAN HACK A SOLUTION. A *CURE*.
SNIFF...
THEN I'LL FIGURE OUT WHAT TO DO WITH YOU.
THAT'S RIGHT, THIS IS *ONLY* TEMPORARY! SO DON'T GET COMFORTABLE.
I'm not going to let *me* down.
RRRRRRR...
SNIFF SNIFF SNIFF SNIFF...
GRRRR...
HEY! ARE YOU EVEN LISTENING?!
SNIFF SNIFF SNIFF...
NOW, I'VE GOT TO ADMIT *KREE ENGINEERING* IS PRETTY INTERESTING. RADICALLY--
YOU GOT A *COLD* OR SOMETHING?

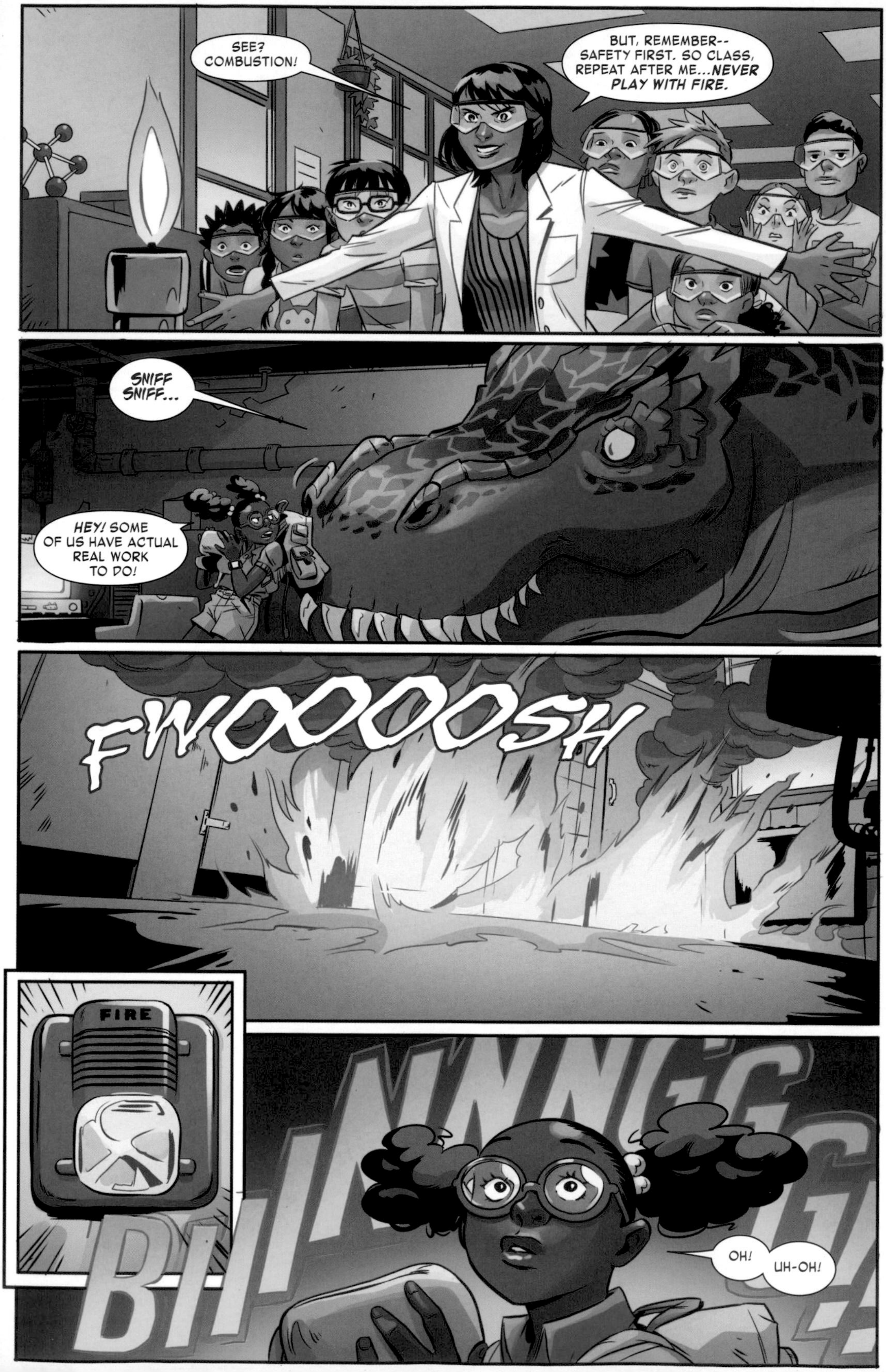
SEE? COMBUSTION!
BUT, REMEMBER-- SAFETY FIRST. SO CLASS, REPEAT AFTER ME...NEVER PLAY WITH FIRE.
SNIFF SNIFF...
HEY! SOME OF US HAVE ACTUAL REAL WORK TO DO!
FWOOOOSH
FIRE
OH!
UH-OH!

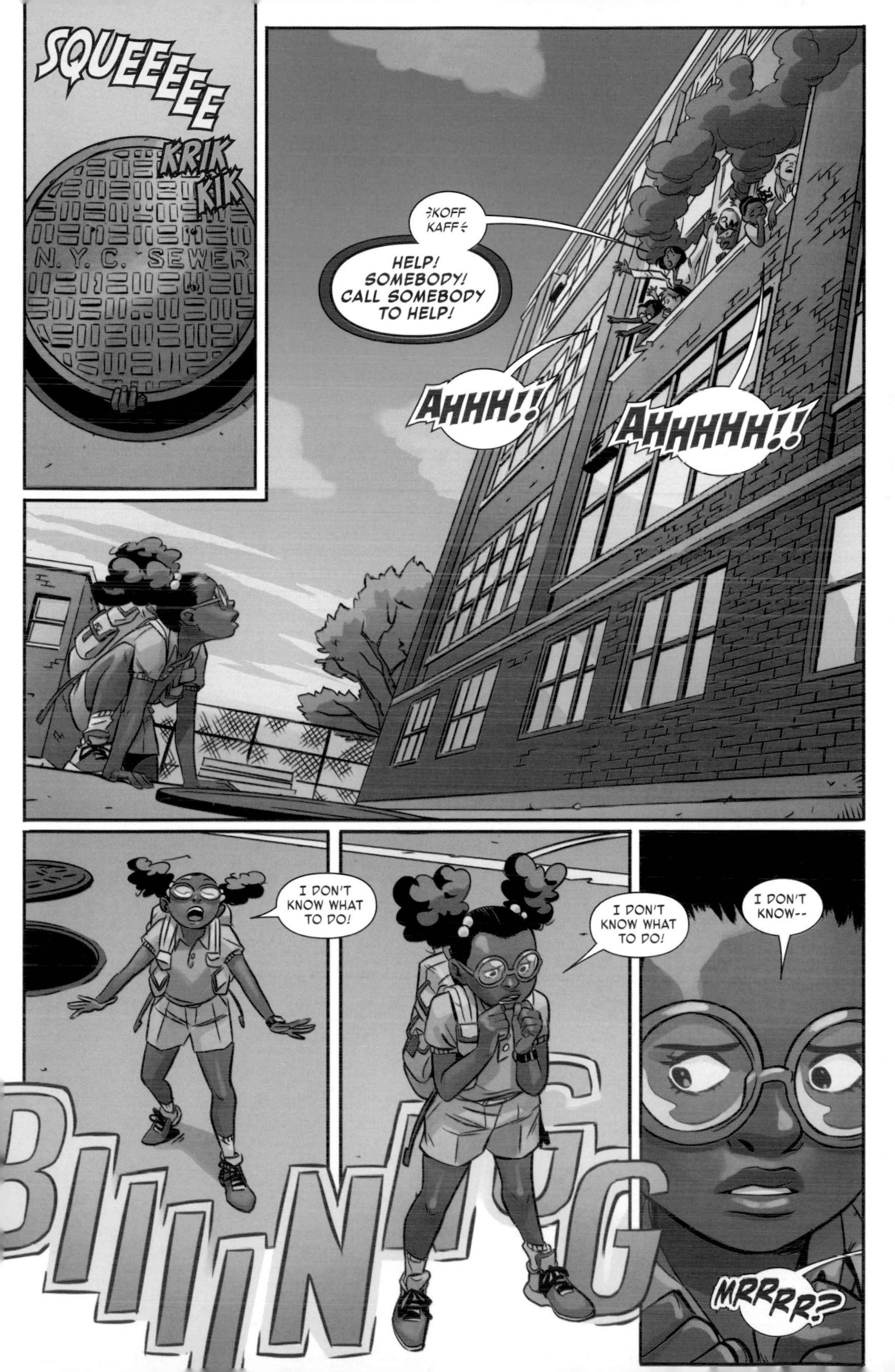
SQUEEEEEE
KRIK
KIK
N. Y. C. SEWER
KOFF KAFF
HELP! SOMEBODY! CALL SOMEBODY TO HELP!
AHHH!!
AHHHHH!!
I DON'T KNOW WHAT TO DO!
I DON'T KNOW WHAT TO DO!
I DON'T KNOW--
MRRRR?

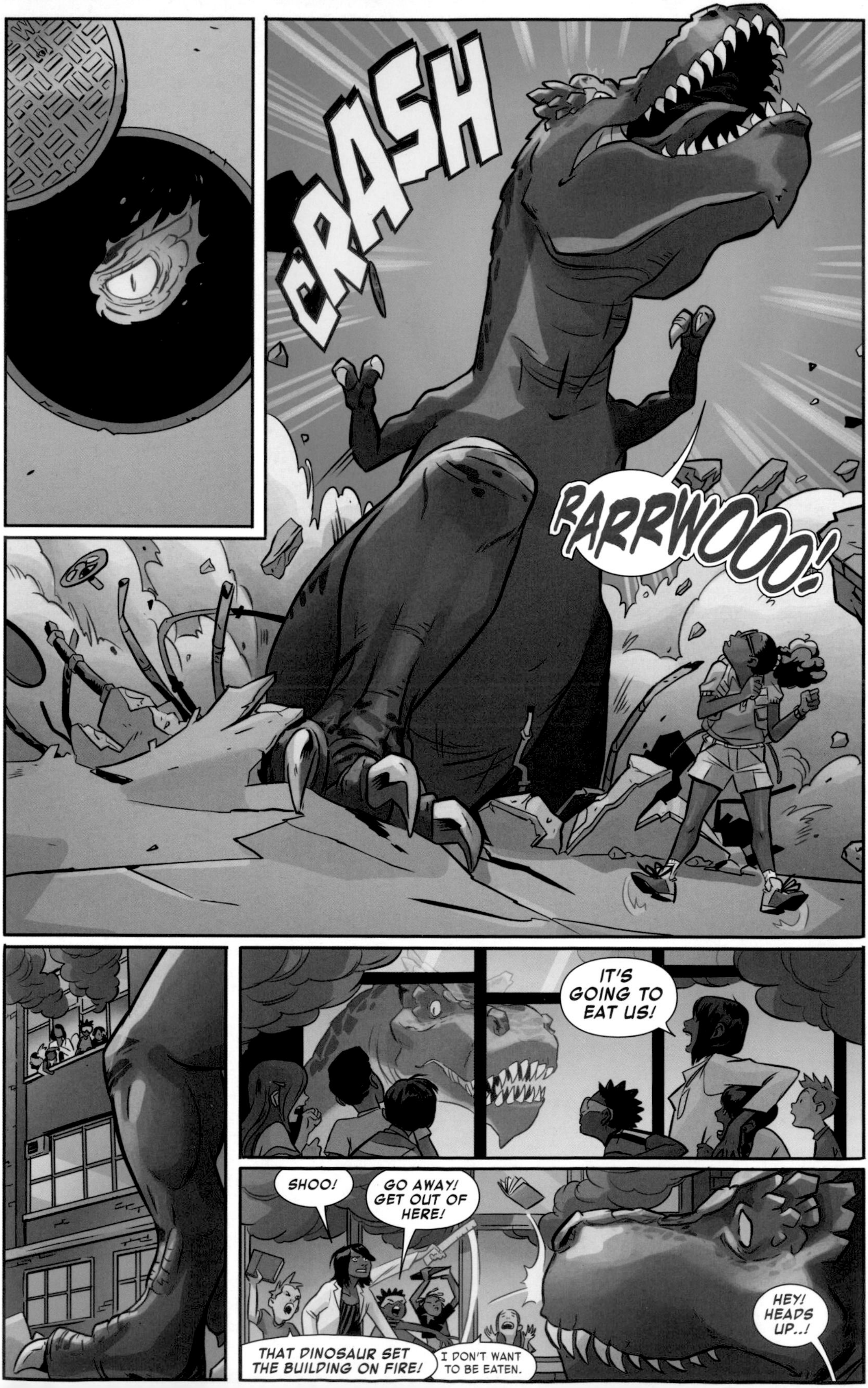
CRASH
RARRWOOOO!
IT'S GOING TO EAT US!
SHOO!
GO AWAY! GET OUT OF HERE!
HEY! HEADS UP..!
THAT DINOSAUR SET THE BUILDING ON FIRE!
I DON'T WANT TO BE EATEN.

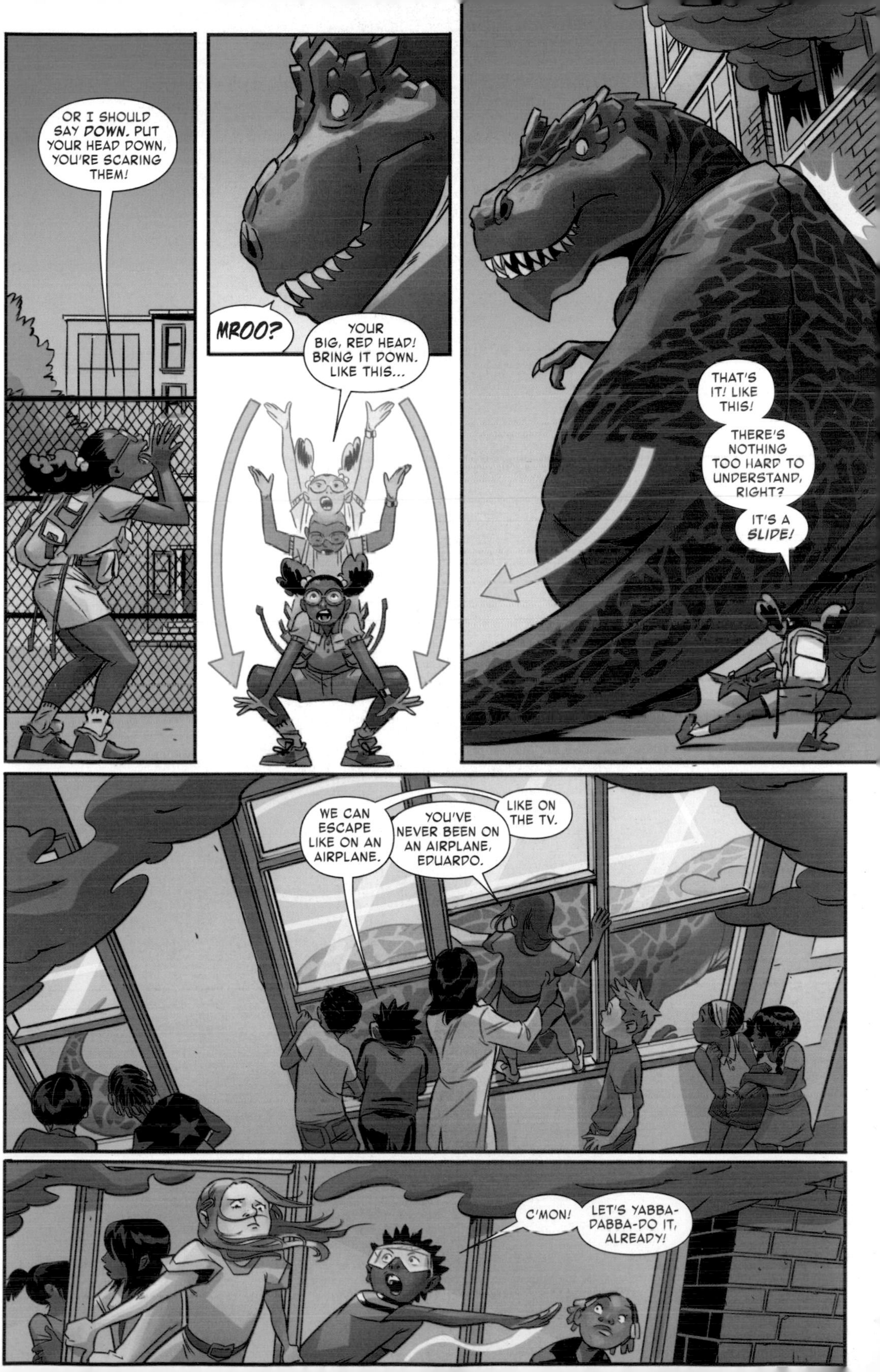
OR I SHOULD SAY DOWN. PUT YOUR HEAD DOWN, YOU'RE SCARING THEM!
MROO?
YOUR BIG, RED HEAD! BRING IT DOWN. LIKE THIS...
THAT'S IT! LIKE THIS!
THERE'S NOTHING TOO HARD TO UNDERSTAND, RIGHT?
IT'S A SLIDE!
WE CAN ESCAPE LIKE ON AN AIRPLANE.
YOU'VE NEVER BEEN ON AN AIRPLANE, EDUARDO.
LIKE ON THE TV.
C'MON!
LET'S YABBA-DABBA-DO IT, ALREADY!

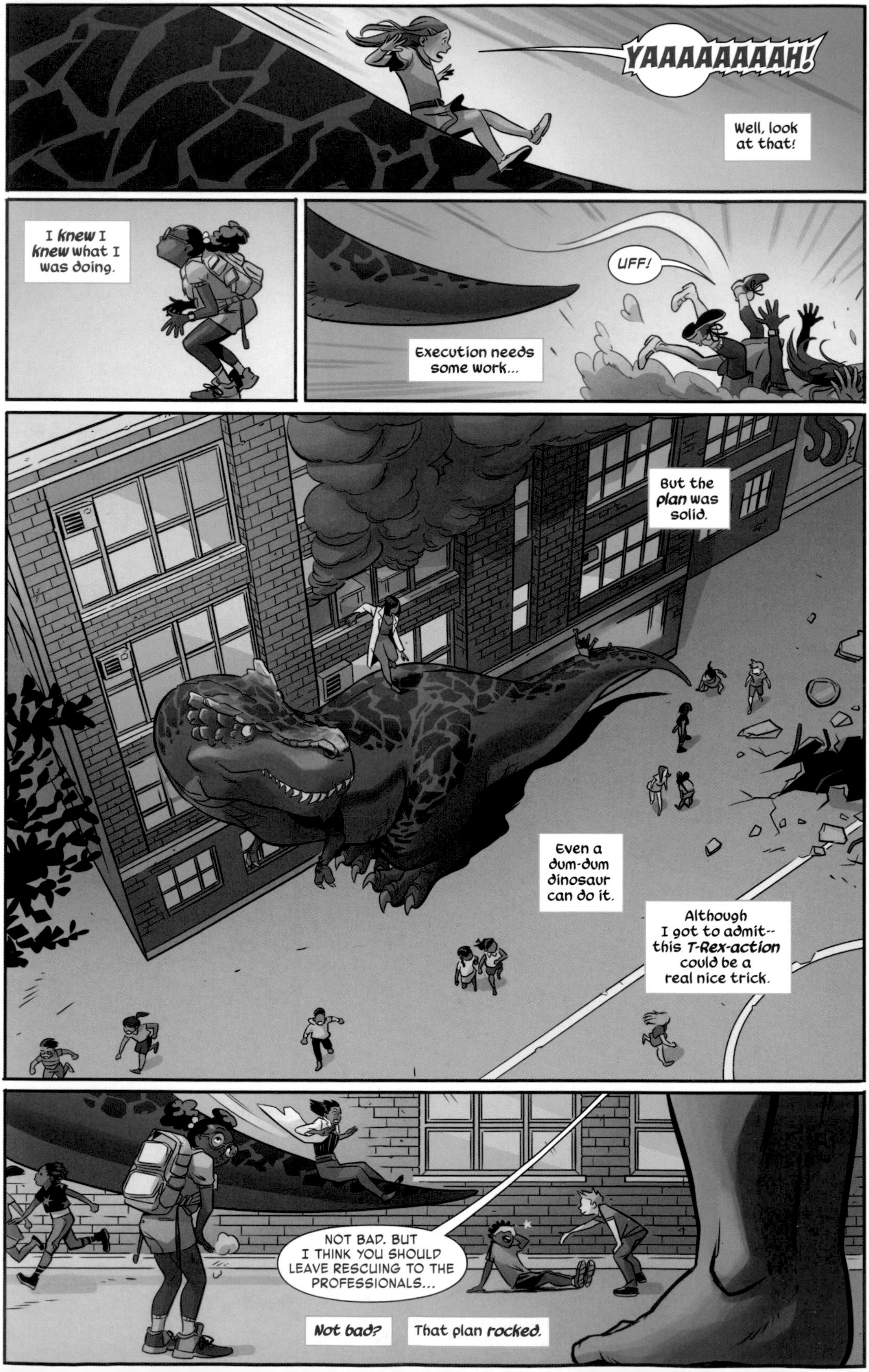
YAAAAAAAAH!
Well, look at that!
I *knew* I *knew* what I was doing.
UFF!
Execution needs some work...
But the *plan* was solid.
Even a dum-dum dinosaur can do it.
Although I got to admit-- this *T-Rex-action* could be a real nice trick.
NOT BAD. BUT I THINK YOU SHOULD LEAVE RESCUING TO THE PROFESSIONALS...
Not bad?
That plan *rocked.*

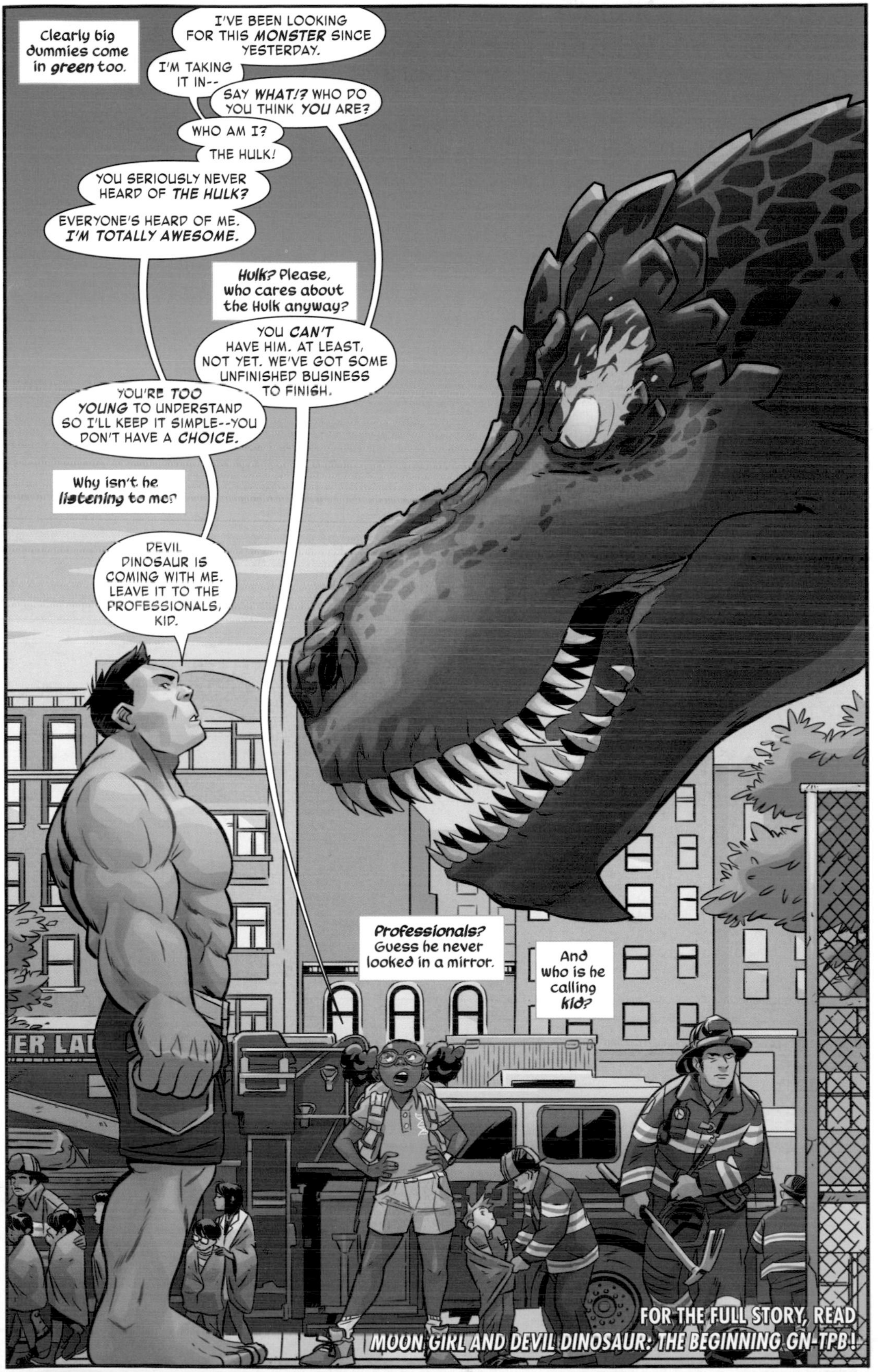
Clearly big dummies come in green too.
I'VE BEEN LOOKING FOR THIS MONSTER SINCE YESTERDAY.
I'M TAKING IT IN--
SAY WHAT!? WHO DO YOU THINK YOU ARE?
WHO AM I?
THE HULK!
YOU SERIOUSLY NEVER HEARD OF THE HULK?
EVERYONE'S HEARD OF ME. I'M TOTALLY AWESOME.
Hulk? Please, who cares about the Hulk anyway?
YOU CAN'T HAVE HIM. AT LEAST, NOT YET. WE'VE GOT SOME UNFINISHED BUSINESS TO FINISH.
YOU'RE TOO YOUNG TO UNDERSTAND SO I'LL KEEP IT SIMPLE--YOU DON'T HAVE A CHOICE.
Why isn't he listening to me?
DEVIL DINOSAUR IS COMING WITH ME. LEAVE IT TO THE PROFESSIONALS, KID.
Professionals? Guess he never looked in a mirror.
And who is he calling kid?
FOR THE FULL STORY, READ
MOON GIRL AND DEVIL DINOSAUR: THE BEGINNING GN-TPB!

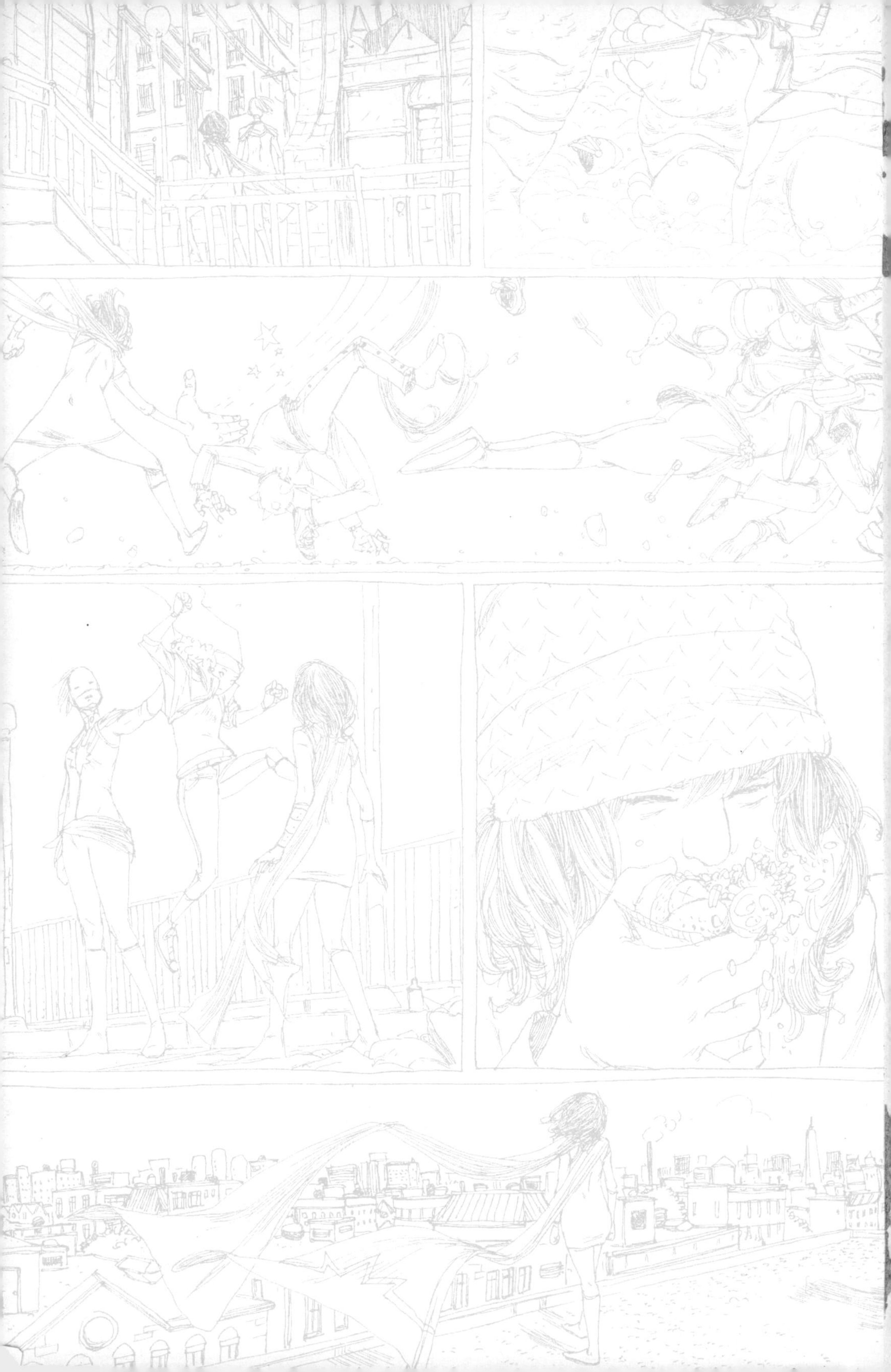